P

A HABI

Lois Battle is the author of seven novels, including
Bed & Breakfast, *Storyville*, and most recently *The
Florabama Ladies' Auxiliary & Sewing Circle*. She lives
in Beaufort, South Carolina.

A Habit
of the
Blood

Lois Battle

PENGUIN BOOKS

PENGUIN BOOKS
Published by the Penguin Group
Penguin Putnam Inc., 375 Hudson Street,
New York, New York 10014, U.S.A.
Penguin Books Ltd, 27 Wrights Lane, London W8 5TZ, England
Penguin Books Australia Ltd, Ringwood, Victoria, Australia
Penguin Books Canada Ltd, 10 Alcorn Avenue,
Toronto, Ontario, Canada M4V 3B2
Penguin Books (N.Z.) Ltd, 182–190 Wairau Road,
Auckland 10, New Zealand

Penguin Books Ltd, Registered Offices: Harmondsworth, Middlesex, England

First published in the United States of America by St. Martin's Press, 1987
Published in Penguin Books 2001

10 9 8 7 6 5 4 3 2 1

Grateful acknowledgement is made for permission to use:

"Sitting in Limbo" by Jimmy Cliff © 1971 Island Music Ltd. All rights for
the USA & Canada controlled by Island Music, Inc. (BMI) All rights reserved.
Reprinted by permission.

"Can't Help Lovin' Dat Man" written by Jerome Kern and Oscar Hammerstein, II
Copyright © 1927 T.B. Harms Company. Copyright Renewed.
(c/o The Welk Music Group, Santa Monica California, 90401).
International Copyright Secured. All Rights Reserved. Used by permission.

"Rum and Coca Cola" Lyric by Morey Amsterdam, Music by Jeri Sullavan and
Paul Baron, additional lyrics by Al Stillman © 1944, 1956, 1957
Renewed 1972 Leo Feist Inc. Rights assigned to CBS Catalogue Partnership
All Rights controlled & administered by CBS Feist Catalog Inc.
All rights reserved. International Copyright Secured. Used by permission.

THE LIBRARY OF CONGRESS HAS CATALOGED THE HARDCOVER EDITION AS FOLLOWS:
Battle, Lois.
    A habit of the blood.
    "A Thomas Dunne book."
    I. Title
PS3552.A8325H3   1987   813'.54   86–26221
ISBN 0-312-00128-2 (hc.)
ISBN 0 14 02.6169 9 (pbk.)

Printed in the United States of America
Set in Janson
Designed by Giorgetta Bell McRee/ Early Birds

To
Alma Nunes

A Habit
of the—
Blood

One

The woman's pace was leisurely, almost aimless, but because of the length of her legs and the straightness of her spine, she gave the impression of walking with purpose. She crossed the street, looking neither to left nor right, her hands stuffed into the pockets of her slacks, her oversized mackintosh and aviator's scarf billowing behind her. A car slammed on its brakes; she moved on, oblivious. Altogether she had an air of scruffy, devil-may-care elegance and, even as people heard the thunder and scurried for the protection of the shops, more than a few turned to look at her. Those who came close enough to study her face might have noticed that the purplish shadows beneath her eyes blended with the whiteness of her cheeks, giving her an acutely observant but dreamy expression, as though she suffered from permanent jet lag.

She stopped in front of a tea and pastry shop, toying with a loose button on her mackintosh. That car had almost hit her, and it was her fault. You're a right fool, Ceci Baron, she thought. She was so preoccupied that she had no mind for her safety. But she'd been preoccupied even before the telegram had come. For almost a week her intuition had been signaling that something was about to happen. She'd found herself staring out of windows or having to ask people to repeat what they'd just said to her. She'd been stomach-grumbling hungry, but nothing had tempted her appetite. She'd opened newspapers with vague apprehension, thinking she might recognize a face in a photo or a name on a list of hijacked passengers. She had even dreamt of the Mexican woman with the silver charms.

Spells of apprehensive restlessness were as much a part of her as blue eyes, wanderlust, or a tendency to overtip, and if she'd given this one any thought she had attributed it to Max's ultimatum that she either marry him or call it quits. The thought of marrying again made her feel as though she'd been nudged to the edge of a high dive and was staring down into a mere puddle of water. She'd left New York for London to think it over, or, as Max had put it, she'd resumed her pattern of "fright and flight." Now, after three weeks, she was no closer to a decision.

When she had started to live with Max, some ten months ago, it had been more by circumstance than design. She'd just returned to New York, had been scouting around for a temporary job, and a decorator friend had hired her to help out with the three-story maisonette Max had recently bought near the East River. When a studio apartment she'd been hoping to rent in SoHo had gone co-op, Max had invited her to live on the ground floor of his place while she looked for something else. Even before they became lovers they'd shared an easygoing domesticity. After the decorating had been completed and Max had thrown his first big party to show it off, he'd told her that he was in love with her. She'd seen the situation so clearly that it had been difficult for her to take his avowal personally. Despite the entrée into New York society that Max's money afforded him, he was a lonely man and an intensely domestic one. Having left his marriage of fifteen years back in Texas, he'd had his flings with actresses, young execs, and divorcées, though this, she guessed, was just a more open practice of what he'd been doing covertly during the last years of his marriage. Now he'd reached the two-years-divorced phase that was so hard on essentially monogamous men. He'd exhausted the possibilities of bachelorhood. He needed order. He wanted to sleep in his own bed. And there she was, the younger woman, worldly enough to entertain his guests, eccentric enough to mystify him, who'd helped to create his new nest. It wasn't really the sex but rather those moments of domesticity—choosing from drapery swatches, arguing with the carpenters—that had constituted his real infidelity and final break from his ex-wife. And infidelity was an infallible rejuvenator. Max had declared that she'd given him a new lease on life. She'd pointed out that it was purely circumstantial; he'd countered that the best partnerships often were and that her honesty in pointing it out was one of the things that made him love her. And so she'd stayed on. In spite of, or perhaps because of, the fact that she was not bound to any notion of a future with him, she'd grown very fond of him, assuming that they would live together until wanderlust or disinterest parted them. Now he'd spoiled all that by wanting her to say "forever."

The waitress inside the tea shop was now smiling at her through the glass as though encouraging her to come in. She looked away, catching sight of her reflection in the glass, her face ringed with meringues, scones, and babas au rhum. She'd succeeded in worrying the loose button off her mackintosh. Pocketing it, she ignored another clap of thunder and walked on.

Walking was the solitary activity she most enjoyed. Max thought it strange that she liked to walk alone for hours, and the fact that she had done so in cities all over the world had not persuaded him that she did not need his protection. She hadn't minded his company, though his desire to avoid any but the best sections of town had given their strolls a dull predictability. He admired what he called her adventurousness, but couldn't understand why she'd want to venture into neighborhoods where slack-breasted women sat on stoops, men loitered about guzzling rotgut from brown paper bags, and latchkey children waited in the gutters. It was, he thought, especially perverse for her because the sight of such people often brought her to anger or tears. He treasured her compassionate nature (that finer grain of feeling was appealing in a woman), but it made no sense to submit herself to sights that only made her miserable. Though generous with

a handout, Max was a social Darwinist: Those who were
down and out must deserve to be so, just as animals who
couldn't adapt weren't fit for survival. They'd had many bitter arguments about that one, she saying that if earning ability was the standard by which he judged people she herself
must be considered inferior; he countering that she must
know that wasn't what he meant. Their ways of looking at the
world were so deeply at odds and she became so "emotional"
about them that it was usually Max who backed off from the
argument. And of course she could see his point about her
perversity. It wasn't as though she were Mother Teresa, ready
to carry unfortunates into her, or rather his, home. And it *was*
indisputably more pleasant to window-shop on Madison, ad-
mire the flower beds on Park Avenue, or chat with a doorman
or a neighbor walking a pedigreed dog. So why did she feel
as though something vital in her was being chipped away?
"Because it's like confining yourself to only seeing movies
with happy endings, that's why."

   She must have muttered part of that out loud because the
man standing next to her on the curb looked at her as though
she'd greeted him, then realized she was a stranger and looked
away. She crossed the street, conscious of the freedom with
which she was swinging her arms. That was another thing:
Max always wanted to hold her hand when they walked and
took her desire to walk free as a lack of affection. He'd given
up on the hand-holding, but he'd adopted the habit of walking
too close to her and veering into her. That this was an unconscious habit of his had made it more instead of less irritating,
and one evening, in fact, the evening he'd proposed, they'd
gone only a few blocks from his apartment when Ceci had to
stop and point out that he'd crowded her to within a few feet
of the buildings. He'd apologized, but within another few
blocks, he was doing the same thing again. Surely there was
something wrong with her if she found fault with an otherwise decent and desirable man just because of his walking
habits, and yet . . . she felt that if she continued to live with
him he'd begin to crowd her in more important ways. She
questioned the authenticity of her affection for him. Was she
really fond of him, or was he just the biggest "built-in" in the

nest she'd created for herself and which she could never hope to afford without him?

When Max had asked her what she was thinking about, she'd mentioned the offer she'd had the previous day: Audrey Springer, a London friend, had called to say that she and her husband were going to Italy and asked if she would like to come, keep an eye on their flat and also keep an eye on Audrey's Mayfair boutique. "So you told her you couldn't?" Max had asked. "I told her I'd think about it," she'd answered. They'd walked the rest of the way in silence, Max, for once, giving her a wide berth and, she'd later realized, preparing his ultimatum.

That he'd stood in the door of her bathroom while she prepared for bed should have made her realize that something was in the offing. Max usually showered in his own bathroom and waited for her in bed; he liked the end product of female grooming, but had no interest in the process. He'd watched without talking as she'd removed her makeup. Had she been in a more tractable mood, she might have spared him the sight of flossing her teeth, but she'd gone on doing it, as slowly and deliberately as if she'd just come from her annual checkup and had embarked on one of those programs of improved dental hygiene that never lasted more than a week. As she'd squeezed the toothpaste onto her brush she'd noticed, out of the corner of her eye, that he was running his hand through his hair (now worn, at her suggestion, several inches longer than it had been when they'd first met). Max was about to make a decision. He'd then nodded his head twice and raised his index finger. This, too, was a gesture she recognized. He made it at estate auctions to indicate his final bid. Mouth full, she'd turned to hear his proposal. When he'd added, "or else call it quits," she'd swallowed some of the toothpaste, which may have explained why she'd felt slightly nauseated for hours afterward.

She'd rinsed her mouth and turned to him. "The trouble with you, Ceci," he'd said as he'd handed her one of his monogramed towels, "is that you're morally uncomfortable with a life-style you'd be aesthetically uncomfortable without." She'd quoted something about people who talked about life-style not having either, but the remark had stopped her. It was the most insightful thing Max had ever said to her. It occurred to her that perhaps he really did understand her. At least he'd continued, over the months they'd lived together, to observe her carefully, and acute observation, even when negative, was an indication of love. She could do far worse than Max Bargeron.

She'd put her arms around him, ready to explain herself, even ready to kiss, when he'd made the mistake of continuing: from what he knew of her background, she'd been right to cut herself off from her family, but her pattern of never making commitments showed that she had never really resolved her feelings toward them. She was the privileged girl who still posed as the rebel. She was still defining herself by being the opposite of her aunt. She would never really trust a man until she'd come to grips with her anger toward her father. And on and on. One neatly packaged psychological cliché after another, made to sound even more superficial and sententious by having been delivered in a Texas drawl, making her sorry that she'd ever told him anything about herself but glad she'd withheld the really important confessions. Disengaging herself from the embrace, she'd told him she wished he'd bring as much originality to his psychological profiles as he brought to his business deals. And yet . . .

Max was no fool. In all likelihood the accusation he'd aimed at her as she'd packed for London was true: she didn't want to be with any man. Not really. Not permanently. Not if it meant changing. But there was the hope that she wouldn't have to change. Max, either in love (as he claimed) or in lust (as she suspected) had missed her, or so he had confessed in their almost nightly phone conversations. He might be willing to accept their live-in relationship without pressuring her for marriage. If he continued to push (the image of the high dive came to mind, bringing on the queasy feeling in her stomach) she might take the plunge. Experience had given her a sort of psychic life preserver. She had been around too much to have any great expectations. And she was certain that she would never again be passionately in love. So she should have known that it wasn't Max's ultimatum that had triggered her jitters, or sent her on these afternoon-stretching-into-evening walks throughout London so that she'd arrive back at the Springers' flat tired enough to sleep. Somehow she'd intuited contact with her family, felt those invisible tentacles reaching out across continents. And last night they had finally taken hold of her in the form of a telegram: AUNTIE SICK. PLEASE COME HOME.

Even before she'd opened the telegram she'd known it had come from Jamaica because it was addressed to Miss Cecily Baron Nettleton. Ceci had never been a Nettleton in name, her father having changed his name from Angus Nettleton to Archie Baron decades before her birth, when he'd started his theatrical career. Aunt Vivie, who believed that the Nettletons were part of the great chain of history and could never grasp why someone would want to deny that they were a link, always tacked it on.

Poor old Aunt Vivie! The adjectives attached themselves to her as readily as "handsome" fixed itself to Robert Redford or "bald" went with Yul Brynner, for Aunt Vivie was poor in every sense but the financial and she must have appeared old before she'd pulled on her first pair of stockings. Reading the telegram, Ceci had been struck by a wave of remorse. Why had she been so neglectful? She couldn't even recall sending Vivian a change of address card when she'd left New York, though obviously she must've done so. Out of habit she complied with Vivian's request to always keep her informed of her whereabouts "in case of emergency"—Aunt Vivie being primed for emergency as only an old woman leading an unchanging and uneventful life on a decaying sugar plantation could be.

In her early globe-trotting days she'd written to Vivie frequently and sent her a host of postcards. Aunt Vivie had left Jamaica only once, a coming-out visit to "the homeland," where, she'd confessed, the chilly cliffs of Cornwall had seemed more alien than would the savannas of the Transvaal. But, like many island inhabitants, Vivie was an armchair voyager. She devoured travel books and talked of the world's capitals as though she'd actually visited them, though she was far too timid to test her imagination of how things might be to discover them as they really were. In recent years their correspondence had dwindled to an annual exchange of letters.

Around holiday time Ceci would send a gift and write an expurgated account of her life during the past year, the sort of impersonal chronicle a housewife might mimeograph and mail to fifty acquaintances. And sometime in January she would receive a reply written on the heavy, ivory-turned-yellowish stationery that seemed to have been made limp by the tropical climate. She suspected that the stationery must have been ordered by the ton around the time of her birth, for the embossed letterhead said only "Nettleton House, Jamaica, West Indies," and, witness to the Nettleton's continuing glory, that seemed to be sufficient address. The letters had all the intimacy of a report to the stockholders. In a hand grown spidery but still showing the careful up and down strokes of a bygone age of penmanship, Aunt Vivie began with "Salutations of the Season" and went on to record acreage under cultivation, market fluctuations in the price of sugar, and labor disputes. This was followed by detailed descriptions of the weather and jumbled reminiscences of better times, and then, by the third page, as the writing lapsed into a backhand scrawl, gossip about people Ceci had either never known or had ceased to remember. And the conclusion was always the same: Best wishes for her continued health and happiness in the coming year and a P.S. inviting her "home" for a visit, discreetly ignoring the fact that she had not been on the island for over fifteen years and never gave the slightest indication that she would return.

And yet, in a strange way, she did think of the plantation as home. She had lived there for a longer period of time than she had anywhere else, unless she counted the California years before her mother's death, which were almost completely lost to her memory. At the age of eleven, when Archie had tired of his role as grieving widower and responsible parent and she had failed to make an adjustment to an English boarding school, she'd been told that she was being sent on "a lovely holiday" and shipped off to Jamaica. The holiday had lasted for four years.

At first Archie had postponed her return to Hollywood on the excuse that he was working on a movie. Then he had put it off because he wasn't working and was short of funds. After a time he had ceased to give excuses. Though Aunt Vivie viewed children as an alien and possibly dangerous sub-species, she was mindful of her responsibilities as the sole female relative. She explained that men were neglectful by nature, insisted that Ceci write a weekly letter to Archie (though she often went months without a reply), and said they must "carry on." The pain of Archie's abandonment had not initially manifested itself because life on the plantation had been much like an extended picnic.

Aunt Vivie had an aristocratic disregard for both housekeeping and formal education. Meals were served any old time. Dust-mice grew under the beds. The silver was polished but the table napkins were often stained with mildew. Flower arrangements abounded but were allowed to rot in smelly water until someone remembered to throw them out. It was decided that no school on the island was of sufficient caliber to educate a Nettleton, so Mr. Hayward Pembroke, distant cousin to Lady Pembroke, was pressed into service as Ceci's tutor. Three mornings a week he wobbled into the yard on his bicycle to intruct Ceci in Latin, algebra and history, but after a few hours of desultory quizzing he would complain of his weak eyes, accept what he called a libation, and drift into bookish conversation with Aunt Vivie. Then Ceci would be permitted to enjoy another day of glorious freedom.

She swam and fished, picked her lunch off the trees, ran in the fields, and chomped sugar cane. With her best friend Jesmina, a girl of her own age with mahogany skin and beautiful slanting eyes, she milked the goats, collected the still-warm chicken eggs, and napped in the hammock. After the emerald flash of evening she sat, barefooted and wide-eyed, on the steps of the servants' cabins while Icilda, the housekeeper, sipped herb tea and told stories. Icilda's tales were fantastical, full of "duppies" or spirits, with an occasional Bible story thrown in for good measure. Though Ceci prided herself on being less gullible than the other listeners, she sometimes shivered and had to hold Jesmina's hand when told of the doings of the duppies. But the stories she liked best, and could elicit from Icilda with a vow of secrecy and a promise of good behavior, were about her own family. Aunt Vivie had instructed her in her genealogy, but Aunt Vivie's stories were much like Mr. Hayward's history lessons, paeans to the industry, courage, and civilizing influences of her forebears, interspersed with dates. Listening to them, it was impossible to think of a Nettleton having a weak bladder or a rotten temper. In Icilda's tales the Nettletons were all too human: they had murderous fights, secret dealings in land and money, illegitimate children, and (always Ceci's favorites) love affairs blighted by abandonment and revenge.

But this idyllic existence came to an abrupt end around the time of her thirteenth birthday. (In retrospect she understood that it was not the birthday itself but the appearance of her first menstrual period that had changed Aunt Vivie from absentminded custodian to jailer.) She was told that she must wear a nightgown to bed and could no longer run about without shoes, that she must leave off playing and concentrate on her studies, that she could no longer sit on the cabin steps at night, that—and this was like a shaft of iron entering her heart—she must leave off helping Jesmina with her chores and must stop hugging and kissing her. These restrictions came at a time when Ceci was naturally becoming more withdrawn and introspective and her observations of the adult world had taken a precociously cynical turn.

She saw that the overseer, though ostensibly polite, softsoaped Aunt Vivie and made fun of her behind her back. She noticed that "Wayward Hayward" Pembroke's eyes were red and watery even before he began to parse Latin, that the smell of gin came not from his libations but from his very pores, that as he discussed Jane Austen or Daphne Du Maurier with Aunt Vivie his gaze wandered to the arms and backs of the boys who tended the gardens. She sensed the continual backstairs plots and jockeying for position among the servants; discovered that Icilda's loyalty was paid for in hard emotional coin. Even her beloved Jesmina seemed to have gone over to the adult side, for after a brief exchange of clandestine notes and a few meetings behind the wash house, Jesmina became standoffish. She began to call her "Miss Ceci" instead of "Appleblossom"; she took to flirting and holding hands with boys. More and more, Ceci began to feel as though she were under house arrest, her kingdom having been shrunk to her bedroom and the cupola overlooking the surf, where she read and wrote and dreamt of escape.

The boredom of her imprisonment was sometimes broken when Marsden, her half-brother from one of Archie's earlier marriages whom she had not previously known, came from Virginia to visit. Ten years her senior, he had just graduated from West Point. He smoked strong French cigarettes called Gauloises (which Ceci sometimes stole); he listened to Wagner on the old trumpet-horned record player; he had blond body hair that curled above the line of his swimming trunks. Ceci was proud that she was related to such a glamorous figure. Her fantasies were divided between a hope that he would come and take over the plantation or love her so much that he would take her back to America with him. After one of his visits she was so bereft that she threatened to run off into the hills.

And then, on the basis of another whim that she'd never understood, Archie wrote to say that he wanted her sent back to Hollywood. This was around the time when it was discovered that Jesmina had become pregnant, an event that both disgusted and fascinated Ceci. She had never known if Aunt Vivie had written to Archie voicing fears she sometimes muttered in Ceci's presence—that Ceci had become moody and intractable, that her education was being neglected, that the plantation was not a fit place for a young girl, by which, Ceci knew, Vivian meant that pregnancy, like measles, might be contagious—or if Archie had just woken up one morning, remembered that he had left a daughter somewhere, and decided that he wanted her back. Ironically, after years of longing to return to him, she'd felt only anger. It was as though she were some object that could be shifted from place to place. No one thought to ask her what she wanted, and after her first week back in California, she knew that she didn't want to be there. Archie claimed an affection he hadn't earned, exercised an authority she felt he had no right to possess. She complied, just as Icilda outwardly complied with Aunt Vivie's wishes, but she buried her loneliness deep. She guarded her solitude with a jealous and anxious passion. And as she had sat in the chintz and ruffled child's bedroom she'd been forced to leave years before, she'd dreamt of returning to Jamaica.

Even now, as she strode along the streets of London's Holland Park, her shoulders hunched against the wet, her eyes fixed on her boots, she was warmed by the memory of the place. She wanted to see the plantation again. She wanted to see poor old Aunt Vivie. And yet her very survival was predicated on never looking back. If she looked back—

"Yoo hoo, Ceci. I say, Ceci!"

She looked up. She stopped and looked across the street. A clot of people were sheltered under the awning of a greengrocer's shop. A woman raised a red umbrella and began to wave it, then stepped forward, almost knocking over a pyramid of lemons. Still waving the umbrella, she stepped off the curb, moved through the stalled traffic as though she was doing a cakewalk and arrived, breathless and laughing, at Ceci's side.

"Well, blow me down with a feather," she said with a sucking exclamation. "It *is* you. Ceci! What in the world are you doing in London? Why didn't you let me know you were here? How long have you been here?" She brought her lips to Ceci's cheek.

The smell of Coty face powder and nicotine brought a glistening recognition to Ceci's eyes. "Phoebe. Dear, dear Phoebe. It's wonderful to see you! I heard you call but at first I didn't recognize your voice."

"Why should you, ducks? I used to be able to pitch it to the top of the balcony as easily as if I were spinning out a spool of silk, but now I sound like the proverbial fish wi—"

"And even when I saw you crossing the street," Ceci overlapped her, "I didn't . . ." She stopped, pulling back from the embrace. The last time she'd seen her, Phoebe had still been in the artful maintenance stage. She'd hennaed her hair, lined her eyes, and watched her weight. Now wisps of gray protruded from beneath her plastic rain scarf. Her eyes, though still lustrous, seemed smaller, and she wore only a dusting of powder to tone the ruddiness of her cheeks. Always a tall woman, Phoebe was now a large one; her body almost cubic from shoulder to hip. Except for her laugh, which was still throaty and youthful, she'd attained the comfortable but almost sexless dignity of a healthy old woman.

"I know I've changed," Phoebe said, "but it's all for the better. You can't imagine the bliss of total surrender. But you . . ." She reached out, taking a strand of wet hair that trailed Ceci's cheek and tucking it behind her ear. "I do believe you're lovelier than ever." Ceci's face had now attained full maturity and had that highly individual look that passed for real beauty. The mouth was a bit too wide and the jaw a trifle too prominent (Ceci always did lead with her jaw), but the eyes . . . perhaps it was the chic, unhealthy leanness of the face that made her eyes so prominent. . . . No, it was the expression, that looking out of herself. . . . "Imagine running into you like this."

"It is strange, isn't it? I was just wandering about, lost in thought, and then you appeared like the fairy godmother."

"More like a troll in my present condition." Phoebe shifted her shopping basket and linked her arm through Ceci's. "Why didn't you let me know you were here?"

"I rang as soon as I arrived, oh, about three weeks ago. Then I ran into—oh, I forget his name—and he told me you were off doing a play in Edinburgh."

"And so I was, witness to my bloody stupidity. Just got home day before yesterday and was out doing a bit of a shop. I thought I'd gone round the bend when I saw you. Can't possibly be Ceci, I said to myself. Ceci's in New York. Yet in a way I wasn't at all surprised. Call it ESP, but I've been thinking about you ever since I got home. Oh, I know what it was: Your father called night before last, so naturally that put me in mind of you. Have you been in touch? With Archie, I mean."

"No. No. Not for years."

"And, goodness," Phoebe went on hurriedly, "how long has it been since we've seen each other? Four years? Five? You were living in New York, weren't you?"

"Yes. I had a job there. Well, a sort of job."

"And a man too, I'll warrant."

"And a man too." Ceci laughed. "I thought I'd written you."

"I wouldn't dare to scold. You've been a far better correspondent than I, but you move so often I've had to get a new address book because you've taken up the entire B section." Phoebe knew better than to ask about either the job or the man. Both would have been temporary. Ceci had many—perhaps too many—talents, but no particular calling. At one time she'd been keen to be a journalist, a career for which she would have been suited in both intelligence and temperament, but for reasons that weren't entirely clear she'd abandoned that idea. She still wrote the occasional travel or fashion piece for the slick magazines, but she'd also worked as a translator in Paris and Brussels, traveled to South America to buy artifacts, designed jewelry in San Francisco. Then there'd been the times it seemed she would settle in with one of her men; six months with a newspaper publisher in Sydney, an entire year and a half with an archaeologist in Mexico.

The girl (but could Ceci properly be called a girl? She must be thirty-one, or was it thirty-three?) didn't seem to be able to make anything stick. She had an unfortunate combination of idealism and recklessness as well as a taste for the high life. She'd gotten on and off enough planes, shared enough apartments in the world's capitals, known (and probably slept with) enough famous men to be, apart from her heartfelt but unsustained efforts with the underpriviledged, part of that raggle-taggle group the gossip columnists called the jet set. Yet, as Phoebe would put it only to herself, Ceci didn't have "a pot to piss in or a window to throw it out of." Much to her credit, Ceci had never taken any money from the family, and she even seemed to walk away from affairs without so much as a token from her lovers.

Phoebe sighed, directing her eyes to the curtain of rain that fell from the cornice of the building under which they'd sheltered themselves, as though it was the weather that was bothering her. "Well, let's not stand about like two wet hens. You know my old flat's just around the corner. Let's make a dash for it."

Drenched and laughing, they reached the front door. Phoebe caught her breath, complained about being winded but said it was her own bloody fault. In the entrance hall she took off her coat and scarf, handed them to Ceci, then walked into the front room. The storm had grown in intensity, and the interior of the flat was dark. Phoebe switched on a standing lamp and went to the fireplace. After striking a match to the kindling, she looked back at Ceci, who was still poised on the threshold. "You'd best go and dry your hair, love. I'll put the kettle on. Just put our coats in the bathroom. You know the place. Hasn't changed a bit."

The furniture was the put-your-feet-up variety, well made but of no particular period or design. The dark wainscoting set off the flowered wallpaper, which fought for attention with the equally colorful carpet. Books, papers, and pieces of Phoebe's shell collection were strewn about on tables that looked as though they'd gone some time without seeing a dust cloth. A faint but not unpleasant odor of cooking hung in the close air. Indeed, the room seemed not to have changed, from either the last time Ceci had seen it or that first time, shortly after her mother's death, some twenty-odd years ago. Then Archie had guided her across the threshold; then, as now, her feet had been wet.

"This is Phoebe," Archie had said, putting his hands on Ceci's shoulders and moving her into the room. "I've told you all about Phoebe, remember?" He had never mentioned any Phoebe, yet the woman with the funny nose and eyes the color of bittersweet chocolate had come toward her, arms outstretched. She'd noticed that Ceci's shoes were soaked and had given her a pair of men's woolly socks. Archie had laughed at the way they had fallen about her ankles. Plates of raspberries, scones, and clotted cream had been brought out. Ceci had dribbled some of the raspberry juice on her jumper. Archie had pulled Phoebe to him but she'd pushed him away, rolling her eyes in Ceci's direction and calling him "a case." Then Phoebe had given her a book to read and she and Archie had disappeared into the rear of the flat. She had known better than to follow them. Defiantly, she'd licked the cream from her plate and set about "spying." Rummaging through drawers and book shelves, she'd discovered a clue: a photo of Phoebe and Archie, both much younger and wearing stage makeup. Phoebe was dressed as a maid. Archie, the dapper master of the house, was ogling her. The inscription, in Archie's hand, said, "When we lived on hope and tuppence, those were the days," and was signed "S.B."

That she remembered this scene so clearly did not convince her that it had actually happened. In reconstructing the past she knew that she might take a scrap from one scene and attach it to another. The raspberries and cream, the fire in the hearth, and the men's woolly socks—of these she was reasonably sure; the photo she'd probably discovered later, when she was staying with Phoebe. Archie and Phoebe may have gone off into the bedroom, but since she'd been eleven at the time, they would have been in their fifties—hardly the age for instantaneous and undeniable passion. She had probably given their disappearance a sexual innuendo because she had intuited their previous relationship, though at that first meeting she had not known that Phoebe had been the first of Archie's four wives, as her mother, Mabs, had been the last.

If Archie and Phoebe had gone off, it had probably been to discuss what Archie should do with her. He had brought her along on what was to be a grand European tour. Their first stop had been London, but after the initial euphoria of return, Archie had fallen into a galloping melancholia. The theatrical success of some of his old chums had made him lament his choice of Hollywood. Having a child in tow had curtailed his activities, and the fact that people often took him to be her grandfather instead of her father had put a further dent in his ego. He'd taken to staying out late at night. Sometimes he hadn't come back to the hotel at all, and Ceci had been increasingly left in the care of hotel employees who were charmed by her Americanisms. Finally, Phoebe had been pressed into service. She'd let Ceci stay with her while Archie had gone off to tour the Continent alone. Later, he'd stopped off in London on his way back to Hollywood and settled her into boarding school at Roedean.

Ceci watched the drops of water fall from the tip of the umbrella onto the linoleum of the entrance hall. The kindling had started to catch, giving a flickering illumination to the seascape above the mantelpiece. The lamp made a circle on the rose-colored carpet. These scraps of warmth and light gave her not just a feeling of comfort but one of deliverance. Perhaps, she thought as she dispersed the puddle with the tip of her boot, it was not just an accident that had led her to walk in Holland Park. Perhaps she had been unconsciously haunting the neighborhood, waiting for Phoebe's return.

"Oh, Ceci," Phoebe's voice trumpeted from the kitchen. "Is tea all you want? Are you hungry? Would you like a nip?"

Ceci roused herself. "No, just tea will be lovely." She crossed the living room into the passageway. The walls were decorated with the occasional flower print bearing the flower's Latin name. Phoebe's flat was a real home, so different from the Pacific Palisades house where Ceci had spent her early and teenage years. Even as a child she'd known that that place was a museum to Archie's career, as though he might forget who he was if not surrounded by wall-to-wall reminders.

As part of the 1930s exodus of British talent lured to Hollywood by the hope of riches and worldwide fame, Archie had been constantly and lucratively employed, but his star had never risen to what he'd hoped would be its zenith. Instead he had quickly reached, and for several decades remained on, that dubious plateau between fame and anonymity. (His face would be recognized by any film buff, but that same film buff would be hard put to give the face a name.) So Archie treasured every scrap of evidence of his celebrity. His living room was papered with studio stills of his myriad, but to all save him, forgettable roles: the leading man's best friend in the society romance, the courtier to various Antoinettes, du Barrys, and Elizabeths in the costume drama; the second commanding officer in the empire epics and World War II patriotic films. Much later he'd played a dour-faced butler on a television series, but he'd kept no mementos of this. His library was given over to photos of his social life, most of which had centered around the British community: Archie lunching with Vivien and Larry, clowning with Elsa and Charles, drinking with George Sanders or David Niven, dining with

Noël Coward. Even the bathroom had not escaped decoration since, Archie quipped, the likeness of Jack Warner had a loosening effect on the bowels.

She could imagine Archie at this very moment, posed in front of his fireplace, telling one of the stories that she'd come to despise. His guests would be poised and attentive (those who weren't were never asked back), ready to ask him to repeat how he'd told C. B. De Mille to go to hell or what he'd done to save Michael Wilding from slipping off the deck of Errol Flynn's yacht. Just thinking about it made her skin go prickly with the sort of embarrassment only an adolescent would feel.

She threw the raincoats over the shower stall and began to towel her hair, pleased to see that the only things on the wall were a print of a Bonnard nude and a note in Phoebe's bold hand reminding her to TAKE YOUR BLOOD PRESSURE PILLS.

As she returned to the living room, the clatter of dishes from the kitchen felt as soothing as a solo piano in a softly lit bar. The tea service had already been set: porcelain and silver, daffodils in a crystal vase. She smoothed the embroidered tablecloth and picked up a matching napkin. Phoebe, who had an almost stoic disregard for material things, had managed to accumulate them. Even in lean times, Phoebe knew how to "be poor without feeling poor." Ceci was just the opposite. She'd left reminders of her taste on several continents, most recently in Max's apartment. She lived high, but she always felt poor.

"So here we are." Phoebe carried in the water kettle and a plate of cucumber and tomato sandwiches. She set the kettle on the burner, wrapped her cardigan around her bosom, and settled into her chair, picking up the teapot. "You're lemon, no sugar, aren't you?"

"Yes, please. Lemon, no sugar." This remembrance of her tastes touched her. Her hand trembled slightly as she accepted the cup, took a sip and leaned back.

"Just listen to it coming down," Phoebe said after a moment.

Ceci nodded, her eyes moving about the room and fixing on

a photo of her other half-brother, Archie and Phoebe's only child. She had met him only once, and that had been at least a decade ago. "How is . . ." Her mind went blank. Was it Eric or Ian? ". . . Eric?"

"Oh, Eric. Eric's lovely. Never had any trouble with Eric. Deciding to have him was the biggest decision I ever made, but after that he more or less took care of himself. He became a grandfather last month. I was supposed to go to the christening but I was working. There's a picture of the baby somewhere around here." She started to rise, then decided against it. "Can't remember where I put it. I may have sent it to Archie. Don't suppose it matters. They all look much alike when they first come out, don't they? I've never been soft on babies. But this production—not the baby—I meant this latest play I did in Edinburgh, what a dreary piece of business that was. Rained the entire bloody time. And I had trouble remembering my lines. Dried up time after time, I did. It was stupid of me to take the job, but at my age one can't be too particular."

"What do you mean," Ceci remonstrated. "I'm sure you still get more offers than you want to accept." She supposed this was the truth, but she winced inwardly as she said it. Trained to pander to people's egos, she never felt quite truthful even when she was sincere in her praise.

"Have to keep my hand in, shaky though it may be. I've got that little house in the country to support now."

"I caught a few segments of that BBC series. The one where you were playing the queen mother. No, not the queen mother. Some Roman emperor's mother."

"Same difference." Phoebe laughed. "Yes, I was rather good in that one, if I do say so myself. Wouldn't Archie be shocked to hear me say that I love working on the telly? But it's money for jam, I don't have to worry about remembering my lines, and it's so nice when your neighbors can talk to you about your performance." She noted that Ceci had ignored all of her references to Archie, but she was determined to talk about him, even if she had to do it by a circuitous route. "You know I based my characterization for the empress on Archie's mother. Oh, she was a dragon, was that one. Be glad she shuffled off this mortal coil before you were born."

"But you met her only once, didn't you?" Ceci had heard the story many times but knew Phoebe wouldn't resist telling it again.

"Ah, yes, but once was enough." Phoebe poured herself some tea, scooped sugar from the bowl, and held the spoon above the cup, studying it. It was clear that Ceci didn't want to talk about Archie so perhaps it would be best to set them both afloat on a tide of remembrance. "You know the first time I took tea with Archie he said 'Give us some of our sugar.' At the time I thought the 'our' was a slip of the tongue. Little did I know that he did consider it his. His and his family's. He was still going by the family name then. Still called himself Angus Archibald Nettleton. But he hadn't told me anything about the sugar plantation in Jamaica. I knew that he'd been born there because he still had that strangely soft way of pronouncing his vowels. But I didn't know that the Nettletons practically owned the entire bloody island. You know Archie told me that when he was sent to England to go to school he expected the boys to treat him with special respect because he thought that the entire British Empire would be without jam and lollies if it weren't for the Nettletons. I nicknamed him S.B. for Sugar Baron. Always called him that. Though later, as I told him, it meant Selfish Bastard. That's what ruined Archie, you know. Being born in the tropics. Gave him a sense of entitlement just because of the color of his skin. Gave him the habit of command without any of the sense of responsibility that should go with it. But now I'm off the track. I was telling you about the meeting with Lady Mother." Whether out of concern for her diet or a renewed distaste for anything that reminded her of the Nettletons, Phoebe dumped the spoonful of sugar back into the bowl and took a cigarette.

"Archie and I were well into our affair at that point. Virgins both of us, so you can imagine that it hit us rather hard. He'd courted me for ever so long. Played the toff-who's-seen-the-error-of-his-ways routine. Even went to a few socialist meetings with me. Little did he realize that he didn't really have to court me at all. One good squeeze in the right place would have done it. Oh, he was handsome in those days." She inhaled and coughed, staring at the ripple of smoke with misty remembrance. "And more than handsome. He had some spirit. Wanted to set his own path in the world. He told me how shocked he was when he found out that one of the little pickaninnys who was working around the plantation was related to him. It wasn't so much that his grandfather had had a mistress—if there was one thing Archie understood even before he knew he understood it, it was the weakness of the flesh—and besides, that sort of thing, as you well know, is accepted on the island. Not talked about; but accepted. No, it was the fact that his grandfather had more or less abandoned the boy. That shocked him. Archie wanted to break away from all that privilege and hypocrisy. And there were times when I actually thought he might." Her lips twitched into a smile where resignation still fought with regret. "His going on the stage was, at the beginning at least, a gesture of spite. And I was the red flag he waved in front of the family. Some people never have the courage to say no to their family outright, so they pick a mate they know will offend, if you know what I mean."

"Yes, I had one like that a few years back."

Phoebe waited for her to elaborate, but Ceci picked up a sandwich instead. "So there we were, about to meet Lady Mother. It was a strain for us to get out of bed to get to Claridges on time, but that didn't matter because Mother was predictably late. So we fortified ourselves with a bottle of champers. I'd borrowed a hat from the costume room. It was horribly worn, of course. Only made my dress look like the rag it was. And owing to the champers and Archie's repeated embraces it was all askew by the time Lady Mother and sister Vivie arrived. The only time Lady Mother looked directly at me was to comment on that hat. She said something about pheasant feathers being so appropriate for winter, and of course we were coming into spring. Most men wouldn't have caught that. Most men are purblind when it comes to female backbiting. But Archie, give him his due, rose to the occasion. In one fell swoop he told her that he'd decided to make the theater his career, that he was going to marry me, and that he'd changed his name to Archie Baron. He must've decided the name change on the spot, because I remember him winking at me as he refilled my champagne glass. The name change was the thing that almost made the old girl drop her knickers. More tea, my dear?" Phoebe affected a tight-lipped, gelid-eyed imitation of Lady Mother as she picked up the teapot. "But surely, out of family loyalty, you will take two lumps, won't you?"

Ceci smiled and shook her head. The rain was less insistent now and she had a silly anxiety that once it stopped, Phoebe would stop talking and she would be forced to leave. She rose from her chair and put another log on the fire. Phoebe asked if she might get her a cardigan, but Ceci shook her head again, and asked her to continue the story.

"Ah, it was all so long ago. You can't imagine the sense of power those people had in those days."

"Rich people usually have a sense of power. As well they might," Ceci said dryly.

"But the Nettletons! They had it all sewed up, as you Americans would say. They grew the sugar. They shipped the sugar. They even had a factory in Nottingham where they made it into lollies. It took a certain courage, as well as a certain youthful ignorance for Archie to walk away from all that." Again, she looked to see if Ceci had any reaction to Archie's name, but Ceci, back turned, continued to poke at the fire. "Nevertheless, Archie made his manifesto. I don't think it worried Lady Mother that he planned to marry me. She'd dismissed that with a single blink of her hooded eyes. She'd lived her whole life ignoring the flings her menfolk had had with the lower orders, and I suppose she thought of me as a native girl of another stripe. She did send a note around to my flat asking me to meet with her privately, but I assumed that was to offer me a bribe so I never went. One good thing about impractical people such as ourselves is that we know others don't share our values. And the great weakness of people like Lady Mother is that they assume everyone shares theirs. That everyone has a price. She thought I'd care more for money than I did for Archie and sometimes . . ." A fit of violent coughing caused Phoebe to break off. Red in the face, regaining her breath slowly, as though she were counting backward, she turned away.

Ceci averted her eyes and gazed into the flames. It was painful to see Phoebe, so strong in so many ways, continuing an addiction that not only hurt her health but affected her professional life. Why was it so impossible to break old habits? Why couldn't people do what was good for them? She herself worked hard at keeping her addictions in hand. Sometimes she was able to go for weeks without a cigarette or a drink. Of course, when she hit a rough spot . . .

"And sometimes," Phoebe continued, having recovered herself at last, "sometimes I did curse myself for my impracticality. But as I was saying, Lady Mother could have taken our affair in stride. She didn't mind the theater business either, since the young master was supposed to have his fling and she supposed that after a year or two Archie would come back, tail between his legs, asking for some position with Nettleton Limited. But the prospect of Archie abandoning the family name! That was heresy. That was unthinkable."

"Yes." Ceci threw her head back. "I remember when I was sent to live with Aunt Vivie. She expected me to memorize when the great house had been built, when the sugar market had peaked and fallen. The sad thing was that it had all peaked even before she was born."

"It must've been dreadful for you. I warned Archie at the time. It was absolutely brutal to uproot you like that. First dragging you to England, then shipping you off to Jamaica, then dragging you back to Hollywood. The adjustments you had to make!"

"Or didn't make." Her fingers played with the silver heart on the long chain around her neck. "Did I tell you I got a telegram from Jamaica yesterday?"

"No." Phoebe leaned forward. "What . . . ?"

"It was typically Nettleton, cryptic and demanding. Just 'Auntie sick. Please come home.' Naturally they were too tightfisted to make a phone call. So I did. I was surprised when Vivie herself picked up the phone. She said 'Oh, what a lovely surprise,' as though nothing at all had happened.

Then she ignored all my questions about her health and proceeded to dredge up some trivial incident from my childhood. When I asked her again how she was feeling, she started into something about the outlying acreage showing a sluggish profit. I suggested she best consult Marsden about that. He's been living down there for a couple of years now. I tried again to find out what had happened to her but she got very strange —her voice dropped to a whisper and she started talking in a rush of words, with certain words and phrases given special emphasis, as though she were talking in code and I was expected to decipher it. I had the distinct impression that someone, perhaps one of the servants, had come into the room. Because she started to blather about her garden. I mean! I don't mind paying international rates, but not to hear about aphid infestation. Then Marsden took over the phone, and after the usual preliminaries, *he* started talking in a whisper. Can you imagine: fourteen rooms and they all go about whispering. He said the doctors suspected Vivian had suffered a partial stroke. Apparently the physical manifestations are so slight as to be unnoticeable, but the old girl is somewhat disoriented, though if I remember correctly, disorientation is nothing new. I volunteered to come but he brushed it aside. Said the staff had been increased and that he and his fiancée —Hilary I think her name is—were seeing to everything. It was all very strange. I had the impression that I'd misdialed a number and interrupted a dinner party."

"It all sounds a bit fishy to me." Phoebe narrowed her eyes. "Don't you think you should go anyway? I mean if you can spare the time. Perhaps Vivian sent the telegram herself. Perhaps . . ."

"I don't know." Ceci shook her head slowly. "I would like to see her but . . ."

"Of course you would. And you should go. Apart from your concern with Vivian, there is the estate. When she dies—"

"Please, let's not start worrying about my inheritance." Ceci laughed.

"I must say that for a woman without any real money of her own you're taking a very cavalier attitude to . . ." Phoebe stubbed out her cigarette. There was no point in souring their reunion by turning preachy. She'd get to that later. "Don't you have any desire just to see Jamaica again? I should think . . ."

"Jamaica, Paris, Istanbul, New York." Ceci waved a languid hand. "It doesn't much matter. So there's a mosque in one and a cathedral in the other. It's all the same earth, isn't it? And an American Express card will get you a scotch in most places. Do you remember when I worked as a translator in Brussels? I sat in on lots of important meetings there. Great, important things were discussed—population control, hunger, trade agreements. And it didn't really matter if the delegates were from Nigeria or Iraq or West Berlin or the U.S.A. They all railed against '*your* country's policies' being responsible for '*my* country's problems' but when the television cameras were turned off, they all drank together and ate together. And slept together. They're the only country, really. The world elite."

Phoebe shrugged and allowed herself to look confused. Ceci was deflecting the conversation from her personal concerns in a very clumsy way.

"Love of country is just a pose," Ceci went on, leaning forward to show that she was getting to a point. "It's like Archie becoming more British the longer he stayed away. Boodles gin and tweeds in a California climate, no less. Sausage rolls and Earl Grey tea from the English deli in Beverly Hills when he couldn't even pay my school tuition. And his accent getting thicker every year, even when he wasn't playing a part. Oh, yes, the country squire with his bloody, bloody dogs! Mind if I have one of your cigarettes?"

Phoebe handed her the pack. If only in a spurt of anger, Ceci had finally mentioned Archie. "You're being very hard on the old boy," Phoebe plunged in. "Archie has his faults, as I'd be the first to admit, but . . ."

"Nonsense, you'd be the last to admit them. I should think that after the way he treated you . . ." She stood, arms across her breast, puffing on the cigarette.

Even as Ceci denigrated her father, Phoebe was struck by her likeness to him. Her dark hair and delicate nose, these she'd gotten from her mother Mabs, but everything that distinguished her most—her long limbs, her wide-set eyes, her large hands and feet—was Archie's. And the resemblance went beyond mere physical appearance to that indefinable thing called breeding: that quality that made you notice a particular horse when it was led to the starting gate and made you want to bet on that horse even though you knew it was too high-strung, too skittish to be controlled. Much as Ceci disapproved of Archie, she had also inherited his style. She acted as though living beyond her means was almost an heroic gesture, she could create unlimited effect with very little money, and her hedonism was always fighting a covert war with her conscience. And just now, as she lifted her chin and straightened her spine, there was even a bit of Lady Mother there. Her pose might be one of never making demands, but there was something very demanding in her.

"As I said," Phoebe said finally, feeling the impotence of the peacemaker, "Archie is not without fault. But then, which of us is? And you didn't see him in his finer hours. I'm not just talking about his performances. He went all over the place during the war. And he didn't just entertain in the U.S.O.s as some of them did. He put himself in danger. He made great sacrifices. He went to the combat zones. And afterward, he did that tour of the hospitals and read Shakespeare to the boys."

Ceci rolled her eyes upward. "Spare me."

"I expect he told them a few dirty stories, too. Just to keep their spirits up. He got a declaration of thanks from the President himself."

"Which he promptly displayed on his bedroom wall."

"It doesn't mean someone isn't courageous just because he needs the odd reminder of his courage. And . . ." Phoebe continued breathlessly, not wanting to give up the floor until she'd made her point, "no matter what you think, he did love your mother very much."

"Archie's never loved anybody but himself. If he married my mother it was because *she'd* fallen in love with him before she'd even got to Hollywood. When she was sixteen and worked as an usher at a Loews theater in Brooklyn, she saw him up there, thirty feet high, and despite all evidence to the contrary she continued to think of him as thirty feet high until the day she died. *And* she was fifteen years younger and not particularly demanding, and I suppose he thought she'd take care of him in his declining years since he'd squandered most of his energy and nearly all of his money on the women who'd preceded her." She threw her half-smoked cigarette into the fire and moved back to the couch to pick up her teacup. Her eyes over the rim of the cup met Phoebe's and challenged them.

"Perhaps you're right. Perhaps I have grown sentimental. You know, when Archie brought you here that first time, I was still a bit in love with him. I still entertained illusions about our getting back together. Not in the old ways, of course, no champers at noon and destroying the mattress, but . . ."

"And don't you know that when you were willing to forgive and forget, Archie was chasing after girls who were younger than I am now?"

"It was his last dip in the pool before the sun went down. If you were older . . . I don't know. You reach a stage where it isn't important to assign blame anymore. There has to be forgiveness, or there's no going on."

"And it's always the woman who forgives, right?"

"So it seems. But that may be the best thing for her to do. Even for herself. After all, you forgave Adam."

"Adam?" Ceci looked as though she had some difficulty remembering the name. "Oh, Adam. What was there to forgive?"

"I remember when I came to visit you shortly after you married him. You were living in that tiny apartment near the Santa Monica beach. You'd tried so hard to turn it into a home. You baked . . ."

"Unsuccessfully."

"You cleaned."

"I thought that was what wives were supposed to do. Though Adam always took his laundry back to his mother's place in Beverly Hills because he liked the way the maid did his shirts." She laughed. "Oh, dear me. Adam! Well, what could I have expected?" She had expected a great deal, deliverance, happiness, love. She'd been the misfit. The gawk. The girl who wore braids and spoke with a funny accent while her peers had flowing hippie hair and tight jeans and communicated with signs and slang she hadn't understood. Living on the island had left her in another era. The first time someone had given her a V sign, she'd thought it had something to do with Winston Churchill. One of her greatest fears, that she would not be able to keep up academically, had turned out to be groundless, but she hadn't been able to score points by reading Cicero or listening to *Parsifal* when the others were "into" Ken Kesey if they read at all, and singing along with Bob Dylan and the Stones. It wasn't as though any of her school mates were unkind to her. She'd never seen the snicker that would have at least acknowledged her presence because she was invisible, beneath ridicule. And then Adam Goldman, boss of the surfing crowd, had noticed her. And since she was the only remaining virgin on the high school campus, Adam had decided to score. "Did I ever tell you how we decided to get married?" she asked. Phoebe shook her head.

"Well," she went on, enjoying the self-mockery, "Adam and I were sitting in my bedroom at the Palisades house smoking joints while Archie and Adam's father Mort and a few other knights of the round table were knocking back the gin on the patio." How frightened she'd been, taking that first drag. How grateful that Adam had wanted her to. "And we got to giggling about them and adding up their marriages. Two little Hollywood brats dishing the Hollywood gossip. We thought they all belonged in the dinosaur graveyard, swearing 'till death do us part,' then a year or two later, more lawyers and custody fights. Then we smoked another joint . . . and another. Adam said he wished life could be like those Walt Disney movies where the animals mate and then live together for the rest of their lives. I think he even called me Bambi." She laughed. "Imagine being seduced by a boy who couldn't even get the gender of a cartoon character right." He had also said that he loved her—something no one but her mother had ever expressed—and when she'd pushed his hand away from the zipper of her jeans, he'd said that he wanted to marry her. "Then we got it on, or as you English would say, we had it off. Goodness." She put down her cup and opened her eyes wide. "That must've been the root of my confusion. All these years I've never known if I was getting it on or having it off. But now I'm losing the thread of my story."

"But now you're being flip."

"What other can I be? Marrying Adam at eighteen. Thinking I'd have a life of babies and health food picnics and intellectual companionship. With Adam? Adam, who didn't have enough concentration to read the headlines in *Variety*, who thought culture was something you started yogurt with? But it wasn't Adam's fault. Adam was the same at the end of the marriage as he was at the beginning. I can't say he ever led me on."

"No. From what I remember of Adam he didn't have mind enough to be a plotter. But you were desperate to get away from Archie."

"Well, certainly." Ceci shrugged. "Certainly that too. I'm just glad Adam chose his surfboard over parenthood. Even after a year and a half of marriage, we knew we couldn't stand each other."

"I must say you're consistent. You're as hard on yourself as you are on everybody else. But then, you always have been." From the first time she'd met her, a girl whose eyes begged affection but were wary of trusting it, Phoebe had known that Ceci would have trouble with men. But Ceci had bounced back from that ridiculous early marriage. She'd come back to England, enrolled in the London School of Journalism, gotten a part-time job. It seemed that she'd taken charge of her life. Then Paul Strangman had come along. He was the one who had really broken Ceci's heart, though she knew Ceci would scoff at such an expression. It was after Paul Strangman that Ceci had become a bird of passage, going from continent to continent and bed to bed, behaving as though she'd thrown out the rules when, in fact, she'd just adopted that modern rule of controlled intimacy. Ceci now pretended that love and sacrifice and desperation about sex gave one a hopelessly neu-

rotic way of looking at the world, that any expectation of a
future was naive, that commitment, even to a career, might
rob her of spontaneity and freedom. It was, Phoebe thought,
a seemingly worldly but sad view of life; more importantly,
it went entirely counter to what she saw as Ceci's true nature.

"Oh, stop looking at me like that, Phoebe."

"Like what?"

"With all that patience and expectation on your face. As
though I were a two-year-old you'd just put on the potty and
you were waiting for me to *do* something."

"I'm not waiting for you to do anything but tell me what's
going on in your life. And the potty? Really, Ceci. We're
beyond the anal stage. I'm beyond the genital stage myself. So
I suppose we should talk about something spiritual."

"Don't play coy with me. I know you want to talk about
love. Even the brightest women always revert to love gossip."

Phoebe's deep breath lifted her bosom several inches. "You
may call it gossip if you wish, but isn't gossip just a way of
expressing interest in other people's lives? I'm far too close to
the end of mine to waste time pretending that I'm interested
in things I'm not interested in. I prefer a good action movie
to the opera. I'd rather work on telly than in the theater. And
I'm still interested in love. It's one of my favorite topics. So
if you want to denigrate that by calling it gossip, that doesn't
offend me."

"All right. I give." Ceci laughed. "What do you want
to know about? The man I've been living with? His name
is Max. I've been living with him for about ten months,
and . . ."

"Is he rich and famous? Does he have a heart like a motor
and hands like velvet?"

"Phoebe, you do go on. He is rich, yes. Famous, no. He
buys and sells companies. Calls himself a venture capitalist,
though I tease him by calling him a vulture capitalist." She
went on to give a description of Max, wondering why she
sounded so halfhearted while saying mainly positive things.

"And does he love you?"

"Yes, I think so."

"Well, that's half the battle." She wouldn't put Ceci on the spot by asking the other side of the question. "Perhaps it's the better half. I'm not lucky enough to know from experience." She shifted in her chair, reaching for another cigarette. "Do you ever hear anything of Paul Strangman?"

The name dropped through Ceci's consciousness like a stone falling to the bottom of a clear pond, but she arched her eyebrows and shrugged. "Paul Strangman? That was a long, long time ago. You could find out more about Paul Strangman from reading the papers than you could from me. The last time I saw him was about a year and a half ago, on a television interview show."

"He had the most unusual coloring. I shall never forget his eyes. You used to say they were the color of the water around the shores of Jamaica."

"When in heat I have been known to resort to hyperbole. His eyes were greenish, I believe. One was idealistic; the other was ambitious. At close range I'm afraid I didn't notice the difference."

"Now that's unfair, Ceci. Paul was one of the most charismatic men I've ever met. Just listening to him talk made me want to go out and be a revolutionary. And you can't accuse him of not having integrity. He damn near reeked of integrity. Perhaps not always in his dealings with you, but . . ."

"I should have anticipated that. I could hardly expect him to take our little affair too seriously. He had other things on his mind. Becoming Prime Minister of Jamaica principally. Despite all their political cant about equality I think that for men like Paul, women fall under the heading of 'Rest and Relaxation.' "

"I don't think so, Ceci. He did love you. I could see that. They say there are two things you can't hide: love and a cough." As if on cue she began to cough, covering her mouth with her hands and rolling her eyes at the timing of her joke. "No," she continued, "you and Paul Strangman touched a very deep chord in each other. I knew that from the few times I saw you together. One could sense the excitement, the respect and concern."

"Were my less pleasant emotions of jealousy, anxiety, and possessiveness equally obvious?"

Phoebe sighed. "It's been my observation that they're like fish and chips. Is that why you don't want to go back to Jamaica? Because Paul's there?"

"Good heavens, no. I hadn't even thought about that."

The room became so quiet that only the ticking of the hall clock and the patter of rain against the panes was heard. The flames caught the resin from one of the logs, causing it to sizzle and pop. Ceci blinked. "Funny thing about sitting by a fire," she said softly. "It makes me feel very old and very young at the same time. I do have a birthday coming up in a few days."

"Bless me, so you do. Thirty . . . ?"

"Three. I didn't feel much when I turned thirty, but now . . ."

"I'm sure if Archie knew where to reach you he'd want to give you a call. Perhaps if I . . ."

Ceci picked up the pack of cigarettes, began to shake one out, shoved it back in and raised her face to the ceiling with a please-release-me-oh-Lord look. "Dear Phoebe. You've talked about Archie, you've talked about Paul Strangman. Could we please get on to something else?"

"But you haven't heard what Archie had to say when he called the other night."

"You are like a dog with a bone, aren't you?"

"He was very down. He doesn't know what to do with himself. He even mentioned selling up and going to live at the actors' home. You can see how depressed he must be. I think he'd like to go back to Jamaica for a visit, but I don't think he wants to go alone. He says Marsden's invited him. Marsden's got some scheme for turning that ancient house into a convention center or something."

Ceci looked as though she'd just sucked on a lemon. "Christ. To think we'd end up in the bed and breakfast business."

"A bit grander than that, I think."

"I don't care. It has nothing to do with me."

"Of course it does. Part of that property is bound to come to you. You really should take an interest, find out what's going on with it. I'm not saying that if you marry this Max you'd be the bird in the gilded cage; but a little cash of one's own never hurt a partnership. The money's not the only thing. Archie is getting older."

"That, I hear, is the human condition."

"Precisely. One can't put these things off."

"With all due respect, I don't see why someone's getting older entitles them to special treatment. If they're a selfish bore at fifty they're likely to be an even bigger one at seventy. You said a bit ago that you weren't particularly fond of babies because it's only sentimental to be so. I couldn't agree more. I'm not going to put a wreath on Archie's head just because he's lost his hair."

"Regret is one of the most painful emotions, Ceci."

"Phoebe, please."

"No. Our time together is brief." Phoebe got up and came to sit on the couch. She wanted to put her arm around Ceci, but remembering that Ceci rejected comfort as much as she craved it, she folded her hands in her lap. "Regret is one of the most painful emotions—I know I just said that—I repeat myself a good deal these days and it's far more annoying to me than it can be to you, so do be quiet." She pushed a few wisps of hair back from her forehead and stared into the flames. "Don't think I'm advising you just out of concern for Archie. The case could be made that Archie doesn't deserve your concern. The most anger I've ever felt toward Archie wasn't because of how he treated me, or even because he sold his own talent short. It was the way he treated you, and . . ."

"I'm not going back to Jamaica," Ceci cut her off in a soft, even voice.

"I always disliked my father," Phoebe said after a long pause.

"Yes. You've told me that."

"He was an accountant and my mother was a wild Irishwoman with red, red hair and a temper to match. Why they married I'll never know because she never suited his habits of strict accounting either with the housekeeping money or on issues of morality. I didn't suit them either. He practically called me a whore when I decided to go on the stage. The point . . . the point is that I was so unforgiving that when he was dying I refused to go to see him in the hospital. I know all the reasons why I didn't go. I can even forgive myself for not going. I don't think he would have acknowledged me if I had gone. But he's dead now. If I'd gone . . . well, at least I would have known that I'd tried."

"And he probably would have rejected you and acted like a shit and you'd have felt angry as well as regretful," Ceci said as she got up and walked to the window.

Phoebe laughed. "You do love to win an argument, don't you?"

"Yes. And you must admit I'm pretty good at it."

"You're good at lots of things, Ceci. Many, many things." She sighed. "All right. I won't say anymore. I've probably said too much already." She was hoping that when she gave ground, Ceci would relent and ask her to continue, but Ceci shoved her hands into her hip pockets, looked out the window, said "Right," then softened her dismissal with "My, it is getting murky out there."

"Perhaps I could warm up some soup." Phoebe picked up the tea tray.

"Yes. I could do with a drop of homemade soup, and perhaps I'll take a nip of brandy and you can tell me all about your show in Edinburgh."

"I was playing Mrs. Alving in *Ghosts*. I know the part's far too young for me, but when they offered and the money was good I thought this is your last chance, Phoebe, old girl, and ego absolutely ran over common sense. My dear, it took me a bloody hour every night just to get ready to go on! Chin straps and wigs and corselettes that pushed my titties into my armpits and squeezed my guts so I couldn't breathe enough to get the lines out, presuming I could remember them, which of course I couldn't." She lifted the kettle onto the tray and began to gather up the cups. "And I couldn't abide the young man who was playing my son. He fell on his knees and mewled about clutching at my skirts when he was supposed to *resist* my entreaties. I simply wanted to thrash him. But . . ." If only she could nudge Ceci in some positive direction, help her to put her energies into something or someone before it was too late. Before passionate disappointment turned into permanent bitterness. ". . . but I remembered a little hint a director told me ages ago when I was having trouble being vulnerable. He said 'Phoebe, dearest, try going on without your underpants, you'll be surprised how much it will change your performance.' At the time—well, as I said it *was* light years ago—I suspected he had ulterior motives in getting me to drop my undies but . . ." She glanced into Ceci's cup, brought it close to her nose. "I say, Ceci, look at this."

Ceci turned. "What?"

"Here. In your teacup. See how the leaves go up the side like this? That's a sign you're going on a journey."

"I go on lots of journeys. Does it also say I'll win the sweepstakes?"

"No. All I see is the journey."

"And all I see is that the fog's getting worse and I should swallow that soup and get on my way. I could meet you for supper tomorrow night if you like. Oh, Phoebe, do stop staring into that damned cup, otherwise I'll think the only role you can play is one of the witches in *Macbeth*. You Irish are so superstitious. I remember when you told me that if I opened an umbrella in the house or put my hat on the bed I'd have bad luck."

"And have I been proven wrong?" Phoebe asked as she put the plate of sandwiches onto the tray and continued to look into Ceci's cup. "A journey. I definitely see a journey." Satisfied, she carried the tray to the kitchen.

TWO

The ball of the sun was sinking into the Pacific, streaking both water and sky with a pyrotechnic display of golds and corals, but as Angus Archibald Nettleton, known to others and now even to himself as Archie Baron, walked onto the patio of his Palisades home he paid little attention to its magnificence.

Though he was alone and knew he was likely to remain so for the rest of the evening, he had showered, patted his jaws with cologne, combed his hair and mustache, and changed into fresh clothes. This same force of habit had made him bring a full bucket of ice and a plate of limes to the outdoor bar. As he opened the drinks' cabinet, the slanting rays of the sun hit a large assortment of bottles, all but two of which were dusty. He reminded himself to ask Manuela to wipe them off, then, remembering that she now came only once a week, decided that it would be better to point out the mildewed tile around the kitchen sink or the dog hair that matted the library carpet. He poured himself his usual gin and tonic, briefly turned to take in the view, then went back into the kitchen to get the portable TV set.

At one time he had fancied that he would come to an age where, released from the cares of the world, he would be able to devote himself to sunsets and suchlike. But instead of the calm and peace that contemplation of nature was supposed to bring, the waning of the day had the opposite effect. It filled him with uneasiness that often slipped into foreboding, and this evening threatened to slide into anxiety and regret. The fading petals of the hibiscus and oleander made him feel that his sight was going; the flagstones lost the heat they'd absorbed during the day and made his bare feet numb; the rustling on the hillside made him think not of the gentle breath of nature but of some lurking, malevolent presence. Well, his eyes weren't what they used to be. Neither was his circulation. And there had been break-ins in the neighborhood.

He placed the television on the wicker table in front of his chair and looked at his drink. He had a mind to get drunk tonight. Ever since he'd gotten that letter from his son Marsden, his life had been disrupted, and today had just put the capper on it. But he knew he wouldn't get drunk. He'd stop at his usual "one and a fresh-up." Drowning his sorrows would be as inappropriate as speeding along the Pacific Coast Highway with the top down. Those days were over. His stomach couldn't take it any more than present-day traffic on the highway would allow it.

He plugged the TV into the extension cord and sat back, waiting for the picture to emerge. The fact that he owned a television (in fact, not one but three) still surprised him. The advent of television had marked a downturn in his career and, he had once superstitiously believed, in his private life as well. He had sworn never to buy one. But somehow, over the years, though he would never admit to liking it, he'd gotten into the habit of turning a set on as soon as he got up in the morning and letting it drone almost continually until he went to bed.

The newscaster, baby-faced, sprayed, and smiling, was telling of another oil spill near Santa Barbara. Archie wondered vaguely if the tides would bring the spill to the beaches in front of his property, but his thoughts were distracted by the appearance of a young woman in shorts stroking a can of diet soda. Not that he looked at women in that way anymore. When he saw a pretty woman these days he felt like the chef who's prepared the banquet: the display delighted his eye but he didn't salivate. But this particular girl—he wouldn't deign to call her an actress—reminded him of his third and most troublesome wife, Alicia. She had the same vacant but simultaneously intent look, like a cat whose attention has been galvanized by a bird. The animal metaphor ended there, since a cat's expression did not change into one of petulant rage if the bird flew away. But when Alicia was crossed, somebody ended up paying for it. When he'd first bought the house, back in the forties, Alicia had wanted to have a swimming pool put in. He had explained that the hill was too steep for excavation and the natural underbrush was a protection against mud slides, but Alicia had gone ahead with her plans, firing the first architect because he'd agreed with Archie and revenging herself by having an affair with the second.

Perhaps because he'd always associated the house with Alicia's discontents, he had always thought of it as a burden. After their divorce (Alicia, *sans* makeup and jewelry but showing quite a bit of leg, had only to sob into her handkerchief about "this cesspool called Hollywood" to be awarded custody of four-year-old Marsden and most of Archie's money) he'd sworn to get rid of it. But he'd stayed on for what he told himself were practical reasons. The house still looked impressive when he drove his old Bentley up the hill toward it, but the most casual examination showed just how much work needed to be done. It was absurdly large for a man living alone. He had long since had to let the gardener go and to cut back on Manuela's hours. The taxes were eating him alive. He knew that all he'd have to do was pick up the phone and call the real estate man, that same man who'd been dropping by for years, inquiring solicitously about Archie's health and watching him with the calculating eye of a shipwreck victim who knew the water rations were down to the last pint. Yet it had only been during this last week, since Marsden's letter, that he'd actually thought of selling the house.

He took the first swallow of his gin and tonic and realized that he'd forgotten to squeeze in the lime—a trivial omission but a further sign that he was losing control. As he got up and went to the bar, his leg began to tremble. He'd been in a funk ever since that blasted letter. The dividend check that had floated to the floor when he'd opened it had been even smaller than he'd expected, and then there had been the news of Vivian's minor stroke and advancing senility. On a more positive note, Marsden had said that his plans for restoring the great house and turning it into a convention center were going great guns. The sugar market, as Archie must know, was a thing of the past. Something had to be done with the estate. Archie must come to Jamaica and help to convince Vivian to turn over power of attorney to Marsden, otherwise the family's holdings would drift into a further state of decay.

Reading the letter, he'd been seized by a wild notion. He would sell up everything and go to live in Jamaica. Bring his life full circle. End up in the same place in which he'd begun. There was a symmetry in that plan that appealed to him, plus the hope that he might live out his days in a grander style. But then the doubts had begun to creep in. It had been ages since he'd visited the island. He knew nothing of Jamaica anymore. He knew Marsden less well than he knew his barber. And if Vivian had really gone dotty, he didn't know if he could cope with it. He had such an aversion to suffering that he could hardly bring himself to put in an appearance when one of his friends was hospitalized. He surely wasn't up for a sister who'd gone soft in the head.

Though Vivian was his only sibling, he'd never been particularly fond of her. In his mind she was still associated with his mother, and if that association brought about any feeling it was the desire for escape. The only memory he had of their early years together was a vague sensation of having been spied on, for Vivian, always a goody-two-shoes, had liked to catch him in some misdemeanor and rat on him to the adults. The fact that she'd helped to raise Ceci did not mean that he had any particular trust or affection for Vivian, but that she'd been the childless female relative who had a strong sense of family. That Marsden had decided to take up residence in Jamaica and manage the estate was a stroke of luck. It absolved him of responsibility, guaranteed that Vivian's needs would be seen to, and assured him of at least a pittance from the estate. His mother had followed through on her threat to cut him out of all but a fourth of the property, and he had no idea what Vivian planned to do with the remaining three-quarters she controlled, at least legally. He'd dropped Marsden a line, thanking him for the check, sending his best wishes to Vivian, and saying that he couldn't commit himself to a visit because he thought he might begin work on a film—a prospect so devoutly wished for that it hadn't seemed to constitute a lie.

He'd moped about, turning all of this over in his mind, then, feeling the need to talk to someone he trusted, he'd called Phoebe in London. He'd known in advance that he wouldn't want to hear everything she'd have to say, but her advice would at least have the comfort of predictability. Of course he should visit Jamaica, she'd said. Of course he owed it to Vivian to see her, especially if the old girl was going senile. Of course he shouldn't be foolish enough to leave the disposition of the plantation to Marsden. She would countenance no talk of his retirement. Retirement was to Phoebe as the Last Judgment was to most Christians: it might be coming but it was far too formidable and far too remote to be considered. She'd encouraged him to call his agent and, in closing, she'd switched to another predictable question: Had he been in touch with Cecily? He'd answered that he didn't even know his daughter's whereabouts, had mentioned the cost of the call, thanked her, and hung up.

Relieved at having discussed all the things he might do, he'd spent the next few days doing nothing. Intending to write to Vivian, he'd managed to convince himself that he'd already done so. He had pushed all thoughts of Vivian's mental health, Marsden's schemes, and the visit to Jamaica out of his mind in order to make room for his more manageable concerns: a call to his agent, a lube job on the Bentley, a rebroadcast of *Brideshead Revisited*. Then, just last night, when he was sure that he'd brought his life back to a normal if humdrum routine, he'd had a dream that had brought him to trembling wakefulness.

Mabs, his last wife, had appeared to him in this dream. She had urged him, again and again, to perform some minor but neglected household task. He grew increasingly frustrated because he couldn't get her to tell him what this task was. She continued to stare at him, tears welling in her eyes. The rest of the dream was lost to his conscious mind; but as he'd lain there, not knowing if he was hearing a sea sound or just his own blood whispering in his ears, her presence had become so real that he'd almost expected to see her at the bedroom door carrying his breakfast tray, as she'd done throughout their marriage and as she'd done on the last day of her life. He could almost hear the dogs barking on the patio and see Mabs, red-faced, rubbing her coccyx, telling him that he would have to feed the dogs himself. She had gone out with their food bowls. The flagstones had been slippery with dew. The largest dog, Marcus, had lept up and knocked her back-ward, so that she'd fallen, hitting her head on the concrete retaining wall. She'd insisted that only her dignity was hurt, but that perhaps he should wake Ceci, get dressed, and drive her to the hospital for X-rays. That afternoon she had gone into a coma from which she'd never recovered.

As he'd watched the dawn seep in through the windows, the reminder that life could be so quickly and so freakishly snuffed out seemed cause for action. Throwing the sheet from his legs, he'd gotten up, showered and shaved, fixed his break-fast, and, finding himself ready to go but with no particular destination in mind, he'd decided to drive out to Woodland Hills to visit his old friend Mort Goldman at the Screen Actors' home.

The drive itself had exhausted him. The smog was like pea soup, so he'd had to keep the windows up. Both he and the Bentley had stalled on the on-ramp. Even when he'd joined the stream of freeway traffic he'd had trouble keeping up. Other drivers had honked at him, passed him, and almost rear-ended him. So great was the imperative to uniform speed that they hadn't even acknowledged him with the shaking fist or raised middle finger that are the hallmarks of fleeting aggression. This had left him with the feeling that he was both invisible yet threatened, and as he'd escaped to the relative quiet of Calabasas Road he'd found that his neck was tense, his vision blurred, and the crease in his slacks destroyed. Sinking into one of the deckchairs in front of Mort's bungalow, he'd felt that he could stay there, not just for the rest of the afternoon but for the rest of his life.

The operation on Mort's voice box should have ensured that Mort would be more listener than talker, but Mort was in no mood for the give and take of conversation. The surgeon's knife had impaired his capacity, but it hadn't changed his character. Raised on Chicago's South Side, Mort had made a career playing the gangsters he'd known as a child, and if Mort wanted to talk, then by God he would talk. All he'd been waiting for was an audience. With eye-bulging effort, his ascot sucked in and pushed out by the gusts of air coming from the tube in his throat (before his operation he'd referred to Archie's ascots as "fairy ties"), he croaked on, hands gesticulating to illustrate whatever points might be lost. He railed against his family, most particularly his son Adam ("My shiksa wife gave him the wrong name 'cause if he'd been in the Garden of Eden he woulda been the snake. And you let a beautiful girl like Ceci marry that schmuck!"), drifted into his dirty old man routine ("We got a new nurse here with dyed black hair an' melons out to here!"), then ranted about the injustices of Medicare. Just watching him made Archie feel tired. When Archie tried to talk about Jamaica, Mort rasped, "Ain't that the place where Noël Coward died?", then tried to enlist Archie in the Gray Panthers. Fortunately, Mary Astor had wandered by. Revived by a lemonade and the sight of Mary's still beautiful face, Archie bade his farewells and prepared for another two hours on the freeway. Gunning the motor to get back into the four-lane traffic, he'd seen a billboard: "Religion Is the On-Ramp to Eternity." How in hell had he managed to end up in such a place?

He had stopped at an Alpha Beta market on the way home. Waiting in the checkout line, wondering if he would ever find a tomato that tasted like a tomato again or if fruit and vegetables, like actors, were now bred for looks instead of taste, he noticed that the man standing behind him was giving him that "I know who you are but I'm trying to place you" look. Flattered by the incipient recognition, he'd turned so that his profile was more visible. The man, clutching a six-pack to his chest and moving from foot to foot, studied him with undisguised curiosity. Finally, just as the pregnant teenager in front of Archie grabbed the piece of plastic used to separate one customer's goods from the next and slapped it down with fierce territorial imperative, the man spoke. "Didn't you used to be on that TV show? You know the one." He snapped his fingers close to Archie's face. Archie turned away. The man, with a satisfied snort, slapped him on the shoulder. "Yeah, that was you. You were the snooty butler. You used to say 'If that's your pleasure, sir.' That was your line. That used to be you, didn't it? Only in those days you had more hair." Archie pocketed his change. "Yes," he said dryly, "in those days I was more hirsute. And the public had better manners." The man laughed uproariously. "Yeah, I knew that used to be you." Archie took up his package and walked to the exit. Society, he concluded, was now so boorish that it was no longer possible to insult someone. Raised on a diet of television violence, people were now insensitive to verbal displeasure. Either you slugged them or you forgot about it. He'd come home in a mood of desperation that was so intense it had almost made him feel young.

He got up abruptly and switched off the television set. There was a moment when, deprived of its sound, he felt himself to be in a vacuum. Then the insect sounds and the susurrating of the waves closed in around him. The moon was full and he shifted his chair so that his legs were in its light but his upper body was in the shadow of the awning. He put his head in his hands and felt that he was about to weep. He had been called upon only once to cry on camera, and he hadn't been able to do it. In fact, he could count on the fingers of one hand the times in his life when he had been brought to tears. As a boy he'd been told that his moods were self-dramatizing, that he only claimed to feel things deeply in order to call attention to himself. Some of the women in his life and not a few of his friends had said much the same thing, so that even while he'd denied it, he had come to accept their judgment. And he had played so many scenes, in real bedrooms and living rooms as well as on sets, that he wondered if it was possible to tell an authentic emotion from a feigned but deeply felt one. For now, though his eyes were dry, he felt a shudder go through his body and an ache strangle his throat.

He remembered one of the first times he'd been on stage, swearing that he would die of love, and Phoebe, playing opposite him, had delivered the speech that ended, "Men have died from time to time and worms have eaten them, but not for love." Though she had been only twenty, she'd struck just the right note: knowing, subtly mocking, but not unkind.

Phoebe, dear Phoebe. She was the one who had lived with him in bed-sitters whose very seediness had secretly delighted him but had driven her mad. She was the one who had talked him into going to Ealing Studios to find work, who'd sat with him in the stalls of cinemas and told him that of course he stood out in the crowd scenes. She was the one who'd come to Hollywood because he'd had an offer. Had she lived in the days when plastic surgery was perfected, she might have had the bulb removed from the end of her nose and caught some director's eye. As it was she had only a few walk-ons and a single part as a comic headmistress. Yet she'd turned up at the studio at the end of his workday, wearing her brogues and dungarees, her hair cockled from walking on the beach, always laughing, always without pretense. Indeed too much without pretense, since the steady parade of womanflesh at parties, the studio commissary, and poolside at the Garden of Allah (where they'd taken an apartment and marveled at the bathroom tile) had begun to make Archie think that he'd married too young. Yes, Phoebe was game, was Phoebe. She'd even continued to laugh when she'd come in one afternoon and found him on those same bathroom tiles with a tap dancer named Kay. In his innocence, he had believed Kay to be a natural blonde. His shock upon undressing her was only slightly less than his shock at Phoebe's unexpected appearance at the bathroom door.

Phoebe had returned to London the week after the Kay incident, saying only that she was fed up with not working. The divorce had been decided via the mails. It was only after the divorce, when Archie had already married Kay, that Phoebe had shown that her flair for the dramatic was the real thing. She'd let him know that she'd had a baby and had no intention of going through the courts for money but would rely on his sense of decency to support the child. Decades later, when Mabs' death brought him to a short-lived desire to put his life in order, he'd tried to beg Phoebe's forgiveness. "Don't bother, old cock. It's all water under the bridge," she'd said in casual absolution, depriving him of the only heartfelt apology he'd ever wanted to make.

He rubbed his hand over his eyes, then let it drop over the side of his chair, expecting to find his dog Horton's head. The moon had disappeared behind a bank of clouds and he peered around the now dark patio. Horton was not to be seen. He took the last swallow of his drink. "Horton!" he bellowed, rising to his feet, his actor's ear aware of the bullying tone in his voice. Surely the directors had missed their bet by not casting him as a tyrant. He felt his way along the wall to turn on the lights. The patio and hillside were instantly ablaze. He had asked Manuela to replace the lights on the patio and she, with the same delight in primary colors that had caused her to replace the white kitchen shutters with polka-dot curtains and plaster fruit decals on the cabinets, had turned the patio into something resembling an amusement park. He wandered through the kitchen, the dining room, the library, switching on lights as he went, taking in the piles of newspapers, scripts, paintings, photographs, framed fan letters and awards, scarcely daring to breathe lest he choke on Manuela's liberal use of Lysol and floral air fresheners. "Horton!" he called again, stopping by the piano and looking up at the portrait of a six-year-old Cecily above the mantelpiece. It was not a good likeness, the artist having insisted on a cherubic passivity that had never been part of Ceci's character.

In retrospect the years after Cecily's birth had been the happiest of his life, though he'd refused to enjoy them and had moped about, bemoaning his financial troubles and his moribund career. The pride and affection he'd felt for her, sole daughter of his house and heart. The way she'd reached out, seizing his face with both hands for her good-night kiss, fascinated by the mystery of his whiskers. And her strange habit of banging her head against the bars of her crib, but not crying. Her frown of fierce determination as she'd chewed the end of her pencil and learned to write her name. Her precocious but natural social graces—the way she'd looked at him from the corner of her clear, wide eyes when she was being introduced to strangers, then lifted her chin when he indicated approval. Later, when she'd been all knees and elbows, her tennis racket at the ready, imploring, "Don't just *let* me win, Daddy. Play fair." Yes, she had been clever and affectionate and angel-faced. But when he'd reclaimed her after sending her off to boarding schools and Jamaica, she'd returned a different girl. The trusting look in her eyes had turned inward, as though at fifteen, she'd moved into a world of her own making and was prepared to take all shocks. Later, he could see her drifting, squandering her talents, making alliances with the wrong men, yet he had felt powerless to do anything about it. And the last time he had seen her she seemed to have, by a concentrated act of perversity, turned herself into a casually glamorous, brittle but vulnerable woman. The sort of woman he might have picked up and had an affair with.

Not that he was going to assume sole responsibility for the way she'd turned out. He wasn't one of those American parents, interspersing guilt with psychologizing and overindulgence. No. Ceci was her own person. (There had been that early habit of beating her head against the bars of her crib). He knew that all children began by loving their parents; after a time came to judge them and rarely if ever forgave them. Ceci had broken with him just as he'd broken with his own family, though of course he'd had ample justification. Yet as he turned away from the portrait and moved to the staircase in the foyer, he could not help but feel a certain remorse, his pride's substitute for repentance, as he remembered how Ceci had been and the promise of what she might have become.

"Horton!" he called again, grasping the handrail and mounting the stairs, breathing hard as he reached the upstairs landing. He was about to turn on the light in the master bedroom when he saw Horton's front paws protruding from beneath the bed. "Horton!" he commanded. Horton crawled out slowly and, as though coming out of anesthesia, wobbled to his feet and followed Archie down the stairs and out onto the patio. As Archie freshened his drink, Horton shambled to the side of his chair, settled down, and closed his eyes. Turning from the bar, Archie realized that he'd left almost every light in the house burning. He stood for a full ten seconds imagining the next electric bill, then eased himself back into his chair. "That's all right, old boy." His hand caressed his companion's ear, then slid down to hold his muzzle. "I shouldn't have disturbed you. Nothing decent on the telly tonight. We'll both turn in as soon as I've finished my nightcap."

Knowing that he wouldn't be able to sleep, he turned on the television set in the bedroom, watching yet another news report and wondering if the current administration was going to bullyrag itself into another nasty little war. At last he dozed, staring not at the screen but at the window, where Ceci's face, at least twenty years younger, blended into the features of his Jamaican nanny, Mary. The two faces, so different in feature, age, and color, had an about-to-be-abandoned stoicism, arousing a seducer's guilt that would have been more appropriate toward the other women in his life.

Three

Ceci looked up at the face of a watery moon. It had stopped raining but there was a penetrating dampness in the air and the soup and brandy she'd had at Phoebe's warmed her for only a few blocks. Fog was beginning to shroud the small shops and row houses. Children with the elbows out of their cardigans played beneath the halo of the street lamp. A faint strain of reggae drifted from the record shop next to the storefront that promised "Inexpensive Funerals." Refuse clogged the gutter. Pungent cooking smells hung in the air. What would London be without the culinary legacy of Empire, the couscous, khichari, chapatis, curries, and Jamaican meat pies?

At a food counter that opened onto the street, a tall man in a navy trench coat was taking a piece of coconut cake from a fat black woman wearing a yellow, green, and black woolly hat. Ceci paused, listening to their soft patois, pretending to look into the window of a bakery where two black dolls, in tuxedo and white satin, perched on top of an elaborate wedding cake. Out of the corner of her eye she watched as the man put some coins on the counter and turned away. Something about him—the shape of his head, the erect but thoroughly relaxed way he had of carrying his body—had reminded her of Paul Strangman. But this man was mulatto, much darker skinned than Paul. To any but the knowledgeable observer, Paul was an exotic combination of complexion and feature but decidedly white.

She'd met Paul at the home of a professor from the London School of Economics. When he'd come into the room she'd looked up from her sherry and stale biscuits and even before she'd heard him speak—which was not much of a clue since his accent was more Oxford than Kingston—she'd thought *mustefino*. She hadn't thought of the word for years. She'd read it in a volume she'd found in Auntie Vivian's room, a book so old that the pages had crumbled in her hands: "The offspring of a white man and a black woman is a mulatto; the mulatto and black produce a sambo; from the mulatto and white comes the quadroon; from the quadroon and white comes the mustee; the child of a mustee by a white man is called a mustefino and ranks as a white person." She'd been delighted by this variety and had gone about trying to classify everyone she saw until Aunt Vivian had told her that such terms were no longer in use and that it was exceedingly impolite to mention them. Now the handsome stranger with his green eyes, straight nose but full lips, tightly curled hair and swarthy skin brought the word back to her. He was mustefino. He could have "passed."

She was, therefore, somewhat surprised when, moving to the periphery of the group in which he was standing, she had heard him refer to his mixed blood. A man with a pencil mustache and a clerical collar said, "I suppose it's understandable that you should be proud, Mr. Strangman. If I had political ambitions on an island where eighty-five percent of the population is black or colored, I shouldn't mind a touch of the tar brush myself." Paul's face remained impassive as the man continued, "We all understand that the race question is part of the very woof and warp of the Jamaican social fabric, but even if they're wearing T-shirts proclaiming the beauty of negritude in America, there will be no black leadership in Jamaica in your lifetime. But a light-skinned colored such as yourself . . ." Her eyes met Paul's over the man's head, communicating not just an instantaneous attraction, but the understanding that they could afford to tolerate the man's rudeness because they were young, enlightened, and free from prejudice and inhibition. With that first glance they had shrunk the world to the magic space of their own intimacy. "It's an interesting possibility," the reverend continued. "A very light-skinned colored getting votes from all sectors. After all, the British Labour Party used to draw its leadership from the public schools. . . ."

"Yes, Reverend. We are all God's creatures and we are all created equal in his sight. That is your teaching, isn't it? But, as Mr. Orwell said, some are more equal than others." Paul said this with such gentleness that his irony seemed to be lost on everyone save her. "And now, if you'll excuse me." He came to her side, whispering, "Perhaps we could share one of those stale biscuits. And you could tell me your name."

In the taxi going back to her flat she was acutely aware of him, wanting him to take her hand or put his arm around her shoulder. But only their words touched, nudging, teasing, overlapping. They talked about the people at the party, pleased and perhaps even a little smug at the similarity of their assessments, and started into question-and-answer about backgrounds. So great was her eagerness to find out about him that she couldn't help giving elliptical answers to his questions and leaping ahead with her own. After she'd interrupted him and excused herself for the second time, she said, "I don't know whether to talk or listen. I want to do everything at once."

"Then I suppose we shall have to resign ourselves to meeting again."

"I suppose so." Her heart expanded. "But you were telling me about your family." It turned out that his mother was white, his father of mixed blood. "Your father sounds like a Jamaican Joe Kennedy, substituting Oxford for Harvard and cricket for touch football. Was he ambitious for you from the day you were born?"

Even in the shadows of the back seat, she could see his face take on the same impassive expression it had worn while listening to the reverend. "To call my purpose ambitious would be like saying that Caruso sang to show off. It is ambitious only because we struggle against seemingly impossible odds. Perhaps because you're an American you are too cynical to differentiate between ambitious politicians and those who have the gift and discipline of leadership and care about the people."

"No," she protested, while thinking that he was probably right. "I didn't mean . . ."

But the taxi had already drawn up to the curb. She asked if he would like to come in for a drink, but he said he had to get up early the next morning. He touched her only to help her out of the taxi. As she let herself into the flat she thought, "You bungled it, Ceci," and then, "He's a self-righteous bastard, that's what he is."

He phoned the next day. A month later, they'd moved into a flat together. Never before had she known a man of such intellect and purpose. A man who literally believed that he was going to change the world. He had an abundance of energy, a passion for justice, and a genuine compassion for others. And he expected that she should pursue equally high standards. Why shouldn't she strive to be the top of her class at school? Why shouldn't she give up her part-time receptionist's job that was little more than decorating the lobby of a publisher's office and work in a shelter for runaway girls? She did both and felt more challenged than put upon in doing so, because never before had anyone told her that she was gifted and called out the best in her. And there was another side to Paul: he was playful and affectionate; he listened to her; he bought her thoughtful gifts—a tiny ivory monkey with a sorrowful expression, a white satin slip, the poems of Pablo Neruda. And he made her laugh.

All the elements of their affair—the intimacy, the eagerness, the possibility of loss—had been there from that first night. She'd understood very early on that though Paul loved her he was unlikely to marry her. Had he wanted a life in almost any other field or almost any other country it might have been possible, but if he was to become Prime Minister of Jamaica, she was a disastrous political liability. Not only was she white, American, and divorced, she was (even though her connection with her genealogy was so tenuous she never thought of herself as such) a Nettleton. The opposition would do a lot with the fact that Strangman, candidate of reform, branded a revolutionary by some, had chosen a woman whose family symbolized the old order.

That there was no place for her in his future and never enough time for her in his present increased the immediacy that any couple who'd just fallen in love would feel. Any time apart was anxious, wasted time; time spent with others (though she loved watching him in action, talking with equal ease to a street vendor or a cabinet minister) was spent grudgingly. When they arrived home after an evening out, she felt the same eagerness to talk and desire to be silent as she had on that first night. It was only in the act of love that they conquered time, and with a variety she'd never thought possible. They could be fierce or gentle, raunchy or sweet, so that she sometimes felt shy as a young girl, at other times wild as a pick-up, at still others proud as a beloved consort. Then they would lie silent, steeped in each other's flesh, the cup of contentment so brimful that it threatened to overflow into a melancholy as subtle and potent as the first hint of frost on an autumn day. Paul would fall asleep—he dropped off with the ease of a child and claimed never to dream—and she would lie still, regarding their future bleakly, knowing the impossibility of it all, until his breath against her neck or the touch of his leg forced her to believe that they must and would stay together.

But in the mornings, left alone, she would criticize their pleasures, find fault where there was none, dismiss their love as terrific sex. She would imagine scenes in which she left him: she would be serious and noble (It's best for both of us); punishing (I've been seeing a man who wants to marry me); frivolous (This has been such fun, but . . .). Anything that would give her some measure of protection and pride, anything that would soften the inevitable blow. But of course she knew that she'd never be able to do any of those things. And in the end, after almost a year together, it was as she'd always known it would be. He had left her.

It had been a Sunday when they'd planned to go to the zoo.

She'd reached for him before she was fully awake, found the bed empty, and assumed he'd gone out for the papers. It had snowed the previous Sunday and they'd spent the day in bed and now again it had snowed, so that when she first got up she attributed the eerie quiet to the weather. But as she showered she had a strange premonition, remembering for the first time in years how as a child she would get up and go into Archie's room in some hotel suite and find the bed unslept in and Archie gone. She returned to the bedroom and flung back the covers, then noticed an envelope on the bedside table. Slowly and methodically, she finished making the bed. She dressed and put on her makeup. She even took the trouble of going to her desk and finding the letter opener.

His message barely filled a page of notepaper. He had gone back to Jamaica. He hadn't told her in advance because he feared she'd have the power to talk him out of it. He loved her.

She had imagined many endings, but not this one. Paul—courageous, confrontational, principled Paul—had taken the coward's way out. Not that it mattered. What mattered was that he was gone.

She wrapped her scarf more tightly around her throat, stuffed her hands deep into her pockets, and continued to walk on, congratulating herself on her mental health. Half a mile back, when she'd seen the man in the navy trench coat, she'd instantly identified those features that reminded her of Paul, but not for a moment had she thought it was him.

For months after he'd left her, she'd been like a drug addict going through withdrawal. She had dropped out of the London School of Journalism. A week after that she had quit her part-time job. Her periods had stopped, sending her into a frenzy of fear and, in insane moments, hope that she might be pregnant. Unsupported by what she'd known or how she'd felt, she'd groped toward reunion. When the phone rang, she hoped it would be him. When she collected the mail, she looked for his letter. Even after she'd weaned herself away from these daily humiliations, she had still been so obsessed that she'd imagined seeing him. In movie lobbies and grocery stores, at chic little parties he'd never waste his time on, she'd

turn and for a split second believe that he was there. There
would be a flash of pure joy. Adrenaline would course
through her. And then, realizing her mistake, her stomach
would turn and she'd feel as though she'd just escaped a
collision on the highway. Once she'd even thought she'd seen
him gazing into the monkey cage at the zoo. She'd rushed
forward calling his name. The man with the peanuts in his
hand had looked at her as though she was a madwoman and
almost run away. She couldn't imagine why she'd produced
such an extreme reaction until she'd put her hand up to cover
her eyes and brought it away wet. She'd left London for Paris
the next week.

After several months she'd accepted a dinner invitation
from an artist who exhibited in the gallery where she worked.
Thinking that being with another man might help to break
her obsession with Paul, she'd made up her mind to go to bed
with him. She'd hinted as much over the bouillabaisse and
he'd suggested they go back to her flat. Somehow that seemed
to be too intimate a setting. Brazening it out, she'd said she
would prefer a hotel. She'd started to undress herself as soon
as they'd gotten into the room, and by the time he'd come out
of the bathroom, she'd been lying on the bed. She'd convinced
herself that she was ready. Her body felt ready. And yet, as
he'd reached for her she'd started to cry. He'd been very
decent about it, showing a sort of seductive consolation with
only a touch of bullying, the best that any man in a state of
frustrated arousal could be expected to provide. When he'd
seen that it wasn't going to happen that night, he had told her
to get dressed and gone to order a taxi. The next week, fortifying herself with a few drinks, she'd been able to get through
it with no tears and a modicum of enjoyment. A month later,
when he'd left France for the Far East, she'd left with him.
In Singapore she'd met the Australian journalist and . . . And
ever since then she had been safe. The initial excitement of
any affair was always overshadowed by her very explicit no-
tions of how that affair might end; her intuition of potential
incompatibilities was always stronger than feelings that
might have enabled her to ignore them.

The last time she had seen Paul Strangman had been on a television program called "Report from the Caribbean." She'd been in the New York apartment alone, walking through the living room to turn off the set Max had left on. The image on the screen had stopped her in midstride. Paul Strangman's face filled the screen. He had aged considerably. Not just because his hairline had receded (they'd joked about that inevitability years ago) but because his features had a look of fatigue and grim determination. The expression in his eyes was wary, ironic, the look of a man who expected challenge instead of understanding. He was introduced as the man who had become Prime Minister of Jamaica, had directed the country through four years of sweeping reforms, and had just lost his bid for reelection. The camera pulled back. Paul sat forward in his chair, leading with his jaw, on the ready. He was wearing a bush jacket and slacks, the casual clothes he'd always said were more appropriate for the tropics than a three-piece suit and which had become the "uniform" of his administration. One of the reporters asked about the significance of his "revolutionary garb." Paul answered that he hadn't known he was being invited to a fashion show and that they must have more pressing issues to put before him. The questions became hostile. Was he a friend to Fidel Castro? Cuba was a neighbor, he answered, wasn't it best to talk to one's neighbors? What about the South African Peoples' Congress, another reporter, his lip already curled in appreciation of his own wit, inquired, did he consider Africa to be a neighbor? Africa, Paul reminded him, was part of the Third World, as was Jamaica. A flurry of questions followed: Would he continue to deny that he was a communist? Why had tourism fallen off during his administration? Was it true that gangs roamed the streets of Kingston during his election and only his conservative opponent could restore order? Did he really believe the CIA had toppled his government?

Ceci had groped her way to the couch, losing the thread of the questioning as she studied him. Paul began to sum up his position: He sought nonviolent change, following neither the revolutionary Cuban model nor the colonial dependence of

Puerto Rico. He wanted to steer an independent course between the two superpowers. He would run for office again and he would win. She felt proud and angry and close to tears. Even if she hadn't known him, his integrity came across. She wanted to scream at the sneering reporter. She laughed at herself. Apart from everything else she would have made a lousy political wife. She wouldn't have been able to keep her mouth shut. But Paul didn't need a wife. The close of the show was a film clip: Paul Strangman and Mrs. Strangman, a slim, self-contained mulatto woman with wide-set eyes, walking on the lawn of their Kingston home with their seven-year-old son.

As she moved through another block of sightless windows and cat-haunted alleys, she realized that she didn't know where she was. Rounding a corner, she heard raucous, off-key singing and saw the frosted windows of a pub. Two men, tough-looking, wobbly from too many pints of stout, pushed their way out of the doors and started toward her. They sized her up, instantly knowing that she was not one of their own.

"Oh gawd, look at this, will you? She didn't get that outfit in a jumble sale, now did you, love?"

"Lost yer way, 'have you, pussy cat?"

"She can come 'ome with me. I'd know 'ow to keep her warm."

They were blocking her path. She looked from one to the other, judged the older to be a father of three who didn't want to look old-fashioned in front of his buddy, and looked him straight in the eye. "Yes. I have lost my way. And I must've lost my mind too, to be out in such weather." She smiled, still looking at the older man. "Would one of you gentlemen be kind enough to direct me to a taxi?"

The man's expression changed from self-conscious leer to boozy gallantry. He threw his arm back, hitting his companion in the chest. "Go easy 'here, Dave. Let's find the lady a taxi."

Once safely inside the taxi, she slumped back in the seat and closed her eyes. Lemon tea and a hot bath, that's what she needed and that's what she'd have as soon as she reached the Springers'.

Just as they rounded the corner of the Springers' street, she was shaken by a violent sneeze, the sort of sneeze that told her not that she might be getting a cold, but that she definitely had one.

She handed the driver a bill and told him to keep the change. Pleased by the size of the tip, he gave her his wife's favorite cold remedy while she wavered, one foot already on the curb, noticing the lights in the front room. The Springers' housekeeper, Mrs. Davidson, who was more interested in the racing forms than in thrift, had apparently neglected to turn off the lights.

As she turned her key in the lock she was surprised and not a little chagrined to hear Audrey's husband, Roger. "Ceci, my dear," he said as he appeared in the archway to the living room. "We were afraid you weren't coming home."

She put her hand to her throat. "Roger. What on earth are you doing here?"

"We live here, remember? Of course, we didn't plan to live here again until next month, but Fate has decided otherwise."

"Don't make it sound so grand, Roger," Audrey's voice called from the living room. "Fate has nothing to do with it. Come in here, Ceci, and I'll tell you the unadulterated truth."

Ceci let Roger help her off with her coat, smiled her thanks, and walked to the threshold. Audrey was stretched out on the Regency sofa. Wearing one of the combat-chic jumpsuits and matching leather gunbelts sold in her shop, her face vivid with punky makeup, she posed a startling incongruity to the silken opulence and studied tokens of wealth of her own living room. On the coffee table, next to the pile of mail she and Roger must have just gone through, a third glass, obviously awaiting Ceci's arrival, was on the drinks' tray.

"As I said—and welcome, Ceci—Fate had nothing to do with it. We were in this most enchanting little villa in Florence, I had every intention of going to that fashion show in Rome next week, but Roger's tummy starting playing up. I told him that if he'd just had some restraint and not gorged himself with garlic and tomato sauces . . ."

"I never gorge myself. And I'm not a sissy about illness, but once you've had amoebic dysentery . . ."

"The trots," Audrey insisted. "You have a minor case of the trots."

"Galloping, racing, totally debilitating dysentery. Got it in Delhi years ago. Never been the same since."

"There I was, Mediterranean moonlight bathing my body, feeling oh, so romantic. And there he was, cowering in the bathroom, hugging his bottle of Kaopectate."

Ceci drew in her breath. Audrey and Roger always batted lines back and forth in this exhausting but infectious rhythm, as though they were doing a run-through of a Noël Coward comedy. When she interrupted, her own voice had taken on the same rapid lightness. "I'm sure Roger wasn't gorging himself, Audrey." Roger was a dyspeptic. The mere mention of butter or red meat made him blanch. Ceci had watched him cross-examine hostesses, badger waiters, scrape sauces off fish, pick tomatoes out of salads. "But whatever you've been eating hasn't agreed with you, Roger. You do look a bit green around the gills."

"There, what did I tell you, Audrey? Someone who was blind in one eye and couldn't see out of the other would know I was ill."

"If you've had amoebic dysentery," Ceci said, "you mustn't take it lightly. I had a touch of it in Mexico. Montezuma's Revenge, they call it. I was doubled over in pain. But doubled over. Until I got to the local *farmacia* and they gave me some highly effective native concoction."

"You see!" Audrey sat up and ran her hands through her hair. "Ceci didn't come rushing home squalling for her nanny. Ceci stuck it out."

"I had to stick it out. I was living there at the time."

"Roger couldn't hope to live anywhere that wasn't within a two-mile radius of his birthplace, could you, dear? I don't see how I could have married a man who is so totally lacking in adventure. He just flopped about that villa mewling like a cat. Fortunately George and Ruth Edgeworth were in Florence, too, so I went about with them. Ended up dancing with a twenty-year-old saxophone player who wanted me to get him a visa. Believe me, if I'd had time to get him a barium enema and found his bowels were in working order, I would have brought him home with me. Now, Ceci, you will have a drink, won't you?" Audrey said all this in the consciously teasing tone she used toward her husband when they were in company. She put great store in playing the free spirit who would not be altered by the demands of marriage. And Roger kept up his side of the act as well. He regularly pinched Audrey's bottom, and complained about her faults so openly that people assumed there could never be any real trouble between them.

"I shan't bother to plead my case any further," Roger said, easing himself into a chair and crossing his legs. "You're here now, Ceci, so at least I shall get a modicum of the sympathy to which I'm entitled. I *do* have a severe case of dysentery, or what my charming but not unduly delicate wife calls 'the trots.' In fact, I shall probably have to exit the room very shortly."

"Oh, please. Neither of you should stay up on my account," Ceci said. "You must be exhausted. If I'd known that you were—"

"We did cable you in case you were entertaining the United Nations and we'd have to book a bed in advance." Audrey drained her glass and held it out to be refilled. "But the little man at the telegraph office was quite flummoxed. There was this perfectly awful French couple ahead of us. Well, you know the French. Worst travelers in the entire world. Make the Americans look positively humble by comparison. So the little man was all in a dither. I'm sorry you didn't get the telegram. He sent something. Probably a birthday message to his mother in Sicily. And with our money." She looked down into the glass Roger had just refilled. "Where is the ice, darling? You know I drink brandy with ice. And what about Ceci? Ceci, do have a drink with us."

"I don't feel much like having a drink."

"Oh, give her one," Audrey insisted. "You must share a welcome home drink with us. Oh!" She groaned, flinging her head backward. "I can't believe we're home again. I shall have a case of the blue meanies tomorrow. I'm so disappointed! I don't want to hear another word about your physical problems, Roger. If you were at all sensitive you'd know my emotional distress is ten times worse."

Roger sighed. "Especially for those around you, pet."

"Here, I'll run out to the kitchen and get some ice," Ceci volunteered. She was afraid to think what the kitchen might look like. Mrs. Davidson's efficiency had fallen off rapidly after her employers had left and Ceci, as a guest, had not wanted to pressure her. In all probability the breakfast dishes were still in the sink and the refrigerator was empty. She started to get to her feet. A few years ago she'd thought little about being surrounded by the luxury of others. She'd enjoyed her pleasures without worrying about who provided them. Now she'd become conscious of offering a hundred little favors that came not from her natural good manners, but from a sense of paying her way.

"Nonsense. Stay where you are, Ceci. Roger, you will get the ice, won't you, Roger? After all, the downstairs loo is right next to the pantry. You can kill two birds with one stone. But don't forget to wash your hands afterward."

"Your concern for my health is always touching, duchess." Roger got up, bowed, and left the room.

Audrey poured Ceci a brandy and settled back into the pillows. "Ceci. Dear Ceci. Do forgive us for jumbling in on you."

"Nonsense." Ceci picked up her bag and started to rummage through it, looking for some vitamin C. "It's your house, after all. How could I possibly object to your coming home? Besides, I'm glad to see you." Her first statement was indisputably true; her expression of pleasure somewhat less so. She found the bottle of vitamins, tipped two into her hand, and gulped them down with the brandy.

"I expect poor Roger really is ill." Audrey dropped her voice and reached for Ceci's hand. "It's colitis, I expect. Or perhaps an ulcer. I've been exhausted by it. If you ever do marry, Ceci, insist on separate bedrooms. The old ways are the best ways. After all, what can you do when someone's thrashing about in pain? I'm not a doctor." She bent forward, smiled wickedly, and whispered, "I did have a bit of a fling with the dago saxophone player, but that story will have to wait until Roger's out of the house," then, resuming a conversational tone, "But it was such a relief for me to know that you were in charge of things here."

"I'm afraid the house isn't . . ."

"Not the house, dear. I'll have a few words with Mrs. Davidson tomorrow. One naturally expects them to slack off. I was more concerned about the shop. How are things going at Sally Forth?"

"Profits up. We've almost sold out of the Chinese pajamas. And those T-shirts, the ones that say 'Living Well Is the Best Revenge' in rhinestones, they're almost gone too. I wouldn't have believed it. I'd never even understood what they bloody meant. The best revenge against whom? And at those prices? But, as I said, they're almost gone. I would have started a proper inventory but . . ."

"You're a treasure. Really. I expect your just standing there at the front of the shop, looking piss elegant, must've brought up the sales. I wonder why you don't do it yourself. Buy a shop, I mean."

Ceci took another sip of her brandy. She wouldn't point out her lack of capital. That wasn't the real problem. She could round up the capital if she had a mind to. But she didn't want to own a boutique.

"I hope you didn't have too much trouble with Sue," Audrey continued. "I wanted to give her the sack before I left, but I knew it wasn't fair to ask you to break in a new girl. But she is hopeless. I'm always having to ask her to stand aside so customers can use the full-length mirrors. She fancies herself a model, I believe, which is rather sad because she's not much taller than a mushroom. Now someone like you, Ceci—you could have been a model. Or an actress."

Ceci put her glass on the table. An actress was the last thing she'd ever wanted to be.

"Then again," Audrey continued, "I suppose someone will take a fancy to Sue. She'll give up her discount at the store and find some man to buy her clothes. Of course it's always nice to have a man buy your clothes, isn't it? I just hope Sue catches someone before the bloom is off the rose—I mean the mushroom—she won't hold up much past twenty-five. But some man . . ."

Ceci picked up her glass. Max had wanted to buy her a leopard skin coat last Christmas. He'd praised her sensitivity when she'd said no and given him a lecture on endangered species. But it hadn't just been her conscience about some poor animal that had stopped her; she hadn't wanted to feel indebted. If there were no free lunches, there were certainly no free fur coats.

". . . and speaking of men, your current one, Max, called just after we got back. He said it was nothing important, but you should call when you could."

"Thanks," Ceci took another swallow of her drink. The sensation as the liquor went down was burning instead of merely warming. As Audrey chatted on, complaining about the delay at the airport, counting off the people they knew in common that she'd run into, enthusing about the new fashions from the Italian designers, Ceci nodded periodically and wondered if her throat was really infected. If she just had the sniffles she'd be able to get through the next few days, dripping and dabbing, nursing a low-grade misery. But if the infection settled in her chest . . . it would be one thing to convalesce with Mrs. Davidson, vacant-eyed but benign, puttering about; it was quite another to contemplate being sick with Audrey and Roger at home. She shook out another vitamin and tutted her agreement about delayed flights, wondering how long it would be before she could excuse herself and go to bed. She was just at the point of interrupting Audrey to tell her that *she* must be exhausted when Roger appeared, ice bucket in hand.

"Here we are, ladies. I do feel better now. Really I do." He dropped a cube into Audrey's glass, then reached for Ceci's. She put her hand over it and smiled too brightly into his face. As soon as she removed her hand, he refilled her glass, saying "When I went to the loo just now . . ."

"Please, darling, please." Audrey raised her hand as though she was stopping traffic. "If I'd wanted a baby I would have had one. Let's not limit the conversation to your bowels. Ceci may be an intimate friend, but there is a limit."

Roger waved away her objection and sat on the edge of his chair, bouncing to show that he was really quite hearty, or at least not willing to suffer his wife's displeasure. "I am feeling better. Whoever said that women were the ones who crave domesticity was entirely mistaken. It's we poor men who suffer when we're away from home. You women can carry whatever you need with you. I suppose it has something to do with your blessed internal organs. You are self-contained, so to speak. Well, look at those bag ladies in New York. You don't see men living on the streets carrying their domiciles about in shopping bags, do you? An orderly home, a setting if you will, that's what I need. That's what most men need. Though looking at the pantry just now, I can't say that our home is all that orderly."

"That's my fault," Ceci said. "I told Mrs. Davidson she could take the night off. She said her daughter was having a difficult pregnancy."

"Ah, Mrs. Davidson and her daughters," Roger laughed. "Children pop out of them like weeds after the spring rain. We need never worry about fecundity in the British Isles whilst the Davidson girls are about."

Audrey's laughter, whether from travel fatigue or too much brandy, rose to an almost hysterical pitch. Roger, pleased with himself, settled back, his features relaxing into a sort of amiable passivity before they twitched with discomfort and he clutched his abdomen.

"I'm awfully sorry that you're not feeling well, Roger." Feeling so physically miserable herself, it was easy for Ceci to empathize. "But it's all to the good that you've come home. I'd actually thought about leaving sooner but—"

"Where do you want to go?" Audrey asked. "Back to New York?"

"I don't mean I'm leaving tonight," Ceci said. She felt suddenly dizzy.

"I should think not," Roger said stolidly. "The idea."

"I saw Phoebe today." They looked at her blankly. "Phoebe is one of my father's ex-wives. Archie . . . my father . . ." She

realized that though she'd known the Springers for several
years, they had never discussed anything as personal as families. "And I got a telegram last night. Apparently my Aunt
in Jamaica isn't well and . . ."

"How ill is the old girl?" Audrey asked, fishing an ice cube
from her glass.

"Not seriously. At least I don't think it's serious. She's . . ."
Why, she asked herself, had she mentioned her family? Why
did she feel close to tears? "She's just getting older."

"We're all of us getting older." Roger stifled a yawn.

"And that's another reason why I'm so upset about cutting
this trip short," Audrey complained. "Ruth told me about this
new spa in Fiesole. I could have done with a week of mud
baths, massage, and collagen shots. And I won't hear of you
leaving, Ceci. I just won't hear of it. There are scads of people
who know you're back in town and want to see you. And you
and I will have a chance to go round to things together. You
know Roger won't be good for anything. And you know we
both love having you here. No one's as entertaining as you
are, dear, if you're not in one of your serious moods." She
reached forward and touched Roger's knee, cuing him.

"We won't hear of your leaving. Audrey's so much more
tolerable when you're about that I'd pay you to stay on."

Their entreaties were genuine. Too genuine. Considering
that they had been married for only nine months and had
never lived together before that, they displayed an unnatural
appetite for the company of others. Beneath their playfulness
Ceci sensed a creeping boredom, a fear that they'd have nothing to say if there weren't a third person to enjoy their performance. She stood up and put her hand to her throat, illus-
trating the soreness she actually felt. "I'm terribly sorry to
desert you, but I think I'm getting a cold and I really must go
to bed."

"Dear lord," Audrey sighed. "I might as well be in a National Health clinic. All right, Ceci, I'll see you first thing in
the morning."

Ceci kissed her cheek, picked up her bag, and squeezed
Roger's shoulder. "Good night, darlings. And welcome
home."

As she went up the stairs, she felt a childish desire to cry. Deprived of the small comforts of lemon tea and a hot bath, it was as though she'd been ordered to bed instead of choosing to go. But she knew that if she started mucking about in the kitchen or lingered in the bathroom, Audrey, who was a garrulous drinker, would join her and she'd be up half the night.

Undressed, she searched through the top drawers of the dresser for her warm pajamas, but couldn't find them. She gave up on the idea of going through the suitcase she hadn't yet unpacked, turned out the light, and slipped naked into bed. Her teeth chattering, she tried to add up how much money she had on hand. There was a check for a couple of thousand dollars, a royalty payment for *How to Speak Slang in Five Languages*, which she'd ghost written for a friend who was a syndicated travel columnist; another eight hundred to so in "savings" and . . . But there was no point in trying to tally without pencil and paper. She would do that in the morning. By then she would have decided what her next move was going to be.

She could hear Roger and Audrey on the landing. Their voices no longer had a staccato lightness but sounded tired and irritable. They seemed to be arguing about who was going to use the bathroom first. Shivering, she got up and without turning on the light, retrieved a handkerchief from her purse and felt her way to the closet where, she thought, Mrs. Davidson stored extra blankets. She reached up, bringing a pile of things onto the floor. A mohair cardigan that must have belonged to Audrey was in her hand. She tried to put things back into the closet but couldn't see what she was doing. Cursing, she groped her way back to the bed, pulling on the cardigan.

The chilliness of the room reminded her of the Palisades house. Archie, always mindful of what he referred to as "needless expense," had demanded that the thermostat be left at fifty-five. Even in the California climate there had been nights when she'd complained and called him Scrooge. Archie insisted that she have tennis lessons and riding lessons. She could run up clothing bills at the best Beverly Hills stores. But God help her if she left the lights on when she went out of a room or turned up the thermostat. It was this same perverse attitude that had stopped him from giving her a regular allowance when she'd been away at school, so that she'd been forced to either borrow from the other girls or go without. His reasoning, if it could be called that, must have been that she would have to say "thank you, Daddy" for the lessons and the clothes, whereas there would be no obligation for gratitude if she'd been allowed to keep her room at a comfortable temperature. "Archie, you silly bugger," she thought, as she settled back into bed. "You never had the foggiest idea of what was important. No wonder I never learned how to handle money." But at her age it was both useless and irresponsible to blame Archie for her own bad habits.

She heard the toilet flush. Audrey, now at the whimpering stage, was calling to Roger to help her find her toothbrush. Roger, in a flash of temper Ceci hadn't supposed him capable of, yelled that he didn't care if Audrey's teeth rotted in her head so long as she went to bed and let him get some rest. Another toilet flush, Roger now bellowing that since they didn't live in a Third World country there was no excuse for the deplorable lack of toilet paper. Ceci bit her lip and pulled the pillow over her ear. Were Audrey and Roger able to carry on this way because they considered her part of the family, or were they so completely wrapped up in themselves that they just disregarded her presence? The latter, she supposed. Come to think of it, she had never really liked them. She had drifted toward them initially because they knew many people in common. They were part of the globe-trotting set. They had the same self-assurance, the same open expression of self-gratification and general lightheartedness. Cushioned by their wealth, they saw the world through a soft lens, and if the human race was going to hell in a wheelbarrow, if there was famine, overpopulation, wars, rumors of wars, this was none of their concern. They still moved freely, despite fluctuations in currency, revolutions, and airline strikes, in the only world they cared to inhabit. Their *joie de vivre* was often stimulated by drugs and alcohol, but they weren't seriously addicted; or, if they were, they could retreat to hideaways with pleasant grounds and a genteel staff for "cures." If they were self-assured it was because they were what they believed themselves to be: lucky if not blessed, worldly wise if not actually intelligent; stylishly up-to-date if not original. They took their privileged status as a sign of their natural superiority.

Still shivering, she wondered when her acceptance of their limitations had started to wane. Despite her conviction that she was not as superficial as they (did anyone ever admit to being superficial?), she had lived much the same feckless life, congratulating herself on her ability to move with style and avoid all the obligations that a settled life implied. By constantly traveling it had been possible for her to feel not just that she'd escaped her problems but that she'd actually solved them. Traveling sharpened her senses, gave her a sense of command, made it possible for her to observe things without having to do anything about them. In new scenes she'd felt herself renewed. Until recently.

"Neti-neti," she whispered. She had learned the expression from a woman named Maya. She and Maya had met while stranded in the Calcutta airport and had shared a hotel room for the night. Maya was a professor of comparative religions at a California university, and though Ceci had less than a passing interest in Eastern philosophies, they'd stayed up all night talking. Freed by the knowledge that their paths were unlikely to cross again, Ceci had spoken with uncharacteristic openness. They'd finished the cognac Ceci had brought from a duty-free shop as they'd watched the sky turn orange through the tiny oculus window. Maya had embraced her and shaken her head, "Neti neti, that's the name I shall give you." She'd told Ceci that it literally meant "not this, not this" and characterized the process of negative discrimination. "One decides what one *doesn't* want, what *isn't* true. It seems you have fashioned your life in this way. But when you come to know that to which you are truly connected, life will really begin. First negation; then affirmation." Ceci had thought about this for a long time after they'd parted. One of the disadvantages of a life of travel was that she had many acquaintances but few intimate friends. Intimacy took time. She still wrote to Maya. And she still signed her letters "Neti neti." The list of things she didn't want had only continued to grow. Just now she didn't want to stay on with Audrey and Roger; didn't want to look for a flat of her own; didn't want to accept any of the numerous invitations to stay with others. Didn't want to make any decisions about Max.

Her throat now felt as though tiny needles were being pricked into it. She willed herself to sleep, though Roger was still in possession of the bathroom, complaining loudly if unintelligibly. The toilet flushed yet again. She bit her lip and cursed Roger's tummy. But, after all, it was their house. She had played "neti neti" for so long that she had no house. No husband to yell at her about the lack of toilet paper. No child. No real job. She had nothing, in fact, but an increasingly low regard for herself. And in forty-eight hours she would pretend to ignore her thirty-third birthday.

The house was quiet. Rain lashed against the windows. The prickle of a gathering sneeze sent her hand searching for the handkerchief she'd wadded into the sleeve of the cardigan. Oh, how she wanted that hot tea. She waited, snuffling, handkerchief at the ready. Strange how she had known in the taxi, known with that very first sneeze, that she was sick when moments before she'd felt quite healthy. All those germs had been working away, multiplying and gaining strength quite unbeknownst to her. And they had announced themselves in a single little explosion and now had to be dealt with. But, she thought, shifting about irritably, life was full of those turning points: the first gray hair, the bank statement that confirms that you were overdrawn, the single vote that decides the election, the touch that changes the flirtation into an affair, the bitter word that can never be retracted. The heartbeat between life and death. And—achoo! water streaming from her eyes and nose—that moment when you know you are bloody fed up with yourself. That you won't take it anymore. That you have to change your life or you might as well give yourself up for good. Seize the day or go under.

She flicked on the light; tried to calculate the time difference between London and California. Between London and

Jamaica. Whatever time it was, it was the right time. If she didn't accept some responsibility now, she never would.

Archie reached for the phone in a single movement, surprised to see that the television screen had gone blank. "Baron here," he answered with quick assent, as though responding to the rowing team captain's roll call or the assistant director's order to return to the set.

"Archie? Is that you? This is Ceci."

"Ceci?" He grasped his knee, stared about him.

"Your daughter. Remember?"

He heard a snuffling and a sneeze, and then the voice continued. "I suppose I've woken you up and I apologize. I'm calling from London. . . . Is the connection bad at your end? Shall I have the operator place the call again?"

There was no crackling on the wire, just this strange sinus-plagued, unfamiliar voice. "No. no. So it's you, is it?"

"Yes. It's me. Cecily."

"Loud and clear. Everything right at this end. Anything the matter there?"

There was another pause. He sat up, alert now, ready to dial "O" and ask for assistance if they were interrupted. "I say," he repeated, "anything the matter there?"

"I saw Phoebe tonight."

"Is she . . .?"

"No. She's fine. She said she'd heard from you and that you were a bit depressed."

"Not a bit of it. Everything fine at this end."

"Well, in that case . . ."

He could feel his heart beating fast. "Cecily, are you crying?"

"No. No, I'm not."

"Sounds as if . . ."

"Just . . . bloody awful cold. I got a telegram from Jamaica. It seems Aunt Vivie . . ."

"Yes. I heard."

"I've been worried about her. I thought . . . or rather, it had occurred to me . . ."

"Nothing to worry about. I'm surprised Marsden bothered

to contact you. He said he'd like me to come down, but that was just for business reasons. Vivie's quite all—"

Her words came in a rush. "I thought, that is if you'd like, that we might meet down there. We might go back together."

Four

The whining, swooshing sound brought Ceci out of her doze. The flaps and wing gear were being lowered. The pilot's voice came over the intercom: "Ladies and gentlemen, we will be landing in Montego Bay in approximately five minutes." There was a general flurry of anticipation. Briefcases clicked shut, plastic glasses were offered up, magazines closed. The family sitting opposite, Jamaicans who had obviously "gone a foreign" and were returning for a triumphal visit, were already struggling to retrieve the mess of packages they'd stashed under their own seats and those in front of them. The stewardess rushed down the aisle and in a voice that was about to lose its cool pleaded with them to remain calm and stay in their seats.

Ceci pressed her forehead to the window and squinted against the glare. The ocean's deep blue disappeared into the pellucid aquamarine, pale gold, and vivid greens of the shoreline. "Jamaica is in technicolor; the rest of the world is just black and white." So she had written in a high school essay that had earned her only a passing mark. Remembering this, seeing the eye-smarting palette beneath her, she felt an unexpected excitement, the poignant joy of a homecoming.

The plane dipped and circled, then rose again to hover above the tiny airport. The pilot was back on the intercom, his voice jovial, soothing the passengers with information about plans to enlarge the runways. Then they were gliding downward, wheels touching, moving forward with the gentle thrump, bump, bump of a ball that had been tossed to earth. The motors revved and became silent. The tall grass on the side of the runway undulated and stilled as they came to a stop.

The Jamaican family, jabbering like magpies, were unhooking their seat belts and arguing over who should carry what. Ceci stayed in her seat, looking beyond the runway to the fringe of palm trees and the clear expanse of the bay. She waited until the cabin had almost emptied, but just as she was about to get up, the stocky man with the slicked-back hair who'd tried to start a conversation with her earlier in the trip came out of the first-class cabin and rested his arm on the back of her seat. "So, we finally made it. We're here." She was about to answer, "That's an indisputable observation," but reached for her purse instead.

He had boarded the plane at the Kingston stopover and had settled into the empty seat next to hers and started to chat her up. His heavy gold jewelry spoiled the effect of his expensive suit, and his gaze had a too obvious sexual intent. So many millions of men in the world, she'd thought, and so few originals. Though he'd taken a cigarette from an initialed case instead of chomping a cigar and opened the conversation with "I suppose I'll have to call you Ms. until I get your name" instead of calling her girlie, he was what women of Phoebe's generation would have called "a masher." She'd pretended to be absorbed in the book she carried as a shield against just such advances, but he'd kept on. Where was she from? How long would she be staying on the island? Had she ever been here before? Knowing he was the type whose interest would be fueled by her lack of response, she'd been about to tell him that she was married when the stewardess had informed him that his seat was in first class and had invited him to move. "Hey, I know what I pay for. I know where my seat is," he'd smiled. In her chilliest English accent, Ceci had excused herself to go to the bathroom, where she'd stayed, sitting on the edge of the toilet and reading her book, until another passenger had knocked on the door. Returning to her seat she'd found his card: "Albert Lupon, Tax Advisor & International Business Consultant." A telephone number where he could be reached on the island had been scrawled beneath his Miami address. She'd put the card into the seat pocket, adjusted the nozzle of the air-conditioning so that it blew into her face, and slept. Some of her most restful sleeps came while in the air. She yielded herself up, the transcendent, trustful virgin being carried off on the flying white horse, like the finale of Cocteau's *Beauty and the Beast.*

"So we're finally here," he repeated.

She pushed a pair of sunglasses onto her nose and turned to face him, amiable but distant. "Yes. Are we much behind schedule? My husband's picking me up and he's not the patient sort."

He removed his arm and stepped aside to let her into the aisle. Breaking her own rule never to examine her face in public, she took a compact out of her bag.

"Don't get sunburned in your bikini," he called over his shoulder as he walked to the exit.

She was one of the last passengers to descend the metal stairway. Waves of heat smelling of damp earth and gasoline rose from the tarmac. The afternoon thundershower, usual this time of year, had apparently just finished. There was a crowd on the roof of the terminal, their black skins and light-colored clothing vivid against the newly washed sky. Some of them were waving; not, it appeared, to anyone in particular, but in the general excitement of having seen a plane land. She waved back. Unencumbered, not hurrying, but moving with her usual long-legged stride, she overtook passengers who had exited before her, and mindful of another encounter with Mr. Lupon, lingered at the terminal door to let them pass.

Inside the terminal she saw a line of girls dressed in the loose blouses, long skirts, and bandannas that had been slave attire of a hundred and fifty years ago but now passed for native costume. They were swaying back and forth, singing a welcoming song that had probably been written on Madison Avenue. She tipped a porter, told him how to identify her bags, and asked him to meet her upstairs in the emigration line. Passport already in hand, she refused a paper cup of complimentary rum punch and got into line. The porter joined her with her bags; an emigration officer waved her forward. He smiled seductively as he flipped through her passport. It seemed everyone was on the make today. Why was she so put off? There were days when she basked in the knowledge that she was a desirable woman and others when the attention was a mere irritation. Suddenly serious, the emigration officer handed back her passport with a little bow of his head. His attitude had apparently been chastened by having seen "Nettleton House, Westmoreland Parish" scribbled on her destination form. Yes, it was still a tight little island. The Nettleton name was still to be respected.

As she left the terminal the heat was so intense that she felt she had been dunked into a hot bath. Crowds of tourists struggled with their luggage, boarded minibuses with hotel names on them, scolded children, embraced relatives. Signaling to one of the horde of taxi drivers, she followed him to a dilapidated Chevy. Just as they were about to drive out of the parking lot, a black Toyota cut across their path and she saw Albert Lupon, already bent over some papers, in the back seat.

The Chevy chugged up the hillside onto the bluff that overlooked the bay. Here on the rise were homes of the almost affluent, along with guest houses and restaurants, all nestled amidst and partly hidden by the vegetation. "Oh, what's the name of that flower?" she asked. "That bright purple one. Not the bougainvillea, but the one next to it." The taxi driver's eyes, reflected in the rearview mirror that sported a Playboy trinket, were blurred with boredom. Horticultural information obviously didn't come with the fare. "Don't know. What hotel you say?"

"The Tradewinds. It's—"

"I know it."

Unfortunately, Archie had not been able to coordinate his flight from the States until the following day. At first she had thought it rude that Marsden had not offered to send the car for her, but now, as the taxi reached the crest of the hill and rattled down the other side toward the town, she was just as glad to have the time alone. Each reunion that was coming up, with Archie, Vivian, and Marsden, was fraught with bewildering possibilities. It was, as Marsden had suggested, best for Archie to meet her at her hotel and have the family car pick them up there.

She had not been all that familiar with Montego Bay, but still its sprawl and street activity surprised her. Billboards for discos, bars, waterfalls, caves, and other tourist attractions vied for attention with the streams of sunburnt, scantily clad tourists and native street vendors or higglers selling cashews, coconuts, chewing gum, cans of Coca-Cola, and crudely carved "African" masks. Beyond the main road, where taxis careened with reckless abandon, as though they were playing bumper crash in an amusement park, were the rutted, unpaved streets, sun-bleached shops, and buildings of the town. And beyond that, crowded onto the rise of another hill, Montego's shantytown of wood, cinderblock, and corrugated tin shacks.

A young Rastaman, jeans tight and dreadlocks flying, darted in front of the Chevy. The taxi driver, his eyes momentarily ablaze with the power of being behind the wheel, almost ran him down. As they screeched to a stop, the young man put his head into the window. "Great ganja. Great herb," he insisted. "Come on, American, you want?" The driver cursed at him in patois. The Rastaman cursed back, thumped the hood, and strode off, waving his arms. The driver honked and swerved to avoid a stray dog, honked again and floored the accelerator.

They skirted the town and passed by stretches of flattened-out land, pocked with the lone abandoned automobile or box-like concrete houses. And then they were rounding the bay again, out past waving palm trees, clusters of lavender plumbago, orange trumpet vine, pink oleander. The homes hugged the water's edge, protected by high concrete walls with shards of glass embedded in them. A marina with several small pleasure craft and a few impressive yachts came into view. The driver slowed at a kiosk and a guard in pseudomilitary uniform, his brass buttons and white teeth glistening in the sun, looked into the back seat, asked if Ceci were a hotel guest, and waved them on.

Her traveling suit already stained with sweat, Ceci got out of the taxi. The doors of the hotel lobby swung open and a cooling blast of processed air greeted her. A Muzak rendition of "Tonight I Celebrate My Love" was playing. The desk clerk, an Indian girl with muddy skin and a sulky manner, pushed a registration form across the desk and stood toying with the tail of her long braid. "Would you like to exchange your currency for sharks' teeth?" she asked when Ceci returned the form. Ceci raised her head without speaking, sure that her expression conveyed her question. "It's so you won't have to worry about money," the girl insisted.

Ceci laughed. "Would that our financial worries could be so easily overcome."

"All currency has to be exchanged for Jamaican dollars. It's the law. Here at the Tradewinds we make everything easy for you. We exchange Jamaican dollars for sharks' teeth. You can wear them around your neck when you're on the beach. Say you want a rum punch, you just take off one of the teeth and pay the boy with that. You can trade like the natives do."

Ceci now saw the loops of multicolored plastic "teeth" locked in the cabinet next to the room keys. Trade like the natives, indeed. The taxi driver had offered to give her a black market exchange rate that was higher than what she could get at a bank. "No, thank you. I'll only be staying overnight."

A bellboy wearing tight-fitting white pants and a floral shirt was already reaching for her key. She followed him across the courtyard, glimpsing a circular bar with a thatched roof and a swimming pool between the hotel shops. The lobby of the building where she would be sleeping was painted with stalks of metallic bamboo. She stood silent while the boy punched the elevator button. They rose to the strains of "Rocky Mountain High."

Alone in the room, she threw her bag, key, and card for complimentary drinks in the Swinging Plantation Lounge onto the bureau and walked to the balcony. From the courts to her left came the soft thrup of tennis balls; near the registration building to her right, the gardener left off pruning the border of multicolored flowers and called to a taxi driver in lilting, unintelligible patois. A yacht glided on the marina directly in front of her. Unlike so many places she'd visited, this was everything the postcards promised. Max would love it, she thought as she went back into the room. Part of her was sorry that she'd turned down his offer to come with her.

The bellboy had switched on the TV, proudly telling her that programs were beamed by satellite from the States so she wouldn't have to miss her favorite soap operas. On the screen a man who'd apparently just finished the sex act without ruffling his hair was telling a sobbing blond, "I don't care if it means losing my position with the firm, I'm going to marry you, Kimberly." She switched off the set and took a bottle of Johnnie Walker from her bag. The ice bucket was empty but she felt too tired to call for room service. Later, when she'd showered and napped, she'd have food and ice brought up and would spend the evening in the room reading. She sat on the bed sipping the neat whiskey and looking around. Twin Gauguin prints hung, slightly askew, above the double bed, which was covered with an aqua polished cotton spread. If she opened the bureau drawer she'd probably find a Gideon Bible. She wouldn't mind. She was in a mood for Ecclesiastes: "I returned and saw under the sun, that the race is not to the swift, nor the battle to the strong, neither yet bread to the wise, nor yet riches to men of understanding, nor yet favor to men of skill; but time and chance happeneth to them all." Time and chance. Here she was, in another hotel room, wondering why she'd come.

Once they'd reached the planning stage for the trip, she'd had only the most cursory conversations with Archie. Marsden, he'd told her, would be more than happy to have them. "Not happy enough to bother sending the car," she thought as she slipped off her shoes. She had no idea what to expect from Marsden. It seemed that he was now devoting all of his time to the estate. Prior to that he'd been a Washington consultant, though whom he consulted and what he consulted them about she'd never been able to determine. But her world was full of artists who didn't paint, actors who didn't act, businessmen who never went to an office. It was probably just as well that she'd been raised to vanity, absurdity, and chaos. What better preparation for the real world? She knew who she was. Well, most of the time.

She stripped off her clothes and went into the bathroom. Lining up the mud pack, shampoo, and conditioner on the sink, she knew that she was not just about to restore herself after a long journey, but that she was preparing to look pretty for Archie. One of the least pleasant memories was of her mother Mabs, face void of makeup, hair pulled back, dusting photographs of Archie embracing famous beauties. As a child she'd imagined that had Mabs made herself more glamorous, Archie would have loved her more, would not have been able, after a few tears, to have embraced his widowhood with such fervor.

The last time she had seen Archie, some three years ago, the first thing he had said to her had been, "Ceci, your hair is greasy." He had said it offhandedly—and there was no question that she had looked like hell—but it had cut her to the quick, making her feel small and childish, as though she could never, no matter how hard she tried, measure up to his standards. The remark had, she could see in retrospect, sent them on a collision course that had culminated in one of the worst fights they'd ever had.

She'd been traveling to San Francisco after having lived in Mexico for two years, and had arranged a three-day stopover in Los Angeles. Despite the fact that Archie had ignored most of her letters on the excuse that "only George Bernard Shaw and a few nancy poets ever kept up a correspondence," she'd wanted to see him. He wasn't able to pick her up at the airport because the American Film Institute was doing a retrospective honoring one of his cronies and he was "obliged" to attend. Her ex-husband Adam had promised to pick her up, but was nowhere to be seen. She'd called his apartment and a woman identifying herself as Mrs. Goldman had answered. Two short weeks before, Adam had written to her c/o American Express, and said that he couldn't wait for her visit. Apparently he really hadn't been able to wait. "Two weeks ago he was panting; now there's a new Mrs. Goldman," she'd thought. Well, things moved fast in L.A.

She'd arrived there giddy with fatigue, having refused the airline food but accepting the free drinks given to numb the passengers after a delayed departure. She'd taken a handful of pesos, pounds, and cruzedas out of her purse and stared at them. She had legal tender, but it was nonnegotiable, just as she had some value but didn't have the vaguest idea about how to trade it, use it, or make it count.

She'd felt orphaned. Bereft. A violent, undirected anger frothed up in her. Catching a glimpse of herself in a plate glass window, she'd seen that the color had drained from her face so that her makeup stood out in patches. She'd gone to the restroom and washed her face with the foul-smelling liquid soap before she'd gone to the Rent-a-Car booth.

The first half-hour behind the wheel, when a wrong turn could have sent her to hell or San Bernardino, she'd used up the steam of her rage. Then, nerves jangling, with the homing instincts of a pigeon and just about as much consciousness, she'd found her way to the Palisades and up the hill to the house. The porch and patio lights had been turned off. For a moment, as she saw only a dull gleam from the library window, she'd thought perhaps Archie had gone to bed.

He'd met her at the door, gin and tonic in hand, wearing an expression of disappointment and a fine dinner jacket. She couldn't remember their initial exchange, but when he'd finally kissed her and she'd rested her head on his shoulder he'd said, "Ceci, your hair is greasy." Had he offered the smallest thread of kindliness or concern, she might have stayed up half the night, the prodigal returned. As it was, she'd declined his offer of a drink and had gone upstairs to her old room. She hadn't expected it to have been preserved as a shrine, but she was not prepared to see that it had been stripped of any reminder of her presence and turned into den *cum* TV room suitable for either sex.

They'd agreed to breakfast together, but she hadn't woken up until early afternoon. Archie had left the house. Manuela, the Chicana cleaning woman, told her that Mr. Baron had gone to play bowls "like he always do on Wednesday afternoon." She also said a Mr. Goldman had called. Wearing Archie's robe, Ceci roamed the house, eating crackers out of the box and trying to stay out of Manuela's way. Adam called again. Why, he asked, had she hung up on his mother? She apologized and said she'd thought perhaps it was his new wife. But hadn't she recognized the number? He had just gone through a divorce and was living back at his mother's Beverly Hills place until his new apartment was decorated. She apologized again and accepted his invitation to meet at a Malibu restaurant for a late lunch.

Adam had changed so much that she hadn't recognized him as he'd come into the restaurant. His laid-back surfer image had disappeared along with his shoulder-length hair and beard. He explained that it had taken him a year of therapy to realize that he was "hiding behind all that hair." Looking at his less than impressive chin, she'd been tempted to tell him that he would have been better off if he'd kept hiding. He gave her his business card (he was an exec for some film distribution company), fingered his worry beads, and talked at such a clip that she thought he must be on uppers. On her third drink she realized, albeit with relief, that he hadn't asked a single question about her life. After lunch (he'd taken out his pocket calculator to check the bill), he'd suggested they take a ride up the coast. As it grew dark, his mind lapsed into a shadowy nostalgia. He took down the top of the car, stopped talking about his recent divorce and started singing old Beach Boys songs. She asked him to turn back. He pulled onto the beach, turned off the motor, and reached for her, his eyes expressionless as marbles. She turned her head away and felt his open mouth on her neck. The Villa del Sol (where they had spent a luxurious honeymoon on his father's money) was just up the road. He asked if she remembered the mirror over the bed and couldn't they "check it out" for old times' sake? The suggestion made her feel as though some lout had just yelled a proposition across a crowded street. Was it possible that she'd been married to this man?

Seeing that it was a no-go, he looked at her pityingly and said that although he still considered her a "significant other" he refused to take her rejection personally. *He* had come to grips with his socially imposed macho image and he really hoped she would get some therapy so that she could come to

grips with her ambivalence about interphysical relationships.
He'd then shoved the gears into reverse, peeled out onto the
highway and, blessedly, driven back to the restaurant at such
a speed that conversation was impossible over the roar of
wind and motor. Driving back to the Palisades house, she'd
stopped and bought a pizza, thinking that instead of going out
to dinner, she and Archie would spend the evening at home
and make up for the previous night's disaster.

When she'd let herself in she'd found him sitting at the
dining table. He was wearing his sports jacket and ascot. The
table, dim in the light of candles that had already dripped
onto its shining surface, had been set with the good china. A
dried-up roast and a lettuce and tomato salad, clearly of Archie's making, sat untouched. Even before she'd noticed that
the gin bottle had been left unceremoniously at the end of the
table, she knew he'd had more than his usual "one and a
fresh-up," because the first words out of his mouth were, "I
can't seem to find the carving knife."

She was relieved to see that he was a little drunk. It would
make her apologies easier. "It's right there. Under the platter
the roast is sitting on."

"The roast is cold."

"I'm sorry. I had no idea that . . ." She put the pizza box
on the table, swept back her hair, and smiled at him.
"Couldn't we save it for sandwiches tomorrow? If you're not
busy we could go down to the beach for a picnic. I'm in a junk
food mood myself." She opened the box with flamboyant
"ta-da!"

"Cecily." He straightened up to ramrod rigidity, his eyes
both blurred and intent. "You know that dinner is always
served at eight. And I don't believe you are properly attired
for dinner."

Her full name, pronounced in that clipped, airy accent,
made her want to giggle. "Angus Archibald," she said in a
mocking tone. "Couldn't you invite the archbishop to confer
his blessing while I slip upstairs and put on the family jew-
els?"

His eyes had shut tight, in what she'd imagined was a
caricatured yielding to her clowning. "You will exhibit some

respect or you will leave this table," he said, without opening them. She had felt her cheeks distend in an explosion of laughter. "You can't be . . ." "I will not," he cut in, with deadly, melodramatic calm, "I repeat, I will not have my daughter coming to table as though she were something the cat dragged in."

"Archie, you can't possibly be serious! Had I known that you were preparing . . ." She broke off. Why was he always like this? Why was it necessary to be grovelingly contrite about every silly misunderstanding? "Here." She opened the box, tore a slice of pizza from the circle and held it toward him. "Let's have a pepperoni and mushroom and make up."

He took up the carving fork, plunged it into the meat as though it was still a living animal that had to be put out of its misery, fumbled for the knife, and began to cut. She thought the moment of confrontation had passed. "Carving meat," she said offhandedly. "It's something men feel they have to master. Like bringing home the bacon." He was hacking away against the grain, the veins in his temples standing out with the frustration of not being able to perform a simple task. She couldn't stop herself from adding, "It's so much easier to just tear off a piece."

"Shut up. Shut up. You disgusting, spoiled slut of a girl. Just shut up!"

He hurled the fork at her. Not directly at her. Rather, he threw it in her direction. It bounced off the side of the table and landed on the floor with a thud. He gripped the edge of the table and pulled himself up, leaning into her so that the flame from the candle transformed his features into a grotesque mask. "You have no respect for anything."

"You are quite wrong," she said, her voice calm with shock. "I have spent my entire life looking for something to respect. But I have never been able to find it in this house." Some force seemed to yank her up, so that she stood, the roots of her hair tingling, her eyes bulging. "The sad thing, the really pathetic thing . . ." She was going at him now, her voice rising, her hand pounding the table, then making a sweeping gesture that sent the pizza flying. ". . . is that I keep coming back here to play out these little kitchen-sink dramas you've cast us both in so that your alleged dramatic abilities won't go entirely to waste. But let me tell you something, Archie. It's over. I won't be sucked into this again. Not ever."

She ran out of the room and up the stairs. All she knew was that she had to get out. To that end she was lucid, concise, and determined. She got out her plane tickets, dialed the airline and asked if she could exchange her booking for a flight that left that night. She even had the presence of mind to enlist the clerk's sympathy by saying that her mother was ill and she had to get to a hospital in San Francisco. The clerk called another airline and arranged a transfer. She was booked for a midnight flight.

Stuffing the few things she'd removed back into her bag, she sat still long enough to smoke one cigarette. She'd given up smoking six months ago but, mercifully, she found a crushed pack of Adam's Marlboros in her back pocket, though she couldn't remember having picked them up. Dizzy from the cigarette and the rebellious pleasure of returning to a destructive habit, she picked up her bags and went downstairs. At the front door, as she dropped the bags and reached for the doorknob, she heard the soft sound of running water and the clink of a dish. She stopped. Archie had never washed a dish until Mabs had died. She knew just how Archie washed dishes, rubbing the sponge on both sides of the plate, bringing it to the light to inspect it, rinsing it methodically, gingerly placing it in the rack—as though he was performing some intricate ritual of repentance. But then he would leave the pots in the sink and forget to wipe the countertops. That's right, she thought, that's you, Archie: make the show of doing something but leave the dirty work to someone else. She'd wrenched the door back and let it slam against the wall, half-hoping that he would hear her and come. She'd heard him turn off the faucet and had stood, waiting for him. After a full minute, imagining them both poised but unmoving, fighting a desire to turn back, she'd kicked her bags onto the porch and slammed the door behind her.

Faint strains of a calypso band playing "Banana Boat Song" drifted in from the balcony and woke her from her nap. The lined draperies kept the hotel room so dark that she had no idea what time it was. She reached for the bedside lamp. Click. Click. Nothing. She felt her way over to the wall switch. Again nothing. A power outage. Of course. Power outages were such regular occurrences in Jamaica she couldn't imagine how she'd forgotten about them. Groping her way to the balcony, she pulled back the draperies and stepped out. Stars spangled the sky. The moon, watery but bright, brought enough light into the room for her to find her clothes and a flashlight stashed in the top bureau drawer. She made her way to the hall, where she heard a deep voice telling Doris that he had found the stairwell and that she shouldn't be scared. With the aid of her flashlight and Doris' giggles, she felt her way down seven flights to the ground floor.

The emergency power supply had been reserved for the pool and bar area. Putting her flashlight into her purse, she walked toward the giant aqua kidney. Colored lanterns bobbed in a breeze so moisture-laden that it might have come from an atomizer. The band gallumphed through "Some Enchanted Evening," complete with steel drums. She took a table on the periphery (could any woman feel comfortable eating alone in a resort?) and told the waiter that she was in a hurry. There was an antic restlessness in the crowd. Sipping their fruit-garnished drinks, their shell necklaces and sharks' teeth dangling, flowers tucked behind their ears, they were like children at a birthday party. The power failure had delighted them, whetting their appetite for the unexpected. Halfway through her lobster salad, the lights came back on, causing whoops, a smattering of applause, and a few groans. "Okay, ladies and gentlemen," the bandleader said and laughed. "Everything is A-okay. Let's get on with the fun. Dancing going on here and in ten minutes you can place your bets for the crab race, which will take place on the Bamboo Walk." She quickly paid her bill, left the remainder of her salad, and walked down to the beach.

The breeze was sea and flower-scented. Beyond the fringe of palm trees, the sand looked like powdered sugar. Taking off her shoes, she began to walk briskly, wanting to distance herself from the band and hear only the gentle pounding of the surf. She felt a shock of delight as the first wave hit her legs. Tucking her skirt into her underpants, she waded out and stood, toes gripping the ribbed bottom. Her skin felt both moist and taut. She closed her eyes and fingered the tiny silver heart around her neck. She had bought it in Guadalajara, and though she had seen the beggar woman who had sold it to her for only a few minutes, she could remember her high Indian cheekbones and sad, black, slanted eyes more vividly than she could call to mind the faces of people she'd known for years. The woman had been standing in the nave of the cathedral, and as Ceci had passed, she had shyly offered a piece of worn purple velvet to which miniature silver ornaments in the shape of limbs and organs had been attached. With no more than a dozen words and a dumb show, she had explained to Ceci that a supplicant bought an ornament corresponding to that part of the body in which she, or a loved one, was afflicted. The ornament was then pinned to the cloak of the Virgin and if prayers were sincere, one was healed. Ceci had shaken her head but the woman had reached out, touched her between her breasts, then pressed the little silver heart into her hand. Though she'd given the woman money, she'd always thought of the heart as a gift. As she touched it now she fantasized meeting Paul Strangman, walking with him on a beach such as this. But she knew this wouldn't be. And upon reflection, she didn't even want it to be. Just to invoke his memory gave her a sense of the vastness and mystery of life.

She walked on until she could hear nothing but the rhythm of the waves. Farther up the beach was a fire with a group of people, whites, circled around it. As she grew closer, she saw that they were naked, but decided to keep on walking. She had no objection to a skinny-dip. She would just avert her eyes as she passed. She then saw that one of the men was standing in a particularly exhibitionistic attitude and realized that the group was made up entirely of men. American homosexuals, who, like their heterosexual counterparts back at the hotel, had shed their inhibitions along with their winter clothes and would have looked better in both. She turned back. What must it do to a country's psyche to be so dependent on tourism? Jamaicans who mostly saw Americans on vacation wouldn't understand that some of those Americans had worked an entire year to have two weeks of spendthrift abandon. They would see all Americans as rich, lazy, and demanding, and that would produce that dull look of hostility and envy she'd already seen on native faces.

Turning her back on the ocean, she looked past the lights of the hotels to the distant hills. The tourists had claimed the shoreline, but the hills still belonged to the natives, if not legally then in fact. Archie had mentioned that Marsden wanted to make the great house into a convention center, and though she had mixed emotions about the Nettleton plantation she was sorry to think that the cane fields she'd walked as a girl might soon be the site of another, more opulent Swinging Plantation Lounge. But places, like people, had their karmas, and Jamaica's had always been an unhappy one. It had been fought over, abused, abandoned, and fought over again for almost five hundred years. The Spaniards had discovered it, killed off the native Arawaks, and settled in, only to be killed off by the British. The British had made it theirs, importing African slaves to work it for them, supressing revolts that were seldom mentioned in the history books. And even before Jamaica had attained independence from Britain, it had already come under the cultural and economic dominance of the United States. Always struggle, exploitation, and bloodshed. Why, on this very spot where she was now standing, conquistadors, pirates, and real estate agents had said, "This is beautiful and this is mine," and then— She was startled by a sound from the trees. A man darted out, necklaces draped on his outstretched arm. Would the beautiful lady like to buy? She walked on, only half-hearing the added offer of first-class ganja, coke, sex. . . .

Returning to her room, she found a pretty woman with a broad bottom turning down her bed. The woman eyed some packages Ceci had brought from Harrod's and began to ask her questions. Did the lady come from England? She wanted very much to get a visa to "the homeland" because her mother lived in Brixton and worked for a hospital taking care of the old ones. Did Miss need a maid back home? Ceci smiled, shook her head, said she was very tired, and unpacked a dress that needed pressing. Was the Miss traveling alone? Did the Miss have a photo of her children? Knowing it was acceptable to be unmarried but that for a woman her age to be childless made her "a mule," Ceci lied and said yes, she had a little girl but didn't have her picture. The woman sighed. Ceci handed her the dress and asked that it be returned by ten the next morning. (She wouldn't be dressing until eleven but calculated that the extra hour might help her get the dress on time.) The woman wished her good-night and shut the door.

Five

The next day was both overcast and full of glare. Ceci sat on the hotel balcony trying to concentrate on the *Daily Gleaner*. Fatigue and the anticipation of Archie's arrival had left her senses raw. The sounds of outboard motors and shouts from the tennis courts seemed intrusively loud; the smell of her fruit salad too sticky sweet; the clots of papaya clinging to the glass, the dregs of coffee, the yellow plastic carafe eye-smartingly bright. She had fallen asleep the moment her head had hit the pillow but had been awakened by a dream in which she was stranded in an airport, had missed a connecting flight, and couldn't remember her destination. She'd flicked on the light, thinking that she'd now come to the point where her waking life and her unconscious had become interchangeable. She'd checked her watch, smoked a cigarette, and had been about to go to sleep again when a couple had made a boisterous entrance into the adjoining room and proceeded to have a fight. Though she couldn't make out most of the words, the nature of the argument seemed clear enough: a struggle over vacation sex, exacerbated by booze and vacation crankiness. The man had bellowed at Dora or Doris while she showered and just as Ceci had given up on getting back to sleep and started to sympathize with poor

Dora or Doris, they'd reversed roles and the woman had yelled at the man while he showered. Score evened, a blissful quiet had ensued. Ceci had moved around to find a cool place on the sheets, settled into a comfortable position, and just begun to drift off when the couple's headboard began to bump steadily against her own. The thumping, which had all the variety of a metronome and lasted a scant three minutes, left her awake for another half hour.

She tackled the paper again, passing over the cricket scores on the front page and the birth and death announcements on the second. A smattering of international news was on the third. Her eye caught a column about labor disputes in the bauxite mines near Mandeville. Next to it, in a smaller column, was a statement from Mr. Paul Strangman, former Prime Minister. "The moral legitimacy of the current government is sharply brought into question by their decision to grant tax abatements to multinational firms while closing wards at the Kingston Public Hospital. The citizens of Kingston—"

There was a rap on the door. She started toward it, stopping in front of the mirror, approving the fit of her peach linen dress. Even Archie would have to admit she looked smashing. Flinging open the door, she saw a lanky young man, his skin dark as an eggplant, so that it seemed to disappear into the shadows of the hallway, exaggerating the whites of his lemurlike eyes.

"Miss Cecily." He bobbed his head. "I come with the car."

"Oh, yes, do come in. Mr. Archie . . ." She had quickly fallen into the habit of first names plus titles. ". . . my father, isn't here yet, though I expect him any minute. I had a bit of trouble telephoning the airline but I assume his plane is on time, so . . . your name is?"

He took a few steps into the room. "Percy." He said it with a "you remember" emphasis and she was embarrassed to find that she didn't. "I Miss Icilda's grandson."

She remembered that Icilda, Vivian's housekeeper, had had a virtual nursery school of grandchildren. "You used to play around the big tree, didn't you?" This was a safe guess. The big tree had been the unofficial demarcation between the house and the staff's quarters; all the children had played around it.

"Sure. I was only a little guy. When you know me, I don't yet got me khaki," he said, referring to the school uniform, "but you . . ." She had been a tall, skinny girl who got sun spots on her pink skin and tried to get rid of them by rubbing them with lemon juice. and a brave girl, too. She had explored the abandoned great house while he and the other children had hidden in the trees trembling with fright. But she had not spent much time with the children. She had lain in the cupola out in the water, reading, reading, until he thought her eyes would drop out. She had told him his people came from Africa, though he had been born in the village not twenty miles from the house. Once she had given him a tin of purple candies that smelt like flowers.

"Well, it's lovely to see you again, Percy. Won't you sit down."

"We get news you go everywhere. All over the world." He made a round shape with his hands and shook his head in amazement. "Everywhere you go, Mrs. Pinto says to us and shows us pictures, too."

"Ah, yes." It took her a moment to identify Mrs. Pinto as Aunt Vivian. Though she knew that Vivian had, around the age of thirty, been married, then quickly widowed by one Jacob Pintosuan (a Portuguese Jew who had, probably at the insistence of the Nettletons, Anglicized his name to John Pinto) she could never think of her aunt as anything other than Vivian Nettleton, spinster. "Yes, I have traveled a great deal, and I used to send Mrs. Pinto letters and photographs."

They stood awkwardly, she giving back his smile, wondering how to put him at ease. His eyes left hers, fixed on the blank screen of the television set, shifted to the balcony. A perplexed and morose expression came across his face. "Percy," she said, testing to see if the name nudged her memory. Something about his expression certainly did. She judged him to be about twenty-five and so, she calculated quickly, he would have been about six and therefore beneath her notice when she'd been an almost adult, disdainful thirteen, and yet . . . a sad-eyed boy with bird ankles and wrists, following Icilda around her herb garden with a leaky watering can, left by his mother (had there ever been a father around?), called "Shoe Polish" by the other children because he was the darkest of the brood. "You're *Percy*. Of course."

"You remember me now." He smiled with gratitude.

"But of course I remember you. It just took me a minute to make the connection. Is your grandmother well?"

"She like the big tree, miss. Tremble in the storm but roots still deep."

"That's good. And oh, Jesmina. Do you know Jesmina? When we were girls we used to be the best of friends. I wonder if she . . ."

His smile broadened to show a set of perfect teeth and his eyes widened with pleasure. "Yes, miss. I know Jesmina. She workin' at the place sometimes all these years, but she don't work there no more."

"Do you know where she is?"

"In the village."

"She wanted to be a postmistress," Ceci laughed. "I remember we used to walk together to the post office and Jesmina always said she wanted to be a postmistress. I was always waiting for letters from my father and she used to say that when she became postmistress I'd get a letter every day."

"She got no work now. Living in the village and takin' care of her children." The morose expression she'd noticed just minutes ago again returned to his face. It was, she supposed, this immediate reflection of emotion in the features that led people to use the word "childlike" in the pejorative sense when describing natives. Personally, she found such open expression appealing, though she was at a loss to know why Percy had become so upset. She broke their eye contact and stepped toward the balcony. "Do come out and sit. The view is lovely."

"Always Americans say 'view.' "

"I suppose it is rather silly. Always trying to find some scene you can prop yourself up in front of or take a picture of, but Jamaica is beautiful. It's a jewel of a place."

"Maybe, miss. Maybe."

"Do sit down. Are you hungry? Would you like me to order you some breakfast?"

"No, thank you. Already had me lunch."

"Then perhaps a bottle of Red Stripe?"

"Can't drink beer when driving, miss."

"No. I suppose not."

As the conversation stalled again, she looked down toward the hotel office, her attention arrested by a man getting out of a taxi. He was wearing a white tropical suit and a Panama hat and carrying a cane. He straightened up, waved the cane in the direction of the office and stood as though waiting for something to happen.

"I do believe that's my father down there." Who else but Archie would dress in such a fashion? Who else would prepare himself to make an entrance into a hotel lobby?

Since the desk clerk had not been efficient enough to let her know that Percy was coming up, she assumed Archie would also make his appearance unannounced. She excused herself, went into the bathroom, and whipped a brush through her hair. She checked her suitcases and made sure everything was ready to go. Archie hated to be kept waiting.

Moments later there was a knock at the door.

As she opened it she could feel his stare like a pressure on her face. "Archie!" He made the slightest gesture—was he going to stroke her face, shake hands with her?—then drew back, the seasoned actor commanding attention with immobility. He swept off his hat and stood so erect that his spine might have served as a carpenter's plumb line. His large head was fuzzed with a tonsure of pure white that matched his mustache. He had lost some flesh in the face, making his eye sockets deeper, intensifying the blue of his irises. "Cecily," he said at last, "You're looking very well."

Though she hated his restraint as much as she hated the pathetic vanity of the few wisps of hair combed over the top of his head, she felt a rush of affection.

"Oh, Archie." She kissed his cheek. He straightened up even more, threatening to tip backward, his eyes going past her to Percy. She pulled away. "Excuse me, Archie. This is Percy. . . . I'm sorry, Percy, I don't remember your last name."

"I'm Mrs. Pinto's driver," Percy offered.

"Percy and I knew each other as children, Archie. He's one of Icilda's grandsons."

"Good, very good. Well, my man, let's get these bags together, shall we?"

Ceci winced. "My man" was as dated as Archie's tropical getup. She started to go for one of the bags, but Archie caught her elbow, holding her back. "No use dawdling, is there." He nodded in Percy's direction. Percy picked up her bags and moved to the door. "I had to spend the night in Miami, as you know, and I'm anxious to get home. Have you been in the Miami airport, Cecily? Yes, I suppose you have. Dreadful place. Shops full of geegaws and the most bilious-looking carpet." He paused and nodded a gracious "after you" as she went into the hallway. "Have you settled up your bill yet, my dear?"

"No. But it will only take a minute. I'll . . ."

"No. I'll take care of that. I've left my things in the lobby. You'll go ahead with Percy and bring the car round to the entrance."

"There's really no need for you to . . ." No, don't start any arguments about money. "Thank you, Archie."

Percy went to ring for the elevator. She closed the door, caught another glimpse of Archie's cane, and asked if his legs had been bothering him. "Not a bit of it," he boomed. "Cane's a bit of a prop. I brought it along for sentimental reasons. One of the boys at the house carved it for me as a going-away present when I left for England. S'pose it's outlasted him."

The door to the adjoining room was flung back and a burly man stepped into the hall. "Aw, c'mon, Doris. Get yourself in gear, for god's sake. You can loll around at home," he called over his shoulder, then, catching Archie's eye, warned, "Ya gotta catch the sun." Archie gave Ceci a wry smile, said, "I shouldn't worry, it's here for most of the daylight hours," and moved toward the elevator. He held the Door Open button

while Ceci and the man arranged themselves in front of Percy
and the luggage. Doris, struggling with purse, beach bag,
straw hat, folding chair, and paperback book, tested their
door handle to make sure it was locked and hurried to join
them. As Archie punched the lobby button, Doris pulled at
the seat of her bathing suit to cover an escaping buttock and
dropped her book. Ceci bent to retrieve it. Seeing the title,
Ecstacy's Slave, and remembering the 1-2-3-rabbit coupling
she'd heard the night before, she had an impulse to put her
arm around the hapless Doris. "Gee, thanks, I'm so clumsy!"
"Don't know why you need to take a book with you," her
mate grunted, then, with a leer in Archie's direction,
"There's plenty to look at on the beach." "Especially if you're
an oceanographer," Archie responded in the clipped voice of
a visiting professor. It was eyes-front, close-formation all the
way down. When they reached the lobby, the man bounded
away and Doris, still juggling her belongings, tried to catch
up. "Talk about the Ugly American," Archie sighed as soon
as they were out of earshot. Then, turning to Percy, "Now
run off and get the Rolls and I'll be along in a tick."

"No Rolls, sir."

"No Rolls?"

"Just for special occasions. Gasoline too high."

"Very good then."

Ceci waited on the curb until Archie joined her and Percy
drove up in a black Toyota. As they got into the back seat, she
thought she saw Archie favoring his right leg but said nothing. Like strangers thrown together on a tour, they exchanged desultory comments about airline schedules and the
weather as they passed marinas, tennis courts, and other hotels. When they started up the narrow curving road that
climbed into the hills, they fell silent as if by mutual agreement.

The haze evaporated as suddenly as if a filter had been
removed from a lens. The lush growth beside the road glinted
and sparkled. They climbed higher, enclosed by dense forest,
rarely seeing another car, glimpsing shacks of bamboo, tarpa-
per, and flattened kerosene tins. Barefoot children called and
waved as the car sped past; some of the bolder ones danced

into the road, begging a ride. There was the occasional sign advertising local products—Ting soda pop, Appleton rum, Black Panther condoms (not, judging from the number of children, a big seller in these parts). Percy, proud of his prowess behind the wheel, negotiated the turns with skill, honking on the blind curves, slowing when a donkey strayed too far from the shoulder. Ceci, jolted by countless recognitions, felt a burst of energy.

"Oh, that's it! The bauhinia, the orchid tree. I saw it yesterday but for the life of me I couldn't remember its name. And that yellow one. That's poui, isn't it?"

Archie sat forward, his leonine head moving slowly from side to side. "And the pepper hibiscus. There. That one." He chuckled to himself.

They slowed while a boy drove a small herd of goats in front of them. "I can't wait to have some curried goat," Ceci said. "I suppose Icilda still makes it."

Percy's head swiveled back for a brief, warning glance. "Got a new cook."

"Yes. I'm sure there must be all sorts of changes," she agreed. "Though now we're in the hills, it all looks the same to me."

"Many changes, man," Percy said as he accelerated.

They sped past a waterfall where women knelt in the shallows, pounding clothes on the rocks, then rounded a sharp curve to the little village: saw children chasing each other across the parched schoolyard, the pink stucco spire of St. Andrew's church, a cluster of shacks that looked as though they could be blown away by a stiff breeze, men lounging against the doorless entrance of the grog shop, women crouched on the ground beside pyramids of breadfruit, akee, and bananas, an old woman stirring a cauldron of soup on a stone fireplace. The entire scene was like a painting by one of the primitives: bright, shadowless, bursting with life yet somehow static.

"Now look at that." Archie gestured toward a girl in a flowered cotton shift who walked, spine straight as a ballet dancer's, arms loose, with a large basket balanced on her head.

"The Jamaican women are among the most beautiful in the world."

"The men are pretty impressive, too," Ceci said, seeing an old man, his machete swinging at his side, moving with the same easy gait. "They're probably in such good condition because they walk so much."

"Nothing for it but to walk," Percy said.

Archie asked Percy to turn on the air-conditioning, rolled up the windows, and grew silent. Seeing his impassive features, the mottled flush of his skin, and his misty eyes, Ceci decided that he must be feeling his own homecoming emotions. She had read somewhere that old people could be jolted into a better state of health by returning to the scenes of their youth, and wondered if that meant they came to grips with their past, or if the mere sight of familiar yet changed scenery had a tonic effect. For her own part she was content to give up on conversation to relish her own recognition.

They crested several hills, then descended to flatter land. Lean cattle grazed on rough pastures amidst small plots of ginger and citrus. A broken-down fence ran the distance of several miles and ended in a gravel driveway where a sun-bleached sign, YOUNG PEOPLES' AGRICULTURAL COOPERATIVE, dangled next to a powder puff tree. Despite the greenery and the red pompoms of the tree, the place reminded Ceci of a Dorothea Lange photo of some Depression farm in the Texas Panhandle. "What was . . ." she turned her head swiftly, looking out of the rear window ". . . that?"

"Be Mr. Paul's place to teach farming."

Her heart tripped. By Mr. Paul, Percy must mean Paul Strangman.

"Whose place?" Archie queried. "I should have thought we were near the Edisons'."

"From Mr. Paul. To teach farming. Now it all fallin' down."

"But who did you say the land belonged to?"

Percy shifted forward in the seat, pulled his sweaty shirt away from his back, then squinted his eyes, seemingly intent on the blind curve that was coming up. "Mr. Paul," he said in a quieter voice. "He get it for the kids to learn. Man who own it, maybe Edison, say he shoot cattle and go to Miami when Mr. Paul come in. There be much intrigue. But over now."

"The last Prime Minister was a reform candidate," Ceci explained. "He moved rather more quickly than some of the local gentry deemed correct. His agricultural program . . ."

"Yes. Surely. Seem to remember hearing something about that." Archie's tone was authorative but dismissive, which, Ceci knew, meant that he didn't know a damn about the subject. At least he didn't think of Paul as an enemy. But then she knew Archie prided himself on being apolitical, though he clung to some code of personal honor that did not always permit him to stay entirely above the fray. When Ceci had not yet been old enough to understand, Mabs had told her that Archie had sent telegrams of support to acquaintances who'd been indicted when the House Un-American Activities Committee had purged the Hollywood elite. Archie had even sent a check to the wife of his dentist when the man had gone underground, saying it was a damned shame that a honest professional should be forced to abandon his practice. Smiling to herself, Ceci reached over and took Archie's hand. Percy, still nervous, asked if he might turn on the radio. "No, none of that bloody calypso stuff," Archie declared. "It's not calypso," Ceci laughed. "It's reggae, and I don't see why you don't like it. It's all the rage in New York and . . ."

Archie's attention left her entirely. He leaned forward and told Percy to slow down. High above them, commanding a view of the bay, stood the great house. Ceci too stopped, so imposing and incongruous was the structure. From this distance it was impossible to tell that it was a ruin, uninhabitable since before Archie's time. Dwarfing the few paltry shacks that dotted the hills around it, it seemed, with its height, its stone columns, its double flights of steps leading to massive doors, the habitation of giants, a glowing white temple dropped by a Divine hand into the jungle. In its heyday, the house had been the focal point of what constituted an entire village. There had been a mill, a boiling house, stables for the grinding cattle, lodging for the overseers, workshops for the smiths and carpenters and coopers as well as the slave shacks. Vivian had pointed all of this out when she had taken Ceci on a tour of the grounds, though they had not, for safety's sake, approached the house itself. It was only later, on a muggy afternoon Ceci could still remember, that she'd gone with some of Icilda's children or grandchildren on her own dangerous mission of exploration. The black children had shivered with the excitement of fear. They had told her of murders and beatings and of the duppies, or spirits, who still dwelt in the great house. Ceci, half believing their stories and therefore under a stronger obligation to prove her courage, had left them cowering in the underbrush while she had walked forward, blazing in the sun, climbing onto the crumbling piazza, pushing aside the hairy vines. Knowing that she was being watched she hadn't been able to back out, even though her heart had been pounding. She had finally crawled up the stairs and pressed her face, shielding it with her hands, to the weathered boards that covered a window on the lower floor. A dank, underground smell had titillated and stiffened her nostrils. Reason had told her that the place was now occupied by rats, bats, and birds, but when she'd heard the dull thud of God knew what—a lump of plaster dropping? a bird's nest falling? or perhaps the ghostly tread of her great-great-grandmother (who was said to be a witch)—she'd scurried back, full of bravado, to assure the others that it was just an old plantation house and nothing to be afraid of.

". . . and seven kinds of wood imported for the dining room paneling alone," Archie was saying. "Rosewood and mahogany, cedar, teak, and—"

"But imagine the backbreaking labor. Just getting the building materials up that hill. And in this heat."

"All the more reason for it being so impressive. It took, I believe, over three years to complete. It was one of the most outstanding examples of colonial architecture on the entire island."

Their conversation trailed off, for they had looped down through another forest of bamboo and were driving parallel to the coast, approaching what was always referred to as "the guest house," though it had been the family's residence for over a century. A high stone wall, sturdy but overgrown with vines and creepers, blocked off the view of the sea for several miles. The car slowed and turned into a driveway that ended at wooden gates so warped with age they hardly closed together. Percy pulled on the brake, jumped out, and slipped the loop of rope from the top posts. Pushing the gates open, he yelled for someone to come and close them and jumped back into the driver's seat. They moved over a lumpy gravel road, past hissing sprinklers that seemed to be redundant in this climate but guaranteed a green lawn right up to the water's edge even in the dry season. It seemed as though they were about to drive straight into the surf when Percy swung the wheel sharply to the left, bringing them to the massive tree whose roots twisted as high as a foot from the earth.

The "guest house" was now in front of them, a sprawling two-storied, white-washed structure that shone in the sun, pristine and smooth as a wedding cake. The architecture could charitably be described as eclectic. The house had been built onto countless times. Its upper floor had the jalousied windows and decorative, nonfunctional ironwork balconies of the turn of the century. Its lower floor had a series of French doors that opened onto a wide, semi-enclosed veranda that ran the entire perimeter of the house. The veranda, with its reddish tile floors, Moorish arches, and roof decorated with small-scale minarets, had been added by Archie's father, who had spent much of World War I in a Turkish prison but had returned to Jamaica with an inexplicable affection for Middle Eastern design.

Without waiting for Percy to assist him, Archie got out, left the car door open, and crunched up the pebbled path swinging his cane. Ceci stood for a moment, turning in the other direction to see the outbuildings—the row of single-room cabins that made up the servants' quarters, the stables that had been converted into garages, the laundry room and privy —then followed him. She paused again at the little pool. When she'd lived here, mildewed leaves had encrusted the dry bottom. Now it was clean and full of carp. The nereid statue at the center of the pool had been painted but seemed not to be laughing, as Ceci had remembered her, but to be gasping for breath. Shading her eyes, Ceci looked out at the narrow footbridge that led to the cupola some hundred feet into the water. How could she have forgotten the cupola? It had been her retreat, her hideaway. She'd spent countless afternoons there, reading, writing in her diary, rocking in the hammock, imagining herself a mermaid.

A girl wearing a smartly starched uniform waited on the front steps. She was barely out of her teens, so Ceci did not recognize her. The girl bobbed her head and reached for Archie's hat.

"My sister . . ." Archie faltered, then tapped his cane impatiently on the tile.

"Yes, sir. We expecting you, sir. Miss Vivian still be in her room."

"Then I suggest you go and tell her that we've arrived. Cecily, do come in out of the heat. You'll faint dead away."

"Not bloody likely. I love the sun. I was wondering if it was too late to put on my bathing suit and go out to the gazebo."

"Perhaps it would be more polite if you greeted your aunt first."

"Of course. I didn't mean I was going to strip down immediately. Of course I want to see Aunt Vivian. And Marsden, too. Though neither of them seem to be around."

The girl started across the veranda but retraced her steps. "Mr. Marsden say tell you he go on important business but sure be back for dinner."

"Very well. Now go and tell Miss Vivian." Archie waved her away, his features sagging in disappointment before he drew himself up. Avoiding Ceci's eyes, he looked around at the polished tile, the wicker chairs and tables, and the potted plants, emitting little grunts of approval. "Marsden's kept the place up."

"It was always a bit much for Aunt Vivie to handle," she said gently.

"Don't know why it should have been if she'd known how to handle the staff. Of course she's in no condition now, judging from the reception we're getting."

"Don't take it as a rejection, Archie. Don't be disappointed."

"I am not disappointed. I'm merely commenting that Mars-den has taken a real interest in the place. I don't recall the girls' wearing uniforms before, do you?"

"No. That's probably Marsden's idea. All those years in military school, I expect he'd like to see us all in uniform."

"There's no need to be snide about it, Cecily. Marsden's taken a real interest in the place." He put a special emphasis on Marsden's name, implying that she'd somehow been re-miss.

She was conscious of her own discomfort, standing about on the veranda, neither guest nor resident. Archie removed his hat. The band had left a welt of red on his already flushed face. He took a handkerchief from his breast pocket and mopped his neck.

"Come on, Archie. Let's go in. You're beginning to get a boiled look."

The front room did little to put them at their ease. Since the family was opposed to any ostentatious display and the room was rarely used, it had, despite the fact that it opened onto the bright veranda, a feeling of a somewhat musty recep-tion area. An old horsehair sofa and several armchairs were pushed back against the walls. There was a breakfront in which the good plate and a few inconsequential pieces of silver were locked, a low coffee table on which two ashtrays, a copy of Naipaul's *The Middle Passage*, and several recent copies of *Fortune* magazine were placed. The walls were bare except for three small eighteenth-century prints of slaves, naked except for loincloths, slashing the cane with long ma-chetes, and large portraits of the most famous Nettletons. The only change that Ceci could see was that a carved mahogany table had been replaced by a chrome and glass drinks' cart. A rum punch had been prepared for them, (or perhaps drinks were now available round the clock since brother Marsden had taken "such an interest"). Next to the ice bucket and the pitcher of punch, which was protected by an embroidered, beaded cloth, stood English gin, American scotch, and Irish whiskey. "Ah, the tropics," Ceci said. "If the heat don't get you, the liquor will. Shall we have one while we wait, Archie?"

Without waiting for his reply she poured two punches and carried them over to where he stood, fingering the brim of his hat and looking up at the portraits. "Cheers." She touched her glass to his, took a long swallow, and raised it to the paintings. "To Izzy and Maude, without whom none of this would have been possible." Isaac (later Sir Isaac) Nettleton and his first wife Maude Parr had been painted against a background of the English countryside, which Isaac had seen only once in his life, when he had gone "home" to be knighted and to claim Maude. Except for the fact that Maude was wearing a dress and a lace kerchief and Isaac carried a musket, they might have been identical twins, so alike was the set of their large jaws and the boldly confident look in their steely blue eyes. Isaac had built the great house. Maude had been its mistress, at least until the seven-wood paneling had been installed. She had then returned to England, taking their children with her and leaving Isaac to fight with Colonel Grignon in the slave uprising of 1832. Isaac, it was told, had witnessed the burning of many Montego Bay plantations, but his great house had been spared by what he attributed to Divine Intervention. "To Izzy and Maude," Ceci repeated. "Come on, Archie, drink up."

"Damn it all." Archie put his glass down on the coffee table and gave Ceci one withering glance. She blinked and set her glass down as well. Did he disapprove of her draining an entire glass of punch midafternoon or did her mere proximity make her the recipient of his angry feelings? He threw his hat onto the sofa, and walked into the passageway, calling "Vivian! Vivian, where are you?" Ceci followed, almost bumping into him as he stopped, momentarily confused at a division in the dark passageway, then abruptly turned left. The young servant girl pressed herself into the wall as he passed her. He checked two closed doors and arrived at a third that had been left ajar.

Vivian was sitting by a window, her back to them. Icilda stood at her side, holding an open jewel case. "I think the garnet, don't you, Icilda? Yes, I shall wear mother's garnet necklace."

"Miss," Icilda whispered, "they already be here." She

smiled nervously, acknowledging them, her fingers fumbling as she fastened the necklace around Vivian's throat.

"Vivian! Are you off your chump completely? I'm here. It's Angus."

"Oh, Angus." Vivian turned slowly. "So nice of you to come." She said it as though they'd just walked across the road to say hello. "You mustn't scold me because my toilette has taken so much time. I know how important it is that I look well when I see you."

Ceci held her tongue firmly behind her teeth to stop from laughing. To some observers her aunt's greeting would be proof of senility; others might see it as a sly sort of one-upmanship. Her guess was that Vivian had reached a new, if more eccentric stage of consciousness. Coming to the end of her life, Vivian had finally abandoned the social constraints that had always bound and baffled her. If her brother Angus hadn't bothered to see her for over a decade, what difference could a few more minutes make? And Vivian was right on target about the importance Archie attached to appearance, especially that of "his women," which included female relatives.

"Cecily, you naughty girl! You're here too." Vivian's eyes watered with recognition. She clutched the arms of her chair and pulled herself up. She was wearing her usual dark print dress, stockings, and sensible brogues (which were not at all sensible in the tropics). Her chestnut hair had whitened in patches and was pulled back into a bun. She had carefully powdered her face, though she had been less successful with the application of rouge. Her body still had an indentation at the waistline and was beautifully proportioned, though too rigidly held to be graceful. Yet, even as a young woman she had never been considered beautiful because one of her eyes was slightly crossed, giving her a look of focusing inward, as though constantly drawn to some long past but irredeemable tragedy. As she drew Ceci to her she muttered, "How you've changed. You are lovely, lovely, lovely."

Ceci, feeling the softness of her own flesh against her aunt's bony frame, thought, "I've inherited all these crazy, powerful genes. If I don't do myself in, I shall probably live to an advanced age and I too shall make people who've neglected me wait until I'm damn well ready to see them." But as she drew back and looked into Vivian's face, another thought intruded: Vivian might be more than eccentric. Perhaps it was because of Vivian's wayward eye, but Ceci had the strong feeling that though Vivian was staring at her and holding her hands, she was not really aware of her presence; that she, and perhaps everyone else in the world, was somehow peripheral to Vivian's inner life.

"And Angus. My, how handsome you look. Your color is excellent. And you're still so tall." Though they were approximately the same height, Vivian bowed her head to receive his brotherly kiss. Archie, placated, let his hands fall on her shoulders. "Now see here, Viv"—a brief look in Ceci's direction to show that he was being firm but not chastising —"you shouldn't have made us come looking for you. And we can't stand about in your bedroom."

"No, indeed. Come to the front room. Icilda's made some of her famous punch. We're all so glad to see you. Your arrival will cause quite a stir. Mrs. Cleardon has insisted on arranging a party."

"Mrs. who?"

"You wouldn't know her, Angus."

Ceci recognized the "not quite one of us" tone in her aunt's voice.

"But, as I was saying, Mrs. Cleardon has insisted. It's to take place tomorrow evening and absolutely everyone in the parish is invited." She arched her eyebrows and pursed her lips, teasingly censorious. "And please refrain from going about puffed up like a toad because there's going to be a party in your honor, Angus. Life here is, as you know, very quiet, so the appearance of anyone—perhaps not anyone, but an actor—is cause for celebration. Almost 'the prodigal returns,' eh, Icilda?"

Icilda stood quiet as a tree, her starched uniform hanging away from her thin arms but pulled taut across her thickened trunk. She lowered her head.

"Now, Icilda," Archie boomed, "where's that smile for me?"

The old woman raised her head in a dreamy fashion, her mouth immobile, her eyes full.

"The smile, Icilda. The smile," Archie insisted.

She obliged, but hesitantly, like a child who had just lost her front teeth.

"And lest you remind me of my poor manners," Vivian said, bringing one hand to her throat and taking Archie's arm, "I shall now go and station myself at the front door and you can make a proper entrance." She led him off down the hall.

Ceci turned back into the room. It might have been preserved in a time capsule. There was the four-poster bed with the plain white coverlet, its headboard carved with swans inclining their necks. (The headboard that had always frightened her because she'd imagined that the swans pecked at Aunt Vivian in her sleep.) There was the old wardrobe, large enough for a full-grown man to hide in; the end table with its glass of water, lamp, and opened book; the bookshelf holding the same leather-bound classics and battered travel books that Vivian read and reread; the dressing table with its silver brush, comb, and mirror set. And Icilda.

"Dear Icilda. How are you? How have you been?"

"Wishing God's precious blessing on you, miss. For true I think I don't see you or Mr. Angus this side of heaven." She lowered her head again, her eyes brimming. Her manner changed abruptly as she saw the young girl still standing by the door. "Thelda! What you stand for? Go get sandwiches. Go get fruit. What you think Mr. Marsden say me if ice bucket empty?"

Thelda remained motionless, captivated by the sight of Ceci's dress.

"Go," Icilda commanded. "Jackass who gallop an' kick muss get cucoo macca tik."

With a look both obsequious and insolent, the girl sauntered off.

Ceci laughed. "I know what that means. 'Donkey that gallops and kicks must be punished with the stick.' You used to tell me that when I threw my clothes under my bed instead of giving them to you to wash. But you never punished me."

"No, miss. But that one, she terrible. Everyday a fuss in the yard. Mr. Marsden want everything be nice. Two more girl come. Cook from a school. But everyday a fuss in the yard."

Ceci knew that she was about to get an earful. There had always been intrigue and jockeying for position with the staff, and now that Marsden had apparently decided to turn the house into his version of a four-star hotel, conflicts were bound to be exacerbated. Knowing what pride Icilda took in her cooking, she offered a small word of consolation. "New cook or no, I want some of your curried goat. My mouth has been watering for it all day."

"No, miss. We have French food now. Only I buy all things to cook but don't cook. We all tested. If we good, we go to the great house when it come open."

"You mean he really plans to restore the great house? Archie mentioned something about that but I didn't really listen because it seemed so improbable. That would cost such a lot of money, and frankly I don't think Marsden has . . ." She stopped. It wasn't seemly to spill all the family business to Icilda. "I mean, why does he want to do that? What for?"

"For a better class of tourists to come," Icilda recited what she had either overheard or been told. "Important people, so we all be rich."

"*All* of us?" Ceci asked archly. "I didn't know Marsden was so concerned with the general good. But what about Aunt Vivian? What does she think of all this?" Having vowed only moments ago not to get involved, she was now pumping the old housekeeper for information. "Has Marsden actually started work on the house?"

"Sure, miss. Men be there from last Christmas, hammer and saw, pull down everything, put up—"

Archie's voice was heard, summoning Ceci.

"Sorry, Icilda. I must go and see Aunt Vivie. You can tell me more later. Come to my room. I have a little gift for you."

Icilda beamed, all concerns banished. "Thank you, miss. It is a true child of God who loveth the poor."

Ceci swept her hair from her forehead and looked away. "I wish you wouldn't say things like that, Icilda." Such abject gratitude embarrassed her. But as Icilda dropped her head, Ceci realized that her own embarrassment was just another form of self-indulgence. Icilda's thanks was no less heartfelt because her expression of it came from a child's prayer book, and since six months of Icilda's salary wouldn't have bought the purse Ceci had slung over her shoulder, of course Icilda would be pleased with any gift. "I just dropped by Harrod's to get something for Auntie and I thought of you, too. Now, listen . . ." She took Icilda's hand as Archie called out to her again. ". . . I'll be staying for a while, so we'll have plenty of time to talk."

"If you want the goat curry, miss, I have Percy bring from my daughter's house."

"That would be lovely." She tried to disengage her hand but Icilda held on, so that they went through the motions of a gentle tug-of-war.

"So many things to tell you, miss. Please only, only talk with me. I tell God's truth."

Ceci kissed the old woman's cheek, patted her hand, and assured her that they would talk.

A simple lunch of cheese, potted meat sandwiches, cold lobster, and fruit had been set on the dining room table. Vivian closed both the doors to the living room and the one to the kitchen and dismissed the new girl, Thelda. When Archie said he wanted some mayonnaise, she rose from her chair and went to the kitchen to get it. Vivian had always instructed Ceci that one did not impose on the servants to do anything one could do for oneself. This code of self-sufficiency had mostly to do with manners. It did not include cooking, washing, cleaning, or serving meals, so when Vivian returned with the mayonnaise and carefully closed the kitchen door behind her, Ceci assumed that they were about to have an intimate conversation.

But Vivian only asked if the food was to their taste, then launched into stories of the peccadilloes of local personalities, some of whom, Ceci suspected, were no longer alive. As Vivian warmed to her subject, her Jamaican dialect became more pronounced. Ceci could not help but smile. Her aunt, in appearance so much the proper British matron, sounded very much like her servants. Archie joined in the conversational badminton, recalling the drowning death of Pastor

Stokes, the mismanagement that had led to the loss of the Blair's shipping line, the hurricane of 1923. Ceci drank more rum punch. Once or twice she tried to nudge the conversation to more personal topics, but this was largely ignored. At one point, Vivian interrupted her appraisal of that year's pineapple crop and stared at her with an anxious expression. Vivian began, "What I've really been meaning to tell you—" but then broke off, scanning Ceci's face as though looking for a blemish.

After an hour, her bottom numb, her skin beginning to itch, Ceci rubbed her shoulder blades against the rungs of the chair and was about to excuse herself when Vivian got up abruptly, looked at both of them as though they were pieces of furniture she'd just inspected but decided not to buy, and announced that she was going to her bedroom for her afternoon "flop."

"Well, what do you think?" Ceci inquired when the door had been shut.

"About what?"

"About Aunt Vivian. About everything."

"It's perhaps worse than Marsden has led me to believe."

" 'It's'? I suppose you mean 'she.' "

"Yes. Very well, she. Never been anything like this in the family. Our minds have always held out to the end."

"That's your opinion," she kidded. When he didn't smile, she rested her chin in her hand and leaned closer to him. "Isn't it strange to be back? Don't you feel a hundred little shocks and surprises? Just seeing the big tree sent a shiver through me, and the portraits—I'd completely forgotten about the portraits—and then Aunt Vivie herself. When I first saw her . . ."

"Yes. It's worse than Marsden led me to believe."

"I don't know what he led you to believe, but I should think, at least I hope, that part of her behavior is attributable to seeing both of us after so many years. I don't think the Nettletons could win any prizes for expressing spontaneous emotion. And speaking of Marsden, I wonder what was so pressing that it prevented him from being here to meet us. I should think that . . ."

Archie pushed back his chair and reached to touch the leg of the table. "When I was a boy, our housekeeper, Mary, used to set the legs of this table in little tins of ant killer. I used to watch the ants. They never got any further than this curve about midway up the leg, then they'd topple off. Don't s'pose there's a need for that anymore. Better insecticides nowdays."

So the massacre of the ants helped you to ignore what was going on at the table then, just as remembering it aids your avoidance now, Ceci thought. She realized that she shouldn't have mentioned Marsden's absence. She merely thought it cold and ill mannered, but it must've wounded Archie. "But back to Aunt Vivie," she said, lowering her voice. "I admit she did act strangely, but even as a younger woman she was always . . ." She searched for the gentle word, but couldn't find it. "She does seem, I can't quite put my finger on it, anxious or fearful. But then, look at how she lives."

"What's wrong with the way she lives?"

"I just meant she's so isolated. She has no one to talk to."

"Nonsense. There's Marsden. And this girl he's going to marry—Hilary, isn't it?"

"I think that's her name. The other thing I noticed was that Aunt Vivie didn't say a word about her health. Or this business of restoring the great house. Neither did you, for that matter. Did you realize that it's well underway?"

Archie grunted noncommittally and returned his attention to the table leg.

"I wonder," Ceci went on, "where he's getting the money for it. I should think it would be prohibitively expensive. Has he sold off any of the property?"

"I should say not. We've never . . ."

"I know, I know. 'Not since 1836' and all that."

"Wonderful idea, this restoration. Once that convention center is opened, this estate will begin to show a profit again. A substantial profit, I should think."

"You know, you haven't discussed any of this with me."

"Hardly had the opportunity, have we?" he asked reasonably. "All we've had are a few telephone calls to arrange our travel plans. I certainly haven't known where to contact *you*, have I?" Though she knew that he bore equal responsibility

for their estrangement, she felt a prick of guilt. "That's one
of the reasons I came down here," he went on after seeing the
subtle change in her expression. "Have to consult with Marsden about the future of the estate. So far as I can see, he's right
about one thing: Vivian is certainly not capable of handling
any financial affairs. He should have full legal responsibility,
power of attorney or whatever it's called."

She looked up. "Is that his idea or yours?"

By way of answer, Archie began to push at a pineapple rind
with his fork.

"What would be the need for that?" Ceci persisted. "She
gives him a free hand, doesn't she?"

"You don't understand. Sometimes decisions must be made
on the spot, documents need to be signed, responsibility al-
located. A clear head and a firm hand . . ."

"Archie," Ceci laughed, "you sound as though you're reading from some bad script about executive takeover. And I
certainly wish you'd told me more about what's going on. It's
my feeling—"

"You women and your feelings. This is a straightforward
legal and business problem. If Vivian isn't capable of seeing
the wisdom of it, we shall seek some medical and legal advice
and we shall make short shrift of it. For Vivian's own good.
Did you enjoy your lunch?"

"Oh, shit. My lunch? Oh, shit, Archie!"

"Cecily, I'm aware of the fact that your generation is incapable of expressing itself without the use of gutter language,
but if you could make an effort to communicate without it, I'd
much appreciate it."

She looked at the lobster carcass, so frustrated that she
wanted to pick it up and throw it. But no. Not another mucky
scene with food tossed about and utensils used as weapons.
"Sorry. I'm tired. I expect you must be too with all this
traveling."

"Not a bit of it. Feeling more than fit."

"What's say we go out to the cupola? Loll about, catch up
on what we've been doing lately and talk about—"

"Loll about in the middle of the afternoon? I leave that to
our Latin brothers. I shall take a turn round the grounds."

No point in trying to confront him now. "Very well, sahib. Me, I'm stripping down to a bathing suit and taking my own nap in the hammock." She got up, feeling a heaviness in her limbs that couldn't altogether be attributed to traveling. She longed for some free and open conversation, some expression of feeling and acknowledgment of her return. "Icilda!" She went to the kitchen door and pushed it open. A smooth-faced mulatto wearing earphones and an apron that said Bloomingdale's was moving his feet to unheard music and feeding a carrot into a Cuisinart.

Thelda had trouble remembering where she'd put Archie's hat and cane, but once she'd found them he was off, leaving the house with a sprightly step that slowed only when he was sure he was out of sight. Despite his support socks and the prosthesis in his right shoe, his legs were starting to ache. He cut across the lawn and paused at the big tree. In his time there had always been someone about—the staff's ubiquitous children or grandchildren, their lips smeared with food, their eyes dolorous after a beating or delighted with the prospect of some mischief; visiting cousins, nieces, and nephews (it was impossible to sort out their tangled kinships); and, in crop, cutters who had wandered down from their field barracks looking for food or a woman or an opportunity to loiter and smoke. But now the row of cabins baked in the sun, so quiet it was hard to believe that anyone lived in them.

He turned away, walking down to the ribbon of sand, watching the waves for a minute before moving along the shoreline past the cabins and looping up into the uncultivated property behind them. As soon as he was sure that he was protected by the thick tangle of trees and vines, he found a stump and sat down, mopping his brow. He had meant to seek out Icilda. Being so riled up over Vivian's bizarre greeting, he had barely acknowledged Icilda's presence. He was sure that Icilda's mother, Mary, who had taken care of him in his boyhood, was long since dead, but he'd hoped to inquire after her, slip Icilda a few dollars, and express his condolences.

Mary had been his nanny; the first woman he'd ever loved. Not that she would fit most people's idea of comforting ma-

ternity. She'd had a fierce, omnipresent eye. Her voice, in
anger, had screeched like a parrot's. But she'd let him sit on
the high kitchen stool and watch her cook. He had loved the
way she pounded dough. And when she'd gutted a fish, she
would stand staring into its innards as though she was some
Roman priestess skilled in augury. And sometimes, when he
brought her one of his drawings or showed off his gift for
mimicry by impersonating someone from the village, she
would laugh and hold him to her small, flat breasts. Remembering her, a shadow of guilt crept over him in the bright late
afternoon sun. Not that he had ever done anything to harm
her. Of course he had exaggerated her scoldings to his parents
and thereby gotten her into trouble; he had dipped his finger
into her fancy cake icings and ruined their design, and once
he had stood on a box and peeked through the window of her
cabin to see her naked, sitting on top of Joseph the gardener
and emitting the same little grunts of satisfaction she made
when she took a soufflé out of the oven. He had promised to
write to her when he'd been sent off to England but had used
the fact that she couldn't read as an excuse for never doing so.
These things were hardly reprehensible for a boy. Yet guilt,
for those who are inclined to it, can fix on the most trivial
things and just now, closing his eyes and seeing a mottled red,
the "sponge cake incident" that had led to Mary's dismissal
played on his mind.

He had been about nine at the time, home for the holidays
but about to be packed off again. Evelyn, his mother, had been
complaining about Mary for some time. Mary had a habit of
letting the milk boil over. Mary went to church on Sundays
but secretly consulted her Obeahman for spiritual advice.
And when she was in a black mood, her manners left something to be desired. But her meringues, curries, and tarts were
without equal in the parish and so she had been allowed to
stay on. One day an unexpected guest had arrived for afternoon tea. Evelyn asked that the sponge cake be served. The
cake was nowhere to be found, though the family had cut into
it only the night before and Evelyn was sure that a full third
of it remained. After the guest had gone, Evelyn had ques-

tioned the other servants and had determined that Mary had taken the remains of the cake to her cabin.

"I do not expect thievery from a woman who has been in my employ for fifteen years." Archie could remember his mother's very words. He had stood in the pantry eavesdropping while Evelyn had made her accusation. Even as Mary swore her innocence, he'd been sure that she had, indeed, stolen the cake. Yet the ring of indignation in her voice had been so convincing that he'd almost believed her and had desperately wanted his mother to believe her, too. Was it such a great thing, after all? Half a sponge cake? When Mary had baked thousands of cakes for them over the years? But he also took his mother's side. It was wrong to steal. Evidence of one theft gave rise to suspicions of countless others that might have gone undetected. Or, as Evelyn had more dramatically put it: "A violation of trust between master and servant unravels the entire fabric of civilization." Archie, torn by the insolubility of this moral dilemma, had scratched the scab on his elbow and made it bleed while Evelyn's lecture about society's tattered fabric had continued. He had become aware of another presence: Icilda, Mary's daughter, crouching outside the pantry door. It pained him to think of her hearing her mother being humiliated, but to chase her away would have been to expose his own presence. So he'd remained, stiff between the bags of rice and sugar, while the argument had continued.

Mary had been so snivelingly contrite that he'd become disgusted with her. But then, just as it seemed that Evelyn must relent and come down on the side of forgiveness, Mary had turned vengeful. There had been a great crashing of pots. He'd imagined his mother, pale-faced, pressed into a corner, while Mary, like an elephant in an attack of "must," had destroyed the kitchen. He'd felt he must come out of hiding and go to his mother's aid, but he had been immobilized by fear. The name of God had been invoked by both parties, and then Mary, in a voice so low that he'd had to strain to hear it, had said that she refused to serve in an establishment where, after fifteen years, she wasn't trusted. Evelyn had no choice but to dismiss her.

Shortly after Mary had gone, it was discovered that a wire whisk, a copper bowl, a ten-pound sack of flour, and three silver teaspoons were missing.

The other servants had praised his mother's goodheartedness when she'd allowed the abandoned Icilda to stay on in Mary's cabin. One of them had pointed out that since Icilda had been named after a bleaching face cream, she would stand a better chance of redemption if given a proper Christian name. Someone—Archie had forgotten who—had rebaptized her Rachel, and for a few weeks this was how she was known. But the novelty had worn off, and being summoned in annoyance or in need, or simply out of habit, she had become Icilda again.

Looking up through the leaves of the sea grape, Archie could see that the sponge cake incident had been a turning point in his life. At nine he had not had the words, and therefore could not properly formulate his idea of escape, yet the desire was already in him. In some way he had intuited that if he grew to manhood on the plantation, he would be free to be a gossip, a drunkard, a fornicator, and a bully, as long as he never questioned the code that had made some human beings masters and others slaves. He wanted no such shrunken manhood. He wanted, instead, to treat men as equals. He was not afraid to compete. He would be noble, courageous, a true gentleman, a lover. And he would have a spot of fun doing it. He had begun to petition his parents to send him to England.

Six

Ceci turned in the hammock, simultaneously pulling the towel over her midriff and bringing her other hand up to cover her ear, so that a moment later, when she came to full consciousness, she wasn't sure if the late afternoon breeze or the sound of the car had woken her. Sitting up, she saw two men and a woman getting out of a tan BMW. The woman was slender, wore a brightly colored floral dress, had ear-length hair the color of cornsilk, and appeared to be in her mid-twenties. One of the men was stocky and wore chinos and a black sports shirt, the other—she lowered her sunglasses, trying to reconcile memory with reality—was Marsden. He looked considerably older than his forty-odd years. His close-cropped hair was already silvery and his more casual version of Archie's tropical costume showed that the flesh of his upper body had melted into a slight paunch. "Cecily," he called, shading his eyes, "is that you?"

She called back that indeed it was and got up. She'd made it only halfway across the footbridge before she realized that the man in the black shirt was the same one who'd tried to pick her up on the plane. The chilly breeze made her nipples stand up. She felt as though she was parading on a runway; not just because the man was ogling her but because the woman was staring at her with openly competitive appraisal. She could almost feel her checking off her defects—hips disproportionately larger than bust, hands and feet too big—as though she were a judge in a Miss America contest.

Marsden offered his hand to help her down from the footbridge. "Cecily. It's been such a long, long time." His lips, light and irritating as insect wings, brushed her cheek, but he didn't seem genuinely pleased to see her. He stepped back for the introductions. "This is my fiancée, Hilary Berwith . . ." Hilary's lips stretched into a "say cheese" smile that strained her neck. At close range, Ceci could see that they were about the same age. Hilary had a flawless complexion and regular, pretty features marred by a slightly porcine nose. ". . . and this is Al Lupon. Mr. Lupon is a business associate of mine. Mr. Lupon, my sister, Miss Baron."

Lupon grinned. "It's *Miss* Baron, is it?"

"That's right. But Ceci will do just fine."

"So where's that impatient husband of yours?"

Ceci smiled back at him, then turned to Marsden and Hilary. "Mr. Lupon and I met on the flight in. I'm afraid that I was less than honest when I introduced myself."

"And I was less than gentlemanly. I was trying to pick her up."

"How *was* your trip?" Hilary gushed with a solicitude that would have been appropriate to asking someone's condition after major surgery. "There've been so many delayed flights lately. So much *tedious* waiting about." Her accent said Midwestern childhood, New England education, overlaid with British affectation.

"Just fine."

Lupon held his grin. "Would've been a damned sight finer if you hadn't had to fight off guys like me. I apologize for the nuisance."

"Not at all." In a flash she realized that it had been Percy, driving Marsden's Toyota, who had picked up Al Lupon at the airport while she'd been left to find a taxi.

"What a happy coincidence that you two have already met," Hilary said. "Al's dining with us tonight. Terribly sorry we weren't here to greet you, but we were showing Al around the island." Ceci looked down at her feet. So much for the importance Marsden placed on her and Archie's return. "And what did I tell you, Al?" Hilary went on, "Isn't this one of the loveliest places you've ever seen? When I take my morning coffee on our veranda, I feel as though I'm in transcendental meditation."

All eyes turned out to the bay and Al dutifully commented on the beauty of the view. Ceci noted the sense of ownership with which Hilary had referred to "our" veranda.

"Where's father?" Marsden asked.

"I don't know," Ceci answered. "He wandered off after lunch. I expect he's found his way back by now." She was conscious of lifting her neck and moving her head, trying to establish eye contact, because Marsden focused first on her brow, then on her cheek, but didn't meet her gaze.

Hilary moved toward the veranda. "Shall we go in and have a cool drink?"

Ceci wrapped the towel around her waist, not wanting to give Lupon the pleasure of watching her behind going up the steps or provide Hilary with another chance to judge her less-than-perfect thighs. When they reached the front room, Hilary moved to the drinks' cart, lifted the lid from the ice bucket, and dropped it back with a deep sigh. "They've let the ice melt! I've told them time and time again. . . ." The cords in her neck stretched taut. "Icilda!" She shook her head. "Really! It's like talking to children."

Ceci reached for the bucket. "Here, let me. I know where the kitchen is."

"But they've got to learn," Hilary insisted, clutching the bucket to her chest. She crossed to the threshold of the dining room, yelling "Thelda! Icilda!" with the gusto of a hog-caller, before turning to Lupon and saying in a sugary voice, "Terribly sorry, Al. I suppose the place has just gone too long without a woman in charge."

"Where is Aunt Vivian?" Marsden asked.

"Down for her afternoon flop." Ceci smiled at Lupon. "That's what Aunt Vivian calls her nap."

"My aunt is getting on in years," Marsden explained.

Lupon spread his hands, shrugged, and said something

about the old folks needing a rest after having been in harness for so many years.

"But that's the trouble," Hilary said. "I don't think Aunt Vivian has ever been in harness. You can't imagine the mess things were in before Marsden took over."

Thelda appeared, her face already anticipating a rebuke, but Hilary merely handed over the ice bucket and said "Ice!" as though she were a surgeon demanding a scalpel in the middle of an operation. She then turned back to Lupon. "It isn't just Aunt Vivian's age. My daddy is almost Vivian's age and believe me he has all of his faculties. With Vivian it's— how can I put it politely—" She tapped a fushia nail to her brow and made an idiot face.

"It's not Alzheimer's disease or anything like that, is it?" Lupon asked with concern. "I had an uncle who came down with that and it was a nightmare for everyone concerned."

"I'd say," Ceci cut in, making her tone light to disguise her annoyance, "that Aunt Vivie just exhibits a more pronounced form of an eccentricity that runs in the family."

"If you'd been around her as much as we have, you'd know the problem is far more serious than that," Hilary corrected her. "Sometimes she's silent for days at a time. She just wanders about the house touching the furniture and muttering to herself. Then, when she does talk, it's impossible to follow her. I swear I don't think she knows what year it is. Just the other day—out of the blue—she asked Marsden if he thought there'd been many casualties in the invasion."

"She may have been talking about Grenada," Lupon ventured.

Or her own property, Ceci thought, bending to the coffee table to take a cigarette. She blew the smoke out with Bette Davis flair while Hilary supplied Lupon with further examples of Vivian's senility. It was cruel gossip at best; callous betrayal at worst. When Lupon finally met Vivian he'd expect to find her in a straitjacket. She stared at Marsden, willing him to intervene, but he stood at the doorway, looking out at the bay, oblivious. "I think I'll go in and change," she said when she could stand it no longer. She stubbed out the cigarette.

"Hey, don't run off and leave us. Stay and have at least one drink," Lupon urged. Sensing that he too was uncomfortable, she said she'd have a half glass of punch and sat down next to him on the sofa. She stared down at her feet, wondering if Hilary was going to chide her for tracking in sand.

Thelda appeared with the ice bucket.

"Thank you very much, Thelda. And in the future, you will try to remember what?"

"Ice bucket to be full all times," Thelda mumbled.

"Yes," Hilary continued, articulating each syllable, "the ice bucket is to be full at all times."

"But, miss," Thelda began, "power out for long time today so . . ."

Hilary cut her off. "Not now, Thelda." With a roll of her eyes she directed her back to the kitchen. "Marsden, darling, will you do the honors?"

As Marsden poured the drinks he said, "Hilary's been an invaluable help in getting things shipshape. Once we've finished the restoration on the great house, she'll be able to provide all the finishing touches."

Ceci raised her eyebrows, begging further information.

"You did hear that we're turning the great house into a convention center, didn't you, Ceci?"

"I may have heard something to that effect, but . . ."

"We'll have to take you on the grand tour sometime."

"Yeah," Lupon said, "It's really going to be great."

"If it ever gets done." Hilary sighed.

"Hilary's used to a standard of efficiency we don't have on the island," Marsden said. "She knows a great deal about hotel management. You've probably heard of her father, Harold Berwith."

"Sure," Lupon nodded. "Everyone knows the Berwith chain."

"Yes, Daddy's an innkeeper." Hilary smiled.

Of course, Ceci thought, it would be "Daddy," and "innkeeper" was a coy way of putting it. In reality, the Berwith chain of Family Inns was a blight on the face of America. They stretched from coast to coast, hideous, overpriced, prefab buildings that managed to be both garish and sterile.

Once, when her car had broken down, she'd been forced to
stay in one. Harold Berwith's photo hung in the lobby, alongside the American flag, a Pledge of Service, and a clutter of
plastic ivy. The desk clerk had given her an earful: no liquor
was served in the motel restaurant because of Mr. Berwith's
fundamentalist beliefs, but Daddy Berwith's Christian spirit
didn't extend to his employees. Most of them were illegal
aliens, and management had a habit of calling the immigration authorities if anyone asked for a raise.

"And to think," Hilary laughed after taking a sip of her
gin, "that Granddaddy Berwith started out with a root beer
stand in Missouri! It was back in the early thirties when he
first . . ."

Ceci looked down at her toes. They were in for the Success
Story. It was sad to think that after knowing her future sister-
in-law for less than twenty minutes, there would be no surprises. But some people really were like pieces of stage scenery: the facade was all. She knew Hilary's type: transatlantic
social climber. Hilary would be American enough to spin the
tale of the Berwiths' realization of the American Dream, but
distinctly undemocratic in every other way, panting after
every foible of class and caste. Hilary must've thought she'd
hit the jackpot with the Nettleton plantation. Ceci liked her
not at all; and as Hilary concluded her story and threw her
a veiled, speculative glance, she knew the feeling was mutual.
Ceci tossed off the rest of her punch. "If you'll excuse me,"
she said, getting to her feet. "I must go and change."

"We're very informal here," Hilary informed her. "We
don't dress for dinner. But do be ready in an hour. We're
trying to teach the staff to be punctual."

"And we don't want you to miss the sunset," Marsden
added graciously, then, turning to Al Lupon, "Want to bring
your drink and wander out to the garage with me? We have
a vintage Rolls from the twenties and I know how much you
like anything mechanical."

"Sure thing. Love to see it," Lupon agreed. "See you later,
Ceci. And you too, Hilary."

"Surely. See you in a bit."

"What fun to have another woman around." Hilary turned to her. "I haven't had anyone I could really talk to."

"About . . . ?" Ceci inquired.

"Shopping. Managing the house. Men. You know. Girl talk."

"Perhaps after dinner . . . see you soon."

Ceci started up the passageway, passed Archie's door, thought of knocking but decided against it. Back in her own room she leaned against the door. She'd been in such a rush to get into her bathing suit and get out of the house that she hadn't really taken in the changes in her old room. Her single bed had been replaced with a four-poster, her rolltop desk was gone and iron grillwork had been added to the windows, increasing her feeling that she was being held captive in a rather elegant cell. She stripped off her suit, did a few situps, and went into the bathroom and sat on the toilet, staring at the verdigris stains around the tub drain, turning on the water and letting it run over her hand. She could hear footsteps above her. Hilary in what had been the closed-off master bedroom? Probably so. Did Marsden share it with her? Probably not. Did he steal across the landing after hours from what had been Grandfather Nettleton's bedroom to increase his carnal knowledge of his fiancée? Hard to tell. Nowdays some people thought of sex as an obligation, like regular exercise, good for your health. Yet she couldn't imagine Hilary and Marsden touching, at least not in any emotional way. They both displayed such an aridity of spirit that she couldn't think of any unifying act, unless they went over bank statements together or burned votive candles in front of a photo of Leona Helmsley.

She lowered herself into the tepid water and heard the fearful barking of dogs. Not just a few dogs, but what sounded like an entire pack bringing their quarry to ground, waiting for the hunters. But of course. Everyone who had property had guard dogs these days. Even rich city dwellers had Dobermans or Akitas. Still, the insistent barking made her shudder.

Her bags had been unpacked, her clothes pressed and hung in the big old wardrobe. She stood before it, wondering what she should wear. The peach linen? Too formal. Besides, Archie had already seen her in it. The black strapless sundress? A bit Barefoot Contessa, but yes. She loved the way it slithered over her hips and swung around her calves. She brushed her hair slowly and let it hang loose. She made up her eyes, put some creme on her lips, and brushed her hair again, determined to forstall a reunion dinner that promised to be even more strained than she'd anticipated.

Finally, leaving her room, she found everyone, save Aunt Vivie, assembled on the veranda. Marsden and Hilary sat in twin fan-backed chairs. Marsden, wearing a flowered short-sleeved shirt and white pants, held a puppy on his lap. Hilary was wrapped in a purple sarong, a spray of flowers tucked behind each ear. As Ceci paused on the threshold and spotted Thelda, stationed near the drinks' cart, dressed in a long-sleeved maid's outfit complete with cap, cuffs, and collar, she couldn't help but smile at the contrast: the master and would-be mistress "gone native," the native girl decked out to serve high tea in the London embassy.

Lupon noticed her and rose from his chair, the solid mass of his jaw lifting in a welcoming smile. "Miss Baron."

"Here you are, my dear," Archie said, looking pleased to see her. "We were afraid you'd deserted us."

"Sorry if I've kept you waiting."

"We don't mind," Hilary drawled. "It's just that you've almost missed a glorious sunset."

It was indeed glorious. Ribbons of coral, crimson, and gold streaked the darkening waters, silhouetting the trees.

"But the sunsets here are always great, aren't they?" Lupon asked. "If she missed today's, she'll catch tomorrow's."

The puppy made whimpering sounds as Marsden pulled on its ears and nuzzled it into his belly. "I do wish Vivian would hurry. We've managed to lure this new chef away from the best private hotel in Ocho Rios, but we won't be able to evaluate his performance if we linger much longer. I told him to have dinner prepared for eight."

"Hey, he's on island time," Lupon laughed. "I'm on island time myself. Just as well I have a self-winding watch."

conversation turned, predictably, to food. As Icilda bent close to fill Ceci's wineglass, Ceci noticed that the old woman's eyes were swollen. She wanted to ask what was wrong, but knew that any recognition would embarrass them both. When serving a meal, the servants were supposed to be as invisible as the prop man in a Chinese play, and since Icilda was already nervous about her performance, the only acknowledgment that Ceci could give was to add "Icilda" when she said thank you.

The lobster bisque was brought in, followed by the fish with cream sauce. Ceci guessed that endive salad and crème brûlée would follow. In one of her more domestic phases, she'd cooked the entire menu after seeing it on Julia Child's TV show. And here it was again: French food, demonstrated on American TV, served on the north coast of Jamaica. But she'd seen Jakarta cab drivers sporting Harvard T-shirts, Parisian matrons in "Bloomies" underdrawers, and El Grande Mac con Queso at the Managua McDonald's. Small world. A world dominated by American fads and fashions. She put her fork on her plate. Marsden sat back, watching Al Lupon watch her. She could see that at least for the moment Marsden was pleased with her presence, a good-looking woman being as essential to a dinner party as the correct wine. Hilary was leaning into Archie, hanging on his every word, and Archie, who had a reflexive response to any sort of female attention, was allowing himself to be wooed. Vivian said almost nothing, patting her napkin to her lips and bobbing her head in response to Lupon's pleasantries, but Archie more than compensated for her reserve. The third glass of wine had loosed his tongue and even in the candlelight his face looked florid. "Here's to a grand reunion," he toasted.

Lupon was the only one to respond, lifting his glass and smiling all around. "It was kind of you to include me. Guess it's been ages since you've all seen each other. Did you and Marsden know each other as children, Ceci?"

"Briefly. When he came on vacations."

"So you're from Archie's second marriage, is that right?"

"Oh, no," Archie said. "I didn't have any children from my second marriage."

"And when you really start to think like a Jamaican, you'll forget to put it on," Archie warned.

Ceci lingered in the doorway. "Shall I go and see how Aunt Vivian's coming?"

"No need," Hilary said. "Icilda will shepherd her out. What will you have to drink?"

"Just some tonic water with a twist."

"On the wagon, are you?" Hilary asked.

"I think I had my quota this afternoon."

Archie handed his glass to Thelda. "I might just allow myself a fresh-up. Family reunion and all." The way Marsden was handling the puppy made him uncomfortable. He hated to see animals treated with anything but kindness. "And now, Mr. Lupon, you were about to tell me what you do in . . . Miami, is it?"

"I'd much rather hear from Miss Baron."

"Ceci."

"From Ceci. I understand she's the world traveler." His eyes played over her shoulders, then met hers with a can't-help-but-admire-you smile. "I understand you've been living in London. I went there for the first time last year."

"Did you enjoy yourself? London must've seemed very peaceful after Miami." She took her place in the circle, looking out at the silvery statue of the nereid, listening to the plaintive "ah-ha-ha" of a bird. She knew she could operate within these tame conversational norms without even thinking, but it turned out she didn't even have to speak because Hilary, not to be outdone, launched into her travel experiences, most of which had to do with the lack of goods and services outside New York. She then discussed her plans for the upcoming wedding in exhaustive detail. Lupon, hoping to reengage Ceci, went back to his London trip, which gave rise to Archie's reminiscences of shooting a film on location, which led Marsden into a description of the performance of a Thai dancing girl.

Ceci began to pay attention, recalling Marsden's pride when he'd gotten his officer's commission and his plans for a military career. As far as she knew—Vivian's letters had been

vague at best—he'd been stationed with an intelligence unit
in Laos. Someplace called the Eagle's Nest. The Eagle's Nest.
It sounded like something out of an adventure comic. He
must've been in Vietnam for the last of it. A series of photos
from the war flashed in her mind: the immolated Buddhist
monk; the little naked girl running down the road, flesh
seared with napalm; Kent State; and the picture that had
remained most vivid in her mind because it had shamed her
most of all—Americans wrenching the hands of their Vietnam functionaries from the doors of a departing helicopter
after the fall of Saigon. Had Marsden witnessed any of that?
Was that why he'd chosen to retreat here, to the estate, to live
out his days in neocolonial grandeur?

"How long were you there?" she asked, when he'd paused
for a breath. "In Vietnam, I mean."

"We were all there too long. Or not long enough, depending on your point of view. Refill, anyone?" There was a brief,
embarrassed pause broken only by the zap of the insect-killing machine behind Marsden's chair. "You were asking me
earlier about the history of the plantation, Al," he continued.
"The earliest record we had—though I believe my grandmother gave it to some historical society in England—was a
ledger kept by one of the overseers. That was back in . . ."

Ceci gazed out at the water, while Marsden went into a
detailed monologue. It appeared he knew even more about the
Nettleton history than Vivian did. He had brought them up
to the mid-nineteenth century when Lupon, polite but res-
tive, interrupted. "You're going to have to go slow with me,
Marsden. Until a couple of years ago, the most I knew about
Jamaica was from seeing pirate movies as a kid. You say the
plantation economy went bust here before our Civil War?"

"Yes. Slavery was abolished here in 1838. By decree and
without bloodshed."

"Not entirely without bloodshed," Ceci put in. "The slaves
were emancipated but they didn't have any land, so that led
to a lot of problems. About thirty years after the abolition
there was a very bloody uprising at Morant Bay. It became
a cause célèbre with the Victorian intellectuals. The progres-
sives—Darwin, Huxley, Mill—lined up against the British

governor's suppression of the revolt, and the romantic au-
thoritarians—Ruskin, Carlyle and Tennyson, I believe—took
the opposing view. Then . . ."

"Abolition caused the collapse of the economy," Marsden
overrode her. "The country was thrown into chaos and depression. Great-grandfather Nettleton went back to England
and left the entire place in the hands of the overseers. At one
point he considered abandoning it completely. But then he
rallied round and came back to . . ."

". . . to buy up the property of his less fortunate neighbors,"
Ceci said. "And . . ."

"The real reason he came back . . ." They all turned at the
sound of Vivian's voice, ". . . was because he had a sweetheart
who had a magic hold over him. He built her a house up in
the hills. I've never seen it but I hear it still stands."

Al and Archie rose simultaneously.

"Ah, you're here, Vivie!" Archie said. "Mr. Lupon, may I
introduce my sister, Mrs. Pinto."

Marsden held the puppy at arm's length. "You may take the
dog back to the kennels, Thelda. If Aunt Vivian's ready, I
think we'd best go into dinner."

"Yes, we really must," Hilary echoed.

"Sorry to have kept you waiting. I'm afraid I lost track of
time."

"Hey, no problem," Lupon laughed. "It's easy to do that
down here. We were talking about it earlier."

Ceci touched Vivian's arm. "It doesn't matter, Auntie. We
were just passing the time. Marsden was telling us about
being in the Far East, where he apparently picked up the
custom of ancestor worship."

Marsden stood up. " 'To forget one's ancestors is to be a
brook without a stream, a tree without a root.' "

A man without income property, Ceci added to herself.

The table was set with the good plate, candles, and flowers.
Hilary pointed out where they were to sit and took her place
with such a proprietary air that Ceci thought, I know why
Aunt Vivie goes around touching the furniture: she's afraid
Hilary might move it out from under her. The appetizer of
haricots blancs en salade was generally applauded and the

"You weren't married long enough, were you?" Vivian said. "I didn't even meet that one. She was a cabaret dancer, wasn't she? What was her name?"

"More wine, Al?" Hilary asked quickly.

"Kay. Her name was Kay." Archie's eyes narrowed. He had only the most sketchy memories of her—her tap shoes with the big satin bows, the nasal way she said "Limey," her annoying habit of muddling her cosmetics with his shaving things. He had never quite recovered from the discovery that she was a bottle blond. It had given him a feeling of having been tricked that had stayed with him through the entire six months of the marriage. "Phoebe first; then Kay."

Lupon turned to Marsden. "So your mother's name was Phoebe. That's a pretty name."

"No. My mother was Alicia Winterspan, of the Virginia Winterspans. Her granddaddy had been the governor general of the state."

"And she never let me forget it." Archie winked.

"More wine, Al?" Hilary asked again.

Ceci's lip twitched. It was sad to see such social desperation coupled with so little imagination.

"Mother was . . ." Marsden began.

"A natural blond," Archie said, musing. "She wore blood-red lipstick and Mainbocher suits." Alicia had been the love of his life, if grand passions were to be measured by lust, anxiety, and irregular eating habits. She had not been an easy mark. She wasn't one to give herself in a seedy bed-sitter as Phoebe had done, or on a bathroom floor. He'd convinced himself that only with the vows of marriage and a suitably expensive home would Alicia's desires come to full flower, but to his misery he'd found that the most luxurious surroundings and the most costly gifts did nothing more than feed her discontents, not only with his gifts but with his person. When she'd finally filed for divorce after months of shrieking fights that had brought the cops to the house, her sense of entitlement (which had been a large part of her initial attraction) had proved costly indeed. "She was an extremely beautiful woman. Edith Head saw her poolside once and said her legs were as good as Marlene's."

"Yes," Marsden said. "Mother was beautiful right up until the time she died."

"So . . ." Lupon was still struggling for a sequence but thought better than to pursue the topic. "This is a great meal. Really great."

"Divorced, beheaded, died, divorced, beheaded, survived," Vivian said in a singsong. Though all eyes focused fiercely on their plates, she proceeded with an explanation. "That's how one remembers the wives of Henry the Eighth. Katherine of Aragon, divorced; Anne Boleyn, beheaded; Lady Jane Grey . . . was she next? He only beheaded the unfaithful ones. I suppose Angus would have, too, if it had been allowed. But Angus, I mean Archie, only got up to four."

"I really think we might . . ." Hilary tried again.

"Phoebe, Kay, Alicia," Vivian went on, "and what was your mother's name again, Ceci?"

"Mabs."

"Aunt Vivian," Hilary said through clenched teeth.

"But she wasn't an actress, was she?" Vivian persisted.

"No." Ceci said, tossing back her hair. "She was a secretary at MGM." She smiled. "From an old Brooklyn family."

Lupon returned her smile and buttered another croissant. He ate with such relish that she found it a pleasure to watch him. He had quick reflexes, vigorous appetites, few pretentions, and, she guessed, a violent temper. He was a man of strong, though limited integrity; the sort who would honor his father and mother, treasure a faithful wife, reward his friends, and punish his enemies. She could imagine him screwing a competitor on a business deal and then donating the profit to his local orphanage.

Hilary tasted a spoonful of the crème brûlée, told Icilda to convey her approval to the chef, and pushed back her plate. Marsden leaned forward, lit a small cigar and blew the smoke out through his nostrils. His left hand touched the lemon leaf floating in the finger bowl with almost womanish tenderness while his eyes flitted over Ceci's hair and shoulders.

Ceci looked into the bowl of orchids. Just as that afternoon when she'd noticed his inability to look her in the eye, she felt sorry for him. But there was a danger in that attitude. Marsden would hate anyone he suspected of pitying him almost as much as he would hate anyone who made him appear ridiculous.

Ringing the little silver bell, Hilary told Icilda that they would take their coffee on the veranda. They were about to get up when Vivian, apropos of nothing, said, "Do you remember the night Mother brought her fist down on the table and upset the cruet of mint sauce?" Though her question could only have been addressed to Archie, she looked around the table. "Yes," she continued. "Father had just told her to shut up. I remember he actually said those words. 'Shut up,' he said. Can you imagine Father telling anyone to shut up? He was such a mild man, very much given to his own counsel, especially when he came back from the war. He mostly avoided us. I won't say he drank too much, though he did start before anyone else and usually kept on after others had thrown in the towel. 'Shut up,' he said. 'You know nothing about the business of managing an estate.' Of course he was wrong, not just because he expressed himself in such a vulgar fashion, but because Mother really did know a lot about the estate. I can remember her sitting at her escritoire doing accounts; she even wore one of those little rubber protectors on her finger so as not to stain it with ink, so Father was quite wrong. In fact, I hold the belief that the estate was the only thing Mother did care about. Certainly she cared about it more than she cared about people. Though she was good with animals—not domestic animals; I know for a fact she had my kitty drowned—but she liked large animals, horses particularly. And she brought her fist down on the table and upset the cruet. Surely you remember."

A pause so painful that it stretched time descended on the table. Lupon, whose bottom had risen a few inches from his chair, sat back down and smiled as though waiting for the conclusion of a funny story. Archie took a gulp of his wine. Marsden watched the tip of his cigar.

"So Grandmother was given to knocking the cruets about," Ceci said with a laugh. "I don't think I ever heard that story before. But you know, I was reading somewhere that if families argue they usually argue at mealtimes. I forget where I read . . ." If she was going to come to Vivian's rescue she'd best have more ammunition than a make-believe article.

"But that's what I'm telling you, that's why I remember the incident, because our family—we were very restrained, weren't we, Angus? There was never any . . ." she swallowed ". . . any passion about anything. Except the plantation. If one of us did anything wrong we were sent to Coventry." Lupon inclined his head, begging an explanation. "To Coventry, Mr. Lupon. You're probably not familiar with that expression. It means a wall of silence. You're not spoken to. You're absolutely ignored, as though you were made out of air. As though you didn't exist at all. Mother was very good at sending people to Coventry. She did it as policy. Father sent people to Coventry, too, but not on purpose. He just didn't have anything to say to any of us. Angus used to try to send me to Coventry, too, but it went entirely against his nature because, as you can tell, he loves to hear himself talk. So when Father said shut up, when he became *passionate* . . ."

"Not like my clan," Lupon rushed in. "We can get passionate about the weather report."

"Perhaps that's the difficulty. . . ." Vivian frowned as though reasoning out a problem. "Here in the tropics the weather doesn't change. Germination and fruition are constantly intertwined. I sometimes think that even our planting is an imposition on the natural rhythm of the land. We plant and harvest. After that it's *tempo moto,* or slow time. But in the hills germination is constant. That's why we have so much laziness and that's why there are squatters. From the very first, slaves escaped into the hills. You've probably heard of the Maroons?" Lupon shook his head. Archie, Ceci, and Marsden were absolutely still, aching for the moment when intervention might be possible. "The Maroons were runaway slaves who went to the hills, oh, hundreds of years ago," Vivian rushed on. "You can live off the land in the hills, though the diet of breadfruit and akee and coconuts . . . When I was a little girl, I remember seeing some black children with red hair and I thought it strange until it was explained that

that is what happens because of malnutrition. I expect that you're right, about the seasonal changes being a cue for passion. . . ."

Marsden stubbed out his cigar. "Before you run off into the hills, Vivian, will you take tea or coffee?"

"Coffee, if you please. And that's another thing. The last time I was in a restaurant I was served instant coffee from the States. The idea! Here we have the Blue Mountains, which, as you probably know, produce the best coffee in all the world, but people are so enamored of anything American that they actually buy instant coffee."

"I promise our coffee won't be instant," Hilary cut in. "But I'm not sure if you should have any, Aunt Vivian. You know how you have trouble sleeping."

"I don't mind that because it gives me more time to read. I took to reading as a very young girl. Oh, the eagerness with which I used to wait for the ships to come so that I might see what they were reading in England! But I was always months behind the times. It was the same disappointment when I finally got to England, but in another way. We went just before Angus married his first wife, Flossie—no, Phoebe, Phoebe was her name—and I was so looking forward to it. Mother had spent a great deal of money on my wardrobe but I was hopelessly out of fashion. I had to dogsbody for all our English cousins just to get an invitation to any of the coming-out parties."

"If you do want some coffee, Aunt Vivian, I suggest you take it on the veranda," Marsden interrupted her again, "It's much cooler out there and Father and I have some important things to discuss."

"What things?" Vivian asked.

"Just some catching up on business matters. I promise we won't become too 'passionate.'"

Vivian clasped her hands together and brought them up to her mouth. She had done it again. It had taken her the entire meal to think of something to say, but, judging from everyone's expressions, she'd committed some horrible indiscretion. What had she done? Only talked about her parents, and her trip to England and the weather in the tropics. Yet some-how she'd botched it. She'd be sent to Coventry again.

"Please, let's not spoil the evening with any talk of busi-ness." Ceci smiled round the table. Archie was mopping a dab of syrup from the front of his shirt, a sure sign that he'd gone past his drinking limit. "Perhaps you and I could take a turn round the garden, Archie."

"We won't be long," Marsden insisted.

"I'd like to talk to Marsden," Archie agreed. "It's been ages since we've had a man-to-man. That is, if you don't mind, Mr. Lupon."

"Hey, not me. I'd rather sit and talk to the ladies. Shall we?" He got up and moved to Vivian's chair.

"There's no point in discussing something tonight if you won't remember it tomorrow, Archie." Ceci tried to fix Ar-chie's attention with a level gaze.

Archie held up his wineglass. "If you are implying that I am in any way impaired by having ingested this excellent wine, then I shall have to inform you otherwise; and to bor-row the words of a great playwright: 'Let a man drink ten barrels of rum a day, he is not a drunken skipper until he is a drifting skipper. Whilst he can lay his course and stand on his bridge and steer it, he is no drunkard. It is the man who lies drinking in his bunk and trusts to Providence that I call a drunken skipper, though he drank nothing but the water of the River Jordan.' "

"What's that from?" Lupon wanted to know.

" 'The captain,' " Archie continued, his voice full of convic-tion, " 'is in his bunk, drinking bottled ditch-water; and the crew is gambling in the forecastle. She will strike and sink and split. Do you think the laws of God will be suspended in favor of England because you were born there?' "

Ceci put her head into her hand. If Archie was perform-ing he was in even worse shape than she'd supposed. "Ar-chie . . ."

"Hey, that was great," Lupon said. "What's that from?"

"I've changed my mind," Vivian said quietly. "I shan't be wanting any coffee. I shall leave the young people alone.

Hilary, I'm sure, will see to everything. Perhaps you could show Mr. Lupon the garden, Cecily."

"This is too ridiculous." Ceci thought she might explode. "Why don't we all go out on the veranda . . ."

"No. Show me the garden, will you? I'd really like to see it."

Icilda stood, holding the tray with the coffeepot and cups. Vivian rose with dignity. "Please put the tray on the table, Icilda. It's far too heavy for you. And you may take my cup off. I'm going to bed to read."

Hilary gave a satisfied sniff, her nostrils two little holes in her white face. "That's an excellent idea, Aunt Vivian. And I'm afraid I shall have to say good-night myself, Al. I'm leaving tomorrow morning for a few days' shopping in New York."

Vivian raised her arms and fluttered her fingers. "Everyone flying about. I feel as though I live in an aviary."

"I'm off tomorrow morning, too," Lupon said. "Business trip to the Cayman Islands."

"That's where they have all those new condominiums, isn't it?" Vivian asked.

"Yeah," Lupon assented. "There's quite a bit of development there."

"Lady Pembroke's been telling me about it," Vivian said sweetly. "In the Caymans now they build condominiums and have shady banking and wash money."

Lupon laughed. "I wouldn't exactly say . . ."

"Ah, yes. I got it wrong. It's *launder* money. And tax *shelters*," Vivian cocked her head, "though shelters are by their nature shady, aren't they?" She smiled at each of them in turn, but they had either failed to understand her little pun or else found it inappropriate. "You must come and visit us again, Mr. Lupon. I like to watch you eat. And perhaps next time I can offer you some of our local cuisine."

"I'd like that very much. I'd like to be invited back," Lupon said graciously, looking in Ceci's direction.

"Oh, you shouldn't expect to find Ceci here," Vivian sighed. "She's the most migratory bird of all."

Ceci bit her lip, moving to Vivian's side and kissing her on the cheek. "Good night, Aunt Vivie."

"Please don't chew your lip like that, Cecily. I've tried to break you of that habit ever since you were a child. And please don't be a slug-a-bed in the morning. Your toast and marmalade will be ready at seven. I'll see to *that* myself." She nodded in Hilary's direction. "And now, Mr. Lupon . . . adieu."

Before Vivian had reached the passageway, Hilary was already muttering her apologies, which Lupon brushed aside, saying he'd had a wonderful time. He moved to the threshold of the dining room, waiting for Ceci to walk out with him. She touched Archie's shoulder, said, "Please don't be too long," and nodded for Icilda to precede them.

"Well, what's it to be? A walk round the garden?" Lupon asked as soon as they'd reached the veranda.

"I don't know much about the garden. Would you mind if we just sit here and talk?" It was useless to insist on proximity since she couldn't possibly overhear the conversation in the dining room. She shifted her chair so that the awning shrouded her face.

"Your father's pretty damned good," Lupon said as he settled into his chair. "I'll bet if he weren't . . . well, I just meant he's . . ."

"It's all right. The liquor hits him in the legs first. He has to be far gone before it affects his tongue."

"Yeah, well, like I said, he's still pretty good. Soon as I saw him I thought I recognized him."

"You should have told him. He would have liked that."

"What was he quoting?"

"I think it's from a play called *Heartbreak House.*"

"A love story?"

"No. It's about a family—a group of people—who sit around and talk a great deal. In the last act, the first bombs of the First World War start to drop."

"Oh." The barking of the dogs flowed into the silence.

"You were very kind to my aunt. I appreciate that."

"Hey, families are crazy, know what I mean?"

"Mmmm. When I was about sixteen, I had this fierce craving for normality. I thought all families, save mine, must have it. I befriended a girl at school chiefly because she seemed to have a typical family, and I wangled an invitation to their home for the Christmas holidays. It was all so lovely. Roast turkey and vegetables, singing round the piano. Everyone with that healthy, open look. When I met my friend years later, she told me that her brother had run off to join the Moonies and her mother was a kleptomaniac who only escaped arrest because of her father's connections with the police. I suppose normal families are a myth best reserved for whole-grain cereal commercials and political campaigns."

Al shifted in his chair. "Those dogs can really get to you after a while, can't they?"

"Yes, they can."

"Ah . . . did you go to the theater much when you lived in London?"

"Not really." She could hear Archie's voice and paused long enough to determine that he was declaiming again. "And now," she brought her face into the moonlight, cupped her chin, and batted her eyes. "Now let's talk about *you.*"

"Me? What do you want to know about me?"

She sighed. Few things made her as aware of her loneliness as someone not knowing when she'd made a joke. "Well, your business," she began, attending to the coffee cups. "Just what do you do?"

"Investments. Management. You know."

She didn't know and could see that it would be difficult to find out. She took a stab. "I think Marsden mentioned your interest in turning the old house into a convention center."

"We're talking."

"I don't see why it wouldn't work. Marsden seems confident enough."

"Yeah, well, investments in this part of the world are always risky. I'm cautious because my family lost a bundle in Havana when Castro took over. I was just a kid at the time, but I can remember my uncle coming back from Havana and telling my father 'Hey, all hell's gonna break loose, we'd better cut our losses now.' My father wouldn't listen to him. That's why I was laughing at your aunt's stories about fights at the dinner table. Reminded me of home. Nothin' wrong with it if it's kept in the family. Gets the juices flowing." He rolled his head around to take the tension out of his neck, stretched his hairy arms, and cracked his knuckles. "But Marsden seems to be pretty well connected. If he's convinced that the boys in Washington are gonna underwrite this government, I guess he knows what he's talking about. Long as Jamaica doesn't elect someone like that last guy."

"Yes, there's been a massive increase in aid since the last guy's administration."

"They really cut off his water, didn't they?"

"And Washington's decided to make Jamaica a sort of test case for free enterprise in the Caribbean. They're pumping in about a hundred and ten million in aid. They won't want to look ridiculous, so I suppose they'll keep propping it up."

He leaned forward. "You're very intelligent. I guessed that on the plane. I like intelligence in a woman."

"That's good. I like intelligence in a man." Gone were the days when men praised the beauty of your hair or the sweetness of your smile; nowadays when they wanted to get you into the sack, they always started by talking about your intellect. But Al Lupon wasn't the sort to use a feminist line in seduction. He probably did like intelligent women.

"How come you know so much about Jamaica?" he asked.

"General interest. And I used to live here. And at one time I thought I was going to be an international correspondent. Oriana Fallaci, you know." He didn't. "I read a lot."

"So why didn't you become a reporter?"

"Lazy, I guess. And I couldn't stay in one place long enough."

"You'd be good. Or one of those TV anchorwomen. You've got the class for that and they don't really have to study much."

She said nothing. The bird had set up its "ah-ha-ha" again and she felt like laughing along with it.

"Have you ever been married?" he asked suddenly. "Hey, I don't mean to be nosy, just, I figured, a woman like yourself, you must've had a lot of offers."

"Once. When I was very young."

"Me, I've never said 'I do.' Waiting for the right woman, I

guess. It's real important to get the right woman because I don't believe in divorce. Don't believe in breakin' any contract. A contract is sacred. You make one, you stick by it, know what I mean?"

"I do."

A thin, far-off voice began to sing in the servants' quarters. Ceci caught the line of the melody and hummed a few bars. Lupon shifted in his chair again, stifling a belch. "Sure is beautiful here, isn't it?"

"It is."

"I was reading somewhere that airline stewardesses make the best wives because they've already been around—I mean, they've traveled a lot, so when they settle they really settle."

She stared out at the cupola. In his clumsy way he'd picked up on the fact that she'd "been around" and was letting her know that he didn't mind. As he took a pack of cigarettes from his pocket and offered her one, he was deferential, relaxed. Their fingers touched as he cupped the match for her. She wondered what he'd be like as a lover. Intense but lacking finesse, she guessed.

"Thank you." She inhaled deeply. "I don't know about settling down. To me it sounds like some chemistry experiment where you watch the sediment form in the bottom of the beaker. When I was younger I wanted to travel and everyone said I'd outgrow it. Now they say I'll outgrow it when I'm middle-aged. All I can say is that I hope they have the senior citizens' discount on international flights by the time I reach that age."

"I have a couple of planes."

"Can you fly them yourself?"

"Yeah. I've had my license for years, but mostly I just take the Cessna back and forth to Vegas."

Click. "I'm letting the coffee get cold. Cream or sugar?"

"No, thanks."

Plunge in. "So if you do go in on the gambling casino here, you'll be able to fly down and check up on things."

"Sure enough. We've almost got the runway near the great house completed. We figure a lot of our guests will have private planes," he added quickly. "You should give me your address. That way, when I fly down, if you want to thumb a ride . . ."

"That's very nice of you, Al."

"Hey, what can I tell you?" he laughed as he accepted his cup. "I'm a very nice guy."

"Yes, Al. Yes, I expect you are." For a mafioso.

Seven

There was another half-hour of small talk before Ceci felt
Marsden's presence and turned to see him standing in the
doorway. Before her question could go from her eyes to
her mouth, he answered that he'd put Archie to bed.

"I hope you didn't give him any more to drink," Ceci said,
imagining the humiliation Archie would feel in the morning.

"Sister, where comes this sudden concern? The old man's
in fine condition."

"I know he looks healthy, but we shouldn't forget his age.
He's been traveling for two days and it's an emotional jolt for
him to come back here, so . . ."

"I can assure you that I cut short his rendition of *Lear* and
now he's sleeping it off. Al, would you like a liqueur?"

"Not for me. Much as I'm enjoying the company, I guess
I'd better be gettin' back to the hotel. I'm flying out early in
the morning." He got to his feet and moved to Ceci's chair.
"I hope to be seeing you again. How long did you say you're
planning to stay?"

"The initial plan was for them to stay for two weeks,"
Marsden cut in, "but I doubt if Ceci'll be able to stand it for
that long. Our quiet little island doesn't have much to show
the world traveler."

Ceci offered her hand. "I really can't say, Al. Perhaps I'll stay for the entire time, but then again Marsden's guess may be nearer the mark. It's been very interesting meeting you."

He shook her hand vigorously. "You wouldn't like to ride back to the hotel with us, would you?"

"Thanks, but no. I'm pretty well done in myself."

"I'm going to drive you back, Al. There are still a few things I'd like to iron out with you," Marsden said.

Al turned back to wave as they descended the steps. She raised her hand and smiled, then slumped back in the chair. As the car motor started up the dogs began to bark. There was a single blast of the horn as Marsden summoned one of the servants to open and close the gates and then, except for the whisper of the surf and the call of the bird, all was quiet. She picked up the tray and went inside.

The dining room had already been restored to order. The kitchen was dark. She left the tray on the sink and tiptoed into the passageway, stopping in her own room only long enough to get the smaller package from Harrod's, a pack of cigarettes, and a sweater. Retracing her steps, she left the veranda and moved away from the house, walking on the grass so as to avoid the crunch of the gravel.

Her feet were already wet with dew as she passed the big tree. Three of the five doors in the row of cabins were closed. The dim light from the others silhouetted two figures sitting on the wooden steps. As she drew closer she could see Icilda and the young girl Thelda. They were still wearing their uniforms but had shed aprons, cuffs, and collars and even their shoes and stockings. Thelda was smoking a cigarette.

Icilda got to her feet. "Miss Ceci, why you don't go to bed? You tired."

"You're the one who should be in bed. You must be exhausted."

"I wait and close the gate for Mr. Marsden. Don't sleep till everyone down."

Ceci nodded. Paul Strangman had reformed the Masters and Servants Law and limited the workday, but it seemed that servants of Icilda's generation still clung to the practice of staying up until the master returned home. She looked past Icilda's grizzled head into her room. A low-watt bulb dangled from the ceiling, barely illuminating the picture of the Good Shepherd and the tuftless candlewick spread (once Vivian's) that covered the single bed. Of Thelda's room she could see nothing but a section of wall pasted with magazine photos of rock stars and advertisements for clothes and cars.

"Don't be standing, miss. I get a chair."

"Please don't bother. I can sit on the steps with you."

"Get your pretty dress dutty," Icilda muttered, going into her room and coming back with an old garden chair. Ceci handed her the package from Harrod's and sat down. Icilda took the gift in both hands, shook it close to her ear, clasped it to her chest, and, with a sidelong glance at Thelda, put it on the step unopened. "I thank you for remembering me, miss."

"Now," Ceci said, settling into the chair and taking out a cigarette, "tell me how you've been." Thelda pushed the saucer that was serving as an ashtray along the steps. Ceci offered her a cigarette, and with a nod of her head she took it. As Ceci bent forward to drop the match into the saucer, she saw Icilda's look of disapproval. Ceci repeated her request to hear from Icilda but when it was again ignored, she asked, "And where's Percy? Gone to bed already?"

"No, miss. He gone to the great house. Keep his eye on all going round. Building things there. Thieves come carry them away. Trouble bad in the parish. Rude boys, thieves—these young peoples like the monkey: higher he climb, more he expose 'imself. Just we ladies here. No mens around." Icilda dropped her head but not far enough to hide the sullen look that had come over her face.

"What about the new cook? Doesn't he stay on the property?"

"He's the *chef*," Icilda explained none too happily. "Got him own house in the village. He don't have to guard."

"I see. But you haven't told me anything about your family. How are your children and your grandchildren?" She couldn't remember most of them by name.

Icilda leaned forward and crossed her hands on her bony knees. "Not every day is Christmas, miss. Evelyn she gone to St. Thomas, work for the Chinaman in his shop. She mind

Almyra's babies when Almyra run off to Kingston and don't be back. An' Esmerelda's boy got no work, but got him three childrens by three womens and turn away from everything I teach him. Lloyd cutting the cane. Go one place to other, follow the crop. He got no woman by him—"

"Just some factory ranger," Thelda put in, joking about the semi-prostitutes who followed the harvest.

"Elizabeth marry a carpenter in Mandeville. Good man. Workin' man. They got a television and three babies. I know she get two more. She come to me to deliver the first and I see by the knots she have five, but she don't believe me."

Ceci nodded. It was believed that twists in he firstborn's umbilical chord showed the number of children a woman would bear. She drew on her cigarette to stop from smiling. Most of her early information about sex had come from Icilda and, superstitions aside, it had been remarkably accurate. She could remember the furor when one of Icilda's granddaughters had turned up pregnant. Promiscuity and illegitimacy were the rule rather than the exception, yet a girl's first pregnancy was often greeted with horrified surprise, the girl's mother sometimes turning her out so that she had to seek help from other female relatives. It seemed that that initial fall from grace was punished but subsequent pregnancies were shrugged off as "just nature." "Tell me about Jesmina," she asked, vividly recalling her friend's fall from grace. "Where is she now? What's she doing?"

Icilda pressed her lips together. "You remember Almyra?" she asked, ignoring the question. "Don't know where Almyra is now. All young peoples run and run. Kingston, New York, Tomanto . . ."

"*Toro*nto," Thelda corrected.

"All young peoples run," Icilda went on, ignoring the correction. "Try to find job; only find trouble. Stay where you born, I say. Remember James? James, he go . . ."

Ceci felt Thelda's eyes on her, but as soon as she looked in her direction Thelda turned away. The girl's face was sturdy, placid, seemingly unthinking—she had doubtless heard Icilda's stories before and was not remotely interested in them—yet the deliberate way she pulled on her cigarette and stared into the darkness showed that she was not altogether mentally absent. And Icilda kept on. As though recounting the master script of a long-running soap opera, she told of loves and betrayals, feuds and reconciliations, pregnancies and deaths. Finally, she broke off and leaned forward, scanning Ceci's face. "You don't look good, Miss Ceci."

"Just the dinner, I think. I haven't digested it properly."

"Too much saucy food make you sick," Icilda said firmly. There was a slight fluttering of her eyelids, then, as though she'd heard a noise, she became very still. She got up, shambled to the end of the cabins, and disappeared. Some minutes later, as Ceci sat speechless and Thelda continued to regard her with unabashed curiosity, Icilda reappeared and offered Ceci a branch of bright orange pods. "Cerrassee. Remember it? It purify your blood and free your bowels." Ceci took a pod and popped it open, taking the bright scarlet seeds into her mouth. "Remember, Miss Ceci, I give you calaloo when you a child? That what make your skin so pretty. Now I make you some tea." She turned to Thelda and said, "Time to go to bed," with the sharpness of a prison matron.

"What about the gate?" Thelda asked.

"I close the gate when Mr. Marsden come. You go to bed."

Thelda stubbed out her cigarette, stifled a yawn, nodded good-night to Ceci and closed the door to her cabin.

"Come. Come now, miss," Icilda insisted, smiling for the first time. Ceci picked up the chair and followed her into her room. It was so small that it made her feel clumsy. "Now give me that chair, miss," Icilda ordered. Ceci backed up next to a card table covered with a hot plate and jars of herbs while the old woman pushed the chair beneath the dangling light socket and crawled up onto it. "Now hand me cord to hot plate, if you please. And set the kettle on. It filled with water for me good-night tea." Ceci focused on Icilda's splayed feet as she plugged the cord into the socket, climbed down, and pushed the chair toward her. "You sit in chair. I sit on me bed," she continued ceremoniously. She picked up her gift, unwrapped it, carefully smoothing the wrapping paper and putting it to her side, then lifted the filigreed picture frame from the box. "So beautiful. So beautiful, miss. Now you

must give me your picture so I can kiss you when you gone."
Her shoulders quivered and she dropped her head.

"Icilda, whatever's the matter? I noticed at dinner that
you'd been crying. Are you sad because Percy doesn't stay
down here with you?"

"Percy up there, guarding the place, anything can happen.
It too dangerous." She looked up, her eyes full to the brim.
"And me husband. Going to sleep with me tonight but Mr.
Marsden say I can't have him. Only peoples who work here
can sleep here. But when Percy don't come, I don't sleep.
Worry all the time."

Ceci glanced at the narrow bed, wondering how much
sleep would be possible if two bodies were crammed into it.
"But you're quite safe, Icilda. We're all just across the way."

"Bad things happen all round. Bad people. And me husband, I see one day only. I used to having him by me side. We
not like teenagers, miss. We don't have a party. Just we sleep
together. He get himself in trouble if he don't sleep with me.
Find some other woman. Used to be he come to me but now
not allowed."

"I see." Did Icilda really believe that her old boy would be
out carousing? And what harm could there be in letting the
old people sleep together? "I'm sorry." She was on the verge
of promising to speak to Marsden but decided against raising
Icilda's hopes.

A radio was turned on in Thelda's room and a rocking beat
pounded through the walls and reverberated up through the
floorboards.

"So many changes since you be gone," Icilda went on.
"Everyday a fuss in the yard. That one," she jerked her head
in the direction of the wall, "she be the age of me great-
grandchild but she look 'pon me like d' washer woman look
'pon dutty clothes on Monday mornin'. She got herself set for
Percy, but she no good. She take herself to the clinic an' get
a shot so she play wit d' boys but don't have no baby. I tell
you, she no good. When she work she slow as a parson goin'
to hell, but Mr. Marsden don't trouble her. What her eye see
her mouth tell. Now," she leaned forward whispering, "she
play the music but her ear be to the wall all the same."

"Do you mind if I smoke in here?" It wasn't just the size of the room that was making her feel claustrophobic. She could feel herself being drawn back into the narrow world of rivalries, backbiting and intrigue.

"You do whatever you like, miss."

"Tell me how Aunt Vivian has been."

"Miss Pinto be old, that's all. I pray to the Lord for her every morning and night. I give her bush tea to calm her when she restless. But she worry her mind over all dead things. I love her, miss, but them that have no child of his own be like the child himself." The kettle started to screech. She got up and shuffled to the card table, taking pinches of herbs from several jars and pouring the boiling water over them. "For pain-a-belly," she smiled, handing the cup to Ceci. "Wait for it seeps."

Ceci took the cup, watched the moths circling the bulb, waved a mosquito away from her face.

"Miss Pinto be excited that Mr. Angus come, that why she strange this morning. And to see you. She think you make all right."

"I don't quite understand." Ceci paused, then asked, "What is it I'm supposed to make right?"

Icilda turned her eyes to the floor. "You ever think to live here again, miss?"

Ceci shook her head. "I can't say as I do, Icilda."

This was greeted with a shrug and a slow passing of tongue over teeth. "So what Mrs. Pinto can do? She no can dash 'way she stick 'fore she dun cross river."

"Yes, I see what you mean. She does need someone to run things."

"Best to do somethin' 'fore new queen be set on throne," Icilda warned, still averting her eyes.

"Do you mean Miss Hilary?"

By way of reply, Icilda sucked her teeth.

"But I can't stop Mr. Marsden from getting married." Ceci took a sip of her tea and slapped at another mosquito.

Icilda looked up. "Your scent attract them, miss. They want you pretty skin. When you're in the sun tomorrow, I get the aloe plant."

Ceci laughed. "You with your plants! If you lived in California, you could make a fortune, Icilda, do you know that? Now tell me about Percy."

"Percy the best of me grandchildren. He like me own son. He darker than all the others but he have a true heart. He dream to have a taxi of his own and work at the airport. Work for himself. He can do it. At the school he learn to fix the cars and drive, too."

"You mean that agricultural school up the road on the Edisons' place? The one that's shut down now?" She couldn't help herself from adding, "The one Paul Strangman built?"

"He gone now." Icilda shut her lips tight.

"What's the matter? Didn't you like him?"

"Americans like the man we have now. Lots of fuss when Mr. Paul is there."

"Does that mean that you like the new man?"

"Mr. Paul, he be good, he love the peoples, but . . ."

"But?"

"He don't believe in the Lord."

"How do you know that?"

"He want to change everything. Our pastor say he want make everyone do like he want. Pastor say Mr. Paul don't believe in the Lord."

"I see." Useless to pursue that topic. "What did you think of Mr. Angus? Does he look well to you?"

"Very good. Handsome still," she grinned broadly. "Now the womens don't trouble him so, he be right. He always like the bad womens. Even when he little boy he like the bad womens like me mother."

Ceci finished her tea, put the cup back on the table, and got to her feet. "I'm feeling sleepy now."

"I put a leaf to help you sleep, miss. Bush-medicine good for you."

"Thank you, Icilda." Ceci took her hands. "Thank you so much."

Icilda brought Ceci's hands to her lips. "One thing," she whispered urgently, without looking up. "When me mother Mary was sent off, Mr. Angus' father give her a patch to farm. We have it all this time, but we got no paper. I think now we need the paper. Percy show it to you. Just a little patch of land. Before you go, you help me get the paper?"

"You mean you've been farming it all this time but you don't have a legal document to say it's yours?"

"For true, miss."

Ceci sighed. "I can't promise you anything, Icilda. But I will look into it."

"Thank you, miss. Thank you for remembering this old woman." Moving with her to the door, Icilda inclined her head toward Thelda's room and hissed, "Don't give that girl cigarettes, miss. Remember: Play with puppy, puppy lick yo' mouth." With this injunction against familiarity, the door was closed.

As Ceci reached the big tree she stopped, bending down to remove a pebble that had worked its way into her sandal. A single light was burning on the upper floor. She wondered if Hilary had been watching her. "And I don't give a damn if you are," she muttered to herself.

She leaned against the trunk, looking up, admiring the moonlight gloss of the branches. Icilda's "leaf" had calmed her. She felt as though she could sleep for days. She closed her eyes, listening to the gentle rhythm of the surf. As she opened them, she saw a man come from behind the cabins and glide to Icilda's door as smoothly as if he'd been on roller skates. She drew in her breath. The cabin door opened just wide enough to let the man slide in. Icilda's husband. Waiting in the bushes until the coast was clear. When Icilda had gone to pick the cerrassee she'd probably warned him to wait. Ceci smiled. For all of Icilda's confidences, she hadn't trusted her with that one. She imagined the old lovers nestled front-to-back in the narrow bed, like spoons in a drawer. After waiting a few minutes she crossed the lawn, remembering the nights she'd snuck into dormitories after lights out. Well, the more rules there were, the more ingenuity it took to get around them.

She had barely reached the veranda when the dogs started up and, standing stock still, she heard the motor of a car. Marsden coming back. Quickly and quietly she moved through the front room, past the silvery stares of Sir Isaac and

Lady Maude, into the passageway. She paused at Archie's door just long enough to hear his bassoonlike snores. Poor old bugger. Sleeping it off. Marsden had reeled him in as fast as a fish from a commercially stocked lake. Her sympathy was not without a tinge of contempt for Archie's gullibility; still, if she could find the makings of a Prairie Oyster tomorrow morning, she'd fix him one, sit on the beach with him while he baked out his hangover, and do everything in her power to get him to talk with her.

Eight

Percy turned down the wick of the lantern, set it next to his cot, and began to take off his boots. Pulling one uncovered foot and then the other up to his chest so as not to let them touch the dirt, he lay back, feeling his stomach muscles go hard and then relax. He took the yellow plastic lighter out of his shirt pocket, flipped it into the air, caught it, flipped it again, watching the shadows it made on the tent wall, then brought it close to his face to look at the little lion and the word LEO. Thelda had given him the lighter and told him she'd bought it. At first he hadn't wanted to accept it, thinking that Thelda would take it as a sign that he was sweet on her. But then Icilda had told him that it had been left behind by one of Mr. Marsden's guests and Thelda had merely appropriated it, and so he had taken it. Leo was his sign. It was meant to be his.

The wall of the tent began to shake as the dogs nosed the cardboard box holding the empty cans. "You not dogs, you pigs," he muttered, turning on his side. He knew he should have taken the cans to the stream and washed them to get rid of the food smell, but he'd been too tired. It was almost sunset when he'd driven up to what Mr. Marsden called the "biv-ouac"—this clearing at the end of the road with its U.S. Army tent and the sign that said PRIVATE PROPERTY. VICIOUS DOGS. YOU

HAVE BEEN WARNED. Though Marsden had told him that he must never leave the area unguarded, it was his habit to chain the dogs, feed them, and go off to work the half-acre on the edge of the cane fields that had been given to Icilda by old Mr. Nettleton, and which they had been farming for as long as memory even though they had no paper to say it was theirs. When he'd come back from the plot, it was already dark. He'd given the dogs another can of food, hoping to fill their bellies so they would let him sleep. It was more than their quota— Marsden stressed that they were not to be given enough to really satisfy them and always counted the cans—but that was all right because tomorrow night he would be driving the beautiful Rolls into Montego Bay and Willie, the relief boy, would be in the tent. Let Willie deal with the hungry dogs.

The wall quivered again. "Quiet, you dog. Quiet. You make me head duncy," he called softly, reaching into his pants for the little candy tin in which he kept his ganja. He liked the extra ten dollars a month Mr. Marsden paid him to sleep up here, but there were times like tonight when he longed for the comforts of his cabin: the electric light, the square of carpet on the wooden floor, the bed safe from ants and spiders, his stack of *Mechanic* magazines, and the photo of his mother.

But sometimes it was worse to be up here on the bivouac when he wasn't tired because then he remembered the nights when he'd waited in his cabin until all the lights in the house were out so that he could sneak down to the boats to meet Jesmina. Conjuring the smooth slope of Jesmina's shoulders, he felt a powerful longing mingled with sadness. He could no longer be sure that Jesmina was really his woman. Since she'd been dismissed from the job she'd met him at the boats a few times, but though her thighs still clutched him, she did not look him in the eye so often, and Jesmina was a great one for looking people in the eye. It had been that very habit of hers, that slow, slow gaze, that had offended Miss Hilary and caused Mr. Marsden to dismiss her, even though she did her work and didn't have Thelda's sticky fingers. He had wanted to say something when Marsden had told her to wipe what he called her "insolent look" off her face, wanted to say "Boss, that the face Jah give her. How she goin' to take a rag and wipe it off?" But of course he had said nothing. He had pretended to tinker with the car battery while Jesmina had shoved her things into her airline travel bag and walked off to the village.

It had been a great blow to his manhood to remain silent. When he'd explained that he'd wanted to knock Marsden down with a single blow of his fist but hadn't dared to speak up because he had to keep his job, Jesmina had nodded that she understood, but it had been a slow nod. And she had not met his eyes. He hadn't dared to try to comfort her with his future plans—plans to get enough money to marry her, build a house on the little plot of land—for fear that she would call him a bullshit artist, or, worse yet, give him that look that said she had heard too many promises from too many men. Men's promises were like the slapping of the waves.

He sucked the ganja deep into his lungs and stared at the open tent flap. The dogs had quieted, sniffing the sudden stillness in the air. A big storm was coming, though it was still far off. Not tonight, but day after tomorrow it would visit. He remembered Icilda's stories of Anancy the Spider. Anancy could fight anything, even hurricane happenings, but Anancy's greatest battle was against his own spirit. The most powerful thing a man could do was to conquer himself. Not the boss, or the duppies, but that within the self that warred against the self. Jesmina might think that he had the soul of a servant, but she was wrong. It was just that he understood what Icilda had taught him: "Back of dog is dog; in front of dog is Mister Dog." It was not enough to do your job, you had to look happy doing it because the bosses, especially the American bosses, wanted to believe that everyone was happy all the time. He had been given his Shoe Polish face, as naturally shy-sorrowful as Jesmina's was bold, but he could control his face, and it was better to do this than to hang out at the shops swilling rum as his father had done.

And no matter what face he showed, he had his own plan. He would save his crop money. He would rent a taxi. He would change Jamaican dollars at a black market rate for the tourists. With Icilda's help he would get Miss Ceci to help them get the paper for their land so that it would be all nice and legal. Then he would ask Jesmina to marry him. No more sleeping alone in the tent at night. No more listening to the dogs or dreaming that they would rush in, tear open the cans, and maybe tear him open, too. And he would give Icilda money for her church contribution. And buy mechanic's tools. And a fine satin jacket such as was worn by American basketball players. And . . . and . . . and . . .

His fingertips were burned by the last of the spliff. He dropped it on the dirt and turned off the lantern, watching as its mantel turned ashy. He settled back, staring through the tent flap at the black, black forest and the sliver of sky. His head felt full of liquid, his eyes heavy. It would be good. Jah would guide him. Jah-jah, not the son of Mary, but Jah, son of Jesse, black Jesse Congo, would guide him. He brought the transistor radio close to his ear, turned it low so as not to disturb the dogs, listened to it as he had listened to his grandmother, as Jimmy Cliff sang:

> *Sitting here in Limbo,*
> *But I won't be here for lo-o-ong,*
> *Sitting here in Limbo,*
> *Like a bird without a so-o-ong,*
> *Well they're putting up resistance,*
> *But I know that my faith will lead me on.*

* * *

The sound of a cock crow brought Ceci out of sleep. It had been some time since she'd woken to a cock crow. She threw back the sheet, her feet hitting the tile, stretching herself. Then she heard a great racketing down the stairs and a high-pitched voice. Who else but Hilary? If Hilary was up then everyone should be up. Thank God she'll be out of the way for a few days, Ceci thought, sitting back down on the bed. The day loomed before her, and after the day the evening party at Mrs. Cleardon's. Ignoring her previous night's vow to rouse Archie, she pulled her knees up to her chest and willed herself back to sleep.

Hours later, when the morning heat had made the room stifling and covered her with a film of perspiration, she woke with a start. Vivian was standing not two feet from her holding a bouquet. Ceci clutched the sheet to her breasts. "Oh, my God."

"Don't be startled, my dear. I felt sure the sound of the lawnmower would have woken you."

She blinked, pushing back her hair and catching a glimpse of herself in the wardrobe mirror. Her face looked like dough that had risen during the night. "What time is it?"

"I usually pin my watch to the front of my dress. . . ." Vivian pulled her head back, making a concertina of the folds beneath her chin, and stared down at her bosom. "But it appears that I've been remiss. Are you quite awake?"

"Almost." She gathered the sheet around her and wandered into the bathroom. In passing, she mumbled something about the flowers.

"I'm so glad you like them." Vivian took a few steps toward the bedroom door and trumpeted, "Miss Ceci's awake. Will someone please bring me a vase and a pot of coffee."

Icilda's head popped around the doorjamb, her expression of almost comic surprise betraying the fact that she'd been shadowing her mistress.

"Two cups, Icilda. And I think perhaps some fruit for Miss Ceci."

Icilda bobbed and disappeared.

Ceci splashed cold water on her face, wrapped the sheet more tightly around her, and, seeing that Vivian was not about to leave, got back into bed.

"Do you mind if I sit on your bed?" Vivian asked, though she had already done so. "Would you like me to find your dressing gown?"

"No, that's all right. I'll get dressed in a minute."

"I have taken to sleeping in the nude myself," Vivian announced in a voice that both solicited and defied comment.

"It's cooler," Ceci said, remembering the nightgowns Vivian had forced her to wear when she'd wanted to sleep in her underpants.

"Of course, if there were ever a fire . . ."

"You'd grab your dressing gown as you left the house."

"Yes. I suppose so." Vivian nodded at the wisdom of this advice. "One can only plan so much. 'Man proposes; God disposes.' And I don't suppose women can do much of either." Her wandering eye caressed the flowers. "I was sure that the garden would do well this year, but then we had the heavy rains. . . ." She studied Ceci with sad objectivity, as though Ceci herself was a rose that had unaccountably been attacked by blight. "I was far too strict with you when I had you, Cecily. I can see that now."

"You did your best."

"I have often thought that had Jacob lived we might have raised you properly. I'm sorry you didn't know Jacob. He was very fond of children, though, like me, he preferred raising plants. Well, they are so much quieter." This wasn't what she'd come in to say. When she'd found out that Ceci was coming back, her hopes had flared. She'd spent days imagining what she would say to her. But now her thoughts were scattered and she knew that if she tried to speak she would be neither concise nor impassioned, as she had hoped to be. She looked at her niece, her eyes imploring. *What's to become of me, Ceci? I can't say when being alone came to frighten me. Perhaps it always did; but I used to be braver without knowing it. People don't come to visit anymore. So many are dead or moved away. People like us, that is. And there are robberies and worse. I know you won't like this, Ceci, but I used to think that being a Nettleton, that just having white skin, would protect me. Can you imagine? Makes you want to laugh, doesn't it? On those rare occasions when Percy takes me into town, I can see a look—a look I never expected to see, as though times had changed, which of course I already know—but that somehow they'd all like me to be humiliated, to pay for what I never, personally never, did. Because you'll remember that I was all for Independence and I've never tried to lord it over people or be unkind. If it weren't for Icilda, I don't think I could keep the younger ones in line and . . .*

Ceci was looking at her intently. Vivian cleared her throat and stared into the bouquet, her attention galvanized by a large red ant that was crawling along the stamen of a hibiscus. "Of course I have my books," she said. "It was Jacob who introduced me to real reading. That was one of the reasons Mother disliked him so. She had an aversion to bookishness. She prized physical courage above all else and claimed she could see a man's character in his physique. But of course one can't ride to the hounds on a tropical island, can one?"

"No."

"I was twenty-nine. That's a shocking age to be unmarried. I don't mean for you, Ceci," she added apologetically. "I meant in those days. Jacob's was my one and only offer, so Mother tried to ignore his scholarly side. And she thought that because Jacob was a Jew he'd be good at business. But he wasn't that sort at all. He was studious and dreamy. We were soul mates in that."

Ceci took her little finger and removed some sleep from the corner of her eye. "I'm sorry, but . . . ." She yawned conspicuously, implying that her inability to follow was due to drowsiness, "I don't quite understand. . . ."

"Have many men proposed to you, Ceci?"

"Quite a few."

"How do you get them to?"

"By showing a complete lack of interest in the subject. They're so afraid of being trapped that the less inclined the woman is, the more likely she is to be asked."

"Is *that* how it works," Vivian exclaimed, as though Ceci had just explained the operation of some electrical appliance. "But I can't believe your disinclination is the real reason men want to marry you. I think it's because of your beautiful eyes." She sighed. "Jacob had trouble with his eyes, too. When he first told me that I was beautiful I was sure it was because he couldn't see me properly. But he saw perfectly well with his glasses. Though he did strain his eyes from reading so much. We had lamps on either side of the bed so we could read propped up in our pillows and our hands unclasped only to turn the pages."

Ceci wrapped her arms around her knees and looked down at the rumpled sheets. She had never heard this much about Jacob before, and though Vivian's words were jumbled, her love for the man was palpable, triggering Ceci's own memories.

Paul had read constantly, standing up, sitting down, at his desk or in taxis and buses, but it was only on Sundays that they'd read in bed. Sundays in the London flat: toast crusts, lukewarm tea, scattered pages of the *Guardian* and the *Times*, legs hot from sleep, buttery lips. And one particular Sunday. The Sunday before he'd left her. A morning of an unusual snow. They'd woken early because it was so very quiet, read, breakfasted, and fallen back to sleep. Then . . . Paul rousing her to acute if groggy awareness. Spreading her legs. His weight. She'd come fully awake at his first thrust, turned her head to the window, seen through slitted eyes the swirling, glorious mass of white. It had been eerily silent, peaceful, glittering; and he'd plunged into her, bringing her to sweet, humming release, whispering for her to mount him, but no, she couldn't move—the snow was too lovely, her legs were too weak—so he'd kept on, groaning that he was "past it," thrusting with such determination that his penis had seemed some ungiving substance, wood perhaps, and she'd looked out at the snow until finally he'd been made flesh again and cried out, shattering the stillness.

She'd been lying on a newspaper and the love-sweat had tattoed the print on her buttocks. He'd turned her onto her stomach, caressing her rump, saying this was the only way to read an editorial. She'd wiggled away, hitting at him. They'd rolled over each other, grappling, laughing, until they'd tumbled to the floor. And there they'd stayed, watching the snow until she'd turned, looked into his eyes, and thought that nothing, nothing in the world, not even this first snow, was more beautiful.

". . . and shorter than I was, too," Vivian was saying, "so that I never got over the fact that we didn't look right together. I'd been reading the *Tatler* since I was a girl, you see. Imagining that I was Lady Tottingham in a backless bathing costume with a marvelously tall Lord Tottingham flexing himself beside me. That's a terrible thing about living near the water, you see. Sooner or later everyone has to get into a bathing costume and then it doesn't matter how bright you are or if you can say witty things or if you have pots of money . . . you're there, almost naked. A body. Nothing can save you. So Jacob wasn't what I'd expected to love. I suppose no real man would have been because I didn't know anything about real men. But Jacob, my dear, he might have been a Latin . . ."

Ceci moved her head slightly, indicating that once again, she'd missed the point.

"A Latin. You know how those men are," Vivian insisted. "It doesn't matter if they're short or slight or they can't discuss business or compete as a sportsman. One has a sense that they *appreciate* a woman." The word seemed loaded with erotic implications. "Shortly after Jacob and I were married, it was my time of the month and . . ." Vivian swallowed and looked down. "I had stained the sheet. And do you know what Jacob said?"

Ceci marked again what she'd noticed yesterday: that Vivian no longer inflected her voice with conversational interrogation but questioned as though she expected a real answer. "No. No, I don't," Ceci said softly. "What did he say?"

"He said, 'Don't bother getting up to change the sheet.' Of course I did. I had to. But that," she said emphatically, "that was the sort of man he was."

"You must've loved him very much." She was amazed that Vivian would speak with such intimacy.

"Jacob embarrassed me. Because he wasn't like the imaginary Lord Tottingham. Because Mother thought him foolish. Because he was shorter than I. Or perhaps just because I've always been a goose. When I walked his casket to the grave, I remember straightening up and thinking, At last I can walk at my full height again. The point is that I was never able to *express* my love to him fully." The red ant had made its way to Vivian's hand and had begun to crawl up the sleeve of her dress.

"Yes," Ceci agreed. "It's always hard to express what we really feel."

Vivian leaned forward. "I was about to tell you . . ."

There was a tap on the door and Icilda appeared, balancing the tray of coffee and fruit.

"Just put it here, please," Ceci said, shifting her cigarettes from the bedside table.

"Where's the vase, Icilda?"

"I get it now, missus."

"No. No. Don't make an extra trip. Just take these flowers and fix them and bring them back, if you please."

Ceci looked for her robe while Vivian poured the coffee. "Aunt Vivie, you were saying . . ."

"I can't remember. Ceci, how do you take your coffee?"

"Just cream, no sugar." She rummaged in her overnight bag and came up with a bottle of water pills. Vivian put the pot down and stared at her. "Don't worry," Ceci laughed, "they're just diuretics. You take them when you're retaining water and they . . ."

"Yes. Yes. I'm sure," Vivian answered dubiously.

"Hey, trust me. You know you taught me to be honest. Especially about anything I might get punished for."

"We Nettletons have always prized ourselves on our honesty. I suppose that's why I was blind to so many managers rooking me."

"Then will you please be honest with me? I want you to tell me about your health."

"There's nothing much to tell. I had a bit of a short circuit in the old head works. Nothing serious, believe me."

"When I got the telegram it was so vague."

"What telegram?"

"The telegram you sent, or Marsden sent."

"I can't imagine what you mean."

"The telegram," Ceci insisted. Vivian shook her head. Ceci tried another tack. "And then when I called you, you sounded upset, as though you were speaking to me in code or something."

"Oh, that. Nothing. Bit of a go-round. Marsden had to let one of the girls go and I'm afraid I'm rather brittle about changing things."

"Was she lazy?"

"No. Quite spirited in fact. Almost too energetic. But she had a way of looking at one. A look I usually see only when I go into town—as though I've been told to go into the corner and put on a dunce cap."

"So you didn't mind her being dismissed?"

"I just said, she didn't trouble me personally. But she insulted *her*."

"Who? Hilary?"

"Mmmm. Icilda says 'she step like puss 'pon hot brick.' "
Vivian laughed like a naughty child.

Ceci laughed too. "That's right on. That's how I felt about
Hilary. I didn't know you felt that way too."

Vivian flushed. She felt her dress shields sticking to her
armpits. "I wish you wouldn't interrogate me, Ceci."

"Don't be so touchy. I'm only trying to understand what's
been going on. Let me put it another way: how do you feel
about Marsden's plans?"

"Marsden is my nephew."

Ceci sighed. "Yes. But are you comfortable with the way
he's running things?"

"Blood is blood. When Marsden was just a little tyke . . .
you'll remember that I knew Marsden long before I knew
you, Ceci."

"Since he's ten years older that would seem to be unavoidable."

"Alicia made a point of writing to me when she and Angus
divorced. She was crushed, simply crushed. Angus didn't
treat her at all well. I was so pleased that she was interested
in retaining my friendship."

Which of course she wasn't, Ceci thought as she began to
pace the room.

"I appreciated her desire to retain the family connection.
For Marsden's sake. I thought it very generous of her not to
show malice and to send him down for holidays. He was not
a demonstrative child by nature. Not at all like you. You were
always high-strung. And he wasn't a handsome child either,
which upset Alicia no end. But he was very fond of me. Very
fond. The way he followed me around! We were like kite and
tail."

Ceci reached for a cigarette. Following Vivian through the
marshes of memory was a tedious journey indeed.

"When Alicia remarried and Marsden was sent off to military school . . ."

"Let's not regurgitate all of Marsden's traumas."

"His what? I wasn't about to make excuses by saying things
have been difficult for him, if that's what you mean. He took

to military school like a duck to water. At least from his letters
—which may have been censored, for all I know—he seemed
to like it."

"He would."

"Marsden's first wife was much like you."

"How like me?"

"Intellectually quick. Affectionate but somehow mistrust-
ful. There was a sense that she was judging him in a general
way. He was wildly jealous, of course. He was even jealous
of the gardener and William, the man who was our driver
then. He . . ." She could sense Ceci's impatience. It was such
a vicious cycle. She was never able to express herself properly
and that made people impatient and when people were impatient it made her nervous so she sounded even more the fool.
"He called her his Last Duchess," she rushed on, afraid she'd
lose track of her thought. "She was indiscriminately democratic, the way some liberal Americans are. And perversely,
he seemed to have chosen her *because* she wasn't of his stripe.
But love should be unconditional, shouldn't it?"

"Only from our mothers."

"Which Alicia's *wasn't*," Vivian answered triumphantly as
though she'd just put Ceci in checkmate. "When Marsden was
knee-high to a duck, learning to swim . . ."

"It was my impression . . ." Ceci drew her hands through
her hair, then realized she was holding an unlit cigarette. She
twirled around to look at Vivian. The ant had made its way
to Vivian's bosom now. "It was my impression that you feel
somewhat intimidated by the situation. I can't help but notice
how domineering both he and—"

"Anyone who has responsibility for things may become
short-tempered and lacking in humor."

Ceci reached for the lighter and sat down. "Exactly my
point. Last night I couldn't help but notice that Icilda had
been crying. When I asked her about it, she said that Marsden
had forbidden her to have her husband come and sleep with
her."

Vivian put down the coffee cup. Her good eye studied Ceci
and it seemed as if, by conscious act of the will, she was trying

to bring her wayward eye into focus with it. "Do you take cream and sugar?"

"I just told . . . cream. No sugar. Please. And now about Icilda."

"What are you planning to wear to Mrs. Cleardon's to-night?"

"Something appropriate." Was Vivian making a clumsy attempt to avoid the issue, or had her concentration really gone?

"Then you'd best make your choice now and put out whatever you're planning to wear so that Thelda can press it."

"Are you purposely ignoring me?" she asked gently. "We were talking about Marsden forbidding Icilda's husband to spend the night with her."

Vivian dropped her gaze and busied herself with the plate of fruit, separating the slices of papaya from the wedges of pineapple. Icilda's name caused her grief and humiliation. Icilda loved her. Icilda had come to her with just this problem when Marsden and Hilary had changed the rules. But Icilda's love, well, what sort of protection was that?

"You forget what the servants are like, Ceci. They are like children. They try to take advantage."

"But how can her being with—"

"Things can get out of hand very easily. You permit one visitor in the cabins and before you know it it's a little colony. One of the girls has her man in. The following week it's another man. One knows nothing of his character."

"Yes, I can see the difficulty of that but—"

"As for the protection of manners and respect, things are not what they used to be."

"They never are. They never were."

"You are somewhat of an outsider, Cecily."

"Sometimes outsiders see things more clearly."

"Just two weeks ago . . . just two weeks ago," Vivian repeated, struggling for emphasis, "Betty Sempill was robbed in her own house and thank heaven she escaped with only a lump on her head and her jewelry gone. One feels quite vulnerable."

"But with Icilda. Surely Icilda . . . She's part of the family. She's . . . I may as well come out with it, but promise me you won't be angry with her. She told me last night that there's some plot of land up in the hills that grandfather gave to her mother and she's very anxious about getting the legal papers for it."

"Everything like that is taken care of in my will."

"I just meant that it might be best to take care of it now. If anything in the will was to be contested, where would Icilda stand?"

"It would be unfair and divisive to make an exception with Icilda. You can't imagine the furor, the charges of favoritism, the disruption it would bring with the others. And Icilda herself is likely, with no conscious intention of doing so, to overstep the mark."

"Look, I probably shouldn't have said anything to you, but I can't stand this mystery and intrigue about everything. Couldn't we all just sit down and . . ."

"You *know* I care for Icilda," Vivian said, her voice tremulous. "But truly, before Marsden took over I felt quite inundated. On Sundays I would look over to the cabins and there would be crowds of children." There was a balanced singsong to her speech, as though she was reciting a public address she'd learned by heart. "And you know how they breed." Patches of color stood out on her cheeks. She closed her eyes as though she herself had been forced to witness acts of multiple copulation. The ant had now crawled onto her neck and she shivered, aware of an irritation but unable to make the connection to any particular part of her skin. "Their mothers would leave them with Icilda and then, during the week, I'd come onto the veranda and almost tred on some poor mirasme child. And what then?"

Ceci ran her hand through her hair. "Aunt Vivian," she said, her voice strained, "There's an ant crawling on your neck. There . . . no, there," she pointed as Vivian's hand wandered. "On the left side. There! Near your ear."

"Goodness. Dear me. Yes." Vivian captured the ant, squashed it between thumb and middle finger and brought it up to her nose.

"We were talking about Marsden. About Icilda. About
. . . Bloody hell, I don't know what we were talking about."
Her frustration put her in mind of a time when a woman
friend had asked for her help in leaving a husband who was
beating her up. Against her better judgment Ceci had inter-
vened and taken the friend in. When the woman returned to
her husband, she'd deflected her anger onto Ceci. Since that
time she'd made it a rule never to be involved in lovers' or
families' quarrels. But she was a member of this particular
family. And she still had a strong sense that Vivian wanted
her to act for her. If only Vivian could determine what it was
that she wanted done.

"Yes," Vivian conceded, "we were talking about Marsden.
Marsden wants to be living back in the colonial days. Or the
colonial days as he imagines them to be. He's very good at
organizing things, though I expect he'd rather be running a
plantation than making this convention center or whatever it
is." She wiped the ant onto the napkin, folded it into neat
triangles, and smoothed it on her knee. "I wish you lived here,
Ceci."

"Aunt Vivie, I . . ."

"I wish you did, but you don't."

"Is that all you have to say on the subject?"

"You don't live here."

"That's right. And to tell the truth, I never could." She
turned her back and raised the blinds. Just a few feet away,
beyond the grillwork and sun-drenched bushes, Thelda stood,
broom in hand. At the sound of the blinds being raised, she
began to push the broom along the path, humming to herself.
"I think that new girl Thelda . . ." she began, but broke off.
She was annoyed. Not just because Vivian had refused to
confront whatever issues she was trying to raise, but because
Vivian was right: she wasn't just an outsider; she was a butt-
in-ski, confident enough to analyze other peoples' problems
after fewer than twenty-four hours of observation, but not
committed to solving those problems. The smartass traveling
through. Always traveling through.

"Your coffee's getting cold, Cecily."

She turned. Vivian had opened the napkin again, exposing

the squashed ant, holding it up to her. "I can remember when you used to give funerals. Any bird or mouse you could find. You quite robbed my wardrobe of shoe and hatboxes. And you would force all the servants' children to stand around and sing. Well, you know you can be quite dictatorial in your own way. And you would cry and cry. You were quite a big girl then, but still you cried. There were times when I was quite worried about you."

Ceci let go of the cord, allowing the blind to fall with a crash. "Where's Archie?"

"He left ages ago. Marsden took him up to see the construction on the great house."

"I see. Have you been up there? Do you know what's going on, or how it's being financed?"

"No. The place always gave me the shivers. And what with all the workmen about, it's no place for a woman. I'll admit that I was apprehensive when Marsden first started with his plans. I couldn't help but feel that the idea of a hotel—convention center if you like—seemed somehow vulgar. All those Americans wanting to play golf or watch television, and one never knows how they'll treat the staff because some of them have such hateful attitudes toward coloreds. And I don't think you should go up there either."

"If you don't mind, I think I'll put on my bathing suit and go for a swim. Perhaps Icilda could pack me some sandwiches." She crossed to the wardrobe to look for her suit and saw the other package from Harrod's. "This is for you," she said gently.

"Whatever can it be? I do so love presents."

"It's . . ."

"No, you naughty girl! You're always spoiling things. I'll just take the package to my room and then when I've finished reading my book, I'll open it. Like saving the sweet until I've finished my vegetables." She clapped her hands and held them out. Ceci handed over the box and reached for her coffee, gulping it down as though it were a cool drink. If she didn't get out of this crazy house, there was no telling what she might do. Just as when she was a girl, she wanted to swim until her arms and legs ached, run on the beach, and work herself into a mindless muck-sweat.

As though divining her thoughts, Vivian got up. "I don't mind what you do, Ceci. I'm just terribly happy that you've remembered me. That you're here. You can have funeral services for the ant and make the servants sing if you like. And tonight . . ." her lips worked silently as though trying out her next words ". . . tonight I wouldn't, if I were you . . . just don't bring up things that are bound to make people uncomfortable."

"Such as?"

"You know what I mean, Cecily. Your ideas . . ."

"What do you know about my ideas?"

She brought her face so close to Ceci's that her contrary eye came into line with her good one. "One has only to look at you, my dear." To Ceci's surprise, her aunt's tight little smile broke into one of radiant approval.

Nine

Archie had woken with a hangover so painful that a bird call had made him wince. Cotton-mouthed and crawly-fleshed, he'd managed to pull himself into a sitting position when he'd heard Marsden tapping at the door and asking if he still intended to go to the great house "as planned." The question had compounded his physical agony with mental anguish, for just as Ceci had predicted, he had only the foggiest notion of what had happened the night before. Had he promised cooperation in ventures he knew nothing about? Agreed that Marsden should have power of attorney over Vivian's affairs?

Calling that he would go "as planned" as soon as he'd showered, he'd tottered into the bathroom.

The sunlight on the tile blinded him. Bracing himself against the wall, he'd stepped into the tub. (Once, when he'd had to play a man who shot himself, an old Yiddish actor had given him a tip: The shock of the bullet could be created by remembering what it was like to be hit by cold water in the shower.) He reached for the faucet—"A fitting end to a worthless life, Count Maurice"—and ahhh!—destruction blasted him in the face. After the initial punishing shock, he'd turned on the hot tap. The water needles had a pleasantly numbing effect and he'd been able to come up with an equation: Vivian had been cheated by a series of managers; Marsden had cared enough to come and set it to rights; therefore, Marsden deserved his support. This was clear enough until he'd turned off the water, at which point his mind had become as clouded as the steamed mirror.

Breakfast had been served on the veranda. As he came out into the glaring sunlight he had another moment of lucidity, thinking, There is a uniquely poisonous quality to the tropical hangover. The brightness, the lushness of the landscape, the obscenely vivid colors of water, earth, and sky intensify the guilt. Guilt leads to the desire for oblivion. Oblivion can be found in another drink. Oh, Christ. He'd wanted to share this insight with Marsden, but Marsden, who never looked truly healthy and therefore could never look absolutely dreadful, wouldn't have understood. Indeed, Marsden was creating a hideous spectacle, dipping toast fingers into the goo of coddled eggs. Archie'd averted his eyes, taken one glass of juice and then another. As he'd reached for the pitcher a third time, Marsden noticed that his hand was unsteady and had reached over to pour for him. The gesture, seeming to help but in fact only serving to humiliate, had struck Archie as both unseemly and unmanly. But then, Marsden had never been the son he'd hoped to produce. Perhaps, as his old friend Mort Goldman put it when referring to his own disappointing progeny: "The fuck determines the kid." He had told Mort he thought that a vulgar superstition (though Mort being Mort, vulgarity was hardly the issue), but perhaps he'd only objected to it because he half-believed it.

He closed his eyes on the coddled eggs and saw dancing, phosphorescent spots that had changed into photos of his first son, Eric: Eric in hand-knitted rompers, his fist around a rusk, his eyes merry; Eric at the cricket pitch, on the ready, determined; Eric in long pants, don's robes, a wedding suit. Initially he'd hated getting those photos, suspecting they were Phoebe's way of rubbing salt into his wounds, but then he'd realized that Phoebe sent them out of her own sense of rightness, not for any effect they might have on him. And when he'd finally met his firstborn (Eric had been, by then, a full-grown man who'd treated him with a gruff respect), he'd known that Phoebe had shielded Eric from any knowledge of his wrongdoing. All by herself, Phoebe had managed to bring up Eric to be just the sort of man Archie respected. And Eric had been conceived where? In a rented bed? On the fancy tile of the Garden of Allah? Perhaps on the very spot where he'd betrayed Phoebe with the tapdancer? Perhaps Eric was decent and robust because he'd been conceived in love, because Phoebe was the only woman with whom Archie had laughed in bed.

There had been some laughter with Ceci's conception, but of a different sort. Strange thrashings about, seductions initiated by Mabs that he'd realized only after the fact, had little to do with his desirability. Perhaps because she was a foundling who'd been shunted about in foster homes, Mabs had desperately wanted a family. To that end she'd resorted to raunchy underwear (those transparent panties with the black hand over the crotch), poses she'd seen in blue movies, and books of erotica on the night table. Again, he'd missed the point initially, thinking that because of their age difference Mabs thought his virility might need a spur or that she had some libidinous quirks of her own. But the sheer silliness of it all and Mabs' ineptitude as the femme fatale had tickled him and, bless her, Mabs had been able to laugh at her own clumsiness—at least until they'd gotten into "the act," at which point she would turn super serious and take on something of the bizarre attraction of a human suction machine. Once she'd conceived, her come-hither glances and risqué underwear had been put away. Mabs had fairly wallowed in motherhood; so much so that he'd often felt like an intruder in his own house. But if ever there had been a wanted child, it had been Ceci. Which, he supposed, was all to the good. Otherwise Ceci would never have been able to survive the loss of her mother and the shock of having been moved about so much, or grown to be the independent, self-willed, and adventurous creature she seemed to be.

But Marsden, poor bugger! In what explosion of never-to-be reciprocated passion had that particular sperm fought its way upstream and into that unwilling ovum? It could have been any one of the many, many times he'd forced his attentions on Alicia. He would never forget that afternoon when she'd come home from the doctor's, poured herself a stiff drink, taken a piece of paper he'd thought to be a prescription out of her alligator purse and thrown it at him. It was the rabbit test, or the frog test, or whatever they did in those days. Positive. He'd been almost as disgusted as she. They'd talked of terminating the pregnancy, but it had been too late. He'd felt dismal, knowing that Alicia would never again, even for her own purposes, parade in front of him naked. He'd taken her stretch marks as though they were lashes on his own back. Why then had he let such a woman take his son? Particularly since she'd said she'd let him have the kid as long as it didn't interfere with her alimony payments. Because he knew nothing about children and didn't want to know. Because he'd hoped he still had some chance for adventure, and adventure had nothing to do with regular dentist appointments or tucking some small, needy creature into bed. Because . . . He hadn't even been relieved to get rid of the little blighter. He'd just thought of him in terms of his checkbook.

So perhaps there was something to crazy Mort's cryptomysticims, and if that was the case, what about his own conception? Strange—here he was, an old man, and he'd never considered his parents' sexuality. His mother, Evelyn, must've squeezed her eyes shut and thought about England and Duty. But perhaps not. How could he ever know? His father had probably thought—did men think at all at such times—that he wanted an heir. His father . . .

"Mort who? Who's this Mort?" Marsden asked.

Archie blinked. "What was I saying?"

"You just said 'Mort, you old sod.'"

"Old friend of mine. Good chap. Used to play gangsters. Shall I get started? Where's my hat?"

The ride up the hill road reduced him to a quivering blob of nerves. As he got out of the car, the great house, the men working around it, the cane fields beyond it had the quality of hallucination. Marsden droned on about cost estimates and the inefficiency of the workmen. And indeed the men seemed to be moving as though underwater. They stopped whatever they were doing to stare at him and it took him some time to

realize that their grins and whispers were merely an acknowledgment of his presence, the older ones telling the younger
who he was. He couldn't acknowledge any of them because
he was forced to use all his concentration to avoid stumbling
over pipes and lumber. The sound of the buzz saw fairly
drove him wild. The sight of the cement mixer made him
bilious. The sun beat through the crown of his hat, turning
his head into an incubator of pain. While Marsden went behind the house to see how the swimming pool was coming,
he sank down onto the steps beneath the columns, thinking
that it would be a fitting and ironic punishment were he to
expire on this, the site of the Nettletons' great accomplish-
ment.

Marsden loomed over him. "I was planning to give you a
tour of the fields but . . ." He offered his hand, but Archie,
using his cane to steady himself, managed to get up unaided.
". . . we could postpone that until another day. Not much
point looking at them, really. I told you I've cut back on the
cane production. I might put in flower crops once we get the
operation working. There's a market for orchids and the like
in the States."

"But the island isn't producing its own food supply, is it?"
Archie ventured, wanting to sound knowledgeable. "Strange
that such a fertile place isn't even producing enough for the
populace."

"We're a business, not a charity operation. Not unless we
want the profits to stay at the miserable level they are now."
Marsden placed a moist but cool hand on Archie's and steered
him to the car.

Arriving back at the house, Archie went straight to his
room, ignoring Icilda's message that Miss Ceci was on the
beach near the rowboats and wanted to see him. As he lay on
his bed, mesmerized by the ceiling fan, it seemed as if, in the
space of a day, he'd slipped back into the most disgusting
habits of the old plantation owner: drinking at night, watching workmen during the morning, "flopping" in the afternoon.

By five o'clock, his leg still throbbing but his headache
reduced to a persistent twitch in his right eye, he showered,

shaved, and straggled out onto the veranda. He glanced in the direction of the cabins and saw that the Rolls had been parked beneath the big tree. He could remember the excitement he'd felt when the car had arrived from England. His father had bought it over his mother's objections, saying it was his reward for having survived the war, and he'd spent a lot of his time in it, driving back and forth over the only stretch of paved road, singing, "It's a Long Way to Tipperary" and swigging from a silver hip flask that had been dented by an enemy bullet. At such times Archie had thought his father a very romantic figure indeed.

That the old Rolls was still functioning was a good omen. He walked toward it. The hood was up and the upper part of Percy's body was bent into its works. Percy seemed to be talking to himself, but as Archie got closer, he heard Ceci's laughter. She popped up from behind a fender, her hair trailing, her breasts barely concealed by her bikini, a can of wax and a cleaning rag in her hand. "No, Percy, the polish isn't really made from turtles. It's called Turtle Wax because it has a hard shell. Oh," she caught sight of Archie, "hello, old chap. I'm just trying to make myself useful. Percy's been explaining to me about the car. Do you know how smart he is? He's managed to study the old owner's manual and he's made repairs on the Rolls all by himself."

Straightening up, Percy looked both sheepish and gratified. "She be a beauty for sure. Break me heart not to see her run."

"Good, very good," Archie grunted. "Tell me what you've been doing to her."

"First I adjust her tappets . . ." Percy began.

There was an insistent honking at the gates. "Excuse, please." Percy ran up the incline toward the gate.

"It's such a shame," Ceci said softly. "He really has a gift for machinery. If he'd had an education he might have been an engineer." She put the can of wax on the top of the car and smiled warmly at him. "Seems you got away without my knowing it this morning. And I've been wanting to talk with you. Do you think we might go for a stroll and have a chat?"

He was about to say yes when Marsden pulled the Toyota up next to them and got out.

"Hello, Marsden. Hot enough for you?" Ceci smiled and shook out the cleaning rag. "Just giving the bloody old hearse a bit of a polish."

" 'The bloody old hearse' as you call it happens to be one of the finest examples of engineering—" Marsden began.

"You sound like a used car salesman, Marsden." She broadened her smile, brazening his disapproval. "This relic reminds me of that scene in *Citizen Kane*. You remember the one: They're going off on this picnic, and all the Rolls are lined up as though it were a cortege, and everyone looks as though they'd been stuffed by a taxidermist. You don't know whether to laugh or cry."

"We're due at Mrs. Cleardon's at nine, and since you and Archie are more or less the guests of honor, I suggest that you . . ."

"You don't have to suggest anything, Marsden. I'm quite capable of dressing myself."

"Really, you two," Archie gave his voice a jocular authority. "Brothers and sisters squabble, but you're both past the age when . . ."

"I wanted to give Cecily plenty of time to get ready." Marsden smiled. "I neglected to tell you, Cecily, but Mrs. Cleardon asked if you'd like to stay the night, and I thought perhaps you'd like to pack an overnight bag."

"Do you mean you accepted the invitation for me?" she asked incredulously.

"Not at all. It's entirely up to you. I thought it very gracious of Mrs. Cleardon to offer, and knowing that there's so little here to entertain you, I assumed you'd want to accept. She's the doyenne of society on this side of the island and I—"

"I don't care if she's the First Lady."

He shrugged. "As I said, it's entirely up to you. And First Lady or not, I assume she'd be able to find something more interesting for you to do than wash cars. Really, Cecily," his eyes flitted to the cleaning cloth, "we are adequately staffed, and it's rather disruptive for you to be helping out with the chores. Well . . ." he moved away from them, ". . . I'll see you both in an hour."

Ceci turned to look at the ocean. "Pompous son of a bitch," she said at last.

The fact that Archie was inclined to agree with her but didn't want to fuel the argument prompted him to say, "You might make some effort, Cecily. He said you didn't have to accept the invitation. I expect he was just trying to find something to entertain you."

"He's trying to find something to get me out of the way."

"Now, now. Why would you want to stay up here with all of us old fuddy-duddies when you might be enjoying yourself with people your own age?"

"Archie, I'm not sixteen. I'm capable of 'entertaining' myself, as you put it." She turned to face him. "You've barely spoken to me since we arrived."

"What do you want me to say? There'll be plenty of time to talk when . . ."

"You haven't even asked me about Phoebe. Don't you want to know how she is?"

"I know how she is. I spoke to her on the phone for hours."

"I meant . . ." She laughed. "You know I had the strangest thought when I saw her last. I thought perhaps, now that you're both older, it might be a good idea for you to live together again. You're alone and she's alone and . . ."

"You do say the strangest things. Phoebe lives in London. She has her career and I . . ." He drew himself up, turning away so that she wouldn't see the twitch in his eye. ". . . I have mine."

A dead end. Why bother? She threw the rag onto the fender of the Rolls. "I would like to go up to the great house with you. Do you suppose we might go tomorrow?"

"If the car's available, I suppose . . ."

"I'm not just here for decoration, Archie. I'd like to know what's going on. It's obvious that I can't talk to Marsden. Oh," she wrapped her arms around her breasts and shuddered, "he's such a petty tyrant. He takes the joy out of absolutely everything. I don't mean that he's purposely cruel. He doesn't beat the staff or cut off their wages. He's just a kill joy. I know he doesn't want me around. Last night, for example. He set all of that up, I know he did."

"Set what up?"

"That little tête-à-tête after dinner. Would you mind telling me what that was about?"

"To tell you the truth . . ." He was about to confess that he'd been too drunk to remember it, but honesty failed him. "To tell the truth, I think we'd best go up and dress for the party."

Her face, animated with frustration a moment before, sagged into a resignation that made him realize, perhaps for the first time, that she was no longer a very young woman. He wanted to make it right for her, lighten her mood. "It might not be a bad idea if you stayed the night at this Mrs. Cleardon's. You might meet some amusing people."

She threw back her head and stared into the intense blue of the sky. "Amusing people," she said softly. "If you only knew how much I've been amused by amusing people, let myself be distracted from any decision or responsibility or caring. And you know, I'm really on the edge of it now. Have you ever felt like that? As though you have to do something to change your life but you just don't know where to begin? Have you ever felt like that, Father?"

It was so rare for her to call him Father that it completely took him aback. He was afraid that a confession of turns not taken in his own life would somehow rob him of parental authority. Had she not been so undressed he would have liked to take her in his arms. Instead, he stood speechless.

She waited for some response, some acknowledgment, some gesture that would cut through everything and bring them together. She sighed, turned, and started away.

"Ceci." He reached for her hand but she had already moved past him whispering, "What a balls-up" and striding toward the house.

What a balls-up, indeed.

Ten

Mrs. Austin Cleardon rested her fleshy elbow on her bamboo bar and glanced at her watch. Twenty to eight. She'd staggered the invitations, asking the "extras" for eight so that when the "stars" arrived at nine a good crowd would already be assembled and onto its second drink. She'd toured the kitchen, tasted every variety of hors d'ouevre, plumped up the couch pillows, changed a lamp bulb from a 100-watt to a 60-watt, and removed a wilting flower from an arrangement. As she bit into a lemon wedge, she felt the high anticipation but none of the anxiety she had had in her younger days, when she'd groomed herself more than her home for parties.

Some two years before she had sold her hill house in Westmoreland Parish to a Maryland psychiatrist, Dr. Obfusky, and had moved to this beachfront property in Montego Bay. As luck would have it, the good doctor's desire for the old had intersected her passion for the new. At first she'd taken his enthusiasm for the cumbersome chiffoniers, wormy picture frames, and dining room table that could have been used to disect a whale as mere politeness; but then she'd seen the acquisitive gleam in his eye. After sighing over the "sentimental value" of her "antiques" (which, in fact, called forth nothing but memories of a nasty mother-in-law) just long enough to bring up the price, she'd sold the place lock, stock, and barrel. She'd flown to New York and hired a decorator to give her "everything modern, everything American." The decorator had obliged with low-slung bamboo divans upholstered in a parrot and palm motif, little red and green lacquered tables that strained the eye as well as the back, a plethora of plants that made the inside of her new house more junglelike than the outside, and a grand piano lacquered Chinese red. She knew that most of the old guard disparaged her taste as much as they'd disparaged her person when she'd first come to the island some forty years before; she also knew that those who had the honor to coexist during her lifetime and wanted to be part of the island's social life would never dare to question her. There was only one person whose opinion she gave a fig about and that was her companion Gladys Julowski. But, she reminded herself as she tongued the lemon pulp from her good back teeth, Gladys was her companion partly because Gladys' opinions rarely, if ever, departed from her own.

"Help yourself to a drink before the guests arrive, Jeffrey," she told the middle-aged black man who was polishing an already spotless glass. "And please fix me a double martini." She walked into the hallway and called for Gladys to please hurry up and to put on something more appealing than jeans. Normally she didn't mind Gladys' casual dress because it set her own colorful plumage off to greater advantage, but this evening it would be best to be on the safe side. The guests would be a rather motley assortment: old planters and land-owners; Americans and Canadians involved in imports, tourism, or management of the bauxite mines, a few "entrepreneurs" and "advisors" whose activities didn't bear questioning; an Israeli farmer who was testing the economic waters; some local businessmen, and a smattering of what passed for the artistic and intellectual community. These last were the most pathetic: scholarly, well-intentioned young men who had studied abroad, insisted on discussing the island's social problems, but decided on their third drink that those problems were insuperable. Still, one had to have a few of the intelligentsia, even if one longed for the days when

Jamaica had been the subject of musicals rather than economic analysis.

Whatever music there was nowadays came from those young Rastamen who'd blended religion and protest into a profitable and popular amalgam. They loved both the Bible and ganja, wailed against the evils of "Babylon," and professed a desire to go "Back to Africa," though they'd become so enormously successful that they were more likely to go back to New York or Hollywood for recording sessions. At Gladys' prompting she'd had some of them to parties and had found them congenial if somewhat bizarre. But tonight whatever glamour there would be would have to be provided by Archie Baron and his daughter Cecily. She'd heard that the Baron girl was beautiful, witty, and something of a maverick, so she ought to be able to entertain the men. Archie Baron's celebrity, though somewhat shopworn, would be enough to delight that group she secretly referred to as the Dragon Club: those wealthy widows who'd fulfilled the injunction that to make it in Jamaica a woman should marry well and bury fast. At least circumstantially she herself might have been considered part of the club, but because of her new house, her social life, Gladys, and certain privately held but never publicly expressed attitudes, she knew that she had sufficiently distanced herself from them.

She pulled back the sliding glass doors and stepped out onto the patio. The moon was full; the air balmy. The swimming pool glowed aquamarine. The lights across the bay were a festive backdrop. She took a deep, satisfied breath and plucked a flower from one of the concrete pots at the edge of the flagstones. Having been born in a tiny Welsh village, which she remembered only in terms of muted colors, coal dust, and numb fingertips, she'd been only too happy to follow her first husband, a planter some twenty years her senior, to the tropics. From the very first, she'd looked at most of the island's inhabitants with a jaundiced eye, but she'd never become jaded about the warmth and luxuriance of the island itself.

She strolled across the patio to the rocky abutment that dropped some twenty feet into the surf. Just a few weeks ago some fool from the Department of Tourism had stumbled past the concrete pots and had fallen onto the rocks and gashed his arm. She'd had a few anxious moments until she'd checked his wound, given him another brandy and reminded herself that though Jamaicans were litigious by nature, they usually confined their legal battles to domestic and property disputes.

She reentered the living room, asked Jeffrey to tell one of the boys to put another torch at the edge of the flagstones, and picked up her drink. It was her habit to fortify herself just before the guests arrived and then abstain until she needed another boost to get the stragglers moving. She took a single sip, then moved into the hallway, holding the drink at arm's length, careful not to spill a drop. Her third husband had been a surgeon, dexterous of hand but careless of heart, and he had often chided her for her lack of balance. She had not grieved inordinately when he'd been taken away with a sudden stroke, leaving her the hill property.

"Gladys?" She tapped at the door and, without waiting for a reply, opened it. The pungent smell of ganja hit her. "Gladys, if you're going to smoke, please keep the door closed and don't open the windows. Not everyone who's coming tonight would approve."

"If they don't approve, then they probably wouldn't recognize the smell." Gladys stubbed out the joint and carefully laid the roach in one of the shell-shaped ceramic ashtrays.

"Why are you smoking, dear? Are you nervous?"

In reply Gladys pushed out her lower lip and leaned closer to the mirror. She didn't like having to give her reasons. According to her lights, everything she did had its reason if only people had the sense to perceive it. She had not run away from Bangor, Maine, hitchhiked all the way to Haight Ashbury, and finally gotten herself to Jamaica to give reasons for what she did. She squinted at herself and pulled out a gray hair.

Mrs. Cleardon touched the crown of Gladys' head. Gladys still wore her hair parted in the middle and trailing down her back in the free-flowing style of the late sixties. At a distance she still looked very young. "I like the caftan," she said, letting her hand slide down to finger the cloth.

"You should. It's yours."

"And the lipstick, too." She patted Gladys' shoulder approvingly. "Please try not to smoke during the party. Or if you do, please do it in here. And alone." She picked up her martini and left the room.

Her calm only briefly ruffled by Gladys' truculence, her thoughts now returned to her guests. There were a few unavoidable duds. Betty Sempill, for example. She would have preferred to leave Betty off the list, but knew the Dragon Club would think her coldhearted if she did. Especially since Betty had been the victim of a recent burglary, an event that she was sure had given a perverse excitement to Betty's dull-as-dishwater life. Like many people of limited intelligence, Betty was fascinated by disasters. She could drone on for hours about herself, her relatives, her relatives' friends, all of whom seemed to live on the razor's edge. Now that she'd experienced a real calamity Betty was bound to make social capital out of it. And that would frighten some of the foreigners. Yes, she'd have to keep close tabs on dear, drear Betty.

And there was that Gloria Milst. She was a cheap piece of goods trying to pass herself off as the genuine article. She said she was a decorator but she wouldn't have known *peau de soire* from polyester. She'd been obliged to ask Gloria because rumor had it that Gloria was sleeping with Marsden Baron and Marsden had used his influence to get the new man from the U.S. Embassy to accept. (It never hurt to know someone from the embassy in case one had to get a visa in a hurry.) Well, Gloria deserved some consideration. Any woman sleeping with Marsden Baron deserved some consideration. Just shaking hands with him made you feel you had to wash off fish scales.

Then there was Vivian Nettleton. That poor old dear would turn up in her sensible shoes and a dowdy dress and sit in a corner staring down the end of her nose. Worse yet, she might plunge off into some conversational underbrush from which it would be impossible to rescue her. And please, please God, no one should talk about politics! She was quite fed up with all the grousing and paranoia. What did the privileged few in a poor country expect, for God's sake? There

were members of the Dragon Club who actually accused her
of fomenting revolution just because she treated her servants
as human beings. (In point of fact she purposely left cabinets
unlocked and left her purse lying about to test everyone on
her staff.) It was just too tiresome to live with mistrust. She
felt some sympathy for the old guard because they were too
ossified to, as Gladys would put it, "go with the flow"; but she
had nothing but contempt for the lukewarm reformers, those
who wanted change for the better on the proviso that it
wouldn't affect their personal circumstances for the worse.
No. She refused to be afraid of change. If things went into
another upheaval, she would be ready; for, as that handsome
rascal Paul Strangman had pointed out, "there are five planes
a day to Miami." And she would be on one of them. In the
meantime she proposed to enjoy herself.

The bell at the front gate was being rung as though sound-
ing an alarm. She finished off her martini, returned the glass
to the bar, checked herself in the mirror, and advanced to the
foyer.

One of her boys was opening the door to Nayef Marouf, a
Lebanese in the import business and—she might have known
who'd arrive first—Betty Semphill.

"Oh, no! Don't tell me I'm the first to arrive," Betty cried.

Mrs. Cleardon opened her arms. "That you are, and welcome. Do you two know each other?"

"We met on the pathway," Marouf explained. "Mrs. Sempill, isn't it?"

"Yes. And your name again . . ."

"Marouf. Nayef Marouf."

"Yes. Of course. I was just telling Mr. Marouf that I had to
come early because I'll have to leave early."

Mrs. Cleardon smiled. "That's too bad, Betty."

"Ever since the burglary I haven't felt safe leaving the
house."

Marouf's brows knit with concern. "You were the lady
who was robbed about two weeks ago?"

Betty Sempill brought her hand to her throat, closed her
eyes, and nodded.

"I'm glad to see that you're up and around," Marouf continued. "I understood that you'd been hospitalized."

"Let's not stand about in the foyer," Mrs. Cleardon said, extending her arm toward the interior of the house.

"I decided it was best to recover in my own home," Betty sighed. "I'm physically recovered. Though the emotional scars . . ."

Mrs. Cleardon smiled again and wondered if her lipstick was bleeding. "Shall we . . .?" As she led them into the living room, it crossed her mind that perhaps she enjoyed preparing for parties more than she enjoyed the parties themselves.

"No, I didn't have the pleasure of working with Lon Chaney," Archie said, glancing around the six or seven people standing in front of him, his eyes only briefly resting on the woman who'd pecked her way into the conversation with yet another question about horror films. She reminded him of a speckled hen—all ginger and brown, ruffled and stupid—certainly not an adaptive creature.

"You were talking about the old studio days," the fellow from the embassy—Simpton, or was it Shrimpton?—reminded him in the smooth tone of someone who was schooled in getting others to talk.

"Ah, yes. The old studio days. And I won't call them the good old days because they weren't. We were at the beck and call of those moguls. Proper little czars they were." He paused briefly, acknowledging the sympathetic nods and trying to catch Vivian's eye. She was standing between Mr. and Mrs. Edison, her lifetime neighbors, in the attitude of someone waiting for a bus amidst a crowd of strangers. "One didn't dare refuse a Sam Goldwyn or a Jack Warner," he went on quickly, "even when one knew that one had been improperly cast. Why, in the late forties I was cast as an Egyptian pharaoh! By the time I got my makeup off it was time to go to work again the next morning."

"I suppose someone had to be in charge," the diplomat ventured.

"Yes," his wife said. They were clearly a duo who'd had a lot of practice backing each other up. "And the quality of the movies was quite remarkable, given what you're telling us about the production schedule."

"Those films shaped America's view of the world," her husband offered. "And the whole world's view of itself." His hand circled and paused, unsure if that sounded too chauvinistic.

"But more importantly, you never forgot the actors' faces," Mrs. Edison, her own face an unforgettable shade of vermillion, put in.

"True enough."

"Not that I'd be likely to forget your face," Mrs. Edison continued, surreptitiously elbowing Mr. Edison into greater involvement. "Even before I married Gilbert, I knew that you and he had been boyhood chums because the Nettleton plantation bordered the Edison . . ."

"But did you know Boris Karloff?" the hen-woman interrupted again.

"I met Boris a few times, though I'm sorry to say I never had the pleasure of working with him. The sort of film I was likely to be cast in was quite different from . . . I'm sorry, I seem to have forgotten your name."

"Sempill. Betty Sempill. What was he—Mr. Karloff—like? I can barely bring myself to call him mister. I always think of him as The Monster."

"*Au contraire.* He was the gentlest sort of man. Terribly shy, fond of children, that sort of thing. I believe it was Karloff—his real name was William Pratt and he was a British actor, by the way—I say, I believe it was Karloff's very gentleness that gave depth to his characterizations. We couldn't feel much sympathy for a monster if he was simply monstrous, now could we, Miss Milst?" He smiled at the young redhead with the moon-shaped eyebrows and the cleavage. She smiled back, as he knew she would, eyes uncertain, mouth ready, a creature so abjectly willing to please that she gave him a sharp though insubstantial predatory flash.

"I think Frankenstein's monster elicits our sympathies because he is someone's else's creature who has yearnings of his own," the mulatto sociology professor said slowly. "The monster has been created out of his master's vanity so the master cannot recognize the monster's humanity; therefore he cannot control him." He paused meaningfully, drawing on his pipe. Oh, Christ, Archie thought, this is the one who's going to talk about "Film."

"But how can anyone control a monster?" the perplexed Mrs. Sempill asked. "If you could control a monster, he wouldn't *be* a monster."

"Madam, if I may, I'd like to recommend a book to you," the mulatto went on in a strained, pedantic tone. "It's Kracaur's *From Caligari to Hitler,* and it traces the German psyche as shown in popular film from 1919 to the rise of the Reich. The schism of the mass mind, as portrayed in monsters and psychotics, is not unlike the collective neurosis manifest in current popular films made in the United States, though now the emphasis is on disaster and random violence. This mass neurosis . . ."

A chorus of discordant voices rose:

"What do you mean by collective neurosis?" Mrs. Shrimpton demanded.

" 'Cali' who?" the redhead wanted to know.

"But did you ever know Peter Lorre?" Betty Sempill persisted.

Mrs. Cleardon had been moving through her guests, simultaneously eavesdropping on several conversations, ready to douse any she deemed incendiary. "Archie," she said in a voice that was not to be denied. "You will allow me to call you Archie, won't you, Mr. Baron? I couldn't help but hear . . ." Mr. Edison, who'd had quite enough of his wife's nudging, moved aside to let Mrs. Cleardon enter the circle, ". . . what you were saying a moment ago. Mr. Karloff may have been entirely different from the monster he played, but there has always been something quintessentially 'you' in your characters. For example . . ." she touched Archie's arm and waved to the boy to bring another round of drinks, ". . . when you stayed behind and defended the Khyber Pass with just that handful of natives who were loyal to the Crown: I should be terribly disappointed to hear that there's no such courage in your own character. In fact," she added almost coquettishly, "I shouldn't believe you if you said there wasn't."

Archie executed a small bow. "Only a foolish man would reject the favorable opinion of a charming woman, even if that opinion is too charitable." As she smiled at his compliment, he stripped the years from her face, trying to imagine what she would have been like when young. Handsome rather than pretty, a bit like Phoebe, though with a much more conscious control over her expressions.

"I'm afraid I missed the film to which our hostess is referring," the sociology professor said. He had sensed his small audience's hostility, and determined to extend their captivity. "However, in a retrospective of German and Russian films that I was privileged to see while in London . . ."

"Oh, Clive," Mrs. Cleardon looked at him sympathetically, deftly removing the empty glass from his hand and replacing it with a full one, "you'll have to forgive us. Young men of your generation study the intellectual content of the films. In my time we just had fun going to the flicks. And what fun it was! We went every week, rain or shine. Sometimes we didn't even know what we were going to see. But I shall never forget Mr. Baron's—Archie's—performance in *Reign of Terror*. The part where he sacrificed himself and went to the guillotine so that the young woman might escape? There had to be a large part of you in that role, Archie, otherwise I shouldn't have believed it so completely. I shall never forget the first time I saw that picture. I was a mere slip of a girl . . ." Not according to my calculations, Archie thought. ". . . and when I came out of the theater, I just couldn't stop crying. That brave smile you had on your face as you went through the streets in the tumbrel! I shall never, never forget it."

"Strange that so many American films about the French Revolution identify with the plight of the aristocracy instead of the peasantry," Clive, not to be silenced with a mere glass of punch, said.

"Probably because the aristocracy had nicer costumes," the redhead said.

Archie laughed, thinking perhaps he'd underestimated the girl's wit; then, realizing that she'd made the remark in all seriousness, he smiled at her gently.

"*Reign of Terror?*" Betty Sempill's brow creased. "Wasn't

that the one about the child molester? I remember the scene where they dragged the lake for the victim's body. There was a water lily sticking out of his mouth."

"Dear heavens, Betty, you are confused," Mrs. Cleardon laughed, rolling her eyes to beg forgiveness from the other guests. "*Reign of Terror*, if you'd been listening . . ."

"*Reign of Terror* is what we had in Jamaica a few years ago," Mr. Edison roused himself to complain. "You weren't around then, Shrimpton, but let me tell you . . ."

". . . was about the French Revolution," Mrs. Cleardon insisted. "At the beginning of the picture, Archie plays an aristocrat who's a bit of a wastrel. You see, he's in love with this sweet young thing, but he's not worthy of her love. She . . ."

Sure that Mrs. Cleardon was going to recount the entire plot, Archie glanced across the room to where Ceci sat, her long legs slanted to the side because of the low couch, the light from the table lamp shining on her hair and shoulders. She was wearing a fifties-style white sheath dress. Her head moved from the man on her right to the man on her left, as though checking for traffic before crossing a street. The fact that her teeth held her lower lip was his only clue that she was suffering their conversation. He could remember her lip-biting habit from the days when she'd been allowed, on condition that she remain silent, to stay up for adult dinner parties. And what a little love she had been: decorously sipping her soup; asking "please may I be excused" over and over again on that dreadful night when Madeline and David Shecter had washed twenty years of dirty linen on the dining room table and decided to get a divorce. Why had he exposed her to such things? And why had he been so thoroughly rude to her that afternoon?

". . . so there was Archie, his cravat torn off, this fierce gleam in his eye, being carted through the streets of Paris while the girl was safely escaping in a coach and . . ." She surveyed her audience. Their expressions ranged from delighted attention (Mrs. Edison and the Milst girl) through polite interest (the Shrimptons and one of the Dragons who'd wandered past and mistaken the story for local gossip) to

undisguised boredom (Mr. Edison and Betty Sempill). Vivian
Nettleton's lips moved silently and her eyes betrayed that she
was listening to some internal monologue. The troublesome
Clive had wandered off. Archie Baron was smiling but peer-
ing through the crowd trying to catch someone's eye. ". . . and
who played the girl?" she asked, reeling him back in. "Was it
Sylvia Sidney? Faye Emerson? Do try one of these canapés."

Archie accepted a shrimp concoction and drew in his
breath. Listening to Mrs. Cleardon was rather like a ride in
an open car. He had a sense that, like many brisk and ample
talkers, she was at bottom a very secretive person. "Damned
if I remember her name," he muttered, then flushed, remembering that he'd spent a weekend with the girl. She'd had a
splotchy birthmark on her bottom and delightfully smooth
skin, but ". . . damned if I remember her name."

Through the roomful of posturing and languid bodies, Ceci
saw that Archie was looking at her. She ignored him, inclining her head toward the Israeli businessman on her right who
was answering the questions of the Canadian businessman on
her left. "We don't have the same problems you do. Here in
Jamaica, we hire mostly women, and they're very happy to
work for six to eight dollars a day."

"Are you growing crops for local consumption?" the Canadian asked.

The man shook his head vigorously. "No, no. We grow
fruit and exotic flowers for export only. A 747 picks them up
twice a week and they're on the streets in America within
forty-eight hours. And the government here is helping us."

"Yes. This administration has been very encouraging to
foreign investment. The subsidies . . ." The Canadian turned
to Ceci. "But I'm afraid we're boring Miss Baron."

"Not at all." She smiled at him. His face was as open as an
aquarium. She could virtually see his thoughts—What are
you doing here? What am I doing here? Are you available?—
swimming by. "But if you'll excuse me for a moment, I think
I'll make a trip to the ladies' room." As she got up she glanced
about, looking for Marsden. For some reason she felt it necessary to know his whereabouts at all times. He was standing
on the patio engaged in an intimate conversation with Dr.

Obfusky, a little man with thin legs, a rotund belly, and a face like a frog.

The Canadian rose with her, promising to save her seat and come up with a more amusing topic upon her return. She moved quickly through the room, overhearing snatches of conversation:

". . . that woman standing over there. Hit on the head. And in her own home . . ."

". . . business trip my eye, everyone knows that he's had a girl in Barbados for . . ."

". . . and so slow that I told him I might as well do the lawns myself . . ."

Her own well of polite conversation had all but dried up, and she felt a pleasant release as she moved into the darker, deserted passageway. Her face was burning up and her shoulders smarted. True, she had taken too much sun, but this felt like an internal fever. The drive into Montego had had all the acute awareness and disorientation of a dream. Percy, respectful of the Rolls, had driven at a crawl. At one point, sandwiched in between Vivian and Archie, Vivian's lavender perfume and Marsden's conversation polluting the air, a jeep had honked and passed them and her hand had involuntarily jerked toward the door. She'd wanted to jump out and thumb a ride. Things had not improved once they'd arrived at the party. Even as she smiled and talked and tossed her hair to catch the light, her social doppelgänger had perched on her shoulder whispering intuitions about everyone to whom she was introduced. Shrimpton, the man from the embassy, wore a beard and tilted his face upward to compensate for his weak chin, which in his case was telling of his character. He was anxiously tethered to his pretty wife, who smiled too brightly and nodded incessantly because she'd realized, too late, that if her husband was to get anywhere she would have to be the motive force behind his advancement. The colored member of Parliament (who complained that representatives of the previous administration had done business with their shirts open) continually fussed with his cuffs and tie, desperately hoping that clothes did make the man. His young secretary was in a state of speechless good behavior because she was sleeping with him. Lady Pembroke, the dowager who insistently refused a drink, had had a couple before she'd arrived. Old Edison had no real anger left in him but worked himself up into sputtering rages, subconsciously hoping to be carried off by a decisive paroxysm. She closed the bathroom door behind her. It was easier to be amused by the human comedy if she could distance herself from it for a few minutes.

She took a cigarette out of her purse and sat on the edge of the tub, wondering if her weaknesses had been as obvious to others as theirs were to her. For all her gloss and social grace, was it apparent that she was a weary drifter, desperately wanting something to turn her world on? She got up, wet a washcloth, and wiped it over her throat and shoulders. Turning off the faucets, she heard a soft but compelling patter of laughter coming from outside and moved to the window. It looked out on the circular driveway at the side of the house where the the drivers were waiting. Some lounged against the cars, smoking, others knelt beneath a single torch playing some sort of game, circled by nonparticipants who punctuated the players' gains and losses with giggles and playful slaps. The Nettletons' Rolls was parked up near the gate but she couldn't see Percy anywhere. Since the window was partially covered with vines and she knew she could not be seen, she brought her face close to the wire screen. As though on cue, the door of the Rolls opened and Percy got out, reaching back, offering his hand. A white woman in a flowing, brightly patterned caftan got out, her laughter loud enough to momentarily distract the men from their game. It was Gladys, the woman who had been introduced as Mrs. Cleardon's "companion." Ceci thought of "companion" in quotes because it was impossible to imagine Gladys writing letters, managing the staff, providing convivial conversation or doing any of the other things a companion might do, and Mrs. Cleardon was far too vital to need anyone to see to her personal needs. Was Gladys surrogate daughter, lover, or just some wandering soul who kept Mrs. Cleardon in touch with the younger generation? Or perhaps Mrs. Cleardon for all her verve and vivacity was simply lonely. So lonely that she didn't mind keeping a girl who crawled into cars with her guests' drivers.

There was a knock at the door. The handle was tried. Ceci ran a brush through her hair and went to open it. Gloria Milst rushed past her, hoisting up the skirt of her gold lamé dress. "Oh, I'm just about to burst. My teeth are floating," she cried as she reached the toilet. Ceci automatically shut the door, then opened it a crack, wondering if she could squeeze out. "Excuse me. I was just about to leave."

"Don't go. It's just us girls. Oh," Gloria stared at the wall, shaking her head. "I get so nervous at these parties. My bladder just kills me, but when I finally get to the toilet . . . maybe if you locked the door and turned on the faucet . . . I just can't tinkle."

Ceci turned on the faucet. She couldn't laugh at the baby talk. She'd met too many Glorias for that. She'd met them on yacht trips, at weekend house parties, at conventions. No one paid much attention to them or took them seriously. It was understood that they were the temporary companions of married men or confirmed bachelors, that they didn't have enough caché to ever be part of "the set." Their lives had been disrupted at seventeen when they'd won the hometown Miss Harvest or Miss Motorworld contest. Vistas of glamour and wealth had opened before them. They'd gone onto the state finals, nervously warbling through selections from *Carousel* or dancing the habañera in the talent contests, shrieking and crying as they, runners-up, showed goodwill by hugging the winner. Moved to the city and tried a career as a model. Ended up demonstrating video equipment or leisure vehicles at the coliseum shows. Posed for a centerfold with copy that said, "Though studying to be an archaeologist, my real desire is to be a wife and mother." No, she'd met too many Glorias to laugh at them. She brushed her hair again, waiting to hear the "tinkle." "It's best not to think about bodily functions," she said. "If you intellectualize breathing, for example, it's difficult to breathe. I expect it's the same with . . ."

"I'm not smart enough to think about anything, but I still can't tinkle. . . . I guess it's like men thinking about performing and not being able to. Like my . . . hey, what am I saying? I'm just a little drunk." She lowered her head until it almost touched her knees, her cascade of beautiful red hair entirely covering her face.

"Here." Ceci handed her the washcloth. "Perhaps if you put this on the back of your neck and kept your head down for a minute."

"I'm just . . . it's just . . ."

"There. There." Ceci crouched down next to her. "You're just upset. It'll pass."

"No, it won't." Her shoulders began to tremble.

"Sure it will. In a minute you'll be able to . . ."

"I'm not talking about *that*. He's going to leave me. I know he is. He's ashamed of me."

Ceci got up. If she'd retreated here to get some perspective on the human comedy she'd come to the wrong place. She looked at the woman, so abject, so miserable that she'd lost all control and was pouring her heart out to her, a stranger. Thank God I'll never be like that about a man ever again, she thought.

"Hey, don't pay any attention to me." The woman smiled up at her. "I'm just a little drunk and, like I said, parties always make me nervous. You won't . . ."

"Of course not. Maybe you'd be better if I gave you some privacy."

"I guess so. Thanks."

Ceci unlocked the door and closed it behind her. She had started back toward the living room but had only gone a few feet when Gladys, her eyes looking as though she'd gone round on a merry-go-round too many times, walked up to her. "Hey, hi. You're . . . ?" Gladys tucked her hair behind her ears and tried to focus.

"Cecily Baron."

"Sure. Yeah. We met a coupla hours ago. I remember now. Love your dress. It's so Marilyn. Monroe. Marilyn Monroe."

"Oh . . . yes."

"Your father was in the movies, right? Are you in the movies too?"

"I'm afraid not."

"Hey, don't be afraid. It cuts down your energy flow."

"It's just an expression."

"I know I know him but I can't remember his name."

"It's Archie. Archie Baron." Looking at Gladys more closely, she saw that she was several years older than she'd first taken her to be. Her hair style, round face, and the faint ghost of a lisp had made her appear younger.

"Yeah. That's it. Archie Baron. Say, wouldn't it be great to get some popcorn and pig out and watch old movies? That's my idea of a party. Not all this standin' around looking uncomfortable and wonderin' if you're making the right connection with the other person, know what I mean?"

"Mmmm." Ceci sketched an incomplete gesture with her hand, implying that she was about to move away.

"One thing that's hard to get here is popcorn," Gladys continued. "Bananas they got, but not popcorn." This observation seemed to plunge her into a deep depression. Her head drooped; her lower lip pouted. "Back home, you know, we always got popcorn in a can. That was my old man's idea of a high old time, popping popcorn on a Friday night. Expatriots, that's what we are. Just like in the twenties, you know."

"How long have you been down here?"

"Fifteen years. Came down to escape the winters and never went back."

Ceci nodded, wondering if the winters were all Gladys was escaping.

"Seems longer than fifteen years sometimes, know what I mean? But, 'Time is a river' and all that." She giggled, put her finger to her lips, and looked around as though she expected to find someone lurking in the hall. Moving down the passageway, she stopped before a door and motioned for Ceci to follow. "Hey, Marilyn, I can tell you're cool. Wanta have a joint?"

Drawn by curiosity, Ceci followed Gladys into a pastel and ruffled bedroom. Gladys pulled up the skirt of her caftan and took a plastic baggie full of ganja from her underpants. "This is my room," she said proudly. "Do you like it?"

"It's very pretty."

"It's safe, too. No one will come in." Opening the top drawer of a bureau, Gladys tossed in the bag, rummaged for a little satin pouch, and took a ready-made joint out of it. She lit up, inhaled, and made an exaggerated gesture of thumping her chest. "Just help yourself to that little shell-shaped ashtray on my dressing table." She wheezed with another inhalation, handed the joint to Ceci, and sat cross-legged on the bed. "I made that ashtray myself. Before I started working for Austin—Mrs. Cleardon—I used to make stuff for the gift shops. Shell things, African masks, that sort of stuff. It's important to have a creative outlet 'cause I have this sensitive streak, you know? Though now my main outlet is baking bread and arranging the flowers and like that. Austin's got a mind like a steel trap but she's not so good with her hands, you know?"

Ceci nodded. If she could put up with Gladys' verbal "you know?" tick at the end of every sentence, she could get her talking about anything. Especially if she first got her started talking about herself. "So you've been down here for fifteen years?"

"Yeah. When my brother Richard got back from 'Nam he was sorta strung out so I came down with him to, you know, straighten out his head. It was really cool down here those days. We hung out on the beaches at Negril, just sorta lived outta backpacks. Ol' Richard was used to living in a tent. He loved it. 'Course there weren't so many tourists here then."

"And did he get straightened out?"

"Who? Richard. Hey, too much. He works in a factory making missiles or something in Utah. And he's Born Again." This caused her another moment of morose reflection. "But I was already living with this guy down here, so I didn't go back, you know?"

Ceci put the joint to her lips but didn't inhale. She could imagine Richard and Gladys, two little vessels bobbing on the sea of life waiting to be filled up with whatever flotsam of belief came their way. Another nod brought forth a synopsis of Gladys' life on the island: three Jamaican boyfriends ("Great in the sack but, like, you know, not committed"), jobs as barmaid, desk clerk, and scuba instructor. A case of hepatitis. "But I'm a Cancer, so I gotta have a real home. That's why Austin took me in. She may not look like it, but she's got a real soft spot for anyone in trouble." Gladys took another toke and handed the joint back to Ceci. "Great smoke, huh?"

"Mmm. Hard to come by?"

"Are you kiddin'! They practically give it away. That whole bag only cost me five dollars. You know what that'd go for Stateside? The guy I get it from is so sweet. He's got these big, big eyes and these long, long legs. And he's got such a rough life. Really, you know?" Gladys nodded several times to emphasize her point. "Not only does he have to drive this bastard's car, but he has to sleep in this little tent up in the hills 'cause this bastard he's working for is growing a couple of hundred acres of the stuff and it's in this flatland surrounded by hills so you can only get to it from one road, and my friend, Percy, he's gotta guard this road. His boss has got cane planted all 'round the edges of the fields so's it looks, like, innocent, you know? Hey, are you all right? You look kinda sick or something."

"Fine. I'm fine." Her mind was clicking away at such a speed that it almost made her body shake. "Your friend's not afraid of getting busted?" she asked after a pause.

"Why? You must be kidding. Dope is the biggest cash crop on the island. Mostly the cops look the other way, unless they hold a grudge or something. Then they come after you. But Percy isn't exporting or anything. That's for the big guys. The big guys have got it sewed up. They harvest it by the ton and fly it into Miami. I hear they're expanding to coke now too. And they never get busted 'cause of who they know and who they pay off. It's like everything else. Them that's got shall get," Gladys said with an explosion of populist vehemence. "Don't get me wrong. My friend Percy doesn't steal it from his boss' fields. He's strictly on the up and up. He's got his own little plot—some quarter acre some ol' dude gave to his grandmother 'cause he fired his great-grandmother for stealing a piece of cake or something. It's quite a story. Anyhow, Percy farms this little plot. I mean, what's he supposed to do? Make a profit selling bell peppers?" Gladys inspected the roach, dropped it daintily into the ashtray and rolled off the bed. "What's say, Marilyn? Ready to go back to all the dull, respectable people?"

The draughts of air Ceci had been swallowing to help her control herself burst into hiccoughing laughter. It all seemed too incredible, yet it all fit into place: Marsden's annoyance at her presence; the question of where he was getting the money to rebuild the great house; Al Lupon . . .

"Hey, you okay?" Gladys joined her with a conspiratorial giggle. "You're laughin' now, aren't you, Marilyn? This ganja finally got to you, didn't it?"

"Oh, yes," Ceci continued to gasp and sputter. "Oh, yes. It surely did."

Eleven

Mrs. Cleardon sat at her shiny red piano playing "I'll Get By" while Clive turned the pages of the music and tried to harmonize his shaky tenor with her determined alto. Most of the guests had deserted the living room in favor of the patio or the billiard room. Betty Sempill had started the exodus by announcing her departure as though she were St. Joan being led to the stake. The majority of the old guard had straggled out after her, leaving Lady Pembroke (who was sitting bolt upright on the only straight-backed chair, head thrown back and eyes closed as though giving her full concentration to the music when, in fact, she had passed out) and the Edisons. They had sunk onto one of the low couches, and it appeared they might need a hoist to get them up. Edison's head periodically drooped onto his wife's shoulder, at which point she tried to rouse him but was repeatedly told to bugger off. Nayev Marouf had managed to lure a blonde who owned a swim shop in Ocho Rios behind some of the indoor shrubbery. A few serious drinkers sat at the bar. The Israeli, oblivious to the change of mood, was still booming about tariff regulations to the captive Canadian.

". . . as long as I have yo-oo-u." Mrs. Cleardon held the last note and looked around. The room was like an airport lounge at 3 A.M. Damn that Betty Sempill. Damn anyone whose victimization was their only means of getting attention. "Let's try something a bit more rousing, shall we, Clive?" She put aside her favorite (*English Music Hall Standards*), found *Musical Comedy Hits of the 40's*, and was about to strike the first note of "Happy Talk" when Cecily Baron came into the room. Her eyes were wide but had a guarded look. An ironic little smile played around her mouth. She took a drink from a passing tray and drank it down as if it were water. When she put the glass back and walked over to the Canadian, her face was blank, as though she'd consciously drained its expression just as she'd drained the glass. I'd like to get a look at that one's diary, Mrs. Cleardon thought. Such panache. But such a loner.

The Canadian got up and suggested they take a breath of air. Ceci let him guide her through the sliding glass doors.

Archie, Marsden, and the Shrimptons were lounging in deck chairs at the edge of the flagstones, facing the bay. The redhead, the girlfriend of the colored M.P., and a few of the younger folk were some distance from them, sitting on the edge of the pool, dangling their feet in the water.

"Well, there you are." Archie turned and smiled as Ceci approached. "I was wondering where you'd gotten to. Do join us, Mr. . . .?"

"Thomlinson," the Canadian said.

"Yes, do join us," Shrimpton seconded Archie's invitation and got up to pull two chairs into their circle.

"Where's Aunt Vivian?" Ceci asked, avoiding Marsden's glance.

"Here, my dear. I'm over here." Vivian was seated close to the house, in the shadow of the wall, with Dr. Obfusky. "I've been having a little talk with the good doctor."

Ceci walked over to her aunt and put her arm around her.

"Mrs. Pinto's been telling me about her garden," Obfusky said, his eyes popping with secret meaning.

"Won't you come over and join us instead?" Ceci asked.

Vivian shook her head. "No. No. They're having some sort of argument, and you know how I hate disagreements."

"No argument a'tall, old thing," Archie called across to her. "Just a discussion."

Obfusky shifted his chair so that his back was toward the group. "And apart from your garden, Mrs. Pinto, what else do you do to occupy yourself?" Ceci wasn't pleased by the professional solicitude in his voice.

"But the garden is quite enough, Doctor. Quite enough," Vivian insisted. "If you'd ever done battle with aphids and moths and ants, you'd know that it's a full-time job. And a defeating job. My own Sisyphian fate, if you will. Because it's the small things that defeat us, don't you think? The unkind word. The heedless gesture. The insects. I dream of a heaven that's colorless as an icicle and cold as Lapland, far away from this constant warm smell of growth and decay." She sighed, pulled her shawl closer to her throat, and touched Ceci's hand. "Do go and join the younger people, Ceci."

Ceci patted her shoulder and moved back to the group. She couldn't help staring at Marsden. He was puffing his little cigar and looking out into the bay with almost sentimental dreaminess. Had she expected to find him wrapped in a long black cape and smelling of sulphur? It seemed wrong that evil didn't have a particular face: that it was only after the fact that one "saw" it. Years ago at a cocktail party, Paul had pointed out a roly-poly man with twinkling eyes. She would have pegged him as the proprietor of a chain of food stores, the sort of man who played Santa Claus at Rotary Club Christmas parties. Paul had told her that the man was the most highly placed KGB agent ever to defect to the West. And wasn't it always the baby-faced boy the neighbors said was shy and kind to his mother who turned out to be the mass murderer? And when you saw the front page, did the embezzler or the dictator really look much different from the Nobel Prize winner before you read the caption?

"Miss Baron?" Thomlinson was still standing, waiting for her to sit down.

"Oh, I'm sorry . . ." She settled herself. Shrimpton's chair scraped the flagstones. Mrs. Cleardon could be heard fumbling over a passage, recovering herself and playing on. The sleigh-bell laughter of the younger women drifted from the pool. Thomlinson cleared his throat. "I hope we haven't interrupted your conversation."

" 'The angel of silence is passing over us,' " Archie said; and after a pause, "That quote's from Chekhov."

" 'The natives are restless tonight.' What's that from?" Mrs. Shrimpton asked.

"I think there's some sort of concert over in town," Thomlinson volunteered.

Mrs. Shrimpton laughed, baring small white teeth that shone in the moonlight. "No, no. That's not what I meant. 'The natives are restless' is a quote from some old movie. I wouldn't refer to the Jamaicans as natives," she added, thinking she might have been insensitive.

"But they are," Archie smiled. "For that matter, I am, too."

"What I meant was . . ."

"Yes. I can hear it now." Shrimpton held up his hand and cocked his head. The others fell silent, listening to the faint thrump of drumbeats from across the bay. Ceci mentally transported herself, wishing she were with that throng, dancing to the driving reggae. " 'The people in the cheaper seats can clap your hands. The others, just rattle your jewelry,' " she said.

"What's that?" Mrs. Shrimpton asked.

"It's something John Lennon said at a Royal Command Performance," Ceci answered.

Shrimpton grunted. "I wonder how long they'll keep it up."

"Most likely till dawn," Thomlinson said. "They get stoned, you know. They can keep it up for all hours."

"Ah, yes." Archie shifted in his chair. His actor's ear was so tuned to the pauses and apparent strain of the conversation that he felt obliged to move it along. "As a matter of fact, we were talking about this drug trafficking thing when you joined us. Shrimpton here was giving us the lowdown on some policy problems, weren't you, Shrimpton?"

"Really?" Thomlinson inclined his head to Shrimpton, encouraging him. "Please go on. That is, if it's not top secret."

"Not if you read *The New York Times*," Shrimpton chuckled. "We've been getting the heat from certain representatives at home who have to deal with drug traffic in their states. Particularly from some Republican woman in Florida who's screaming holy hell about the corruption of our youth. Frankly we're between a rock and a hard place. Jamaica is our ally, and we don't want to undermine the fellow who's in now. To tell you the truth, I didn't even realize how much dope was coming into the States until I read this recent report."

Thomlinson looked at him quizzically, wondering if he was hopelessly uninformed or feigning ignorance. Mrs. Shrimpton caught the look and rushed to her husband's defense. "It's not the sort of thing one studies in the diplomatic corps, is it? Of course, we knew these Rastafarians consider it a sacrament, or say they do. But I didn't realize that fifty percent of the population here is smoking marijuana before they're into their teens."

"Mmmm," Thomlinson nodded. "There'd be tremendous economic dislocation if you really tried to stop it. It's the country's largest export crop. Has a billion and a half wholesale value on the Miami market. Officials here may publicly deplore it, but do you think you have the power to force them to crack down?"

"That remains to be seen." Shrimpton toyed with his swizzle stick. "We're going to drop about two hundred thousand dollars into a campaign for crop substitution. It seems the Jamaican government is willing to cooperate."

"At least to the extent of accepting your two hundred thousand," Thomlinson said with a smile. "That, as you would say, is a nice piece of change. But then you Americans are always . . . generous, aren't you?"

Shrimpton bristled. "It's not a matter of generosity. If they're flooding our country with marijuana or whatever the hell they call it down here . . ."

"Ganja," Ceci said softly. The laughter that had exploded in Gladys' room threatened to burst out again. "It's a Hindi word," she added, looking at Marsden. "It was originally brought to Jamaica by Indian indentured workers."

Mrs. Shrimpton signaled to a passing waiter. "I heard you talking before, Miss Baron. You seem to know a lot about Jamaica. I'd enjoy it if we could have lunch sometime."

"Besides the crop substitution program, we're going to

have the cooperation of Jamaican law enforcement and possibly the Jamaican army," Shrimpton went on. "We're not going to violate anyone's civil rights, of course, but we're going to use explosives to blow holes in the dirt airfields, and intercept boats on the coastline and destroy the fields."

"Sounds like a bit of an uphill task, old boy," Archie said.

Thomlinson nodded. "I agree. I was at the Pegasus last week—"

"The what?" Archie asked.

"The Pegasus. It's *the* hotel in Kingston. You might call it the real seat of power in Jamaica. Certainly there's more action there than there is in Parliament. I was attending some meetings sponsored by one of your agencies, the Overseas Private Investment Corporation . . ."

"Then you must know our friend Chuck Kronenburg," Mrs. Shrimpton said quickly as the waiter approached.

"I may have met him."

"Why don't you just leave the pitcher here?" she smiled at the waiter. "We'll go for broke." She ran her hand through her short brown curls. "It's taken me no time to become addicted to this punch. Tastes like fruit juice, but as my granddaddy would say, it packs a wallop. May I pour?" There were grunts, requests, and one refusal (Marsden's) on the refills. Mrs. Shrimpton sipped, gave an audible sigh of satisfaction, and, seeing that the waiter had moved out of earshot, said, "Excuse me for interrupting you, Mr. Thomlinson. You were saying . . ."

"About the meetings at the Pegasus. Yes. They were very optimistic. Very optimistic. But then the electricity went out in the hotel . . ."

"Hell," Shrimpton waved his hand dismissively. "That's a regular occurrence."

"But one you can't take too lightly if you have a factory to run. At any rate, after the conference I left the hotel—against the advice of several people—and wandered about in West Kingston. The ganja was as thick as fog. You could get a contact high just from walking the streets."

"You are an adventurous soul," Mrs. Shrimpton teased.

"Yes. Rather more adventurous than I'd thought at the

time. I stopped when I got to a ghetto called Trench Town. By that time I was passing myself off as a reporter. Then I wandered in Coronation Market. It's one of the most dispiriting places I've ever seen. Rubbish everywhere, flies, stray dogs, potbellied children without shirts or shoes, people actually living on the streets . . ."

Shrimpton shifted in his chair. "You'll see that in any Third World country," he said with a touch of condescension.

"I'm familiar with Third World countries. I've traveled quite a lot," Thomlinson answered quietly. "And as I was saying, from Trench Town I could see the mansions of Beverly Hills."

Archie leaned forward. "Beverly Hills?"

"Yes. There is actually a sort of country club neighborhood in the hills that's called Beverly Hills. But down in the Coronation Market—I didn't like what I saw and heard. There's anger and restlessness and racial hostility. It's all very well to hear optimistic speeches about ambitious redirection of the economy when you're sipping drinks on the eighteenth floor, but the mood closer to the ground, plus the vocal labor movement and the high shipping costs . . . well, I feel bound to tell my company that I advise disinvestment."

"You'd do well to give that further consideration." Marsden had been silent for so long that it appeared he'd dropped out of the conversation, so he was able to galvanize their attention without even turning around. "Real profits are rarely made in a risk-free situation, Mr. Thomlinson, despite what they may have taught you at business school. You have witnessed some unpleasantness, but that doesn't mean that the country is about to explode. There is no real drive toward revolutionary change here. At least," he flicked the ash from his little cigar and turned toward them, "no more than you'd find in the Dominican Republic. Or even certain sections of Detroit. If 'religion is the opiate of the masses;' here in Jamaica opiates are also the religion of the masses. And addicts make very poor revolutionaries."

"I don't pretend to know anything of present conditions, but if they're as bad as Thomlinson here thinks they are . . ." Archie said. Marsden's superior tone annoyed him. He judged

Thomlinson to be a decent and intelligent sort who was too
gentlemanly to come to his own defense. "Back in the thirties
there was a good bit of unrest. . . ."

"A few shots fired on the Frome estate. But let me ask you:
Is the Frome estate still here? Of course it is. Mere discontent
doesn't make for change," Marsden said slowly, as though
giving a lecture to students who had trouble taking notes.

"But discontent fosters change," Ceci heard herself say
with more heat than she'd intended. "If people are miserable,
they must make changes. Imagine living in a lean-to with a
dirt floor and no running water or electricity. Imagine knowing that your children aren't going to learn to read and write.
And look at the parallels, even in one's personal life. You go
on, sometimes for years, drifting, putting up with, denying,
lying to yourself . . . and then one day something snaps. You
know you'll have to do something or else admit that you're
hopeless, good for nothing, not in control of your own des-
tiny, and . . ." She felt as though she'd started to undress in
front of strangers. Though she knew she shouldn't have anymore, she took another swallow of her drink.

"But then what?" Marsden's eyes hovered between her
brow and the bridge of her nose and came to rest on her
throat. "You fall back into the old habits, don't you? That's
so much easier. And there are so many pleasant diversions
here. Ganja, promiscuous sex, sunshine every day, and all
these lovely hills and beaches. It's rather like living in South-
ern California, eh, Ceci?"

Ceci's hand tightened around her glass. She wanted to
throw her drink at him and watch it drip down the waxy
planes of his face. She took another swallow.

"And," Marsden went on, "there are other safety valves for
Jamaicans. Immigration, for example. Those with any get-
up-and-go do just that. They 'go a foreign.' How many Jamaicans have you met in London, or New York, or in your own
country, Mr. Thomlinson? Those who remain . . ." he gestured with his little cigar, ". . . well, they may listen to revolutionary rhetoric but they have no revolutionary plan. When
the people here think of socialism, they think of it as less work

and a bigger handout, and the barrel just isn't deep enough to have handouts for everyone."

"Well, surely the effects of slavery—" Mrs. Shrimpton began.

"One of the effects of slavery," he cut her off, "is to look out for number one. If we go back in history, to the Maroons, for example—they were slaves who escaped into the hills and set up their own primitive social structure, but when the British government decided to come down on them, they had to capitulate. They put up a rather interesting fight, but the treaty they finally signed required that they return runaway slaves to the plantations. 'Give me what I want and I won't care about the others.' Perhaps not a commendable trait in human nature; but a remarkably consistent one. No, the natives don't really want change. They want more. More transistors, more designer jeans, more television sets. That's what they want and that's what we can help them to get, isn't it, my dear?"

Mrs. Shrimpton stiffened. "I've heard your arguments before, Mr. Baron. They seem irrefutable because they're so callously cynical. But as Miss Baron was saying, there must be a desire for change. I only wish our government could be on the right side for a change, instead of propping up people who are dedicated to the status quo because they want our dollars. I think—"

"Let's put it this way, my dear: the United States will not permit a government it doesn't like to exist on this island."

"I don't appreciate your constant interruptions," Mrs. Shrimpton said testily, "And I am not 'your dear.'"

Marsden's features sharpened. "There's no need to get emotional, Mrs. Shrimpton. I should have thought you'd be pleased to hear that I don't expect rape and pillage on the island."

"You've been away from the States too long, Baron," Mr. Shrimpton smiled. "Women don't appreciate being addressed in that way anymore."

"But we often are," Ceci said. "Especially in arguments about the unchangeability of human nature. Then it's always 'my dear' and 'let's not get emotional.' It's a way of shutting people up."

"If I've offended, then I apologize." Marsden tilted his head to Mrs. Shrimpton and twisted his mouth into a smile. "I'm extremely fond of the fair sex, but you ladies do have a way of derailing a conversation. And we were talking about Jamaica."

Archie pulled himself up to his full height and put down his glass. "The entire point of conversation is that it can't be derailed unless it's theatrical dialogue. Conversation is supposed to bounce along like a tennis ball, like . . ." he struggled to come up with something that would take the onus off Marsden's caddish remarks, ". . . like that song our hostess is playing now. From *South Pacific*, isn't it? Perhaps we should go in and enjoy the music." He rose to his feet. Thomlinson got up with him and stood behind Ceci's chair. "Good idea."

"Consider what I've said, Thomlinson," Marsden drawled. "There may be some violence on the island, but it will be random, mostly directed at their fellows and easily quelled."

"Your opinion will be taken under advisement," Thomlinson said. He often wrote these words on interoffice memos he planned to ignore, and he hoped his tone conveyed a similar dismissal.

There was another embarrassed pause as Thomlinson and Ceci walked away.

"Always wanted to be in a musical but I was too tall and too stiff to be a good dancer." Archie executed a bit of a soft-shoe and looked about. Marsden was facing the bay again, his face as smug as the boy who'd robbed the jam jar. Shrimpton was reaching for his wife's hand, but she pretended not to notice his touch. Lord, Archie thought, I wouldn't have listened to that blighter Shrimpton's opinions if I'd known him to be such a fool. No matter how much women may change, they aren't going to give themselves to men who let them be insulted. If Shrimpton sleeps on the couch tonight, he damned well deserves it. "Now I remember that song." He hummed a few bars and offered his arm to Mrs. Shrimpton. "It's called "There Is Nothin' Like a Dame." And you mustn't be offended by that, Mrs. Shrimpton," he caressed her with his eyes, half flirting, half wanting to soothe. "It's a slang expression in America, but in England it's equivalent to a knight's title. Originally it meant the woman who was in authority in a household and . . ." Seeing her thaw enough to permit touch, he reached for her hand.

"Are you sure there's no Irish blood in you, Mr. Baron?" she asked as he led her away. "I can't help thinking you've kissed the Blarney Stone."

"Women." Shrimpton laughed uncomfortably. He drained his glass and started to get to his feet.

"Wait up, Shrimpton."

"Sir?" There was a faint touch of sarcasm in his voice, but he lowered himself back into his chair and pulled it closer to Marsden's.

"Now that we have a few minutes to talk, you might tell me what this narcotics squad is up to," Marsden said.

"I know what you know. They're morons."

"I meant their M.O., not their character. I know they're morons."

"It's already in the works. I thought Fat Jack would have talked to you."

"He has," Marsden lied. He put down his cigar and reached over, refilling their glasses, settling back and waiting to see if Shrimpton would pick up the drink—Shrimpton's fourth, he calculated, though he'd only been keeping track since Shrimpton had come onto the patio so . . . at least his fourth. "Here's to it." He raised his own glass.

" 'Up the Republic,' " Shrimpton obliged.

Yes, at least Shrimpton's fifth. Marsden brought his glass to his lips but didn't drink. "Going to rain," he said offhandedly. Contempt for Shrimpton and his kind constricted his throat. They were soft and ignorant. Prep schoolboys whose fathers' connections ensured them the best overseas posts. Boys who wore beards and read Regis Du Bray and Franz Fanon and were married to loudmouthed, liberal wives. Boys who'd gone to language school but had never lived in a hootch or loaded a gun. Boys who couldn't handle their liquor.

"Doesn't look like it's going to rain."

"Take my word for it. I've been down here a couple of years, you know."

"I know what I read in my mail. Despite what you Company boys think, we're not that loose at State." Shrimpton thrust his chin forward and chug-a-lugged like someone out of a Clint Eastwood movie.

Marsden leaned closer. "So what coast do we start the window dressing on?"

"Oh, this one." Shrimpton burped.

Ceci and Thomlinson had walked to the far end of the patio and stood beneath one of the torches that marked the edge of the flagstones. "Seems we can't get any farther away unless we're willing to swim," he said. She nodded, looking out into the bay and taking deep breaths. "Are you feeling all right?" he asked.

"I think so. I just had too much sun today and too many rum punches tonight and . . ."

". . . and sometimes one can feel claustrophobic even out-of-doors."

"Depending on the company."

"Depending on the company, yes." The mutual understanding in their smiles encouraged him to lead her under the branches of the sea grape. She leaned against the trunk, still breathing deeply, listening to the piano.

"I'm sorry you're only visiting," he said, putting his hand above her head and watching the shadows play across her face. "Though judging from your brother's behavior, it's probably just as well. Does he always have such an overbearing manner?"

"He's my half-brother," she corrected, then shrugged. "Not that that matters. And yes, his perverse streak is usually in evidence." A great gust of wind roiled the waves and all but extinguished the torches. A flash of lightning drew shrieks from the crowd around the swimming pool. Through the swaying branches, Ceci could see them running for cover. Vivian was scanning the sky, while Dr. Obfusky tried to shepherd her into the house. Marsden and Shrimpton got up reluctantly and followed Obfusky and Vivian through the sliding glass doors as a light patter of rain came down.

"I suppose we'd best go in," Thomlinson said.

"Mmm. The weather has come to our rescue. We can finish off the evening early."

"I didn't want it to end so quickly." He moved closer to her. "I have the use of a company house and I'll be staying on for another month. There's plenty of room there. If you'd like to visit." He drew his card out of his wallet.

"I'm not the orphan of the storm," she said, though she felt as though she were just that. "Mrs. Cleardon has asked me to stay, and I think I'll rent a car tomorrow and drive about the island by myself."

"I don't mean to be an alarmist, but you should exercise some caution about where you go."

"Oh, I'll be careful. And I expect I'll leave in a few days anyway."

"Where for?"

She shrugged. "New York, I suppose. But I do appreciate your offer. It's very kind of you."

"Not really. It's obvious that I'm attracted to you and I'd like to get to know you better, isn't it?"

"Yes. It is." A smile softened her features. He kissed her smoothly and lightly and she kissed him back. His loneliness was plain and simple as an unpainted picket fence. She had known a few such men—decent, uncomplicated—and from time to time she'd been grateful for their company. But only for a time. Then their very normality, their desire for permanence had become "neti neti." Not this, she'd said to herself at twenty-six and thirty-one, not monogamy instead of freedom, not security instead of passion, not meals on time and the life insurance paid up. But would she, at forty, be sorry that she hadn't settled for and settled in? Though she felt no disloyalty to Max by being in this stranger's arms, his kiss made her miss Max, really miss him, with catch in the throat emotion, for the first time.

They broke off as if by mutual agreement. She let her head rest against his chest. His shirt had a clean, starchy smell. The hairs at his open collar tickled her nose. She pulled back, scratching it. "I'd like to be alone for a bit, do you mind?"

"But it's going to rain."

"Not yet. That was just a warning flash. See," she disengaged herself, moved from under the tree and held out her hand. "It's just spitting."

"All right then. But don't stay out here too long."

"I won't."

He went in ahead of her. She passed the table and poured herself another glass of punch, then settled into the chair Vivian had occupied. It was close to the wall, and by shifting it slightly she was shadowed by the awning but able to hear and see the entire panorama of the disintegrating party through the open glass doors. Bodies were strewn about like the last scene of *Hamlet*—Mr. Edison sound asleep on Mrs. Edison's lap; the blonde who owned the swim shop was in the pose of an odalisque with Nayef Marouf sprawled at her feet playing with her toes; the M.P.'s girlfriend flat on her stomach, displaying an impressive backside; Gladys reclining on a heap of pillows, toying with a pineapple rind and telling Mrs. Shrimpton, who sat cross-legged in front of her, that she had "the munchies." Marsden and Shrimpton stood at the bar, ignoring the wreckage. The stalwarts who were still on their feet had gathered around the piano.

"Do give us a solo, Gloria," Mrs. Cleardon encouraged. "I could tell on that last that you have a trained voice."

Gloria dimpled but shook her head. "Just a few lessons. Semi-classical."

"Don't be shy. Give it a go," Archie said. "It's not an audition, you know."

Clive knocked out his pipe. "Compromise," he suggested, wiping some ash from his trousers. "You sing it through once, we'll join in on the second chorus." He gave a last wobbly nod to pedantry. "Compromise: the art of the possible."

Mrs. Cleardon tested for the right key. Gloria clasped her hands in front of her and squared her shoulders. "If you really want me to," she said in a twelve-year-old's voice. They all agreed that they did.

" 'Hey, listen, sister . . .' " She began on a quavering note, all nerves and expectation of failure.

> *'I love my Mister Man,*
> *And I can't tell you why,*
> *Hey, listen, sister . . .'*

Her hands clenched and unclenched. Her eyes flitted about seeking, as her old music teacher had told her to seek, a single person in the audience who would help her to focus her energy. " 'I love my Mister Man . . .' " Settling on Marsden, she found her voice and began to croon " 'Fish gotta swim/ Birds gotta fly . . .' " with the abandonment of a seasoned chanteuse. Marsden turned his back but continued to watch her in the mirror above the bar. She raised her eyes a fraction, singing to his image in the mirror, until he shook hands with Shrimpton and moved to the patio door. She faltered, her confidence seeping from her until she stopped in midphrase. "I . . . I can't remember the rest," she said almost inaudibly.

"Come on, everybody," Mrs. Cleardon urged. "We all know this one."

"The men too?" Archie asked while she vamped.

"Yes. Men too," Mrs. Cleardon insisted.

"I did go to an English public school," Archie joked, "I suppose I can manage it." Amidst general laughter that eased them into the next chorus, Gloria moved away from the piano and came to the patio doors.

Ceci stiffened and remained perfectly still. Marsden walked past her without noticing her. She took a sip of her drink and watched Gloria trail him to the deck chairs.

"You haven't talked to me all night," Gloria choked.

"I know you've spent much of your life in cheap bars, Gloria, but it isn't necessary to entertain at private parties."

"What did I do?" Her mouth gaped and her eyes opened so wide that her moon-shaped brows disappeared under her bangs. "They *asked* me to sing."

"And you do what people ask you to do, don't you. Don't

you?" He said it almost gently, running his hands down her arms, then, with a quick movement, pinioning them behind her. She whimpered and lowered her head.

Whatever he said to her was drowned out by applause and requests for another song, but Ceci was glad she couldn't hear what he was saying because she guessed what it must be. She could see that his contempt had made his body taut and sharpened his features into something resembling lust; that Gloria, limp as a kitten, was begging his forgiveness. Her stomach turned. As Mrs. Cleardon started to hammer away at "Knees Up, Mother Brown," she got up, wanting to go inside but galvanized by the spectacle. Marsden let go, almost dropping the girl. Gloria, massaging her arms, limped to the far end of the patio. Marsden watched her go, hitched at the belt of his pants, wrists turned upward, like a young tough, then spun around.

He had advanced a few steps before he saw Ceci. He smiled as though nothing had happened. "I suppose you're out here because you prefer the native music from across the bay," he said. He reached for her arm. "I think we're ready to go home now."

She flung her drink in his face.

Watching him blink, seeing the punch drip down his cheeks, she mirrored the amazement on his face. She'd had no idea she was going to do it, yet her gesture had a certain inevitability, like the reflexive jerk of her knee when hit by the doctor's little hammer.

"There you are. Both of you!" Vivian stepped out onto the patio and moved between them, looking from one to the other. "I've just sent Mrs. Cleardon's houseboy all over the property to look for you. I do apologize for interrupting your conversation but . . ." she drew a handkerchief from the sleeve of her dress, turning to Ceci, ". . . but I'm quite fagged out. I'm afraid I shall have to ask the Edisons to take me home if you wish to stay on with the merrymaking. Here, Marsden." She handed him the handkerchief without looking at him. "Now, Ceci, what shall it be? Are you staying the night? I really think you should. That girl of Mrs.

Cleardon's—the one in the Arab robe that's made out of curtain material—she was telling me how much she enjoyed your company so. . . ."

"Yes. I believe I will stay." Ceci turned, bent down, and put the empty glass on the flagstones.

"Just for the night, of course. We're having visitors to tea tomorrow and Marsden . . ." Vivian turned. "I do believe he's walked off. Probably gone to fetch Percy. So . . . tomorrow afternoon? Tea at four? Won't that be fun?"

Twelve

Ceci woke, hot and dizzy, in a room of polar glamour. Everything save the cluster of red hibiscus on the writing table was white—white circular bed, vertical blinds, easy chairs, tile. She held her neck stiffly, turning her head to the night table, looking for a clock. No clock. But a container of cigarettes and cigars and three books: a history of the West Indies, an update on the tax and shipping code, and the confessions of an aging actress. She stretched, listening to the whooshing sound of the surf, and got up, walking slowly to the bar. The refrigerator was stocked with the usual mixers and she poured herself a glass of grapefruit juice, her favorite wake-up drink. After a few sips she came to full consciousness, but what she saw in her mind's eye—the punch dripping down Marsden's face—was as bad as the nightmare that had roused her. She took a last gulp, hoping to quell her nausea. For all her disgust with Archie, hadn't she behaved exactly as she'd seen him and his friends behave? Drinking too much, carrying on with Thomlinson, causing a scene. She peeked through the blinds, saw that it was later than she'd thought, and retreated to the bathroom. Here, too, was everything a guest in a four-star hotel could require— sauna, bath and shower, shampoos, makeup and lotions, a hair dryer, even a bidet. "Bless you, Mrs. Cleardon," she thought as she lay on the cedar plank, sweating out her hangover, "you're the one who should be innkeeper to the world." Cleaned, powdered, and perfumed, she was surprised at how good she felt, and as she zipped up her dress she remembered her friend Maya's line: "You don't *have* a body; you *are* a body."

Thinking she might disturb the household, she carried her high heels and slipped out of the door. Azure bay, golden sun, purple bougainvillea, and no one about. She passed the swimming pool and there, on the terrace, sat Mrs. Cleardon in a too-youthful eyelet dressing gown, her face already made up, even to the false lashes, her foot propped on the retaining wall, clipping her toenails. "Ceci, good morning. Sleep well? We're the first up. Would you like a dip in the pool? No, I see you've already put yourself together. Ready for breakfast?" All this in a hushed, solicitous voice. "No? Then do sit down." She reached over to the table next to her and placed her finger on the button of a blender. "Put your fingers in your ears, dear." Ceci obeyed. It seemed impossible not to obey Mrs. Cleardon. "There," Mrs. Cleardon said, pouring the creamy, apricot-colored mixture into a glass. "Take some of this. It's my special blend. Papaya juice, egg, coconut milk, ginseng, vitamins B and C, and just a *soupçon* of rum. Fix you up in no time." Ceci sat down, smiling at this Mother Superior of the Order of Overindulgence. "Thanks, Mrs. Cleardon."

"Call me Austin. I'm so glad we have a few moments to ourselves." In answer to Ceci's questioning look, she explained, "The minister of tourism and his girlfriend stayed over. In separate rooms, of course." She sucked in her cheeks and arched her brows. "Adjoining separate rooms. And Gladys is always a late sleeper. And then there's Gloria—do you remember her? Pretty, redheaded girl. The one who was singing. But you weren't in on the singing, were you?"

"No. I was . . . catching a breath of air." She drank down half of the concoction. She didn't want to be around when any of the others made their appearances.

"Yes," Mrs. Cleardon sighed. "I was up with Gloria after everyone had left. She's going through a very bad time. It's sad when you see a girl like that. She really doesn't want much out of life. She doesn't even want to be rich; she just wants to be married and have someone take care of her. But there you are. It never helps to set one's sight on a single thing, does it? Some men take advantage when a girl seems innocent; then again, some men take advantage when she seems experienced, on the grounds that she can take care of herself. Little Gloria has the worst of both worlds—she's both vulnerable and experienced. An unhappy combination. Especially if the I.Q. doesn't go into three digits, and the man she's involved with isn't the honorable sort." She scanned Ceci's face to see if Ceci would admit that she knew what was being talked about. A quick glance of understanding passed between them. "You should have been an actress, my dear," Mrs. Cleardon went on. "On film, I should think. Only the camera captures the subtleties."

"Archie wanted me to be. Or at least he wanted me to do something that would put me in the limelight. When I was sent back to Hollywood, he brought this woman home. Even at sixteen I could see she wasn't the sort who'd turn him on. She was there to devote her attention to me. She taught me how to walk and talk, how to wear my hair. Archie devoted himself to instructing me in what he called "the noble craft" of acting. He taught me how to read blank verse without taking a breath and all that. He didn't want me to be some Hollywood tart. I was supposed to be cultured and, through his contacts, go to the top of the line without compromising myself. He pushed me into a small part on some TV show. All I was supposed to do was look pretty and say about five lines, but I didn't recognize myself after they'd put on my makeup, and the first time I went on the set I missed my marks. The director called out not to worry, let's try another take. I tried again and I missed the marks again. He said try again, a little less patiently the second time. The third time he yelled 'time is money.' I managed to hit my marks and get my five lines out. Then I went and had dry heaves in the dressing room. Archie wanted so much to play Pygmalion to my Galatea; but it was too late."

"I understand perfectly," Mrs. Cleardon said. "Too bad. You do have a natural talent. But back to Gloria. I told her

I thought the situation here was hopeless and that it was high time she went back to the States. Don't you agree?"

"I do. Will she take your advice?"

"I think so. By the way, you're welcome to stay on as long as you like. You can see that there's scads of room. Staying with relatives can try one's patience, and I have several friends who'd adore to meet you."

"Thank you. That's very kind. But I think I must leave. I'd like to go and rent a car. That would at least give me some independence of movement. Might I have someone drive me to get one?"

"The airport's the best bet. In fact, I'll drive you there myself. I know the woman who runs the rental agency and I can get you a discount. And while I'm there, I might just see about a ticket for Gloria."

"You're very considerate of your friends."

Mrs. Cleardon got up. "My dear, at my age the possibilities of pleasure become somewhat more limited. One has to turn one's efforts to social service and you can hardly picture me whipping up a cake for a church bake sale or soliciting for a scholarship fund, now can you?"

Ceci grinned. "No. I think you've found your *métier.*"

"I'll be back in a flash."

She was, carrying a flowered shirt, which she handed to Ceci. "You'd best put this on. Too early for décolletage and you're sunburned to boot."

"You think of everything."

Mrs. Cleardon left her in the airport parking lot, slapping the fender of her rented Toyota and reiterating her invitation to come again. Ceci stopped at a service station, apalled at the price of gasoline and the slowness of the attendent, then drove into Montego Bay. Because it was early, and a Sunday, the town was quiet. A few hawkers, mostly children, were already on the streets with their coconuts, bags of cashews, and newspapers. They ran up to the car, shouting for her to buy, and the sight of them, barefoot and big-eyed, offering up their paltry wares, filled her with such despair that after stopping to give them her loose coins—which brought another group of children to the car as though they were flies lighting on a

piece of fruit—she stepped on the accelerator and drove out
of town as fast as the Toyota would go.

Once she'd started the climb into the hills, she slowed again.
The car felt just the right size, seeming to wrap around her,
making her feel both free and protected. Still, she could not
rid herself of unease. Victim as she was to so many decep-
tions, cover-ups and half-truths, and feeling an obligation to
set things right but having no real idea of how she might do
so, it was no wonder that she suffered from a sense of unreal-
ity. She concentrated on her surroundings. The road, curvy
and narrow, had a calming effect, and from the green intensity of the forest, flowers trumpeted their color. Despite the
previous night's ruckus, as she approached the village she felt
almost content. She would make one last attempt with Archie, putting everything she knew before him, making peace
with him as best she could. And if nothing came of that, she
would drive to Kingston, perhaps spend a few days with
David Thomlinson, and leave the island.

She passed an empty schoolhouse with a parched play-
ground. The road swerved sharply again near the shallows of
the waterfall. There were no women washing clothes today,
but on a scrub ground three boys were improvising a cricket
pitch. She down-shifted as she approached the crest of the
hill, and the miniature spire of the pink stucco church came
into view. A zestful rendition of "All Things Bright and
Beautiful" rang out through the open doors and windows. A
pregnant woman with a baby on her hip stood on the wooden
steps singing along, and as Ceci passed she too joined in
". . . all creatures great and small." As she rounded another
curve, she saw a red sports car with a crowd of people around
it stopped smack in the middle of the road.

Her foot sought the brake but hit the accelerator. She
swerved to the shoulder, grabbing the hand brake and yanking it up. The car jerked to a stop, bouncing her forward so
that her stomach mashed into the steering wheel. Breathing
hard, she squinted through the windshield, waiting for someone to acknowledge her near-accident, but the crowd was so

intent that they didn't seem to notice. Legs weak with fright, she got out and started up the hill toward them.

A young white couple dressed in L.L. Bean camping outfits were backed up against the sports car. Eight or ten blacks, mostly children, clustered around them. They were all focused on the ground—on what Ceci couldn't see—and everyone seemed to be talking at once, though the white man's voice dominated. "Hey, we were coming down the hill and then crash, wham, kaboom. . . ." His hands jerked and his voice sputtered and exploded like a small boy describing a war movie. "We didn't see it run out. I'm real sorry. Honey?" He shot a glance at his companion, "Honey, you okay?"

The woman, stony-faced with shock, tucked her hands into her armpits as though urging him to control his dumb show.

"Just didn't see it run out," the man insisted, still waving his arms. "I just . . . oh, shit."

"Harris, *please,*" the woman hissed. "Cursing won't help!" She looked up and saw Ceci, released a captive hand from her armpit, and waved. "Hi! Oh, hi! Are you an American? We've had this little accident. Just didn't see it run out. Didn't see it run out," she repeated to the blacks, articulating every syllable as though trying to communicate in a foreign language. As Ceci approached, a girl in a ragged yellow dress broke free and hurled herself down the hill, almost colliding with her.

"We were coming 'round that bend up yonder," the man offered, pleading his case to Ceci. The others interrupted, offering other interpretations, moving aside enough to let Ceci see the carcass of a goat, its eyes glassy, its guts mashed into the road. Her eyes followed the rope around the animal's neck to the hand of a boy. He was down on his haunches, arms wrapped around his head, keening over the body. He raised a face smeared with snot and tears, then tucked his head between his legs, sobbing.

"I see." Her voice was hoarse. "I think you should move your car over to the side. There's a blind curve in both directions and . . ."

"We weren't even driving fast, and of course there isn't any traffic," the man went on. "Where'd you say you were from?"

Ceci looked behind her. Just as she'd suspected, the girl in the yellow dress had run to the church. The pregnant woman with the baby was already lumbering up the hill. Soon the entire congregation would be upon them.

"California, er . . . New York. I think you'd best move your car."

"We're from Tennessee. We're Honey and Harris Bartlett." The woman released her other hand, and though she and Ceci were several feet apart, thrust it toward her. "I just feel so bad about this."

"Him dead," the boy whimpered.

"Please pull your car over," Ceci insisted. She took off the shirt Mrs. Cleardon had loaned her and shoved it into the hand of one of the older boys. "Here. Take this. Go and stand down on the road. Near the church. Wave this shirt if you see any cars coming." He looked at her dumbly. "To warn people who are driving up the hill," she explained, giving him a little push. "Otherwise we could have a real pileup."

"There's nothin' we can do now," Honey said, resignation overcoming righteousness. She turned and moved toward the car.

"Honey, Honey, stop. We can't just leave!"

"I'm not leaving, Harris. I'm going to move the damned car like this lady said. I'll move the car and . . . Is there anything like a highway patrol around here? . . . Could you please move aside?" she begged an old man whose rheumy eyes gave no clue as to whether he was blocking the car door on purpose.

The churchgoers were now advancing up the hill. A large woman in wobbly high heels and a flowered hat had overtaken the pregnant one and was leading the charge. "How things happen so?" she wailed, her meaty arms already waving above her head. Oh God, Ceci thought, the grandmother or the aunt. Now we're in for it.

The woman shouldered her way into the circle. Ceci felt herself pushed forward as other newcomers shoved for a better view.

"Him dead," the boy slobbered, caressing the goat's head. "Auntie, him dead."

Auntie stared down at the carcass and immediately brought

her chin up, eyes blazing. "How things happen so?" A caca-
phony of confused, sympathetic, and angry explanations
started up. Auntie raised her hand for silence and fixed Harris
Bartlett with an accusing stare.

"We were coming down the hill and *whammo*, I slammed
on the brakes, scree-ee-ch . . ."

"Harris, *please*," his wife hissed between clenched teeth.
"What happened was . . ." She began her explanation in a
too-quiet, reasoning voice, but Auntie would have none of it.
"You know what this goat cost? This young kid," she cut in,
folding her arms across her immense bosom.

Mr. Bartlett looked at her blankly. "Now, how could we
possibly know what . . ."

"If you'd move your car to the side," Ceci insisted, "and
then make some *small* retribution." She looked directly into
his eyes, brought her hand to her chest, and rubbed her
fingers together.

"Oh. Oh." He laughed as though he'd just gotten the punch
line of a joke and reached for his wallet.

"Move the car first."

"No Jamaican dollars," Auntie insisted, the vein in her
temple writhing like a large dark worm. "U.S. dollars only."

"We don't have U.S. dollars. Honest. We had to change
what we had."

Auntie looked at the goat again, working herself into a
combination of loss and violent anger. "Goat is pet, understand? Not just to eat. This goat is pet. Fifty dollars U.S."

"Now wait just a little minute." Harris' eyes narrowed. "I
told you I don't have U.S. dollars. It's your goddamn currency law and as for the goat being a pet—let's not try to up
the ante too much."

"Can we call the police or something?" Honey wanted to
know.

"No one in the village will have a phone. Now let's get the
car off the road," Ceci commanded. For a split second she
thought the reasonableness of her suggestion had penetrated.
Auntie glared at her. Honey moved to the door. The crowd
stepped back. Then the boy sent up another wail of grief,
triggering another chorus of warring voices. Ceci looked

around. Several teenage boys had come to the periphery, their eyes eager and hostile. She was hemmed in on either side and now judged the crowd to number about forty people. A whiff of sweat, pomade, and gasoline hit her.

"You white peoples," Auntie cried. "Come in the yard like a rooster. Drivin' 'bout killin' things. Don't worry what happen."

"Let's not turn this into a racial issue. It was an accident," Honey said.

"Who do you think you are, Bishop Tutu?" Harris demanded. Anger had stilled his gestures. He planted his feet further apart.

"Trying to take advantage of an accident when we explained . . ." Honey joined in; further indignation was drowned in: "Who take advantage?" "Killed him goat!" "Man don't wanta pay!"

Ceci heard a screech of brakes and looked up. A jeep had slammed to a stop on the hillside above the melee. It coasted to the shoulder and a stocky black man, his blue shirt open almost to the waist, jumped out of the passenger seat and walked toward them. The driver moved from the cab of the jeep in a single coordinated movement. He was tall, muscular, light-skinned, and dressed in khaki. The silver in his close-cropped curly hair caught the sun. He distanced his companion and approached with an easy, determined stride, as though coming forward to accept a prize. One of the teenage boys let out a cheer. Voices hushed. Only Auntie continued to screech, until she too became aware of the change in the atmosphere and stopped, her cry hanging in the air.

Ceci's mouth opened but a rush of blood locked her face and throat. She reached out for support, found her hand on Auntie's arm, looked down at her bare feet to make sure she was still standing, then looked up. Paul was not ten feet away from her, his hand on the shoulder of one of the youths who'd run up to greet him. His eyes met hers, widened and immediately narrowed. She saw him mouth her name. Heads turned, moving from one to the other of them, curious, sensing a connection. She turned away, felt the sun beating on her naked shoulders. When she looked back, Paul was kneeling next to the sobbing boy. As he raised the child to his feet, his eyes—those incredible green eyes—ran up the length of her body, flashed on her face again, and moved on.

He took the rope from the boy's hand and motioned for the teenagers to lift the carcass to the side of the road. The crowd shifted and reformed as the man in the blue shirt got into the Bartlett's car and moved it to the shoulder. Ceci was pushed aside. She felt a sudden coolness on her feet and realized she was standing in a muddy gully. She watched the gestures of negotiation—the Bartletts talking simultaneously, Auntie pleading her case, Paul listening, his hand still on the head of the boy—it was like a film without sound. Finally Harris Bartlett opened his wallet. Auntie, resentful but mollified, held out her hand. As she counted the bills, Paul drew the man in the blue shirt aside, whispered to him, then turned to receive the thanks of the Bartletts. There were handshakes and nods. The crowd pressed forward, pushing, laughing, reaching out to touch Paul.

The man in the blue shirt came toward her. "My name is Winston Smalls. Mr. Strangman has asked if you'd come with me. He want to speak with you." She nodded. "Is that your car down there?" She nodded again, fell in behind him as he started down the hill, then, remembering the Bartletts, she turned back.

"Hey, thanks. Thanks a bunch," Honey called. "Is there any place around here we could all go for a drink?"

Ceci shook her head, waved good-bye, and caught up with Winston Smalls. "You mind if I drive?" he asked. "Be easier since I know the way."

"Not at all."

He closed the door after her and moved quickly to the other side of the car. As he started a U-turn, Auntie and the boy passed them.

"Stupid, stupid boy! Why you run out like that?" As the child started to blubber an answer, Auntie cuffed him fiercely. "No draw me tongue. What you doin' runnin' on the road! Asking for mischief, that's what you do!" She slapped him again, glancing at Ceci, defying intervention as the car pulled away.

They traveled about a quarter of a mile before Ceci could find her voice. "I'm Cecily Baron. I'm . . ."

"An old friend of Mr. Strangman's. Yes, I know."

Had Paul managed to tell him who she was, or was Winston in the habit of picking up "friends" of Paul's? "It's lucky you came along."

Winston laughed. "Sure. Either Auntie rip off the tourists or the tourists rip off Auntie. But poor little boy! Auntie going to make him eat goat tonight and he's going to gag on it."

She felt as though she might gag herself. "Excuse me, where did you say we're going?"

"Mr. Strangman has a little house close by. We were on our way there when we saw the accident." He shot her a quick look out of the corner of his eye. "Don't worry. He be along soon. You know how it is. Someone want to ask him 'bout electric rates or the price of gasoline, or why the chickens aren't laying. Most just want to touch him. What you call charisma—he got it. A most dangerous thing. One day some-one gonna come up to him, call him brother, and blow him away. But you think he listen to me? He don't listen to any-body. He be his own man always, that's for sure. Head like a bull." Such open criticism made her think that Winston might be one of the few Paul might listen to. He was several years older than Paul but still intensely virile, a barrel-chested, lead-with-the-jaw, old-style man's man; the sort who loved a scrap, probably had several regular women but didn't live with any of them. "But don't you worry," Winston laughed, "He be okay back there. This village is his territory. And I've seen him stand his ground in a crowd of thousands when the shots rang. He can deal with a run-over goat."

They pulled onto the scrubby ground near the waterfall. The cricket pitch was deserted now, the accident having claimed the attention of the boys. Winston shifted into low gear and started up a rutted road that hadn't been visible from the highway. Ceci was bounced forward. Branches and vines brushed the car. "Please be careful," she said, twisting around to see that the foliage had already cut off the view of the road. "This is a rented car."

"Don't worry. I've been chased up worse roads than this."

"Where did you say we were going?" she yelled, clutching the window ledge with one hand, holding on to the seat with the other.

"To Paul's house up in the hills. We can't get there without the jeep, but there's a clearing up ahead. We wait for him there."

She remained silent, watching the jungle rock in front of her, until he steered into a space just wide enough to accomodate the car, and turned off the motor. In the astonished quiet she couldn't hear a thing; but moments later, as Winston rolled his head around to take the tension out of his neck and reached for the pack of cigarettes in his shirt pocket, the soft sound of rushing water crept into her ears.

"The waterfall is right over there. Would you like a cigarette?"

She shook her head.

"Sure you all right?" he asked. "Your face is waxy like a candle."

"Probably adrenaline. I almost had an accident myself." She swallowed. "And seeing Paul again. We were friends. A long time ago. In London." Her throat felt as though it had closed over. She swallowed again, looked down past the gaping bodice of her dress to her muddy feet. She had forgotten to reclaim Mrs. Cleardon's shirt. She must look like a hooker after a Saturday night brawl. She found her purse on the floor alongside her high heels. "How did you happen along? You don't just rove the countryside looking for disputes, do you?"

"We come up to the house almost every weekend. Paul's writing a book. We come up yesterday but then we had to go back to Kingston last night."

"A meeting?" she ventured.

"No. Elliot's got an ear infection. Paul drop everything when Elliot need him."

"Elliot's . . . ?"

"His son."

"Yes. Of course."

Winston drew on his cigarette. "Hot in here," he said after a pause. "Maybe you'd like to get out and go look at the waterfall. It's through those trees." He pointed with the cigarette.

"Yes. Thank you. I could use some air."

"Don't slip on the rocks," he yelled after her.

Some twenty minutes later, Paul stood in the trees watching her. She was sitting on a large rock near the bank, her back to him, leaning forward and washing her feet. The sun shone on her bare back and coppered her dark hair. Her breasts drooped forward. His heart came up in his throat. He took an involuntary step forward. A branch crackled underfoot and a bird cried and flew out of its hiding place, but she didn't move. He realized that she couldn't hear him because of the rushing water and waited, willing his presence to turn her. He could already feel her, like cream on his fingertips. She swept back her hair and held it to the crown of her head and slowly turned around. He broke into a beatific grin. Her lips parted, almost answered his smile but couldn't form themselves. She flicked the water from her hands, got up and waded over to him. He reached to help her up onto the bank, but she grasped the branch of a tree and brought herself up, stumbling but regaining her footing as he reached out to steady her. Her eyes lost their surprised delight and challenged him. "And tell me, oh Solomon, what is the price of a goat? Not an eating goat, but 'him pet'?"

"Ceci."

His hands came to rest on her shoulders. And now it was he who looked curiously sad while she smiled brilliantly, gently shrugged off his touch, and stepped over to a patch of moss. "As the man said . . ." his hands dropped slowly, hooking into his belt, ". . .'No one knows more about love and loss than a ten-year-old who has just lost a pet.'"

"And did Mr. Bartlett put the goat on his American Express card?"

"My little capitalist."

"That's how it got settled, isn't it?"

"Please." He watched as she moved her toes in the moss. "You have very big feet," he said, almost to himself.

"Yes. I used to borrow your socks in the winter."

"Will you come to the house?"

"Has your political career reduced you to asking only rhetorical questions? I'm here, aren't I?" She turned from him and started back through the bushes, arms straight at her sides, only her fingers clenched. At the sound of him following her, she quickened her stride as though wanting to distance herself.

Winston was already in the back seat of the jeep with her shoes and purse beside him. "I locked up your car. Keys are in your purse." He laughed as she pulled herself into the front seat. "I tell you to fasten your seatbelt, but there isn't any." Paul turned on the motor. They lurched forward and ground up the hillside, bouncing over potholes with gut-shaking speed. Paul stared straight ahead. She watched his hands on the steering wheel. Winston sang "Drinkin' rum and Coca-cola, workin' for the Yankee doll-a . . ." at the top of his lungs.

A weatherbeaten, single-storied house with an overgrown veranda appeared in a clearing. A wiry young man with woolly hair and a revolver tucked into the waist of his jeans waved and ran down the front steps. Paul pulled the jeep around to the rear next to an old stone cookhouse and jumped out. The young man with the gun embraced him.

"Teddy," Paul said, "this is Miss Baron. She's a friend of mine. How's it been going?"

Teddy greeted Ceci with smiling equanimity. "Very quiet, boss. Everything very quiet."

"I'd like a drink. Ceci, will you have something?"

"Yes, please."

She followed him up the steps and along the veranda. He paused near an open door. "Would you like to go in? The bathroom's through my room. I'll wait along here." He moved to an arrangement of hammock, wicker chairs, and table, whistling to a canary in a cage.

Opening the whining screen door, she stepped into a room that was just as she'd imagined it would be: polished wooden floors, a desk with an old typewriter, a shortwave radio and telephone, a bookcase. Except for the double bed draped with mosquito net, it was as bare as an officer's billet. Beyond it, a primitive bathroom: a washstand with bowl and pitcher, a shaving mirror nailed to the wall, a lead tub with an old-fashioned spigot connected to a cistern outside the house. She moistened a cloth and ran it over her arms, neck, and shoulders. Her face in the mirror was flushed, expectant, and subtly resentful. After all these years, Paul had beckoned, she had followed.

When she came back outside, he was lying in the hammock staring out into the jungle. He didn't turn as she took one of the chairs. "This house," she began, "you'd never know it was here."

"That was the idea. You'll appreciate the irony. Rumor has it that it was a sort of trysting place built for my great-great-grandmother."

"By whom?"

"Your great-great-grandfather. Or so the story goes. But you can't put too much stock in century-old gossip. Whoever he was, he was supposed to have treated her well. Left her the house and a little cash. She had three children by him but only one, my great-grandfather, survived."

"You never told me we were related," she said with mock horror. "Shall I have to add incest to the list of my crimes?"

"Distantly. Distantly related. I didn't know the story when we . . . knew each other." From partially closed lids he watched her turn, her arms looping her head, her face in profile. The veins showed blue in her wrists. He wanted to touch them with just enough pressure to feel her pulse, then trace it up the length of her arms, hunt it down to its source —the heartbeat felt most strongly just at the curve of her left breast. "How long have you been in Jamaica?"

"Only a few days. It feels much longer." She turned back to him. "You're writing a book, is that right?"

"Sorting out my thoughts. Isn't that what every politician does when he's out of office?" He stretched, putting his arms behind his head.

"If you can't practice law, or become a lobbyist or give fund-raisers for the next election, I suppose that's what you do." She paused. "I'm sorry about your losing the reelection."

"In any protracted battle there are bound to be defeats," he said with a tone of self-mockery.

"I think I've heard you say that before."

"That's probably because I'd read it. But I hadn't gone through it. Reading politics is rather like reading about sex. It's no preparation for the real thing." He moved his eyes back to the jungle. Here he was, verbally seducing her, just as he'd made love to her time and time again when he'd already known that he would leave her, but couldn't stop himself. He swung his feet to the floor as he heard Teddy padding along the veranda. "But I understand that sex manuals are very popular in the States now. Along with pornography and the Moral Majority. So apparently sexual schizophrenia is as endemic as madness in their foreign policy."

Teddy put the tray with two glasses and a bottle of Johnnie Walker on the table.

"Sorry, there's no ice," Paul said as he started to pour.

"Quite all right," she answered politely.

"Of course it's not all right. Cecily without the amenities? That's like a portrait without a frame."

"I'll survive. I believe my ancestors colonized the world on warm gin and fizz."

"But Americans bring ice to their colonies. They believe in progress."

Teddy grinned broadly, enjoying their exchange, and said, "Old ale fiah tick easy fe ketch."

"Thanks, Teddy. We don't want anything else just now."

Teddy sauntered off, humming.

"What did he say?" Ceci asked. "I've forgotten whatever patois I ever knew."

" 'Old fire stick is easy to catch': old friendships are easy to ignite." He touched his glass to hers.

"Here's to your reelection," she said, avoiding any toast to reunion.

He took a swallow, sat back in the hammock, legs spread, elbows on his knees. "Have you married?"

"No. I, like you, pursue a policy of aggressive nonalignment."

"I'm surprised. I would have thought you'd marry."

She raised an eyebrow a fraction. "Would you?" She had a touch of condescension in her voice, as if to teach him that he hadn't understood her then and couldn't understand her now. She took a cigarette from a pack lying on the table.

"You didn't use to smoke, Ceci."

"Things change. You were the one who preached the doctrine of continual change, didn't you?"

"What have you been doing with yourself?"

"This and that. I've traveled a lot."

"I meant your work."

"Just this and that."

"To put bread on the table? Or ice in the Johnnie Walker?"

"Oysters in a restaurant *and* ice in the Johnnie Walker."

"Only by doing 'this and that'? You were going to be a journalist."

"Probably because I didn't have any idea what it was really like. I thought it was romantic. I lived with a journalist for a while. It wasn't romantic at all. The profession, I mean. The journalist himself was very romantic." She tossed her head and blew out a stream of smoke and felt as though she might cry. What could she possibly accomplish by trying to make him jealous?

"It's too bad you didn't pursue your work. You would have been good at it."

She looked away while he continued to stare at her, not so much forcing the issue as forcing her to recognize her evasion of it. She'd seen him do this before in debates. Staring down the opposition, asking the same question again and again and waiting for his opponent to give.

"I don't like being tied down. I'm a free spirit."

"Yes. I can see that." He took in her mass of tangled hair, her revealingly chic dress, her awareness of how she moved her shoulders. When they'd lived together she'd gathered her hair into a knot at the nape of her neck, worn baggy sweaters and flat-heeled shoes, never shown herself in décolletage. This had been partly because she was sensitive to the voyeuristic interest in a "mixed" couple, partly because she was shy. Or perhaps, as she'd once said, she didn't want to show herself because she "belonged to him." Now she had a shiny patina of confidence. She was advertisement sexy, the sort of woman who knew men wanted her and enjoyed it because she didn't give a damn. He wondered how many men had succeeded him.

"It's not as though I've disappointed anybody," she said, taking another drag of her cigarette. "Nobody ever expected me to *do* anything."

"What about yourself?" He remembered the care she'd taken with her papers; that it had taken him some time to see that her perfectionism was rooted in fear of failure. "Or did you mean your father? Is he still alive?"

"Very much so. He's down here, too. That's really the reason I came. To see him and my aunt and to . . ." she moved her hand in a vague gesture ". . . sort things out."

"I was surprised that your aunt stayed on."

"Why shouldn't she? She's a Jamaican, after all. Born here the same as you were."

"Yes. But members of the oligarchy seem to love the country only so long as it is indisputably theirs. If things start to change, they'd rather migrate to the Valley of the Fallen."

"The what?"

"Miami."

She laughed, but there was an edge in her voice when she spoke. "Miami? If you knew my aunt, you'd realize what a ridiculous thing that is to say. Of course to me she's a human being and not a—what did you call her—a member of the oligarchy?"

"I was describing her class, not her personality. You could hardly say that the Nettletons weren't part of the oligarchy."

"Since I don't talk like a textbook, it wouldn't occur to me to say it about anybody. And since things didn't change as much as you would have liked them to, I suppose she was justified in remaining." She tensed her legs to stand. What was the point of staying if she couldn't stop herself from sniping at him?

"No. Don't get up," he said without raising his head. "Things didn't change. Or rather they changed in a way I didn't want them to. Of course, I foresaw difficulties. I didn't anticipate people like your brother Marsden."

"I didn't even know that you knew him."

"Let's say I know him intimately but not personally." He

tossed off the rest of his whiskey and set the glass on the floor. "It doesn't matter. I know my time will come. Our time will come."

She bit her lip and turned her head to the passion flower that clung to the railing. Paul Strangman. Ambition out of one eye, idealism out of the other.

"I made a lot of mistakes," he said quietly.

For a split second she thought he might be talking about their love affair, but then, without even looking at him, she knew that he'd been driven back into himself and his attention had left her almost entirely.

"Such as?"

"Right after I was elected. I didn't want to perpetuate the spoils system. Members of both political parties expect to be rewarded with whatever few benefits are available to the winner. Housing, for example—there's only so much available. You can guess what it's like down here even if you haven't actually seen it. I was advised to give whatever I could to the people who'd supported me. It was the practical thing to do, but I didn't want to be accused of being unfair. So I let the housing be decided by lot. Naturally, those who had supported me felt betrayed and those in the opposition took the handout and thought I was a fool. Things like that."

She leaned forward, scanning his face. It was tired, perhaps even a little bored. "And then when I tried to work out trade agreements . . ." he went on, sorting it out for himself. She settled back in her chair, relaxing for the first time, realizing that more than anything, Paul needed to talk without censoring, needed someone he trusted, that he was talking to her as he might talk to Winston. The difference being that she had heard his plans when they were still in the embryonic stage and he was now confessing that many of them had been stillborn.

He spoke at great length, staring at the floorboards before he caught sight of her bare feet. "But I know you're not interested in the International Monetary Fund or the machinations of the CIA."

"But I am. I've tried to follow things through the papers, books and television, but I don't have a real grasp of what's going on down here. I want to hear about it. Please tell me. Tell me, Paul." It was the first time she had said his name, and said it in the old way, like a caress. She poured another shot into her glass and refilled his without asking.

"I managed to get some agricultural and technical schools going and . . ."

"I know something about that. Percy, the driver at the house, learned about cars in one of your schools. He's quite ambitious."

"If he's ambitious he'll probably want to leave the island. There's not much for the young men here."

"What about your father? And your grandfather? They made something here, didn't they? They were able to advance themselves."

"That push started five generations back. Yes, they were able to do it, but for every talent that poverty stimulates, it blights a hundred. I did make some headway in the literacy campaign, for example. When I took office we had a huge adult illiteracy. When we . . ." He began slowly, but soon, as he talked of labor disputes, international alliances, the Grenada invasion, a passionate desperation crept into his voice. She felt an overwhelming tenderness toward him. There was no hint of self-pity in him, and yet he had lived day by day with these problems and disappointments. They had never left him at night. When they had been lovers, she had marveled at his sleeping habits. He could refresh himself with a ten-minute nap as easily as someone else would take a glass of water to quench his thirst. While she'd struggled to lose consciousness and tossed with dreams, Paul had given way the moment he'd closed his eyes. He'd claimed that he didn't dream. When he'd broken from sleep, he'd broken sharply, with no confusion. It wasn't possible that he still surrendered to dreamless sleep. And what must it be like to know that people wanted you dead? That friends like Winston were also bodyguards?

The sun now slanted onto the veranda. She got up, lowered the bamboo shade, and sat back down.

"I don't know when the destabilization campaign began," he said at last. "Before I was aware of it, that's for sure."

She looked past him and saw Winston coming around the side of the house, moving quietly, feigning interest in some distant object so as not to look at them. "When I did find out—" Without the slightest change in his posture, Paul called "Winston, that you?"

"Sure. Sorry to bother you. Thought I might take the jeep down the hill for awhile. Do you mind?"

"No. Go ahead."

"Teddy's out in the cook house."

"Right."

Winston went behind the house. A moment later they heard the jeep start up. Paul smiled at her. "Winston has a woman in the village. He hopes I never finish this damned book." Winston brought the jeep parallel to the veranda and leaned out, grinning, "Best get inside, take some shelter, boss. Big storm comin' up." He gunned the motor and took off down the hill.

"How is the book coming?" Ceci asked.

"With all the speed of a glacier. I only work on it on weekends. But it's important. I don't mean for posterity," he grinned at her. "I know you think I'm a cocky bastard. I know you've always thought that."

"Not *always*. There was a period of six or eight months, back there in the Stone Age, when you'd conned me into believing that you were so wonderful that I was afraid you suffered from an excess of humility." They both laughed and the laughter felt as intimate as touching, so that she broke off, embarrassed. He wiped his hand over his face again and continued his thought. "I know you thought, even back then, 'How can he expect to bring it off?' A democratic mandate for complete change. Who's done it? FDR? Not really. Allende? Yes, but look what happened to him and Aquino." He turned his head sharply away. "It's more for myself than for anyone that I write the book. I have to sort it all out. To see where I have to correct myself. I used to believe that I could bring it off, you see. Not in a year, or even a decade, but in *my* lifetime. Perhaps," he added wryly, "like all young men, I didn't understand the weight of history. Do you understand what I mean?"

"In a way. Certainly in a personal way. I can't overcome the things I hate in my own family. I knew when I came down here what I was coming back to. I mean, I know Vivian. And Archie. I know the setup. I could almost have predicted how they would act; how I would react, but I was hoping for something better. Now, all I can think to do is to run away. Even the servants, and the people at this party last night . . . it was all so predictable. And the worst part is that there's no one who can even laugh at it with you. Today on the road, for example . . . Until you came along, I knew just how everyone was going to act. When the little boy's Auntie came up . . ."

"Ah, yes, the Auntie. I've met her a million times. Always irate, always full of pride, but always with her hand out waiting for the opportunity to get back at the tourists. But after all, she is very poor. It was perhaps more tolerable before she'd seen "Dallas" and "Dynasty," but all that imagined luxury makes for a festering resentment. She thinks all the tourists have millions, and she has to smile at them if she wants to sell them her baskets or hats or cashews. She's powerless unless she thinks of ways to rip them off. Trouble is she merely envies them, though she'll yell about the pride of being Jamaican. The nationalism here is pretty thin, Ceci. Most Jamaicans have come to think of our country as a piece of real estate they can sell for vacation condos." He looked into his empty glass, then smiled at her crookedly. "Enough." He got up and shook out his arms. The blinds moved in the breeze, making a quivering striped pattern on her flesh. Her head was down and her hair fell forward, parting in the back and exposing her neck. Desire sent his blood humming, tingling his fingertips and skull, pooling in his groin. He went to the canary cage, whistling. "Teddy's bird. She keeps him company when he's up here alone. She won't sing for anyone else."

She watched the muscles in his back, let her eyes wander down the sinews of his arms, over the slight thickening of his waist to his high, still taut buttocks.

A patter of raindrops swept onto the corrugated roof. "I'll be forty-four next year," he said at last.

"That isn't old, Paul."

"Do you still pat that stuff around your eyes to stop the wrinkles from coming?" And then, "My father died two weeks after the last election."

"And you think . . ."

"No. It wasn't the election. He was an old man. He'd had to have most of his teeth drawn. It drove him crazy. He wouldn't even eat in front of my son, and he played with him every day. I believe he loved Elliot more than he'd ever loved another human being. I only saw my father cry twice in his life: when my brother was killed and when Elliot gave him some hard candy and he couldn't bite into it. My mother said he was like some old lion and when his teeth went he wanted to lope off into the jungle and die. No, it wasn't the election, but . . ."

"But you would rather he hadn't seen the defeat."

"I would rather he hadn't lost his teeth."

They looked long and deep into each other's eyes, unspoken questions asked, impossible answers given. Memories of having had her were strong and elusive as the smell of smoke. He moved to her, his hand circling the nape of her neck. She stiffened momentarily, but as he stood above her, his thigh pressing into hers, he felt her breath catch and her body lean into him. Old fire stick easy to catch. Remarkable. Inevitable.

A low rumble of thunder echoed from the hills and another gust of rain pelted the roof and shook the bamboo blind. She turned away, reaching for a cigarette.

"Don't smoke."

"Don't tell me what to do." She had gone moist at his first touch, a pang of desire striking her so forcefully that it had knocked the wind out of her. As if he hadn't caused her the greatest pain in her life. As if he hadn't walked out one Sunday morning leaving a paltry note. And here she was, a decade later, listening while he talked and talked, as he had always done; being caught up in his plans and ambitions, as she had always been. If she had been a bitch puppy she would have yelped and whined and wiggled, crazy to get a lick of his hand.

He reached for the lighter, but she scooped it up, lighting

her own cigarette. He moved away and sat on the hammock, sensing that she was somehow angry, and more than a little angry with himself for wanting her so much. "Are you hungry? I could ask Teddy . . ."

"Not particularly."

Even as she took a drag of the cigarette and crossed her legs, he could sense she was poised for flight, but the rain was now coming down like pellets, pitting the earth and battering the roof. She would have to stay at least until the storm was over. "You were telling me about your father," he said. "Do you still dislike him?"

"I think I love him. Not that it does me any good. But then, as you would say, relations are always strained in the oligarchy." She thought her little joke would break the tension, but instead of smiling he nodded and said, "Yes. I believe they are."

Pompous bastard. "On the other hand, you who are of the people, your private life is one of unconditional commitment, isn't it. You love whole nations. You love the march of history. So is trying to lay old girlfriends part of your revolutionary stance, or," she blurted it out, knowing she would hate whatever answer she got, "don't you love your wife?"

He looked at her as though she were a total stranger. "After all this time I thought you would have come to some understanding of why I left."

"Perhaps I'm retarded. You did give me wonderful clues, didn't you? 'Gone back to Jamaica.' That's an explanation, isn't it? But don't think I don't understand. I've done it myself." She took a swig of her drink, dribbling some of it down her chin in her rush to keep talking. "I've done it myself. Good-bye, it's been grand. So long. All of which meant I just don't want it anymore. What is there to understand? I've left men. Lots of them." She cried it proudly, her voice as insistent as the storm, the deceived who has become the deceiver, the woman revenged. There was a hard lump in her chest that nothing could dissolve. Not tears or laughter. Not being taken hold of. And she was glad of that lump. Without it she would be a blob of jelly. She snuffed out the cigarette and got up, moving past the swinging blind to the railing, holding onto it and leaning out, her hair blowing behind her like a flag, the rain washing her face and trickling into her dress. A hurricane gust blew the cigarettes off the table and rattled the glasses. The birdcage swung furiously. Paul unhooked it and put it inside the bedroom door. "You're getting wet," he said in a stony voice.

She leaned farther, sticking her tongue out to catch the water, then turned, one hip jutting, like a streetwalker beckoning a customer. "We did have some wild sex, didn't we, Strangman? Only natural that we'd both want to have some more. So how about it?"

"You put a low priority on sex now. I can see that. I'm sorry." He had to shout to be heard above a sudden clap of thunder. "As soon as the storm is over and Winston gets back, I'll have him drive you down the hill. And yes," he came to within inches of her, his voice low again, ". . . I do love my wife."

Her smile mocked him. "I don't know why I bothered to ask. The answer's always the same. I've heard it in six languages. But shouldn't you add 'but not in the same way'?"

"But not in the same way."

"But of course not. You and . . ."

"Vera."

". . . You and Vera . . ." The name hit her like a blow in the solar plexis ". . . you're comrades, aren't you? She goes into the slums with you. She digs holes at the agricultural centers. She . . ."

"Don't be a bitch." He grabbed her arm. His breath was hot on her face. "Not a week has gone by that I haven't thought of you."

She wrenched free and ran to the steps. "If you run out in the hurricane, I'm not coming after you," he yelled.

She stumbled forward but was blown back. Grasping the railing near the steps, she shut her eyes against the blinding rain, realized that she was crying and began to laugh, moving forward again, reaching the yard. He blocked her, coming up hard against her, standing with his legs apart, bracing them both against the torrents that twisted the tops of the trees and lashed their clothes against them. He kissed her so furiously that their teeth hit against each other. Her shoulders buckled forward and he draped his arm around them protectively, his other hand clutching at her buttocks, pulling her tight, rocking into her so that she could feel where he would join with her again. Oh yes, still and again. On that tidal wave that would drown the world for both of them.

Thirteen

Now what? The thought intruded even as he reared back, gave a final shudder of release, lunged again, and collapsed full onto her. His head fell into the pillow next to hers and a groan—half content, half anguished—gurgled from his throat and funneled into her ear. It was the first sound she had been conscious of hearing since . . .

He had carried her to the bed, pulled up her skirt and skinned off her pants, unzipped himself, run his hand down the length of his penis, and descended onto her—a dozen mouths and uncountable hands, their swarm quickly culminating in a thrust of swift capture. She had been only vaguely aware of the storm lashing the blinds and threatening to take off the roof, and even those sounds had disappeared as he'd eased his stroke to the confident, insistently languid rhythm that had all the familiarity of the known, and the intense shock of the new. Paul. Paul. Paul. The name she had whispered to herself just to hear it. But he, eyes shut, his face contorted into an expression close to pain, might not even know that it was she. Without leaving her he'd brought her on top of him, struggling with the zipper of her dress while she reared back, coming down on him hard. Just as he was yanking the dress over her head, there had been a fearful crash on the veranda. For a split second he had frozen and her mind had become active, thoughts flashing, short-circuiting like a string of lights on a Christmas tree: Someone was coming! He had broken her zipper! Aunt Vivian had expected her for four o'clock tea! Their eyes had met, his startled look changing into one of surprised acknowledgment, as though realizing for the first time who she was. He had cried her name, just once, but the cry came from his gut and threw her into a totally unexpected release. He'd flipped her onto her back again, oaring into her, smooth and weightless as a ship parting the waves and she had loved, loved, loved him. And heard nothing at all.

Now what?

He was a dead weight, growing heavier by the minute. The sweat slick where their bodies joined began to feel sticky. His breath tickled her ear. And yet she wanted him to remain just as he was. If only they could lie here, suspended in the heavy stillness after the storm. Perfect, whole, complete, beyond the reach of the world. She relaxed as much as she could, accepting his weight, feeling nothing but the subsiding pulse between her legs. If only they could remain like this. Stop time.

But the sounds of the world were seeping back: the steady flow of water from the drain spout, the chirp of a bird, and, as the wind swept the trees, a patter overhead as though someone had thrown a handful of pebbles on the roof. There was a soft sucking sound as he pulled out of her, rolled away, and brought her body close to his. She opened her eyes slowly, saw his foreshortened legs and torso, her own arm tapering across his chest, the gauzy loop of mosquito net above them. And beyond the bed, through the screen door, the poisonously green wash of jungle.

The bedsprings creaked as he released her and moved to sit on the side of the bed. He got up, stretched, and walked to his desk. Through slit eyes she watched as he leaned against it, palms down, head bent, so that he seemed to be reading from the pile of typewritten papers. After a time he moved to the door, so unconsciously self-absorbed that he might have been alone. He picked up the birdcage, whistling softly as he went onto the veranda and hooked it onto its chain. Still whistling, he untwisted the mangled hammock and moved out of sight.

She could hear him righting the table (that must have been the awful crash) and picking up the chairs and the bottle. He came back into the room without looking at her and began to pace from the desk to the door and back again. She raised herself on one elbow, thinking that her movement would attract him, but he seemed to have forgotten her entirely. She lay back, surprised at how cold the wet spot in the center of the bed felt against her thigh, and shut her eyes. He must be struggling with his own "now what?" She would let him speak first.

He turned from his desk, stepped on his flung-off pants, reached down to retrieve them, and stopped. He had conjured her image so many times that it was hard to believe that she was here, sprawled in the middle of the bed, one arm extended, palm upward, the other hand clutching the sheet. In the advancing dusk, those parts of her that had been protected by her bathing suit glowed milky white. Her pubic hair was sweated flat against her inner thigh—how had he forgotten how soft and straight that hair was?—her nipples were an incredibly tender pink. Had he just had her? It didn't seem so. How could such triumph be so short-lived? He hadn't felt so passionately energized since he was a young man. He had to have her again. He had to have her often. And . . . the thought went through like a brief electric shock . . . he had to call his wife.

He threw his wet khakis into a corner and got another pair from the wardrobe. Cupping his half-erection, he zipped them up, still looking at the bed. The silver chain she wore had looped over one of her breasts so that the little heart dangled in her armpit, and the glint of the polish on her silly big toes made him smile. He sat down next to her, blowing on the perspiration between her breasts, picking up the heart and centering it on her sternum. Her face looked younger, healed, but there was a crease of a frown between her brows. "Ceci?" She opened her eyes. Their expression was so expectant and yet so guarded that his desire changed to a tenderness that made his throat ache. He cleared it. "I'm hungry."

She managed a flicker of a smile, but when she spoke her

voice was hoarse, barely audible. "Are you really thinking about your stomach?" She closed her eyes again.

"No. Yes." He ran his hand over her belly, captured her pubic bone, let his fingers stroke where leg joined torso. "I was also thinking about the first time I was in the British Museum. . . ." He ran his finger the length of her labia, parted them. "I was about eleven at the time. I was so taken with a nude statue that I started to feel it up. . . ." He sank his finger into her cleft "Oh . . . and one of the guards told me I'd have to leave." Ah. There. A little deeper. He could feel her stirring at his touch ". . . it wasn't as though I could hurt a statue . . ." She sucked in her breath, covered his hand with her own and pulled it away. Her hand was so soft that it seemed not to have any bones, but her gesture had a firm, "this is my body" assertiveness that locked him out, darkened his mood with a surge of aggressiveness. She started to get up but he pushed her back. "Don't"—his hand sought her again—"Don't get up," he said more gently. He brought his face close to her belly. "As I recall, you can't cook anyway."

"I wasn't getting up to cook." She slid away from him and sat up, her back to him. "Though I'm quite an accomplished cook now. Can you cook now?"

He laughed. "We batch it here. Teddy'll have something out there. Why don't you just stay in bed."

She tucked her hair behind her ears and stood up. He noticed that her buttocks had lost some of their youthful firmness, but this softer, more womanly look was belied by the flat, decisive tone of her voice: "I have to telephone my aunt."

"The telephone lines are probably down but you can try." He raised his hand to his nose and sniffed it, but she was rooting around at the foot of the bed, looking for her underpants, purposely ignoring him. He shrugged. He was hungry. Ravenously, boyishly hungry. He walked quickly to the door. "I'll get us some food."

She sat back down on the edge of the bed, her head in her hands. What had she done? Nothing more than have sex with a man. All right, not just a man. Paul. A decade of regret and terrible yearning had culminated in apocalyptic lust. The heavens had opened. When she had heard his *cri de couer*, that single utterance of her name, it had shaken her very soul. She had believed that he loved her as she loved him. But their brief, self-proving intimacy had come and gone like the storm itself and now he was out in the cook house, scrounging around to satisfy another appetite, probably wondering how he might salvage the rest of his day if she was unwilling to go another round. Had Antony gone back to reading dispatches while still warm from Cleopatra's bed? Had Romeo called for a hunk of bread and a chunk of provolone as he'd reached for his codpiece? How was it possible to be so magically transported and so rudely dumped back to earth? She felt disheveled. Her skin, particularly the sunburned parts, felt as though they'd been rubbed raw. She swatted a mosquito, stared at the little smear of blood on her arm, and got up.

Picking up the phone, she heard popping and crackling and a whiningly weak dial tone. Her eyes scanned the top page on the pile of papers: "... a society is anachronistic when it offers old answers to new questions ... the habits of North American consumerism, so powerful and unchallenged, can be mistaken for the norm of life itself ... though in a state of decay, the heirs of the elite society ..." She shook her head. All this bloody theorizing. And yet ... the look on the face of that sobbing boy as Paul had lifted him to his feet. What gentleness of command. What ... There was more crackling on the line and an echo of a woman's voice demanding something from the operator. A party line or just her imagination? She dialed. She could picture Vivian, crazed with worry, skittering about, neighing over drenched curtains, ruined marigolds and her wayward niece. And what would she tell Aunt Vivian? "Sorry, I missed your tea party. I didn't notice the storm because I was thrashing about with my legs in the air, being humped by a man who even in the furthest reaches of his ecstacy wishes you all in hell. Are there any cucumber sandwiches left?"

The phone had rung at least twenty times. She was about to hang up when she heard "Nettleton House. Who may I say is calling?"

She swallowed. Her throat was parched and she could taste the residue of the whiskey. "Thelda?"

"Uh huh."

"This is Miss Ceci. May I please speak to my aunt or my father?"

There was a long pause—Thelda must be taking her own sweet time to summon someone—and then Aunt Vivian's voice, breathy and girlish. "Ceci, is that you?"

"Yes. I . . ."

"We called Mrs. Cleardon and she said you'd left early but that you might be driving to Kingston."

"Well, I . . ." Was Mrs. Cleardon so practiced in intrigue that she automatically made up stories? Or had she just tried to allay the family's fears?

"No matter," Vivian cut in. "We knew you were in the vicinity because one of the boys who's working on the great house came by and told Marsden that he'd seen you on the road in some sort of fracas. But that was hours before the storm so—"

"It was nothing. Just some American tourists who ran over a goat."

"I'm not surprised. They whisk along these roads as though they owned the place and . . . No, Angus, *I'm* talking to her now, so you can see that she's quite all right. You are all right, aren't you, Ceci?" Without waiting for a reply, she rushed on. "He's quite off his chump with worry. Started quoting Lear's speech begging his daughter's forgiveness and then—"

"Aunt Vivie—"

"Angus! Do go and put something in your stomach before you fall down." The voice dropped to a whisper. "We've had quite a time of it, let me tell you. He was even better in the 'Blow winds, blow' speech—of course, he'd hit the gin pretty hard by then and what with the servants trying to bring in the tea things from the veranda and Angus wrapping himself round the posts and challenging the storm . . ." A peal of laughter that bordered on a cackle fought through the line, followed by a sharp inhalation of breath. "Ceci, do come home. The storm was the least of it. Icilda is so upset because

Marsden . . . What? No, Angus. *I'm* talking to her. Where in the world are you, Ceci? Where in the world—"

"I'm quite safe. I'm sorry if I caused you any worry."

"Are the roads washed out where you are?"

"I don't know. I haven't checked yet."

"I must ask Marsden what to do. Marsden will know. Perhaps we can send Percy to fetch you. But no, of course we can't do that. Percy is gone. Gone. Oh, it was awful. Too, too awful. Icilda won't speak to me. She's just mopping up the veranda and pretending that she can't hear me when I speak to her."

"Aunt Vivie, I can't follow what . . . Perhaps you'd best let me speak to Archie."

"I said," the voice hissed in a stage whisper, "that Marsden has given young Percy his walking papers and Icilda's sent me to Coventry. I—"

"Could you please speak up. There must be trouble on the line." But there was no trouble on the line. Vivian's voice had trailed off, exhausted.

"Trouble on the line? I'm not surprised," Vivian came back, almost braying. "Two years ago, when we had a hurricane, Lady Pembroke's lines were down for weeks. The roads to her property were quite washed away and I was afraid the poor dear would have to take to eating breadfruit because, of course, the food deliveries were cut off in the entire western part of the parish. Where did you say you are, Ceci?"

"I'm safe," she stalled. "If you'd just turn the phone over to Archie for a minute."

There was more popping and crackling, then the line went dead. Ceci pressed the receiver closer to her ear and jiggled the plunger in a useless, melodramatic gesture reminiscent of one of Archie's old movies. After more crackling, the eerie singsong of distant female voices resumed. She hung up, then picked up again and was about to dial when she noticed that Paul's desk drawer was slightly open. She slipped her finger into the drawer and stopped. What would Paul think of her spying on him? When they'd lived together, it had taken all of her willpower not to pry into his things, but now . . . She pulled the drawer back a few inches and saw what might have been the treasure box of a boy: rubber bands, several pens and pencils, a corkscrew, a magenta and black bird feather, an ivory-handled pocketknife. A few inches more: bullets, a revolver (the metal dull but intriguing to her touch), an eraser, and a snapshot of a boy with a beautifully shaped head and straight limbs, kneeling, cleaning a fish, too intent to notice the camera. And behind the boy a dark-skinned, full-breasted woman in a one-piece bathing suit, her head was wrapped in a bandanna, one of her arms, laden with bracelets, thrown up as protection against the sun, obscuring her face. Elliot and Vera. She bent closer to examine the photo, not knowing if she envied or pitied the woman but feeling something like a cramp in her belly as she looked at the child.

She was about to close the drawer when her eye caught a glint of gold. She picked up a single garnet drop earring, feeling instinctively that it didn't belong to Vera. But of course. This house wasn't the monkish retreat Paul had led her to believe. It was a hideaway where he, like all swordsmen, led his other life.

She pressed her lips together. This time *she* would walk away, swiftly and conclusively. She would say her good-byes over rice and bitter coffee, finally having accepted the impossibility of it all. She was glad that she'd gone to bed with him. The act had finally cut through the bonds of her compulsion. Taking a deep breath, she dropped the single earring back into the drawer. She felt an incredible lightness. She was free of him at last. As she leaned back in the chair a shadow fell across her. She turned, closing the drawer with her elbow.

He stood in the doorway, a thick slice of bread in one hand, her purse in the other. "You seem to have dropped this." He smiled, tossing the purse onto the desk, then bit into the bread and held it toward her. She shook her head. "Teddy's put the coffee on," he said through a slow, satisfied munching. His eyes swept the desk. She straightened her spine, drawing her breasts up to a you-can't-put-a-pencil-under-the-droop youthfulness, but then, she didn't have those lush, nourishing breasts Vera had. "Yes," she answered the question in his eyes, "the phone is working." She reached back to the foot of the bed and found her dress. The zipper was, surprisingly, intact, but the dress looked as though someone had mopped the floor with it. "Perhaps I could ask Teddy to . . ." Paul's expression stopped her from finishing the request. "Perhaps," she corrected herself, "if there's any soap around I could wash this out."

"In the bathroom. And the cistern will be full of rainwater, if you want to take a bath." He took another bite, preoccupied. "You say the phone is working? Here, let me give you something to put on." He reached into the wardrobe and took out a shirt, his fingers grazing her nipple as he handed it to her, his head bending as if to nuzzle her neck.

She stepped back. "Is the road washed out?"

"It's in pretty bad shape, but I think the jeep can make it up."

"Will Winston . . . ?"

"Yes. He'll be back."

"How long do you think . . . ?"

"Soon. He left about—how long ago would you say? I purposely leave my watch home when I come here."

"I'm not much good at guessing the time."

"I'd say about three hours ago, wouldn't you?"

She nodded. It seemed as though they were strangers, waiting for a delayed departure, stuck for words. "Well, I think I'll take that bath." She turned to the bathroom. "If you'll excuse me."

"Yes, Miss Nettleton. You are excused."

She ignored his playfulness and pulled the bathroom door behind her. The lock had been painted over and wouldn't latch. Typical, she thought. Nothing on this island works except the men's cocks. She tried to raise the tiny window. The sashes had swollen with the rain and she had to struggle to yank it open. The sussurating jungle noises flowed into the room along with thrumping reggae from the cookhouse. The air was fast losing it's cool, clean smell and becoming verdurous and humid. Storm over; everything back to normal. She picked a dead spider from the tub, dropped it into the toilet, and began to pump the handle of the cistern, concentrating on the gush of water in order to blot out the sound of Paul's telephone voice. Finding herself involuntarily straining to hear his conversation, she began to sing Winston's song: "Drinking rum and Coca-Cola/ Working for the Yankee dolla . . ." If Max could see her now, pumping away, looking around for a bar of soap. Max, whose bathroom had wall-to-wall mirrors, a view of Manhattan, a Jacuzzi, air-conditioning, sun lamps, racks to heat monogrammed towels as thick as blankets, apothecary jars filled with oils, shampoos, and conditioners.

She lowered herself into the tub, surprised at the chill of the water, irritated by the rough surface that greeted her bottom. She found the bar of soap and lathered her pubis, realized that she had stopped humming and was again straining to listen. He was still on the phone, but from the pauses, grunts, and monosyllabic responses, she could tell that he wanted to get off. Vera must be keeping him, reporting his messages, talking about Elliot's ear drops or weather conditions in Kingston. Vera, who had slept beside him for years, who had heard him cry out in nightmare fear of death, who had born his child.

She lay back, lowering her head to let the water close her ears and bending her legs so that her toes gripped the end of the tub. In her mind, she could hear Archie's Fats Waller imitation of "Your Feet's Too Big." She stayed like this until she was sure his telephone conversation was over, then got out and began to towel herself. She could feel him on the other side of the door and half hoped that he would come in, be smitten by her nakedness and want her again. This time she would refuse. Pulling out the plug, she watched the water drain as she buttoned on the shirt he had given her. She pumped in more water, knelt on the floor to wash out her dress and underpants, hung them over the tub, thinking that they would take a day to dry in this weather. As she came out of the bathroom, she heard Teddy chattering about the storm and sweeping up the debris on the veranda. She waited behind the mosquito net until he'd gone and Paul came to the doorway carrying a tray. "Shall we eat on the veranda or in the room?" he asked.

"In the room, if you don't mind."

He put the tray of steamed snapper, coconut water, rice and

peas, a hunk of raw ginger, and a pot of coffee on his desk and drew up the chair. "Here," he said, handing her some scraps of paper, "Teddy just gave these to me. Teddy has a fine sense of humor." She looked at the first piece of paper, a cartoon cut out of a pulp magazine. It was a caricature of Paul drowning in the Caribbean Sea, his legs spread, toes gripping the shorelines of Cuba and Nicaragua. His fingers, clutching the coast of Jamaica, were being pecked by a giant eagle. In a bubble over his head the words "History . . . gulp! . . . will vindicate me. Glug. Glug." The other cartoon showed a starving family, faces pressed to the window of an expensive restaurant, watching a wealthy couple eat. The caption read "We hate to see people starve. Could you please move us to another table?" The third piece of paper—a lapse of Teddy's political consciousness, but a reminder of his more personal needs—was an advertisement for a sale on tape decks. Ceci creased the scraps of paper with her fingernail and handed them back. When Paul offered her a plate, she raised her hand and moved it in a gesture of distant but gracious refusal, such as she might have given to a maitre d'. He shrugged and began to heap food onto his own plate.

"You should at least try the snapper. Teddy's an excellent cook. He used to be the leader of a motorcycle gang in Trench Town but the law was after him, so he got himself a job as a kitchen helper at the Sheraton in Ocho Rios. One of the tourists propositioned him and he beat the guy up, so he was on the run. He was squatting on the land here when I met him. He almost blew me away the first time I came up the hill." He smiled, shoveling a forkful of rice into his mouth.

"A dangerous character," she said softly, folding her hands in her lap.

"Not dangerous. Desperate." He wiped his mouth with the back of his hand, mocking her reserve. "Sure you won't try this snapper?"

"I told you I'm not hungry."

"That's all right. Just don't look so offended that I am."

"The further Left you go the worse the manners are."

"Perhaps the appetites are stronger." He chewed appreciatively, eyeing her. "I'll watch my p's and q's, madam, though

I must warn you, my mother taught me to clean my plate. But I can use the finger bowl with the best of them. Remember the night we went to that hotel with all the Common Market bureaucrats and we left as they were serving dessert?"

"You weren't so important then. They'd seated us at the very back of the dining room."

"And we went to the car but it was so foggy we couldn't drive back to the flat? I almost impaled myself on the gear shift trying to get at you."

She shook her head. He had gotten it all wrong. The night of the Common Market dinner they'd left during the speeches, so randy that they'd stopped in the lobby and gotten a room—a depressing little room with lavender spreads on the twin beds, lithos of Kensington Gardens, and a pervasive smell of damp. They'd laughed that their escape from dreary speeches had landed them in a dreary room. They'd made love without taking off their clothes. Afterward they'd gotten up and driven back to their flat. The foggy night he was referring to had been after a dinner with a Jamaican dentist and his wife in Hampstead Heath. The husband had all but salivated every time he looked at Ceci; his wife had been, understandably, less enthusiastic. Because of the poor weather, they'd been invited to stay the night, but she'd signaled Paul that she wanted to go home. It had taken them hours to get there. Paul had become saddened, then angry, about the loutish unemployed youths hanging about the streets. To cheer themselves up they'd tried to remember the lyrics of old popular songs. She had nuzzled his neck and he had held her knee for comfort. When they had finally arrived back at the flat, chilled to the bone, they'd been too tired to do anything but sleep. But she was not disposed to correct his memory.

"What did your aunt have to say?" he asked between munchings.

"Nothing much. The driver I was telling you about—Percy —she said he was gone. Apparently Marsden has given him the sack. I hope that isn't the case. Aunt Vivie was too muddled to explain what had happened. Oh, and she said that one of the men had seen me on the road at the accident. He went to the house and told them. Living in this place is worse than being in a fish bowl."

"One of your brother's boys?"

"I don't know."

"I have to give him credit. He has a pretty tight network. I wonder if he was trailing me or you."

She tilted her chin up and gave him a deprecating smile. "You are paranoid. Why should he be trailing either of us?"

He drank the coconut water, sizing her up over the rim of the glass. "Is it possible that you don't know about brother Marsden?" he asked finally.

She paused, feeling a curious need to delay her answer. She felt as though she was being interrogated. "I know that he's turning the great house into some sort of convention center."

"A casino if the gambling restrictions are lifted, which is what they're lobbying for, a 'private club' if they're not."

"Well," she shrugged, uncomfortable, "I found out last night that he's growing ganja, if that's what you mean."

"Miles of it, right in the middle of the cane fields. But you could have expected that. He can hardly revive the glory of the Nettletons by raising sugarcane, so he's gone from sugar and slaves to drugs and spies. An enterprising jump."

"You seem to have a pretty tight network yourself."

"I hope so." He pushed his plate aside, his eyes narrowing. "You mean you really don't know?"

"There's more?"

"He came down to stay the year I was elected. The gentleman farmer returned. Convenient that he already had a cover. I think he's one of the boys, Ceci. CIA. Surely you must've guessed."

She looked away. Had Paul fallen victim to his own imaginings? Was he trying to blame the failures of his regime on some destabilization plot?

"What do you think?" he asked. "That all agents look like James Bond and carry magic bullets? They're 'advisors,' reporters, businessmen, teachers. . . ."

"Under every bed?"

"Not this one, I hope."

She could tell by his eyes that he was telling the truth. "My brother the CIA agent," she said softly, trying the idea on for size. "Well, why not?" Of course. Yes. "Poor Aunt Vivie. She'd have another stroke if she knew that." She drew her leg up to her chest, pushing her chin into her knee to control her laughter.

Seeing the long, full span of her thigh and the shadow of fur only partially concealed by the flap of the shirt, his mind deserted him. "You told them you were going to stay the night, didn't you?"

His assumption amazed her. Was she some territory that, once regained, was no longer questioned? "No, I didn't. The line went dead. We were cut off." She lowered her leg and pressed her knees together. "But I would like to get back down the hill. In fact, I would like to leave Jamaica entirely. It was a mistake to come back. I think that even as a girl I must've sensed something evil about the place."

"You are superstitious. Unless you're talking about people like your brother, there's no evil here. It's just that once you get away from the tourist compounds and the estates, 'it just isn't pretty anymore.'" He said this last in a mocking tone, and answering the question in her eyes explained, "That's what the mistress of the Mafia don Joey Gallo said when they asked her why she'd left him: 'It just isn't *pretty* anymore.'" He rubbed his hands on his chest and watched her with cynical, amused eyes.

"I've hardly been out of the compounds or the estates, so, on the contrary, almost everything I've seen has been remarkably pretty. It's the contrast between the beauty of the place and what lies beneath the surface that disgusts me."

"Yes, it is dis-gusting." He drawled out the word as though imitating some effete gourmand who had swallowed tepid vichyssoise. "I believe that's why some of the vacation cruises to the Caribbean don't even dock. They just lay anchor in the bays and the natives swim out to provide whatever services the tourists may need."

As surely as the first gusts of rain had announced the storm, his tone signaled another argument. "Paul," she said quietly, "I don't want to be . . ."

"Involved? But why should you?" His face became impassive. "It's not your fight. Come and get some sun and straighten out your family affairs and get to hell out. You'd be miserable if you stayed here. You particularly would be miserable because you have a compassionate soul. You don't like to witness misery."

It was hard to tell if he was judging or absolving her. "You mean I'm like the people in that cartoon. I want to be moved to another table?" She could feel the muscles in her jaw stiffen. She hated him for making her justify herself.

"Let's just say that you are *of* your class but not *for* them, so ignoring things may be the only option for you. Why shouldn't you be like the people in the cartoon? I've often suspected that some of my most vociferous supporters are driven by envy of those who can ask for another table." He tipped back in his chair, arms behind his head, staring at the ceiling. "I always knew I couldn't afford you."

"Afford me?" She raised her eyebrows and wrapped her arms across her chest. "I don't know what you mean. You had more money than I did when we lived together, so I suppose you're referring to my being a Nettleton."

"In part. Though that never bothered me too much. In fact, I used to take a certain delight in that. Sometimes when I'd be fucking you I'd think 'if my grandfather could see me now.'"

"Oh, really." Her voice was polite and icy as a hostess greeting an uninvited guest.

"I don't mean that I couldn't buy you things. I meant I couldn't afford you in the important ways." He knew he'd rankled her by saying fucking instead of using the euphemism *making love*. In bed she might be hot and gritty as a country girl, digging her nails into his buttocks to urge him on, but once out of bed she not only affected but actually took on this mannered complexity. It was, he knew, part of the dynamic that renewed his desire by forcing him into an adversarial position. "When we first met I took your shyness for self-possession, and I believed that you were dedicated to radical change. But then I began to realize that women like you . . ." He had trespassed again, talking of her sex instead of talking of her as an individual, about to mention the moral vacuum that often led young people of the upper classes to take up with revolutionaries. He was even ready to venture into a psychological explanation: a girl who had been catered to but emotionally neglected, looking for a strong man, choosing a lover who was bound to outrage her father. But the thought of Archie's abandonment brought his own too vividly to mind. ". . . that you needed more care than I could afford to give."

"You make it sound as though I'm a child or handicapped. I can assure you—"

"I couldn't have—I wouldn't have wanted to--take the time or put out the energy to give you what you needed. If I'd married you and brought you back to the island, you would have come to hate it. Maybe you would have even come to hate me. Despite your compassionate soul, I knew it wasn't your struggle. That was the reason I left when I did and how I did." The muscles in his jaw relaxed. He tipped the chair forward and rested his arms on his knees.

He had wrapped up his argument, absolving himself with that masculine reasoning that she didn't quite buy but had nevertheless succeeded in deflating her. And so, she thought, you married a woman who would fit in with your plans. "I suppose it's all for the best," she said as though she were reading the words off a condolence card. "I always knew that your career was the most important thing to you."

"The fact that you persist in calling it my 'career' means that you will yourself to misunderstand." He wanted to get up and leave her there, sitting in his shirt, waiting for her fancy dress to dry. That he now craved her forgiveness and understanding as much as he'd craved her body kept him in his chair. "It's my *life*, Ceci. When I met you I believed that I was choosing it. Now I suspect that a man doesn't choose his path any more than he chooses what will make his blood run hot. You will point out that I was groomed by my father for a political career. I don't know if I've ever told you this, but there were times when I hated my father. I wished he would shut up and stop pointing it all out to me. Stop trying to impress my responsibility on me. '*See* the barefoot woman with the swollen belly' he commanded. '*Remember* when you take food into your mouth that other mouths are too dry to salivate. *Imagine* the kid who lives in the slums, who reaches for his spliff before his feet hit the dirt floor because he cannot face the dawn without the numb of ganja.' But I couldn't imagine it. Short of genius, a privileged person can't ever imagine poverty. I have never been hungry except by choice —the choice to toughen myself—but after the third day it wasn't pleasant. I did not feel any spiritual enlightenment. I only felt that my belly had taken over my mind and that was an imprisonment that galvanized me." He pulled his chair closer, leaning into her. "A few years ago I was driving Elliot through the marketplace and he looked around and said 'It's so dirty. Why don't they move?' Despite all my father's preachings, that was how I felt as a child. Why don't they move? Now I know. If there's one thing it's impossible to do when you're really poor, it is to plan. Poor people can't wonder about how to better their future. Their future is only today. Survival doesn't leave room for anything else. Thinking and imagination are very expensive propositions. I have, by choice and design, some ability to move them. With my ideas, with the strength of my convictions. With my plans. I'm here because I want to be here, and I will do what I have to do and I will keep doing it until I die or until they kill me."

"You've become a fatalist."

"Now how," he asked with a wry smile, "can a man with my political beliefs become a fatalist?"

"I meant the 'my head bloody but unbowed' rhetoric." She felt as though he'd sung her a chorus of "Which Side Are You On?" That despite herself, she'd been moved, wanting to explain that she wasn't a stupid or uncaring person. But more than that, she was angry that he'd again put her in the position of justifying herself. "You're right. I have no belief that things will really change. You said that Marsden is recreating the world of his ancestors. In a way you seem to be doing the same thing. What revolution has ever changed anything but the masters? Aren't the poor, as Christ said, always with us?

So now it's the American empire taking over from the British empire." She stopped, knowing that her rebuttal could be shot full of holes; knowing, moreover, that she didn't believe a thing she was saying, that she was mouthing the sort of thing Max might have said and for which she would have derided him. "Politics!" she exploded. "I hate politics. You're right. I couldn't have lived with you for long. You breath it, you eat it, you sleep it. There's no room for anything or anybody else."

"What do you suggest I do with my life, Ceci? Shall I take up golf? Shall I sell my people out and become a palace eunuch for the Pentagon? Make lots of money and drive through Trenchtown in my Mercedes with the smoked glass windows rolled up? And when the riots come, shall I take my family and go to Miami and live off my Swiss bank account? Do you think I talk about all this just to devil *you*? Is your ego really that inflated?"

"No. But we always come back to the same point. Rest from it a moment, can't you? We could talk about . . ." He had enmeshed her, making it less and less likely that she could leave with the dignity she'd wanted to show, making her care about him and everything he cared about. She shrugged. "I don't suppose we have anything to talk about."

He pulled in a deep, chest-expanding breath and turned his head to look out the door. "I think I'll take a shower." He started to get up. "No, goddamn it." He sat back down and reached for her hand. "Once, when your period was late, you told me you couldn't go through an hour without thinking about it. I knew that was true. I could see it on your face, in the way you held yourself. You were utterly and completely occupied with that possibility." At the time he had felt her possible pregnancy to be an obstacle he wasn't sure how to surmount. It was only years later, when Vera had been pregnant with Elliot, that he'd been shaken by memories of Ceci's scare and fantasized about the child they might have produced. For some reason he was sure it would have been a girl, graceful, playful but determined, with Ceci's blue eyes and silky hair. "I was worried too," he went on. "Your being pregnant would have forced me into a decision I didn't want to make. Any choice I made would have been the wrong one."

"No," she corrected him, "the choice would have been mine." How dare he bring up such things now! Had he given any more than lip service to her anguish? As she recalled, it hadn't even changed his habits in bed. He hadn't even seemed to notice that she had been deeply unresponsive to him at the same time she'd loved him more fiercely than before. She had drawn it all down on herself, thinking she might have subconsciously willed herself to be pregnant in order to hold on to him. Never, not even when her mother had died, had she felt more alone.

"Of course the choice would have been yours." He was tempted to ask what that choice would have been, knowing that neither answer would please him. Her hand felt stony. She had drawn so deeply into herself that her eyes were glassy. He had lost her entirely. "I brought that up to explain—"

"Explain?" Her voice was as lifeless as her hand.

"That I couldn't understand, couldn't feel as you did then. There's a Spanish expression—*sensir en carne propia:* to know it in your flesh. I only knew your feelings in my mind. You knew them in your body."

"No man can ever know that feeling."

"But perhaps you have that same limitation, now, when you think about my life."

She was holding herself rigidly, but something inside expanded, felt soft, willing to accept and imagine. "I have never questioned your dedication, Paul. I . . ."

He tightened his grip, at first, she thought, to silence her; then she realized that it was a reflexive gesture, that he had heard something outside. Now she heard it too—a spinning of tires, a down-shifting and engagement of the gears. Winston was back.

He got up, staring down at her. Her head sank to her chest. The moment had come. Now she would get up, walk to the bathroom, put on her clothes, pick up her purse, and leave, never to see him again. Now she would . . . but she continued to sit, scarcely able to breathe. He moved away from her, latched the screen door, pulled the wooden door shut, and twisted the china knob a fraction of an inch, so that she felt rather than heard the lock take hold. "Paul, no."

He turned, his hand still poised above the knob, as though ready to unlock it should she speak again, but their eyes held in the waning light. At last he came toward her. Her arms circled his waist, her forehead pressed into the flesh above his trousers, her mouth against his belt buckle. After a time, they released each other. She lay back on the bed, shutting her eyes, hearing him as he slid and hunched out of his pants. He lay down beside her, his touch feather light as he undid the buttons of her shirt. She felt acutely aware but somehow disembodied, breathing steadily, as though in the final yoga exercise. There was a sensation of white light around and in her head, for here she had already surrendered. Gradually, as he stroked her, the light suffused her shoulders and arms, moved into her trunk and through her legs. As it reached her feet and her soles began to tingle, her legs moved apart. He entered her slowly and gravely and his penetration seemed to complete her body.

Sometime well after nightfall, they heard footsteps on the veranda and saw a light shining above the lintel. When the footsteps had disappeared, he got up and fetched a lantern, and a bottle of wine Teddy had left for them. "Seems Teddy found this in the larder after all," Paul muttered. "Now if I can only find a corkscrew." He began to rummage in the desk drawer.

"You get pretty good service for a revolutionary," she teased.

"I'd do it for them under similar circumstances."

She was tempted to ask if he actually had, and again the suspicion intruded: How many other nights and afternoons had there been in this hideaway? How many other women had been in this bed? The fact that she'd had her own lovers did nothing to ease that gnawing jealousy. She yawned, rolled over, and clutched the pillow to her chest, watching the light from the lantern on his face. She wouldn't permit such petty, grubby suspicion to ruin this, her only time with him. And yet it was a relief to know that she would not be with him, would not be tormented by fears and jealousies. With Max she felt them not at all. In fact she had joked with him before she'd left for London, encouraging him to see other women. She would never be able to feel that way about Paul. Never. That worm would always eat at her heart. "There is no greater or keener pleasure than that of bodily love, and none which is more irrational," she whispered.

"Did you say something?"

"I said I love your body."

"But you used to say you loved my mind."

"I was younger then."

"Here, look at this."

She sat up. He was holding the earring. "We found it under the floorboards when we were fixing the house up. Don't know who it belonged to. I like to think it belonged to my great-grandmother. Take it." He tossed it onto the bed. "If my fantasies are correct, it came from the Nettleton coffers anyway."

She picked it up and began to laugh, quietly, rocking back and forth.

"What amused you?"

"My own stupidity. I can't explain." Nor did she want to. She didn't want him to soothe her, didn't need to hear him say "I love you" any more than she wanted to express her own fears. They were hers. They couldn't, shouldn't be exposed. Whatever she might gain in momentary reassurance would be paid for in the loss of self-respect. Paul had known, back then, what he could afford. She was just beginning to understand what she could afford. "Ah, Paul."

"Yes?"

"Nothing. Just you. Just Paul. That's all."

"Well, then . . ." He turned and looked at her, unsmiling. "Ceci."

"Stop fooling with that wine bottle. I don't want any."

"Nor do I."

"Come back to bed."

"I thought you'd never ask. . . ."

Afterward they slept, waking in drowsy amazement to find each other there. Winston was playing his guitar. She got up and went to the bathroom, blowing out the lantern as she came back to bed.

"Just stand there a minute," he commanded as she started to throw back the sheet.

"And then?"

"And then come to me."

As the last residue of heat seeped from the house, they began to drift off again, talking, half talking, losing the thread. She was vaguely aware of him getting up, covering her, lowering the mosquito net. She curled into his warmth, her back to his chest, her buttocks touching his pacified groin. She cupped his hand over her breast, but it had already fallen away as she began to lose consciousness.

The first light began to brighten from purple to mauve. There was a flap and slap outside the door and then a cock crow—lusty, mindless, heralding the dawn.

Paul stood over her. Dressed. Holding a cup of coffee. Without talking, she took it, sipped it, and got to her feet. In the bathroom she shivered as she pulled on the clammy white dress and panties.

She offered her back to be zipped up just as Winston turned on the motor of the jeep. Bleary-eyed, they moved around the room, picking up, straightening things, like workers from the graveyard shift completing the job.

She slipped into her high heels. He handed her her purse. It seemed as if, by mutual agreement, they had chosen not to speak, had chosen to leave each other with a silent dignity that reflected their better selves. It would be a good-bye befitting the importance of their love.

Winston was gunning the motor, signaling that it was time to get going.

She reached the door and stopped.

He came up behind her, reaching for the handle. She stepped back. The door was opened. The air raised gooseflesh on her arms. The rooster perched on the railing near the hammock looked at them with stupid, malevolent eyes.

She was about to step out onto the veranda when she heard his sharp intake of breath.

When he spoke, he spoke quickly and directly, as though they were spies passing each other on a street corner. "Friday afternoon at three. Can you be here?"

She nodded and stepped out into the chilly green wash of light.

Fourteen

Ceci sat in her rented Toyota listening to the last sounds of the jeep. Unmindful of the silence she and Paul shared, or perhaps acknowledging it in his own way, Winston had sung as lustily and mindlessly as the rooster while they'd lurched down the muddy road to the waterfall to pick up her car. They'd followed her to the main road, then spun off, Paul not looking back, Winston bellowing another chorus of "Be Bop a Lula." Now all was quiet. She drew in her breath, caught a whiff of vinyl upholstery, stale cigarette smoke, and gasoline. It was too early to go back to the house. The sound of her car would rouse the dogs and then there would be hell to pay. She couldn't think clearly enough to frame her alibi. She didn't want to think at all. She got out of the car and walked toward the shallows where she'd seen the women washing clothes.

She felt incredibly light, as though she could lift off and fly over the trees to the ocean, which was just beginning to catch the first rays of the sun. She found a tree trunk and sat down, almost as if to anchor herself, and looked up, watching the light illuminate the trees leaf by leaf. A donkey, grazing near the shallows, looked at her and then went back to his breakfast. The whole world seemed new-washed, uninhabited, fresh-smelling. It might have been the first day of creation and she the first woman.

Finally she got up, her bottom numb, her bare arms feeling chilled, and went back to the car. The donkey shambled over to stand near the hood. She smoked a cigarette so limp with dampness that she had trouble drawing on it, shook her head to wake herself up, and started onto the main road, driving at a crawl. The village was just beginning to come to life— another chorus of cock crows, the squall of a baby, a thin plume of smoke from a shack chimney. Her mouth watered at the thought of food.

She had gone only a few miles when she saw a tall man and a woman walking along the road. The man carried a roll of bedding, a transistor radio, and several shopping bags. The woman, equally burdened, wore tight-fitting jeans and a yellow T-shirt that seemed luminous in the early morning light. Her hair was plaited and studded with plastic beads in a style Ceci had not seen on the island. And there was something strangely familiar about her walk, not quite a limp but a turning in of one foot that gave a lopsided, seductive roll to her hips. She had driven another hundred yards before she realized the man was Percy.

Backing up, she'd already called his name before it hit her that she didn't want to talk to anybody. A look that showed she was sorry she'd recognized him flitted across her face as he came to the car, but now she was looking past him. It was the woman who claimed her attention and, as Percy stuck his head in the window, talking a mile a minute, her curiosity groped toward recognition. "Jesmina? Is it you, Jesmina?" There was a subtle change in the woman's mouth and eye shape, the beginnings of happy surprise, before her features arranged themselves into a cooler acknowledgment. "Yes, Appleblossom. It's me."

"What are you doing out so early?" was all she could come up with.

"I just told you, miss," Percy said. "I just told you. Carryin' m' things from the bivouac."

She had no idea what he was talking about, but she reached behind her to unlock the back door. "Get in. Get in. I'll give you a lift. Jesmina! I can't believe it. I asked after you . . . and when I saw you just now there was something about your walk I recognized and . . ." As a child, Jesmina had cut a tendon in her right foot and since she'd had no proper medical treatment she'd developed a limp that made her acutely self-conscious, but Ceci's mention of that could hardly account for the lazily ironic look in Jesmina's eyes.

"I know you back on the island," Jesmina said, removing the pillowcase stuffed with belongings from her head.

"Get in. Please get in." Ceci turned off the motor and handed the keys to Percy. "Put your things in the trunk. I'll take you wherever you want to go."

"Don't think you can drive that far," Jesmina said.

"Sure she can," Percy insisted, missing the joke. "Goin' to carry m' things to the old agricultural school. Then we go back to the bivouac an' get more." He looked back at Jesmina as though asking her permission, but she had already moved to the trunk, unloading her burdens.

"There's plenty of room. I can take you back there, to wherever the rest of your things are, and then I'll take you to the school."

Percy's face brightened at the wisdom of this plan, then fell into a sorrowful expression. "You know I'm being fired, miss?"

"Yes. Auntie told me when I talked to her on the phone." She shook her head. "But she didn't explain why."

Percy's eyes sought the ground, embarrassed.

"What difference the reason?" Jesmina asked as she got into the back seat. "Move, Percy. Load the car. Want to keep the lady waiting all day? You fired. What difference the reason? Backra say you go, you go. Backra don't need a reason."

Ceci noted Jesmina's use of the old word for white man and the reference to her as "the lady." She turned to meet Jesmina's eyes and when she spoke her voice was pumped up with that smooth geniality she used to deflect the hostility of black civil servants, bus drivers, postal clerks, "I can't tell you how surprised I am to see you again." She smiled, coaxing a response, hoping that Jesmina would acknowledge that in times of shock the most heartfelt sentiment often found expression in clichés. Jesmina gave her a polite nod. Percy slammed down the trunk and got in beside Ceci, still muttering his thanks. She turned the key in the ignition. "Now tell me, where is this bivouac you've been talking about?"

"Where I guard the fields. Take the road to the great house. I tell you where we turn up there."

After several minutes of weighty silence, Percy asked if he might turn on the radio. The car was filled with static as he searched the dial, increasing Ceci's irritability. She supposed Jesmina's snub was in reaction to Percy's deferential manners, but she was damned if she'd let herself be punished just because she was in a position to extend a favor. Lurching up the hill to the great house, she glanced at that massive and ghostly temple of the past, wishing that it would crumble once and for all. The weight of history, as Paul would say. A history that had become an excuse for all sorts of personal failures and disappointments, that still bred fear and resentment for masters and slaves alike. And she would always be in the middle, always be scorned for trying to bridge the gap. A bleeding heart at parties like Mrs. Cleardon's; a honky to this woman she'd shared her childhood with. She wanted to scream, "Could we just get rid of all this shit and get on with life?" A series of incidents that had happened when she was living with Paul flashed through her mind, shattering the "all's right with the world" contentment she'd felt just a half-hour before. Once they had been at a house party in Devon, the sort of gathering of bohemians and academics where she'd felt most protected, and a quite sophisticated white woman who'd spoken knowledgeably about the situation in South Africa had cornered her in the bathroom and asked if it were true that "they" had bigger penises. That the woman's social guard had been lowered by too much gin had not persuaded Ceci to absolve her. Later, when Paul had noticed her mood, she'd reluctantly told him about it. He'd laughed it off, saying it was the one racial myth he had no intention of dispelling, but she had felt soiled and humiliated. Now she glanced in the rearview mirror and saw Jesmina's face. It had relaxed into a watchful sadness. She softened at the sight of it. Whatever she had gone through, it was nothing compared to what Jesmina must feel. She bit her lip, wanting to say something, wary of another rebuff.

"Okay, miss. Here, to the right. Turn here."

There was another, more primitive road, improved only to the extent of twin strips of gravel. She rolled the window up to stop the mud from splattering in and wondered how much it would cost when the rental place discovered that she'd ruined the car's shocks. They lurched into a gully swollen by the storm. She down-shifted but couldn't make it up the grade. Jesmina and Percy got out. Jesmina found rocks to lodge against the back wheels while Percy rocked the car forward with hernia-producing effort. At last they made the embankment. "Best not to go further," Percy advised, heaving from the exertion. "You sit here in the car. Play the radio and turn on the air-conditioning. We be back soon." But curiosity and a desire to prove her mettle forced Ceci out into air that was already losing its coolness. "No. I'll help. I'll come with you."

She took off her shoes and followed them up the track, wincing as the pebbles cut into her feet. After they had trekked about a quarter of a mile, she saw the fields of sugarcane. "Shortcut," Percy shouted, cutting into the tall stalks of cane. They followed on a footpath, and as they reached a rise she could see that the cane was merely a border, concealing acres of ganja. A large sign, PRIVATE PROPERTY. VICIOUS DOGS. YOU HAVE BEEN WARNED, was nailed to a pepper tree. A yapping started up. Percy called out a greeting. A stocky, hooded-eyed black man about Percy's age came out of the tent, zipping up his dungarees. Jesmina hung back near the tree, watching the dogs strain against their chains. "Even animal nature be perverted," she said solemnly. The dogs were horrible, yellow-eyed, both cowed and vicious. Percy shouted something about picking up the rest of his things and the man, wavering between disturbed sleep and surprise at seeing Ceci, motioned them on and squatted in the dirt outside the tent.

Inside, the heat was already oppressive. Ceci stood near the flap while Percy and Jesmina gathered up his few paltry belongings—an army blanket, a pair of Keds, a cardboard box full of callaloo, akee, and tomatoes. "From me own garden," Percy said proudly, holding up a tomato. He exchanged a glance with Jesmina and she slipped out of the tent. Ceci could hear her chatting up the man outside, her voice now fluting and seductive, while Percy reached under a tarpaulin, stuffed a few cans of dog food into the box, and arranged the vegetables on top of them. He looked at Ceci from the corner of his eye and, assured of either her complicity or her ignorance, quickly wrapped one of the Coleman lanterns in the blanket. "Hey, Willie," he called when the booty had been stashed. Willie appeared at the flap. "You can have these." He tossed Willie a pair of socks. "Turn your foots to ice nights up here, man." Willie caught the gift and turned away. Jesmina raised the cardboard box to her head. Ceci made a slight gesture with her hands, indicating her willingness to carry something, and Percy drew a large plastic garbage bag from beneath the cot. "This the lightest." It was indeed light. She could feel the twigs protruding. Percy's real crop. She felt helplessly put upon, wondering what she'd gotten herself into, hearing Aunt Vivie's words, "The more you do for them; the more they expect." She nodded as she passed Willie, wondering if her presence would be reported back or if he took her to be a thrill-hungry tourist of the same ilk as Mrs. Cleardon's Gladys.

Percy drove down the hill. Just being behind the wheel seemed to restore his spirits. Oh, man, he laughed, wasn't he glad to be away from that bivouac! He started telling stories of his lonely nights in the tent, all the while turning his head toward the back seat or glancing into the rearview mirror, taking in Jesmina's reaction, yearning for her approval. When it was not forthcoming, he began to look glum and switched on the radio. "That's right," Jesmina said, "if your head's empty, Percy, just fill it up with noise." He switched the radio off.

As they passed the village again, a group of women were already out, weeding the yard and sweeping the steps of the little church. Jesmina snorted and rolled up her window. "If that place be on fire," she said, "those foolish ones stay in there singing for God to help them while flames make crackling of they rumps." Remembering Jesmina's pleasure in putting on her Sunday dress, and the illustrated Bible tracts she'd press into Ceci's hand in hopes of converting her, Ceci wondered what had changed such a naively trusting girl into such a hardheaded woman.

At the weather-beaten sign for the agricultural school Percy got out, pulled a pair of pliers from his back pocket, and made quick work of the barbed wire that secured the gate. They passed the Edison's PRIVATE PROPERTY. NO TRESPASSING sign and the once-cultivated plots that had already been reclaimed by jungle growth to arrive at a clearing: four wooden barracks spoked to a larger single-storied structure, which, Percy explained, had served as their schoolhouse. Its windows were shattered. Its door stood ajar. Percy's eyes filled. He got out, waving his arms, exposing half-moons of sweat on his already stained shirt, whipping himself up into a strained enthusiasm. "When we be here, I sleep in that one over there." He pointed to one of the barracks. "Sleep in rows like the army. Everything clean. They kick you out if you don't be disciplined. Discipline." He said the word as though it were a mantra. "Five in the morning, get up, rain or shine, go to learn everything."

"Where you gonna squat?" Jesmina cut him off.

He grabbed the plastic bag and started away, angry. The women gathered up the other belongings, sharing a first, thawing glance.

The schoolroom was empty except for a single chair and a zinc washtub. Bleached and torn posters—MANHOOD MEANS RESPONSIBILITY, diagrams of tractor and auto engines, advertisements from a pesticide company—curled on the walls. Percy looked from the water-stained floor to the leaking roof and chose a dry section in a corner. There was a scurrying sound beneath the floorboards as they dumped his things. "Are you sure you'll be all right?" Ceci asked. "Does anyone patrol this place?" Then, remembering Mr. Edison at Mrs. Cleardon's party, that combination of ossification and bluster, she smiled. Edison would need a hoist to get him out of his lounge chair; he wasn't likely to be policing the fringes of his estate. "Hey, man. I'll be fine." Percy drew his lips back in a smile of bravado and looked about him as though wanting to ask them to sit. "Would you like . . . ?" Ceci shook her head, afraid that he would try to repay her in ganja. "You, Jesmina," he touched her arm, "you keep the vegetables in this box. They for you." Ceci turned away, realizing for the first time that they must be lovers. When she reached the door, he called after her. "Maybe you ask Mr. Marsden, when you get back, maybe . . ."

"We goin'," Jesmina stopped him. "Come by m' house tomorrow. Find what else you need."

"I come tonight?"

"No. Enough for this day."

Ceci left them alone and went to the car. Resting her head on the steering wheel, she closed her eyes. She wanted food, a bath, a cool, dark place to lie down. Her thoughts kept going back to Paul even as she raised her head and watched Jesmina cross the yard and get in beside her. She did not look across at Jesmina until they had reached the main road, then, glancing to see if there was any oncoming traffic, she saw an expression of desolate relief. "I'm sure he'll be all right," Ceci said without conviction.

Jesmina muttered. "Can't let him live with me. Can't. Be like havin' 'nother child underfoot. You got a cigarette?"

"In my purse."

"That's another thing. He always stealin' m' cigarettes." Jesmina took a long, slow drag. "I let him in m' place, I never get him out. You ever been with a real young one? You know what I mean. Young man think he can't live without you but be thinking 'bout hisself all the time. Percy got plans for this, plans for that. Think so big, talk so good sometimes he make me believe we're already sittin' in our own little house in the hills. But he still end up squatting, yes? Think he do in a little way what the boss do in a big way. He don't listen. His ears stuffed up with TV dreams. He don't listen to me except when I got something nice to say. I tell by seeing you, you know about men." She sighed, exhaling a cloud of smoke. "When we little girls with only bumps on the chest, remember we talk all the time? All the time, love, love, love. Man gonna come and make every day Christmas for sure. Me, I still love the sweet talk, but I can turn it off like the radio, you know?"

"Do you know why he was fired?"

"*He* . . ." Jesmina said so contemptuously that she could only be referring to Marsden, "he say Percy sellin' ganja makes trouble. That what he say. I know he lookin' for any reason. He get rid of us one by one. That what I think. What you think?"

"I haven't really been here long enough to . . ." What was she protecting? "Yes. Yes, that's what I think." She could feel Jesmina studying her as they approached the slope just before the village.

"We comin' up on m' place now. Drop me off the side of the road. Or . . ." Jesmina took a long pause. "You want to come up?"

"Yes. I'd like that."

"Leave the car here." Jesmina motioned to a turnoff. "Be sure to lock it."

Planks and pieces of tin had been laid over the higgeldy-piggeldy pathway between makeshift houses built so close together that you could hand something from the window of one into the window of another. The bottle borders dividing the garden patches were submerged in mud. As they picked their way up the hill, Ceci could feel eyes watching her from behind doorways and windows. Mosquitoes or perhaps fleas nipped at her ankles. A few besmattered chickens pecked about. An old woman sat by a water pump, an infant in her lap. "Want to wash your feet?" Jesmina asked. While Ceci pumped water onto her feet, Jesmina hoisted the child onto her hip, asked the old woman if Carlotta had gotten off to school, then moved ahead, pushing open a bright yellow door.

The roof of the shack was supported by a wooden pillar that had been carved in crude imitation of African figures. There was a table covered with oilcloth, a vase of plastic flowers, three wooden chairs, a shelf holding six or seven books, a plush love seat covered with plastic, its injured leg supported by cinderblock. A poster of Che Guevara hung next to one of Bob Marley. The linoleum was swept and everything was as orderly as possible, but the very order underlined the hopelessness of keeping anything clean. Through a locked grillwork gate another room was visible: three beds, clothes on hooks.

"You lookin' pale, Appleblossom. Want a fizzy drink?"

Ceci nodded and sat down. Jesmina shifted the child to her other hip, took some keys from her jeans pocket, and undid the padlock on the little refrigerator. She handed Ceci a bottle of Coca Cola. "If you hold Toussaint, I make some breakfast." Ceci held out her arms. After nosing the child's neck, Jesmina handed him over. "Eggs okay? Rice and peas leftover?"

"That would be fine." Toussaint was a warm lump in her lap, his eyes glimmering with milky expectancy. His hand smacked at her breast, caught her silver chain, and tugged it into his mouth. "He's beautiful."

"Me third. Me last," Jesmina said as she took bowls from the refrigerator. "I don't know he in me at first. Got me the shot to take away m' period, so I don't know at first. Didn't want him there, but there he be. So . . . He sweet, i'n't he? You got childrens?" Ceci shook her head. "Ah, you a career woman, huh?" Jesmina made a fist and laughed. "Womens' liberation, huh?"

"I can't say I have a career either. Various jobs. No real career."

"No husband?"

"Not that either."

"We the same in that." She started cracking the eggs into a bowl.

"But you did get married, didn't you? I seem to recall . . ."

"Mmmm. Icilda see m' belly, she chase that boy all the way to St. Elizabeth, catch him, bring him back. We get married, but when Derek, m' oldest, is no bigger than a piglet, m' husband go off to America. For one, two years he send me money, then . . ." She beat the eggs furiously, picked a fragment of shell from the bowl and studied it. "Remember when we go into Auntie's kitchen one time at bedtime? You keep tellin' me 'bout French toast. Tell me it's American. That's enough for me. We make ourselves a big mess for sure, makin' that French toast. Icilda beat m' bottom sore." Laughing, she dumped the rice and peas into a sizzling pan.

"Yes. I wrote to Archie to send us some maple syrup, but he never did."

"He down here now too? He with you?"

"We came together. I think it's a bit late in the game for us to be *with* each other. Did you ever see your father again?"

"He come to m' mother's funeral, but he don't recognize me. He make fuss over Derek, try to give him five dollars. I tell him keep it. Too late for the presents." She cut the omelet in two and flipped it onto the plates, dished out the rice and peas. "Here. I take Touissant now."

They ate in silence, Jesmina feeding herself, then mushing rice with egg yolk and spooning it into Toussaint's mouth. Ceci ate hungrily, the food tasting better than meals she'd had at four-star restaurants. "Thanks. This is good."

"You want more?"

"No, thanks." She pushed her plate aside. "That hit the spot. You said before that you knew I was back on the island. Did Percy tell you?"

Jesmina lowered her eyes, her mouth turning up in a mischievous, almost seductive grin. "I sent the telegram. I pretty sure you come when you get it."

"*You* sent the telegram? You mean you sent it without anyone else knowing about it?"

Jesmina nodded. "Day after Marsden tell me to go, I take Auntie's book, find your address."

Ceci wiped a film of sweat from her forehead and laughed softly. "I guess that goes to show the level of communication in my family. Aunt Vivie said she hadn't sent any telegram, but I just assumed that she'd forgotten about it." She hit the table with the flat of her hand. "No wonder Marsden wasn't glad to see me. He'd never asked me to come!"

"Things get bad at the house. I don't know if you come, but it's worth a try."

"So I have you to thank."

"Don't know if you want to thank me. Just I see Auntie getting caught up like she be a fly in the spiderweb. Bad enough when Marsden here by hisself. He bring down that Hilary, then there trouble for sure. First week she here I workin' late 'cause they have a party. I'm walkin' home, she drive right by me on the road. After midnight, she drive right by me. I see what it gonna be like then." She sighed. "She want me to smile day after that. I have no reason to smile. I do m' work, but she set out to have me do every kind of thing for her so she say I do it wrong. In the morning she have me serve her breakfast in her bed. I put her coffee down she say, 'Jess, you must never look at a lady's body when you serve her. Keep y' eye on the face." I can't help m'self. I have to laugh. Hear bullshit like that, I have to laugh. She think I interested in her tittie? But I know that the end for me when I laugh. Like when you a child an' you know you go too far? It like that. I know I go too far. You know from the look in her eye that her hand be wanting to lay on me, whoop! But she can't hit me. So I know she goin' to see me out the door for good."

"Yes. She would do something like that. Nothing comes easier to the insecure than bullying."

"I don't care 'bout her security, man," Jesmina said derisively. "She got more security than I ever look to have."

"I meant emotional security."

"Hey, c'mon, man."

"I wasn't trying to absolve her, just to understand."

"You kid y'self, Ceci. You understand everythin' better than you think. Some thing you understand when you very young, right? Bein' fair you understand when four or five, when you take turns in a game. Take your turn. We understand bein' fair very young. We understand mean and bully very young. And lies, too. Don't kid y'self. You understand most things. Maybe you want to forget you understand."

The food she'd enjoyed suddenly felt heavy in Ceci's stomach. "I don't know what I can do about any of this. I've tried to talk to Aunt Vivie. I'll try to talk to Archie. What do you want to do? Do you want your job back?"

"Oh, man." Jesmina shook her head and the plastic beads in her braids knocked against one another. "Maybe you don't understand." A long silence followed, punctuated by Toussaint's gurgles and burps. "Only I want you to *know*," Jesmina said solemnly. "Just to know how things is here."

"But what's the point of knowing if . . ." Toussaint stared

up at her. He gaze had a strange glimmer, like the knowing look of a tired old man. "What will you do now?"

Jesmina stared out the door. "Me, I got m' plan. I got some money saved. I have the name of a man in Miami, got him a marriage racket. I pay him some money, he get me a husband. American citizen. Then I get to be a citizen, get a job, probably takin' care of some other women's children. Then I save again and bring over m' own children. Not Derek. He's on his own now." She ran her hand over Toussaint's head and brought his dimpled fist up to her cheek. "All times I stay with Icilda when I'm a girl, I say, 'When I grow up I never leave my children.' And I say, 'They all goin' to have the same father'—that way the brothers and sisters help each other 'stead of being so jealous-feeling and just looking out for theyselves. Now it look like I do same thing m' mother did. Toussaint here not goin' to miss me, are you, boy? See how he love to go to you? He go to any woman. Like his father. I was gettin' ready to kick that one out. Spreeing be the only life he know. I ready to kick him out, but when he sees m' belly, he leaves without m' askin'. I don't think Toussaint cry for me. But Carlotta . . ."

"Your daughter?"

". . . she seven now. She gonna know I'm gone." There was a palpable ring of guilt in her voice. She handed Toussaint back into Ceci's arms and got up, fishing for her keys again, unlocking the gate to the bedroom. "I show you Carlotta's picture," she called. "She's the best. She very loving. Smart like her father."

"And where is he?"

"In Havana. He's a doctor. Come here to work in the clinic, but when the new government come, they send all Cubans back. Americans don't like the Cubans, so we can't have them here no more." She came back to the table, carrying an Instamatic camera and a handful of snapshots, which she spread out on the oilcloth. "See her?" She touched one of the photos with her forefinger. It showed a skinny, light-skinned, serious-looking girl in a ruffled dress. "There she is. Right after I crisp her new dress." Jesmina sat down, hands between her legs. "Carlotta's goin' to miss me. I'll be an old lady 'fore she understand what I do. I tell her about her father all the time, but she don't understand. I love that man so. When he was sent off, I lay on the bed and can't get up. I think, please let me sink into this mattress, let me never get up again. You ever love a man like that?"

"Yes. Yes, I have."

"Only good thing, we know now that it don't happen twice, right? Older and wiser, right?"

Ceci got up. "I suppose so."

"Here, let me take this boy back. Oh, no! He drool on your dress."

"It doesn't matter. This dress belongs in the Smithsonian by now."

"What?"

"In a museum." With her fingertip, Ceci wiped a speck of egg yolk from Toussaint's mouth. He blew a perfect bubble of saliva and reached out, yanking at Jesmina's braid. "No, no," Jesmina scolded, capturing his hand. He arched his back and let out a squall of protest as he was handed back to her. "Some day . . . if you stay, Ceci . . . I'd like you to see Carlotta."

"Yes. I'd like that." They looked at each other for a long time. Ceci wanted to offer Jesmina some money but decided against it. "I must be getting on."

"Before you go, let's have our picture taken together. That old woman in the yard will do it. She love to operate the camera."

Fifteen

"**D**OWN W" were the only letters still visible in the smear of red graffiti on the big wooden gates. Ceci pulled on the brake and got out of the car, but the workman kept scrubbing, making streams of bloody-colored turpentine that dripped into the ground.

"What did it say?" she asked.

By way of reply, he unhooked the rope from the top of the gates and motioned toward her car.

"What did it say?" she asked again.

He dipped the brush into the bucket of turpentine. "Wood wet from storm. Hard to get off. Drive in now, miss."

The guard dogs began to bark. Thelda hurried up the slope. "Rule is honk horn, miss. Honk horn."

"When did this happen?" Ceci inquired again.

"Break rule, cause trouble," Thelda scolded. "Make dogs angry."

"Bugger the dogs. What . . ."

"Break rule . . ." Thelda persisted, "make . . ."

"Then you may close the gate after me," Ceci said sharply.

She pulled up to the big tree. The sun was at its zenith. There was a harsh stillness in the air, interrupted only by the rhythmic pounding of a hammer. Glancing over to the house, she saw another workman up on a ladder, securing an upstairs shutter that had apparently been blown off in the storm. She looked in the rearview mirror. There was no point even running a comb through her hair; she was beyond repair. The veranda seemed to be deserted. She hoped that she might slip into her room unnoticed. Shoes in hand, she walked past the soupy mess of the garden, but just as she mounted the steps, a chair scraped the tile and Hilary's voice rang out. "Cecily, is that you? We're around on the far side." She stopped, sighed, and rounded the corner to see Hilary, chartreuse silk back toward her, seated at a table. A man in battered straw hat and dark glasses, his shirt buttoned up to the neck, hands primly folded on knobby knees that stuck out from oversized Bermuda shorts, sat opposite.

"That is you, isn't it, Cecily?" Hilary asked without turning around.

The man got unsteadily to his feet. "It is herself," he said, taking a few steps toward her. His knees, elbows, and Adam's apple protruded painfully from skin sallow enough to admit a case of jaundice. His spotty gray beard and mustache seemed incongruous with his boyish features. It was Hayward Pembroke, her old tutor. Nodding, he said, "*Salve, discipula mea. Gaudeo, mihi est voluptas, quod venisti.*"

From some forgotten closet of her mind, Ceci pulled out "*Salve, magister. Gratum est mihi te videre.*" and reached for his hand. A giddy laugh escaped her. "I feel as though I'm in the last scene in *8 1/2*, where everybody who's ever been important in the hero's life comes together and forms a giant dancing circle."

Hilary looked her up and down. "It seems you've been dancing already. St. Vitus' dance?" She lifted the silver teapot. "I was about to have luncheon when Mr. Pembroke arrived. Will you join us?"

"I was s-s-sure Vivian invited me for today," Hayward stuttered. "Perhaps I confused the d-d- . . ."

"Date," Hilary supplied. "If there's been any confusion, Mr. Pembroke, I'm sure it hasn't been yours. Do sit down."

"I feel I've c-c-come at an inopportune time."

"If only Aunt Vivian could remember to inform the rest of us what she's up to," Hilary said peevishly.

"Of course you haven't come at an inopportune time," Ceci smiled. "I'm awfully glad to see you, Hayward. I may call you Hayward now, mayn't I? And may I also say that you haven't changed a bit."

"Would that w-w-were a compliment." He sat down after bumping into the side of the table. "And you yourself . . ." His hands flapped up as though wanting to embrace her. "When I last saw you, you were a grubby-faced ragamuffin, running about without your shoes, and lo and b-b-behold, still y-y-y . . ." He gave up the struggle to get the word out and chuckled softly.

"I was caught in the storm."

"Wasn't it wonderful? I d-d-do so look forward to natural disasters."

Hilary looked from one to the other. "You'll want to go in and change, Ceci. But do hurry. As I said, I was about to have luncheon when Mr. Pembroke arrived."

Ceci sat down. "Please don't bother setting an extra place for me. I had a large breakfast. But I would like a glass of juice."

"Icilda," Hilary screeched before turning to Hayward and dropping her voice to a solicitous whisper. "May I pour you some tea, Mr. Pembroke?"

"No, thank you." He held up his glass. "Perhaps another small l-l-libation, in celebration of my star pupil's return."

Hilary's mouth turned up in a smile that did not altogether mask her disapproval.

"Where is Aunt Vivie?" Ceci wanted to know.

"Hiding out in her room. She *says* she has another of her migraines."

"Then she probably does. And where's Archie?"

"Marsden has driven him into Mo Bay on some business."

"I see."

Icilda moved silently to the table. Her face had the shocked and confused expression of a refugee. "Here you are, Icilda." Ceci reached for her hand. "I hope the storm didn't frighten you. I remember you don't like storms."

"Message for you, miss. Man from New York, called Max. Last night he call you."

"Thanks, I—"

Hilary dropped the sugar tongs on the table. "Icilda, all messages are to be written out on the little pink pad. I've told you time and time again: you write the message on the little pink pad and you give it to whomever it is for. Don't you remember?"

Icilda stared in front of her, eyes blank. "Don't bother, Icilda." Ceci patted her hand and released it. Apparently the old woman preferred to have Hilary think her careless rather than to admit that she was illiterate. "I have the message now. Would you please bring me some juice? And Mr. Pembroke would like some more of your famous punch."

"Perhaps you'd best bring out the pitcher," Hilary drawled.

"Yes." Ceci smiled sweetly. "Bring the pitcher. And perhaps you'd best tell that workman to stop hammering. I hear Aunt Vivie isn't feeling well."

"She got she head spots," Icilda explained, referring to the silver dots that Vivian said danced in her eyes when she had a migraine. "See she flowers drowned in she garden and so she get spots."

"The workman isn't a regular employee," Hilary said. "We're paying him by the hour."

"Nevertheless," Ceci insisted.

Icilda looked from one to the other.

"Very well," Hilary conceded, getting up. "I'll go and tell him to clean the leaves out of the pool. You may tell Thelda to serve lunch, Icilda."

As soon as they were alone, Hayward slipped his dark glasses down to the tip of his nose. His eyes—red-rimmed, pale, sardonic—met Ceci's and held them. "It was wise of you to decide not to eat. Your future sister-in-law can induce indigestion *before* the meal."

"Yes. I'm afraid so."

"I do wish Vivian could join us." He slumped back in his chair. "I had no idea just how much I missed my afternoons with her until she started to go off."

"Do you mean when she had that stroke?"

"It was never determined that she did have a stroke. I

checked on t-t-that. They're searching to find a medical explanation for what I believe are s-s-spiritual problems. She started to go off well over a year ago. Just after Marsden came to stay for good. I hadn't really noticed . . . one doesn't notice these things when one is intimate, you know. But one Thursday, when we met here for our usual discussion—our two-member l-l-literary club—she started out quite normally, normally for Vivian, that is, and then she just went to pieces. She'd been reading Emerson's essay on self-reliance and she was telling me about it, a-a-and all at once, she began to weep." His own eyes welled with boozy empathy. "She said she knew that she had never had it and never would—self-reliance, I mean. It all came out in bits and pieces. Things I'd never heard before. Not in all the years I'd known her. The next time I came round, she acted as though nothing had happened. I don't mean to upset you, my dear. But even as a girl you always wanted to know the seamy parts. I-i-in fact, you particularly wanted to know the seamy parts." He combed his straggly beard with his fingers. "It was good of you to come back." Hilary's high heels clicked through the living room. Hayward pushed his glasses back up and said, "Here she comes again, taxing our geniality. And I haven't been naturally genial since 1952. It's quite amusing to watch her. She can't decide if she's to court me because of my connection to Lady Pembroke, or if I'm just another fly in the social ointment."

Hilary swept back her hair and resumed her seat. "Now," she beamed at them, "you must tell me all about Mrs. Cleardon's party. I had so wanted to go, but my father was receiving an award from the National Businessmen's Association, so I flew back to the States for a few days. Daddy said I shouldn't bother to come but I had some shopping to do and Marsden absolutely insisted. Marsden's very fond of Daddy."

And he may not have wanted you to run into his cast-off mistress at the party, Ceci thought.

"Marsden told me the party was absolutely marvelous," Hilary continued. "Did you have a wonderful time? Was absolutely everybody there?"

"I for one was n-n-not," Hayward said. "Mrs. Cleardon and

I are very friendly, but I'm not on her A list for parties. A p-p-poor relation, you see."

Hilary wagged her finger at him. "I do so love that about you English; your droll sense of humour."

"Since when did f-f-facts become funny? If you'd laugh at what I just said, you'd split your s-s-sides if I said the Magna Carta was signed in 1215."

Hilary's mouth twitched, searching for the appropriate response. Was she supposed to smile? One never knew with these people. She'd hoped her social progress on the island would be sure and swift, but so many of those from the old families were distant or, like this Hayward Pembroke, down-right odd. Their very appearance was disreputable and they seemed to take pains to hide whatever wealth they had, living as they did in sparsely furnished houses that often needed paint jobs. She'd mentioned that to Marsden and he'd said, condescendingly she'd thought, that she didn't understand. "You must tell me when Lady Pembroke has her 'at home' days," she went on, hoping she was striking the right note. "I hear she has a marvelous collection of paintings."

"Whoever told you that was lying," Hayward corrected. "The only paintings we have are those I did of her Pekingese and a few c-c-clotted watercolors of the g-garden. When I had a steadier hand." He actually seemed amused as he held his quivering hand before him.

"You've come from London, is that what I hear?" He clasped his hands around his knees and turned to Ceci. "I've always planned to go back. I can't i-i-imagine w-what England is like n-now."

"Much changed, even from when I was first there. The countryside is still very beautiful. There's still the civility and the courtesy, orderly queues for the buses, friendliness in the shops, and all that—but the bobbies are armed for riot duty, you see more burnooses than bowlers, and there are young-sters with shaved heads and fearful-looking makeup sitting about in the Wimpy bars. But I can't speak with any author-ity. I was only visiting London. I really live in New York now."

"Ah, here are our drinks." Hayward smiled up at Thelda

as she set the pitcher of punch on the table, but Thelda, sensing that his stock was shaky with her new mistress, gave the barest nod and turned on her heel. "Vivian u-u-used to keep a map on the kitchen wall and we used to put little pins in it to show where you were traveling. It became quite tattered. H-h-have you seen it all now, Ceci? Tasmania and Outer Mongolia? Was there some design in y-y-your peregrinations?"

"I don't think so. I don't travel to go anywhere; just to go."

"Ah, yes. The soul of a journey should be liberty, p-p-p . . ." he struggled, pursing his lips, cheeks distended, ". . . perfect liberty." He reached for his punch.

"I'm not sure there is such a thing, though travel certainly creates the illusion. When I first started—"

"Daddy sent me on a world tour when I graduated from Smith," Hilary interrupted in a voice designed to gain the attention of a crowded room. "When I came home I said, 'I've seen it all now. Now I just want to put down some roots.' Of course, I didn't know until I met Marsden that I'd be putting my roots down in Jamaica. I won't really feel as though I've done that until we've restored the great house and had the wedding," she rushed on. "It's so frustrating. The construction workers are like snails. Daddy would know how to light a fire under them, but Marsden is just too kind. As soon as we've opened the great house, we'll have to start to work on this place. It is a perfect old wreck, isn't it? I don't mind roughing it for awhile, but very soon I'm afraid I shall have to start cracking the whip."

"I wouldn't use that particular expression if I were you," Hayward cautioned. "Jamaicans are a bit s-s-sensitive about the mention of whips."

Ceci sat up. "Speaking of native sensitivities, I noticed that graffiti on the gates as I came in. What was that about?"

"It's being cleaned up," Hilary said shortly.

"Yes, I saw that. But when was it put there and what did it say?"

"Something unpleasant, naturally."

"There's a rumor going about that the gasoline prices are

about to be raised. Things are very t-t-tense all over the island. I expect—"

"Yes. I expect that explains it. There's always something, isn't there? So it's not surprising that one is the target of random discontent," Hilary cut him off again.

"Hayward was saying . . ." Cecily said politely. Hilary's constant interruptions were beginning to strain her nerves. But Hilary kept on, discussing her decorating plans in compulsive detail, determined to have her share—which meant more than her share—of the conversation. Ceci lifted the hair from her neck and shut her eyes against the glare of silverware, amused to notice that after his third tumbler of punch, Hayward's stutter had all but disappeared and his voice had taken on a mellifluously mocking tone. As Thelda put down the plates of fish and julienned vegetables, Hilary surveyed the table, eyes narrowed to seek out imperfection. "Oh, no, no, no!" she cried, "I distinctly told him not to do lemon wedges. The lemons are to be cut in half, wrapped in gauze, and tied with green ribbon." Thelda reached for the plate. "No. Just leave it. Go and get the iced water. Honestly! By the time they get the meal on the table I'm so nervous my appetite has deserted me. I just don't know what to do."

"Perhaps you should forget about the lemons and have yourself a glass of punch," Hayward suggested. "There's a belief that the equatorial climate dries up the brain. Youngsters have enough natural oils and juices to allow their brains to work efficiently, but as we get older, those of us who use our brains a great deal, such as you do, Miss Berwith, find that our natural juices tend to dry out. A supply of rum can help to lubricate them."

"If you'll excuse me," Hilary said curtly, "I must have a few words with the chef."

"Dear me," Hayward whispered as soon as Hilary had gone through the doors, "if we don't behave ourselves we'll be asked to eat in the kitchen. I wonder where Marsden found her. She's the spitting image of old Lady Maude, had you noticed?"

"That's it. I knew she reminded me of somebody."

"Enough to make you believe in reincarnation. The perfect

consort for the Nettleton's second empire. *Tum Caesar . . . Quia suam uxorem etiam suspicione vacare vellet.*"

"Mmmm. This particular Caesar's wife certainly will be above suspicion. She will never succumb to the deadly sins."

"She's too dyspeptic for gluttony; too ambitious to be slothful . . ."

"Too afraid of losing control to give into drunkenness. And she couldn't give into lust—there's no fashionable costume for it."

"That leaves only anger, envy, and avarice." They smiled at each other. "Oh, and pride. We forgot pride," Hayward added.

"I always forget it. It's one of my own principal sins."

"If I forego d-dessert, might we go and sit in the cupola?"

"That would be a good idea. I want to speak to you more about Aunt Vivian."

Hilary reappeared, carrying a crystal dish. "I do hope your fish isn't cold, Mr. Pembroke," she said as she deposited a gauze-wrapped lemon on each of their plates.

"May we begin now? I'm loathe to rush such an excellent meal," he said after taking a first bite, "but I couldn't ride my bicycle because of the flooding, and since Percy wasn't about, I told Lady Pembroke's driver to pick me up at three."

"I'm sorry to inconvenience you. We had to let Percy go. Marsden feels just awful about it. But there was nothing else for it. I mean, you do the best you can to help them and then they turn around and slap you in the face."

Ceci arched her brows. "Percy slapped someone's face?"

The cords stood out in Hilary's neck. "What I meant to say was that we've given Percy every chance. He's disappointed us rather badly."

Hayward's fork stopped in midair. "Young Percy gone? You mean to say you've s-s-sacked him? Surely not."

"Personally, I think he should be reinstated as soon as possible," Ceci said. "He's polite, he's an excellent driver, and he knows how to service that relic of a Rolls."

"Finding a mechanic is not equivalent to locating a brain surgeon," Hilary said slowly. "Believe me, there are ten others standing in line for the job."

Ceci felt her anger rise. "But Percy—"

"I'm sure Mr. Pembroke didn't come to lunch to hear us wrangle about problems with the staff, did you, Mr. Pembroke?"

Hayward pushed his plate aside. "I've known Percy since he was a boy," he muttered. "Since he was a boy."

"Percy is Icilda's grandson," Ceci said evenly. "He's as much a part of this property as that guango tree."

Hilary affected a look of amazement. "You surprise me, Ceci. I should have thought you'd be the last one to talk about the staff as though they were property. They're paid workers. And as for Percy being Icilda's grandson . . ." she gave a hoarse little laugh, ". . . we'd have to own the entire island to provide employment for all of Icilda's relatives."

"It's extremely upsetting to Aunt Vivie to have all these changes. Was she consulted about any of this? I can't believe that she—"

"Really, we must stop this tiresome chatter. It's ruining Mr. Pembroke's lunch."

Hayward touched his abdomen. "I'm afraid my appetite has deserted me, Miss Berwith. I've had a gippy tummy for days. Would you think it too rude if I forego the sweets? I should like to have a few words with my former pupil."

"Whatever you please." Hilary raised her head, alert. "I believe I hear the car. The men must be back."

Their escape thwarted, Ceci and Hayward exchanged a glance and settled back into their chairs. The car doors slammed and as footsteps crunched on the gravel, Hilary brayed, "I'm over here, darling. On the far side of the veranda."

Ceci steeled herself to look straight into Marsden's face as he and Archie approached. He returned her look, his eyes going from her forehead to her shoulders, a thin smile making a little knot in his chin. As he bent to kiss Hilary's offered cheek, his eyes caught Ceci's for the briefest moment and flashed a palpable hostility. Whatever anger she'd misplaced onto Hilary now turned inward. If she'd kept her wits about her at Mrs. Cleardon's party she might have been able to exercise some leverage in the family's affairs. She would have had to feign ignorance of the really important issues and negotiate her way through half-truths and a good deal of hypocrisy, but she might have achieved something. Instead, she'd thrown that possibility away when she'd tossed the drink in Marsden's face. If he'd considered her an annoyance before, he now considered her an enemy.

She glanced at Archie. He stood at a little distance, leaning on his cane, looking flushed and rumpled. She felt a need to comfort and be comforted by him, to put her head against his chest and say, "I think we've both made a muck of things." She even had an absurd impulse to tell him about Paul.

"I say," he grunted, taking her in, "you look like the Wreck of the Hesperus." His tone dissolved her tenderness. Why did he always persist in putting so much importance on the appearance of things? "We were all terribly worried about you," he went on. "You might have let us know where you were."

"I'm sorry. I thought I'd made it clear when I spoke to Aunt Vivie that I was perfectly safe."

"But where were you?" he wanted to know.

She stood up. "You've never met Mr. Pembroke, have you, Archie? Hayward Pembroke, this is my father, Archie Baron. Archie, this is Hayward Pembroke, my old tutor. I'm sure you remember my speaking about him."

"To be sure," Archie lied, extending his hand to the troll-like man. "Pleasure to meet you, Mr. Pembroke."

"The pleasure is all mine. I've always been a f-f-fan of your art, Mr. Baron," Hayward said in a shyly caressing voice.

Oh, Christ, Archie thought, a doddering poof. He smiled while Hayward reminisced about his performances and stammered on to say what a brilliant pupil Ceci had been, and tried not to look at her. On the drive back from Montego, just as he was relaxing into fantasies about the increased dividends that would be coming his way once the great house was opened, Marsden had insisted on talking about Ceci. Expressing a brotherly concern that Archie could not accept as altogether sincere, Marsden had said how much it pained him to see how Ceci had "turned out." She was wild, unstable, irresponsible. Rumor had it—though Marsden wouldn't be specific about the source of the rumor—that she'd spent the night in the hills with some black men. Not that that was without precedent. Girls of good family often rebelled in a way that was designed to hurt the family most. Didn't Archie recall the scandal—more of Archie's time than Marsden's—of Nancy Cunard, daughter of the famous Cunard shipping family, who'd made herself a subject of international gossip by her blatant affairs and by publishing a book called *Negro?* Ceci seemed to be a similar "type." Archie had been surprised at how much this talk of Ceci as a "type" had wounded him. He had tried, unsuccessfully, to come to her defense, all the time feeling a mounting anger toward her. For where were the weapons with which to defend her? Here she stood, disheveled, with an angry glint in her eye, living proof of all that could be said against her.

". . . and I was never more than two lessons ahead of her, the entire time I t-t-tutored her," Hayward concluded. "I was sure she'd g-g-go on to take honors at Oxford."

A sudden gust of wind flipped the tablecloth up onto one of the plates and swept off Hayward's hat, exposing his baby-bald head. He chased the hat along the tile, knees knocking, a pitiful sight.

"Wind's up. That's good," Marsden said, turning to look up into the hills. "Things will dry out before we know it." He turned in a half-circle, looking out at the bay, a wistful, regretful expression on his face. "I'd like to have just one whole afternoon to sit and look at the bay. Just one."

"Well, it can't be this one," Hilary reminded him. "We have a thousand things to attend to."

"We'll leave you to them," Ceci said, anxious to break away. "Hayward and I are going out to the cupola for a chin-wag, Archie. If you're not tired of hearing Mr. Pembroke sing my praises, why don't you join us?"

"But Archie must be famished," Hilary cooed, touching his arm. "Aren't you famished, Father? Do sit down and have some lunch."

Though he was both exhausted and hungry, Archie shook his head and shrugged off her touch. More and more, Hilary had begun to remind him of a pretty pink pig. "I think I'll go in and change my shirt. Then, perhaps, if you'd send a sandwich out to the cupola."

"Whatever you like. Marsden and I have some business to attend to, don't we, dear? So if you'll excuse us." She smiled all around. "And Mr. Pembroke, do extend my regards to Lady Pembroke."

They scattered in their different directions, Hayward pouring himself another glass of punch and following Ceci across the spongy lawn. "You'd best steady me." He reached for her hand as they got to the footbridge. "The weight of my liver makes me list and there's no point in drowning; I already see my life pass before my eyes every morning when I wake up. What an extraordinarily handsome man your father still is."

"Ah, yes, Archie in his bwana suit."

They reached the cupola and stood at the railing, looking out into the bay. Some native boys rowed by in a skiff, laughing and waving at them.

"I'm surprised Miss Berwith hasn't checked her maritime law and set a twelve-mile limit on this bay," Hayward croaked as he settled himself into a deck chair. "I wonder why Marsden picked this particular Lady Macbeth to prick the sides of his intent. One can see that she'll never be satisfied with anything. Perhaps that's it—bizarre as it sounds—she'll keep him going by constantly reinforcing his own poor opinion of himself. Marriage is such a strange institution, don't you think? It allows people to torture each other in ways that they'd be brought up on charges for if they weren't legally joined. But I'm not surprised. Marsden always had that strain of melancholia. It seems to me that this rushing about trying to restore things is just his attempt to deny a terrible anomie."

"And to think I used to have a crush on him." Ceci sighed as she stretched herself out in the hammock.

"So did I. I did so look forward to his visits." Hayward's Adam's apple bobbled as he took a long swallow of his punch.

"I'm not particularly interested in Marsden's melancholia. Marsden is a reactionary creep."

"Reactionary. Radical. Right wing. Left wing. Why bother to label it? More and more I find that I haven't the energy to take sides. The last time I did was when the local gentry removed the Anglican preacher from the parish. When he counted up the Christmas contribution for the poor, he said, 'God forgive us for pretending that we care about the poor when we do not like them and do not want them in our homes.' Commendable honesty, don't you think? They got rid of him, of course." He took off his dark glasses and studied her with rheumy eyes. "I'm eternally grateful that I've been cast in the role of observer. All I have to do is to wait for Lady Pembroke to die and then I can become a hermit in style. You, too, are an observer, Ceci. You had that stamp on you—that ability to look out of yourself—when you were very young."

"I'm not sure I'm flattered by that analysis. I want to take sides."

"Mmmm. And when you were a girl you told me you wanted to be Joan of Arc. Perhaps if you weren't so attractive you might have been."

"Pretty women don't have to do things?"

"Why should they? Their mere existence is enough."

"You should meet my friend Max. The two of you would see eye to eye." She listened to the surf, trying to calm her heartbeat. "I met Jesmina today. Do you remember Jesmina?"

"Of course. Of course I remember Jesmina."

"Jesmina is pretty. It doesn't seem to have been enough for her." She paused. "Seeing her—I don't know how to say it— it made me feel the same way I did when I was eighteen and in my first philosophy class. Everything important seemed to be beyond my understanding. We loved each other, Jesmina and I. A childish love to be sure, since it never took our considerable differences into account; perhaps a stronger love because of that. We were peas in a pod, The plans we made about how our adult lives would be! Now . . ." She opened her hand and closed it suddenly, as though trying to grasp the air. "Our lives now could not be more different. I don't mean that I pity her. She's strong. Very, very strong. But . . ." She saw Jesmina's rooms, the padlock on the refrigerator, the photos of the little girl ". . . why was I lucky enough to be born with privilege? What toss of the cosmic dice makes it possible for me to develop what you call my 'style'? To float through the world without a care while she . . ."

"Without a care? You? Surely not. It was not my intention to make you sound superficial, though you still, as you yourself pointed out, sound rather like that wet-behind-the-ears philosophy student. People do stop asking themselves these questions after a time."

"Somehow I didn't think you did."

"I don't. Between the third and fourth tumbler, they are always with me." He paused. "Do you recall the Greek word *aidos*, Cecily?" She searched her memory and shook her head. "*Aidos* is . . ." he went on in his boozy, pedantic voice ". . . difficult to translate . . ."

"The good words always are."

". . . in a way it means reverence; then again, it is the shame that holds men back from wrongdoing. But it also means the feeling the fortunate should have in the presence of the wretched of the earth—not compassion exactly, but a sense that the difference between them is not *deserved*. For how could it possibly be? What could one possibly have done to deserve to be whole while others are sick; to be desirable while others scratch for a crumb from love's feast; to be rich while they are poor? You see, what I dislike about Marsden and Miss Berwith, apart from her abominable manners, is not their politics, but their lack of *aidos*."

Ceci swung her feet to the floor, lost in thought, absently stroking her arm.

"I see you've taken too much sun," Hayward said gently.

"So it seems."

"You weren't made for this climate."

"No."

"I suppose you'll be leaving soon."

"I don't know."

"You couldn't possibly think of staying on. What would you do with yourself?"

"I don't know."

"I know how grateful Vivian is that you've visited, but for your own sanity you'll have to get out soon. Marsden and Hilary won't be cruel to the old girl, you know."

"They make her feel dependent and foolish."

"She is both of those things. Even if you love someone you

can't hope to alter their life when they're at the very end of it."

"I know."

"Have your holiday and get out. There's nothing here for you. Let Marsden and his lady galumph about like gorillas, baring their teeth, beating their breasts about their territoriality. You aren't like that."

She gave him a wry smile. "I didn't know how territorial I was until I saw Hilary pawing Auntie's silverware and blathering about redoing everything. And Marsden, bullying everyone about, not caring about anyone, getting his rocks off by . . . no, I didn't think I cared about the plantation at all, but now I, I who've always despised the place, I find I do care about it. When I went into the hills this morning and saw Marsden's crop . . ." She stopped herself, shrugged, got up and moved to the railing. "I care about what's happening here. I care very deeply."

"Ah, yes. 'A human life should be well rooted in some spot of native land where it may get the love of tender kinship for the face of the earth, for the labors men go forth to, for the sounds and accents that haunt it, for whatever will give that early home a familiar unmistakeable difference amidst the future widening of knowledge: a spot where the definiteness of early memories may be in wrought with affection and kindly acquaintance with all neighbors, even to the dogs and donkeys, may spread not by sentimental effort and reflection, but as a sweet habit of the blood.' "

"Yes. Something like that."

"I used to feel that way about Maida Vale and Cambridge." They were silent for a long time. "But," Hayward roused himself, "that's being sentimental. And you can't think of staying here. It's difficult to have a kindly acquaintance with guard dogs. And some of the neighbors? My dear, they're even harder to talk to! There's no future for the island, except as a vacation land for the Americans. They'll keep coming down to get their sun and surf and screw a few natives—like tired old Romans holidaying in Pompeii." He stroked his knees and squinted at her. "Vivian, that day she turned on the waterworks and sobbed for hours, told me she'd made out her will. Funny thing about wills, isn't it? They can tempt the most timorous into assertiveness. There's not much of a surprise in it, if she was telling me the truth. Of course I'm sworn to secrecy, but I think you should know. It's half to you and half to Marsden. My advice—not that you asked for it—is to hire yourself a good solicitor to protect your interests and leave. In the meantime, try to enjoy yourself. Jamaica is a wonderful place to be if you will just let *it* be. No one's ever succeeded in changing it, you know."

Ceci leaned forward, bringing her face from the shadow of the roof, exposing it to the scorching heat of the sun. There was a prickly sensation around her mouth and throat. Paul's whisker burns.

"Ah, I think they've caught something." Hayward got up to stand beside her, looking out into the bay. One of the boys was standing up in the skiff, holding a glittering fish. The other boy made a lunge for it, almost tipping over the boat, and they clutched at each other, shrilling with excitement. "And Marsden wants to find time to enjoy the bay," Hayward shook his head. "He'll never be able to enjoy it as much as those two bootless scalawags."

He looked back toward the house. "It seems your father is going to join us after all."

Turning around, Ceci saw Archie cradling the puppy in his arms, moving gingerly across the footbridge. Thelda followed, carrying a tray.

"Isn't he a remarkable little fellow?" Archie asked, holding the puppy toward them. He lowered himself into a deck chair and caressed the dog's muzzle. "I had to leave my dog Horton in a kennel, or the Hound Hilton, I believe it's called. Appalling place, really. Little doghouses with carpeting and doggy-sized furniture. Something Evelyn Waugh might have thought up. And terribly expensive. Still . . . ." he seemed to be talking mostly to the puppy, "Horton's getting on. Deserves the best money can buy, don't you think?" He brought the puppy up to his face, almost as if he were going to kiss it, then nestled it in his lap and reached over for his sandwich, lifting up the bread to examine its contents. "Ham and cheese. Well, all right," he said with faint disappointment.

"Want me bring something else?" Thelda asked.

"No. I was salivating for a corned beef on rye. Thinking of Greenblatt's delicatessen, actually. My old friend Mort Goldman and I used to drive there. Wonderful sour pickles."

"It sounds to me as if you're homesick, Mr. Baron," Hayward commiserated. "Do you plan to stay long on the island?"

"Love to stay on. Love to," Archie said jovially, "but there's a film deal coming up and my agent won't hear of it."

"That's the wonderful thing about the arts, isn't it?" Hayward said. "One never has to retire."

Thelda handed Ceci a slip of pink paper. "This for you, miss." The name Max was printed on it in large letters.

"Max called again? When?"

"He on the phone now."

Ceci crumpled up the paper, exasperated. "Why didn't you tell me? Oh, don't bother. Please excuse me, gentlemen." She pushed past Thelda and ran across the bridge.

"Max? Max, are you there?"

"I was about to hang up. Where the hell were you, in the east forty?"

"I just got the message. Damn it. How are you?"

"Worried about you, for one thing. I called last . . ."

"I know. I'm sorry. I was staying the night with a woman in Montego Bay. They did tell you that, didn't they?"

"It seemed nobody knew where you were."

"Sorry. It's terribly disorganized here. I stayed a couple of nights in Montego with this woman, Mrs. Cleardon. She gave a party in Archie's honor and . . ." She was surprised at the glibness with which she embellished her lie with details about the party.

"But how's your father? And your aunt? Are you getting along with them all right?"

She glanced about, wondering if anyone was eavesdropping. "Mmmm. Yes. That's right."

"I take it you can't talk."

"That's right."

"They got you between a rock and a hard place, girl? Skeletons sliding out of the ol' family closet?"

"Like Halloween."

He chuckled. "I've got to go to Houston for a coupla days. Thought I'd give you the number in case you needed to call."

She reached for the pink pad. "Shoot."

"Hey, the Groscheks had a dinner party last Friday," he said after giving her the number. She put in little grunts of recognition as he went on to tell her about his life during the past week: he'd gone to the opening night of the opera and yes, he'd fallen asleep, but he'd met Beverly Sills at the party afterward and Beverly was such a charmer that he'd written out a five-thousand-dollar check to the Opera Fund. Nutsy Bernie, his stockbroker, had given him a good tip and he'd cleaned up on Beatrice Foods. And oh, those gardenia plants on the terrace—the ones she liked so much—they'd died even though he'd called in a plant specialist from Green Thumb.

He made no mention of his emotions and for once she didn't prod him with the "But how do you really feel?", which, she was sure, made up at least a third of all intimate male-female conversations. She knew how he felt: lonely, deprived, and holding it in so as not to pressure her. She talked about the storm, her sunburn, the boys she'd seen fishing in the bay—anything to keep up her end of the conversation. But what was really going on, he asked again. Couldn't she give him any clue? She promised to write.

"Do you have any idea how much longer you're going to stay down there?" Without waiting for a reply, he followed up with, "I may have to go to China next month. Wanna come? Might be fun. It would sure be more fun for me if you did. You haven't seen the Great Wall yet, have you?"

"No. I haven't seen the Great Wall." Here was the capitulation she'd hoped for in London. No more ultimatums about marriage but a tacit offer to have her come back under any arrangement she wanted. "Max . . ."

"Yeah?"

"Max . . . you're sweet."

"For Chrissake, you make me sound like a pecan pie."

"All right, you're . . ." She searched for the right word, something that would express her affection and appreciation without committing herself.

"Do you need me to do anything for you, Ceci?"

"No."

"Then I'm gonna sign off. Hey, girl, I'm your friend."

"I love you, too. Bye."

She put the receiver down and leaned back onto the sofa. How had she gotten her lines mixed up? *He* loved her; *she* was his friend. She'd never in all the months they'd lived together said she loved him. It had popped out of her just now. But how cowardly to say she loved him because she had been touched by his concern, and his mention of trivial but shared things had made her feel safe.

She got up and walked to the veranda, looking out at the cupola. Hayward had taken off his glasses, which meant that he must feel welcome in Archie's company, and Archie was standing, talking, one hand gesticulating, the other holding the puppy on his shoulder. He had such a way with animals. He lavished his concern and affection on them in ways he'd never been capable of showing to human beings. Stepping back out of sight, she leaned against the wall. Perhaps it was the fact that she'd been brought up for the most part without a father that had given her this fatal and all-consuming interest in men, as well as her profound mistrust of them. There was hardly a time in her adult life—except for that terrible six-month period after Paul had left her—when she had been without a man. She'd never considered herself promiscuous —not in the root sense of the word, meaning indiscriminate. She had discriminated. By some perverse intuition, she had always chosen men who weren't likely, in the long run, to make a commitment. They were easy enough to find. And she'd worked to make them fall in love with her, putting more energy into her affairs than she ever had into a career, a cause, or a friendship. She had danced and pranced for them. She had listened to their life stories and their career plans. She had been "good" in bed. And when they'd sensed that she too was unlikely to make a commitment, and had therefore decided that they must have her permanently, she had gotten her licks in first and left them. Well, she had been left and she had left. Leaving was better. Now Max, so rooted in the practical and the material that he'd seemed unlikely to have much emotional insight, had tripped her up. He hadn't consciously manipulated her. He had just been the "good daddy," firm but forgiving, offering her all the comforts of home.

She turned quickly, thinking to go and shower, but she continued past her rooms to Vivian's door, tapping on it lightly, then gently pushing it open. The clock was ticking and she could hear a soft, steady snoring. The shutters, closed against the glare, made stripes on the wall. There was a mingled smell of Pear's soap, old books and insect repellent. Vivian lay on the bed dressed in her flowered wrapper. Her face against the pillows had a glazed and withered look.

"Are you awake?"

The head raised itself a few inches, then fell back. "Icilda?"

"No. It's Ceci."

"So you're here safe and sound. That's good."

"I'm sorry if I caused you any worry."

"If you've come to make me drink that herb tea Icilda gave me, I'm not going to. I know it helps, but it tastes vile."

"I hear you've got your spots again."

"Oh, all right. I'll drink it. I'll drink it if you want me to."

"I don't care. That's up to you." But Vivian's hand was already reaching for the glass on the night table. She propped herself up, staring straight ahead, grimacing between sips.

"Did you know Hayward Pembroke's here?"

"Ruined," Vivian muttered, wiping her lips on the hem of the sheet, "absolutely ruined."

"Well, yes, he has had his libation, but he's quite lucid."

"Who's lucid?"

"Hayward. Mr. Pembroke."

"I meant my garden. My Crimson Beauty was so lovely this year. Now she's quite ruined. And Percy, too. He's been selling ganja, you know. That means he's probably been using it, too. Icilda would be heartbroken if she found out."

Ceci sat down and took Vivian's hand. It was moist and cold. "I expect Icilda knows already," she said softly. "It's really not so terrible."

"Not so terrible?" Vivian asked, her iris rolling to the rim of her good eye.

"I just meant . . ." What did she mean? That she too had occasionally smoked ganja, that everybody did it? That would hardly wash with someone of Vivian's generation. Acceptable behavior, Vivian would say, was not determined by what everybody did. And Ceci herself agreed. She released Vivian's hand and reached out to touch one of the swans carved into the headboard. "I used to be so afraid of this bed when I was a girl. I always thought the swans would peck you while you were asleep." She couldn't help herself from yawning. The wind rattled the shutters.

"That's good," Vivian said. "The wind is up. Things will be dry before we know it." She touched Ceci's forehead. "Are you feverish?"

"No. Just sunburned. And very, very tired."

"Come. Put up your feet. Lie here beside me. In a moment I shall get up and visit with Hayward."

Ceci lay down, propping herself up on an elbow lest she give way and drop off to sleep. "Auntie, there's something I must talk to you about. Remember the other morning when we were discussing that little piece of property up in the hills? That plot grandfather apparently gave to Icilda's mother? I was wondering if you could see your way clear to giving Icilda title to that now." She broke off, searching for the right approach. "All the changes that are going on are so disruptive to the servants. It's such a small plot—a half-acre, an acre, whatever it is, and it should be taken care of before—"

"You didn't imagine that I was going to pass away without leaving Icilda something, did you?"

"Of course not. But if it could be attended to now. I could even stay on long enough to help you arrange it with your solicitors. You could just explain to Marsden that it does, by rights, belong to Icilda, and I could help you to arrange everything."

"I don't see the rush in—"

"Icilda is getting on in years and . . ."

"Icilda isn't old. In fact, she's a year younger than I," Vivian exclaimed with tenacity.

"All the same . . ." Ceci began.

"No. Icilda is far too old to want to be grubbing about in the hills," Vivian corrected herself. "She hates to leave the house even to go to the village. Why would she need vegetables from the hills when she can have this chef cook for her in our own kitchen. That's tommyrot."

"But it would be a place for Percy to stay."

"Percy might have stayed on here if he hadn't been up to no good."

"Auntie, I must tell you, I picked Percy up on the road this morning. He was walking along with Jesmina. He has no place to go. Just between us, he's squatting on the Edisons' property in this miserably rundown schoolhouse."

"You saw Jesmina?"

"Yes."

"And I suppose she gave you an earful."

"We talked. Yes. We talked." Ceci sighed. "And she asked after you. She's very concerned with your well-being. She really is."

Vivian pressed her lips together until they all but disappeared, leaving only the network of fine, vertical wrinkles. "I took her back into service so many times, Cecily. So many, many times. I've always been fond of Jesmina, though I must say she's created some terrible problems for herself. You saw her children, I suppose. They're all different colors."

"I saw one of them. The baby."

"A dear little thing, isn't he?" Vivian said with the wistfulness she reserved for her garden, Jane Austen, and black children under the age of twelve. "I knew you'd be upset if you found out she'd been dismissed. That's why I didn't tell you. I personally never had any complaint about Jesmina's work, but you must understand that she overstepped the bounds. She laughed in Hilary's face. Literally laughed in her face."

"I confess that I'm often tempted to do the same thing."

"But you're not in service, Ceci. Nobody pays a servant to laugh openly at them. You can't expect—"

"I don't expect anything. I know Jesmina seems hostile, but then, why shouldn't she? It's remarkable to me that she still has as much concern for us as she has." She stuffed a pillow under her head and drew up her legs. Her limbs were heavy and her brain felt cloudy, drifting back to thoughts of Paul. "I don't want to discuss Jesmina," she continued, fighting to bring them back to the topic. "If you agree that the plot of land is Icilda's, why don't you turn it over to her legally? That way, Percy can at least have a place to stay, something of his own. It would help him to stay out of trouble. I mean, we can't just allow him to be turned out."

"Of course we can't. But we can't have him back here if he's a dope dealer as Marsden says he is."

"Oh, for Chrissake, Marsden! Let he who is without guilt cast the first stone."

"What do you mean by that?"

Ceci shut her eyes. She felt as though she were in some play that could go on indefinitely because a crucial piece of information was being withheld; but she couldn't bring herself to tell what would either be vehemently denied, or, if believed, cause unmeasured pain.

"You've been going out to the cabins, Ceci, haven't you? Hilary saw you the other night after our dinner party. She told Marsden and Marsden told me. That's why you've gotten yourself entangled in all this business about plots of land."

"It's theirs, isn't it?" Ceci said sharply. "Just bloody well give it to them."

"Do you know that in all the years Icilda has been with us she has never, never once, asked for an increase in salary? That's because she knows that her needs will be taken care of. The times I've bailed out her relatives, the mountains of wedding presents and baby clothes and Christmas boxes and church contributions I've provided, even when my own purse was slim!"

"I know you've been generous, Auntie. But it's important to take care of things legally. And people of Percy and Jesmina's generation don't want—" She stopped herself from saying "your handouts."

"What do they want? Tell me, Ceci. They can't really manage for themselves, but they want us out. They want to change everything, but they only succeed in creating chaos. How can they run things if they can't even sustain a decent family life? Jesmina and all those children, for example. She . . ."

"Do you think she ought to have had abortions?"

"Of course not! She should have . . . Well, Icilda and I

understand each other perfectly well. Icilda and I see eye to eye on most of these subjects, even if I am cock-eyed." She covered her wayward eye and winked with the good one.

"The point is . . ."

"Hilary had the gall to ask me where Icilda was going to retire to. The idea! That Icilda would ever leave this house is the most—"

"*That's* the point, Auntie." Here was the wedge. "Hilary doesn't understand your relationship with Icilda." And who could understand that almost feudal mutual dependence that accepted their differences without questioning; that made these two old women cling together as waves of change washed over them, like water over stone?

"Hilary's not . . . though Marsden says she's from a perfectly good family . . . she's not . . ."

"Yes. Quite." Not one of us. Not to the manor born.

"Whenever she's agitated . . ."

"Which is quite often . . ."

". . . a certain gaucheness . . ."

". . . she has the voice of a tram conductor . . ."

". . . and she asked me if, if . . ." Vivian shook with silent laughter, covering her mouth with her hand ". . . if the Nettletons had a coat of arms, and when I said no, she . . ."

". . . wanted to have one made up, right?"

"How did you know?"

Ceci giggled with giddy fatigue. She might not be able to reason with Vivian or appeal to her on moral grounds, but they shared the same sensibility of what was and was not *done*. They stood united against gate-crashers and social climbers. What would Paul say when she told him she'd manipulated Nettleton snobbery to do a good deed? "So you will see to giving Icilda title to the land?"

"That's only fair," Vivian said as blithely as if there had never been any debate. "We, you and I, we'll do it straight away. You will stay long enough to do that, won't you, Ceci?"

"Yes. I'll stay. I'll stay as long as . . ." She shut her eyes. She couldn't see Paul's face as she had last night or even this morning, but she could clearly see a photo, long since destroyed, of him sitting in Hyde Park. His rolled-up shirt sleeves, the thickness of his exposed neck, the challenging look in his eyes, made her weak with joy. She would be with him again. She would be with him until . . .

"Whatever have you been doing with your hair, Cecily?" Vivian's bony fingers stroked some back from Ceci's brow. "Birds could nest in this."

Ceci yawned. "Mmmm. I know. In a minute I'll get up and . . . in a minute . . ."

"You do feel feverish."

"No. I'm happy. Very happy."

"We must have Icilda mix some lemon juice and parsley into the rinse water. It gives your hair such a lovely sheen. Poor Hayward. Have you noticed, he hasn't any hair now. At least on top. Looks like an egg. An egghead. My, that wind is fierce, isn't it?"

"Mmmm." The rattling of the shutters seemed far away, and as the hand kept moving, steadily stroking her forehead, the voice too seemed distant, murmuring "Higgledy-piggledy, my black hen/She lays eggs for gentlemen/Sometimes nine and sometimes . . . I too feel very happy . . . Higgledy piggledy . . ."

Sixteen

Archie, alone on the veranda, his aching leg propped up on a chair, watched the puppy as it skidded along the tile chasing a toy mouse Icilda had given it. The wind came up again, hot and raw, making his skin feel like parchment and his throat dry. He reached for a slice of papaya, took a bite and put it aside. Ever since he'd mentioned the Greenblatt's special, his mouth had been watering for that particular taste. How could anybody live in a place that didn't have a decent delicatessen? He strained forward, picked up the mouse, and tossed it, wondering how old Horton was faring. He longed for the protection of his patio, for his television set, for anything familiar that might ease this feeling of being at odds with the world. He had a mind to put in a call to Phoebe (not that there was a hope of making a call in private) to explain what had happened and ask why, when he had done what seemed to be the intelligent and responsible thing for a change, he felt so desolate.

That morning everything had seemed clear. The doctor had explained that Vivian was the victim of advancing senility that could only be slightly ameliorated by medication, which she had so far refused to take. The lawyer had also been firm in his advice: Archie was fortunate indeed to have a son who was willing to assume legal responsibility and was such a fine administrator. And once they were alone, Marsden had assured him that now he was going to be in complete charge Archie would soon see an improvement in his dividend checks. It had all seemed to fit into place. Why, then, did he feel unmanned? Why did he feel like a party to some undefined betrayal?

He passed his hand over his eyes and turned his thoughts to the benefits those increased checks would provide: he would make repairs on the Palisades house, trade in the old Bentley, visit his tailor Herb (presuming Herb was still alive), and have a truly beautiful suit made, so that when he dropped by his agent's office to say he was back in town (not that his agent would have noticed his absence) he could present himself as in no way needy but willing to work should the right part come along. But instead of buoying him up, these fantasies just made him feel tired. He daren't take a nap. Not at this time of day. If he did, he would wake up in darkness, and he couldn't handle that.

Hearing a step behind him, he turned to see Ceci. She was wearing a full-skirted dress of some soft mauve material. Her hair was damp and her face, without makeup, created an impression of much younger days. She put her hands on his shoulders and kissed him lightly on the top of his head. "What were you thinking about, Archie?"

"Nothing at all."

"That's not possible."

"No, it's not, is it? More's the pity. Actually, I was thinking about my old tailor, Herb Moscowitz. What a sense of humor that man had! He was pinning a vest on me once and made me laugh so hard that I doubled over and he ran a pin into my ribs. Then he told me he was going to sue me for getting blood on such a fine piece of dry goods. Don't know if he's still around." He sighed. "But a really fine suit . . . it gives a man confidence."

"You looked very handsome when you were at Mrs. Cleardon's the other night," she said, determined to get the conversation off on the right foot.

"Ah, if you could see what's happening in Hollywood these days. It's all run by dolts who aren't dry behind the ears. Last time I went in on an interview, the director—he couldn't have been more than twenty-seven—asked me if I had any film of myself. Don't know if he would've been able to focus on it if he had seen it. He looked coked out to me. It strains one's dignity to have to audition for them. And what are the parts? The occasional mad scientist, the snooty butler, the cute grandpapa who's a font of homespun wisdom. Not my meat and drink, would you say? And of course the ubiquitous Nazi officer. I begin to think the writers are grateful for the Third Reich. It provides them with ready-made evil, so they don't have to think. And haven't you noticed it, Ceci? Nobody has conversations in the movies anymore. It's just grunts and gore, rutting and car crashes. It's hard enough for someone over fifty to get work, let alone someone over sixty."

She nodded, noting that he'd just chopped ten years off his age.

"I should have stayed in England," he went on. "Should have, might have. That's what seizes me at nightfall, all the might-have-beens. Phoebe's doing all right for herself. Not that she doesn't deserve it. She just held on until they had to use her. Held on and sort of grew into her face."

"Yes, she has. I don't think I've ever seen her happier than this last time we visited." She looked about before pulling up a chair. "Can it be that we're all alone?"

"Quite alone."

"I apologize for leaving you with Hayward. I meant to come back out but . . ."

"Not to worry. Thought he was a bit of a screamer at first, but he's quite the conversationalist. And you can do no wrong in his eyes." It had been gratifying for Archie to hear some-one praise Ceci for a change, even if it had made him uncom-fortably aware that Ceci had not lived up to her youthful promise and that he'd never given her the slightest help in discovering what her direction might be.

". . . I just lay down with Aunt Vivie and then I dropped off."

"Yes. She told us."

"Where have they all gone?"

"Lady Pembroke's driver called to say he was delayed, so

Marsden volunteered to take Mr. Pembroke home. Hilary wanted to go along . . ."

"Oh, yes."

". . . and that persuaded Vivian that she must go. They called a bit ago to say that Lady Pembroke had invited them to stay for dinner."

"That's a blessing. I don't feel up to facing anybody tonight."

"Nor do I. I've done nothing but eat and drink and sit about since I've arrived and it's quite exhausted me."

"Nothing like enforced leisure to take it out of you. What's say I tell the cook to go home? We can watch the sun go down, then later I'll fix us some scrambled eggs and toast and we'll pop off to bed before they descend on us again."

"Excellent idea."

The puppy wobbled over to lick her foot. She reached down, stroking his head, then leaned forward, her chin in her hand.

"You're looking very pretty, Ceci. Very content with yourself."

"Nothing like hot water and a good scrub."

"And your young man called from New York."

"He's not mine and he's not all that young."

"Have you known him long?"

"I've been living with him for about ten months."

"All this living together. Flitting about from one to the next but never wanting to say 'I do.' "

"I don't see the point of saying 'I do' so that six months later you can say 'maybe I've changed my mind.' "

"I suppose not," he conceded, feeling the sting of what he took to be a reprimand. "I should have given you a proper wedding when you married Adam," he said after a pause.

"I don't think the expense of the ceremony would have changed anything," she shrugged, though she still remembered that he had been so niggardly that Mort Goldman, Adam's father, had offered to pay for her wedding dress. "You might have talked to me about it, or tried to talk me out of it, but I don't suppose that would have changed anything either."

"No. It wouldn't have. You don't remember yourself at eighteen. No one could stop you from doing anything. You haven't changed much in that," he absolved himself. "But to look at you now . . . you seem so mellow . . ." Mellow was a word that young people used, wasn't it? ". . . that can't just be from the salubrious effects of a long bath. Are you in love?"

"Yes, I am. Unutterably." She smiled at the aptness of the word. "But not with Max."

He ran his tongue over his teeth, searching for some way to find out about her private life without seeming to pry, but wary of what he might find out. "I'm sure it'll all work out," he said brightly. "You look content somehow."

"I'm far from content, but I do think I accomplished something this afternoon. I spoke to Aunt Vivie and we reached an agreement of sorts."

"If you've succeeded in having a conversation with Vivian you've done better than most."

"You just have to be patient. She's stopped censoring herself, so things just pop out, then she gets all flustered and she sounds sillier than she really is."

"So what did you accomplish?"

"I talked to her about this plot of land up in the hills. I don't know if you're aware of it, but your father apparently gave it to Icilda's mother."

"To Mary."

"I don't know her name. That was before my time. Did your father have a thing with her?"

"A thing? A thing? You do massacre the language. If you mean an affair, no. How could you think such a thing?"

"It's not exactly without precedent."

He shifted and straightened his spine. "If you'd known Mary . . . She was no beauty. Not by a long shot. She was very cantankerous, even as a young woman. She disappeared from the house for a whole week at one time. Went to Kingston to hear Marcus Garvey speak. Don't 'spose you've ever heard of Marcus Garvey. He was a Jamaican who founded the Back to Africa movement."

"I know who Marcus Garvey was."

"Anyway, my father didn't have 'a thing' with Mary, but

he liked to take her side in household disputes. He and Mother didn't see eye to eye but he could never openly oppose her, and since mother and Mary were always feuding, Father got his licks in by taking Mary's side." It was the first time he'd given voice to the convoluted relationships of his childhood, and he found himself wanting to talk more about them.

"I don't suppose it's important how Mary got it," Ceci interrupted. "I know that Percy has been farming it for years even though they don't have title. Vivian has finally agreed to sign it over to them. It's such a minor thing—an acre or two out of our hundreds—but it will make life so much easier for them. I suspect Vivian wanted to do it all along. She has the right impulses, you know. And now she's agreed to let me get in touch with her solicitor and arrange it."

"Wait a minute. Have you discussed this with Marsden?"

"Archie, you know I can't discuss anything with Marsden. Marsden doesn't even want me here. That first night we were back, I realized how much he disliked me, and I even tried to think of all the terrible things he might have gone through because I thought it might help me to forgive him. But it won't wash. I can't stand what he is or what he's doing. Setting up his little fiefdom, playing God with everyone's lives. You must see it. You do see it, don't you? Getting this land for Icilda and Percy seems to be the one thing I can do to help."

"And you've decided, all by yourself, what needs help?"

"Archie, please. Let's not argue. Let me explain what I know, what I've found out. . . ."

"Will you please keep your voice down? The servants . . ."

She became aware of an unusual silence in the house and got up as quietly as she could, moving through the front room to see the cook sitting at the dining room table, ostensibly reading a recipe book. He smiled profusely and began to move toward the kitchen door. "You may take the evening off," she told him. "Mr. Baron and I will see to ourselves." Returning to the veranda, she stood next to Archie's chair and said, sotto voce, "I'm not comfortable here. And I would like to talk with you some more. Will you come for a ride? We could go up to the great house."

He ran his tongue over his sharpest tooth, a frown of apprehension creasing his forehead. When she pressed his shoulder
and said "Please," he got to his feet without looking at her.

Thelda came around the side of the house in an attitude of
lazy innocence. "You goin' out, miss?"

"Yes. We're going for a drive. Would you be kind enough
to take the puppy to the kennels and then open the gates for
us."

"Goin' far, miss? In case Mr. Marsden ask for you . . ."

"I shouldn't think so. I'll just get my keys. Archie, will you
wait in the car?"

As the gates were closed behind them, Ceci turned her head
before pulling out onto the road. "Did you see that graffiti
before it was cleaned up?" she asked.

"It was still wet when Marsden and I left early this morning. Marsden thought Percy might have done it in reprisal."

"Percy didn't do it. Percy was with me. I picked him up on
the road and gave him a lift. What did it say?"

"Silly little blighters running around with their red paint!
I tell you, you couldn't pay me to live down here. 'Down with
the CIA'—something like that. Nothing to do with us."

"Nothing to do with us? That's our foreign policy, Archie.
The coup in Guatemala in '54, Chile in '73, they destabilized
the last administration in Jamaica, and if we just look across
the Caribbean Sea right now, we could see agents swarming
all over Honduras, El Salvador, Nicaragua, Costa Rica. Nothing to do with us?"

"If you've brought me out to give me a lesson in politics,
Ceci, I must tell you that I will not be your willing pupil."
He turned and stared out of the car window. The hills were
darkening to deep greens and blues and the first insistent,
crepuscular sounds were beginning to creep over the land. He
had an increasing sense of foreboding. His bladder was full
and his leg began to throb. He didn't like the thrust of Ceci's
chin or her determined grip on the wheel and, wanting to
forestall the inevitable resumption of their argument, he said,
almost to himself, "I used to love this time of day. Not as a
boy. As a boy, living here, it meant early bedtimes, the end
of things. But as a young man, when I was first in London,

when Phoebe and I were in rep—oh, the lights came on, lights
everywhere, people everywhere, looking forward to the excitement of the night, lorries everywhere, marquees, women
in their evening clothes, and we, getting ready to go to the
theater, getting ready to give them our best. . . ." His voice
trailed off. They rode on in strained silence.

As they turned off the main road and began the ascent into
the hills, it seemed as though they were moving in slow motion. She turned off the motor when they reached the barbed
wire fence that protected the great house. It looked like a
Maxfield Parrish painting, glorious in the amber wash of
sunset. "Like the dwelling of gods," Archie said softly.

"Unfortunately the inhabitants were always far too
human." She took out a cigarette, rolled down the window,
and turned to him. "Now, Archie . . ."

"Shall we get out?"

"I'd rather not. There are bound to be guards about."

"They'd let us in. All we have to do is identify ourselves."

"I'd just as soon we stayed private." She blew out a ribbon
of smoke and stared at him. "I want to know why you object
to my trying to get that land for Icilda and Percy."

"I don't necessarily object. I just said that since Marsden's
in charge you'd best speak to him about it. With all your good
intentions, you seem to have a most disruptive effect on peoples' lives, Cecily. You come down here, you find nothing to
your satisfaction, though you've never had anything but deri-
sion for the family or the estate. You rush about, you disappear God knows where, though there's already a nasty rumor
about . . ."

"You think I give a damn about gossip?"

". . . about your going into the hills with some black man
and . . ."

"Who do you think started that? Who do you think is spying on me?"

His brow creased momentarily, but he went on with a
laugh. "So this time next week I expect the gossip will have
mushroomed into tales of orgies and witches' sabbaths and . . ."

"Do you want to know where I was, Archie? It's rather a
long story, but I have wanted to tell you. You see . . ."

"I didn't say I believe any such things," he interrupted quickly.

"No, let me tell you."

"I have no desire to pry. If you'd just stop taking responsibility for things that don't concern you, stop getting involved in . . ."

She stubbed out the cigarette. "What the hell's the matter with you? Why are you attacking me? Percy's just been thrown out on his ass on the most paltry and hypocritical excuse because Marsden wants to consolidate his position by having a complete changing of the guard. And why should you object if I try to help him or Icilda? What the hell difference can it make to you if they get their lousy patch of land?"

"Because you're interfering! Because Vivian is not competent!" he shouted. He heard his voice ring out, then calmed himself enough to go on in a sad, measured tone. "I may as well tell you the worst of it. Marsden took me to see Vivian's doctor and lawyer this morning. Vivian is senile. Their professional opinions are—"

"Professional opinions aren't always objective. They can be bought, too, you know."

He shook his head. "Your affection for your aunt has clouded your vision."

"That's why Marsden wanted you down here, isn't it?" she asked slowly. "To put your seal of approval on having Vivian put away."

"Put away? Put away?" he guffawed. "There. Your imagination has led you to misjudge the situation yet again. Marsden has no intention of having Vivie put away. He will let her stay on until she dies."

"Let her? Let her stay on? How noble. How magnanimous. It's still her goddamn property, isn't it?—or has it already been signed away?"

"You may not like Marsden's style. You may not approve of his politics, but you'll have to admit that he has been rather more solicitous of Vivian's well-being than either you or I."

"Marsden is solicitous of Marsden. That's the beginning and the end of it. You'll make a great mistake if you underestimate his ambition. And if you're trying to make me feel

guilty, you needn't bother. I realize how dreadfully I've neglected Aunt Vivie. But now that I understand the situation I
intend to do something about it. How can you be so blind?"
she spluttered. "And think about this: If Marsden gets control
now, he can easily invalidate Vivian's will. Do you think he'll
treat either of us any more kindly than he's treated people
who've worked here for most of their lives?"

His head felt as though it were full of fluid and his leg
throbbed painfully. "You're jealous of him," he lashed out.
"Jealous because he has some purpose, some sense of direction, and . . ."

She bent close to him and asked in a whisper, "How much
money has he promised you?"

The blood rushed to his face, his hands began to sweat.
"The idea!"

"You're willing yourself not to see it, aren't you?" She
knew she had him cornered and pressed her advantage with
all of her pent-up feelings of anger and neglect. "You're turning away from the unpleasantness, aren't you? Just as you've
turned away from every unpleasantness, every goddamn responsibility that's ever crossed your path. You dumped
Phoebe and you dumped me and you'll dump Aunt Vivian."

"Vivian is not competent," he muttered, almost to himself,
then repeated it, enunciating every syllable, his eyes narrowing, wanting to shut her up once and for all. "Vivian is not
competent and Marsden is running the estate at a profit. And
since I'm not being kept by some man in New York, yes,
money is important to me."

She bowed her head, so that her hair fell forward, shroud-
ing her face. He was stung with remorse, wanting to apologize, wanting to touch her.

"Do you know how he's managing to run things at a profit?
Do you?" she asked without raising her head.

"I assume . . . I . . . I shall have the wisdom to leave well
enough—"

"I suspected something that first night, when I met Al
Lupon. And then, when we were at Mrs. Cleardon's party,
her friend Gladys told me."

"That wilted flower child? That little tramp? Surely you wouldn't be stupid enough to—"

"How do you think he's been able to make enough profit to restore the great house? How?" Now she turned to him, her hair burnished by the sun, her face impassive. "Marsden is a CIA operative. He came down here to help destabilize Paul Strangman's government. And he's been making a profit because he's been growing ganja."

"You're worse than your aunt. You're raving!"

"I can't prove the CIA stuff, but the other . . ." She turned the key in the ignition and stepped on the accelerator, lurching them forward. "I'll show you."

"Ceci, I think . . ." They bounced up the road, grimly silent. "I think we'd best go back to the house," he said at last. "I think . . ." He could tell from her expression that she had no intention of turning back, and as they came to a primitive road of two strips of gravel, branches of the darkening trees brushed the windows and he clutched at the dashboard, trying to steady himself. He muttered, "I wouldn't recognize a marijuana plant if I saw one."

"They don't look much like sugarcane," she shouted. "You confiscated some of it from my room once. Right after Adam introduced me to it. You didn't confront me with it, but I knew you'd taken it. Remember?"

He scarcely heard her. His mouth filled with saliva and he thought he might vomit. He swallowed great draughts of air, vaguely wondering what he would do when she showed him the ganja fields. He already knew that they would be there, though what she proposed he might do with that information he couldn't guess. It seemed that knowledge of most of life's miserable secrets was always there, like maggots under the rocks. The lover confessed infidelity, the physician pronounced the fatal diagnosis, the accountant opened the books to reveal the crooked business partner, the President, still crying his innocence, resigned—and the only surprising thing was that there was so little surprise, that the whisper from the deepest recess of the brain was just, I knew it already. Somehow, I already knew.

"This road leads into the fields," she said, pulling on the brake. "I think we'd best walk from here. We won't go as far as the tent. There are guard dogs there and a man with a gun."

She got out and walked to the gully where Percy had had to push the car. The flood water had already subsided and two planks had been thrown across it. "Archie? Will you come?"

He made no answer, but got out, mute, numb. The wind billowed her skirt and blew her hair. She held out her hand to steady him as he reached the planks. He took it, surprised by the strength of her grasp, and began to move, crablike, across the planks. He had an undeniable sense of having crossed this gully before. It wasn't just that it was the time of day when his eyes played tricks on him; he *had* been here before. Mary had brought him here on the way to her "farm." He could see it as clearly as if he'd been watching a film: Mary up ahead, scolding his playfulness, as his boy's feet had jumped from rock to rock. Now he inched along wishing he'd brought his cane. What goes on four legs in the morning, two at noon and three at night? Man. He was an old man.

As they reached the far bank, Ceci released his hand and again moved ahead of him. After they'd advanced a hundred or so yards she stopped. "Am I walking too fast?"

"Not a bit of it. Everything capital here." He pushed his voice from his diaphragm as he'd been taught to do when learning how to project to the balcony, and though he was already winded, he still sounded powerful. Ceci paused, looking about. "Here. I think this is the shortcut. Near this star apple tree. Yes. Come on." She offered her hand but he ignored it, moving steadily but precariously, avoiding creepers and branches, until they came to the border of cane stalks whispering in the breeze. Moving through them, he remembered playing hide and seek, hearing the thwack of the machetes, seeing the sweating backs of the workers, hearing their songs. "Here," Ceci said. "As you can see, it's only a border." She parted the stalks and they stood staring at a vast field that sloped down into a valley. It was a sea of marijuana plants. She plucked off a leaf, holding it up. "Good ol' cannabis. I wonder what the market value is? Enough to let Hilary gold-leaf the entire house, wouldn't you think? Not that I

suspect she knows anything about it." She turned, saw that
Archie was glassy-eyed and his chest was heaving, and felt a
sudden shame. "I shouldn't have put you through this," she
said softly. "It was . . ." The word *inconsiderate* came out with
British reserve. "But I wanted to bring you up here because
I was afraid you wouldn't believe me unless you saw it yourself."

"I believed you," he said almost inaudibly, feeling the wind
on his sweating head. "I already believed you."

"And you're angry with me, aren't you?"

"No," he lied. "I can hardly blame you, can I?"

"I don't know what, if anything, we can do about it. But it's
always better to know the truth no matter how painful it is.
It's always better to know, isn't it?" Hearing the rhetoric of
her question, seeing him, still impassive, gazing up into the
sky, she wanted his forgiveness. Why had she dragged him,
an old man who'd managed to survive because of denial and
illusion, through this ordeal? "I expect you'd like to chop off
my head, wouldn't you? I'm the messenger who brought the
bad news."

"My father used to ride his horse to the fields. And there
was rum for everyone when the cutting was over. And in
London, when I first arrived, when I was suffering from
terrible homesickness, I'd hide a bag of lollies under my pillow—humbugs, licorice, toffees, butterscotch—and I'd think,
I know where they came from. From our fields—as though
we'd made a gift to every schoolboy. I . . ." He shivered and
blinked. Her face was now a blur of white. "No, Ceci. I'm too
tired to want anybody's head. Even Marsden's."

"I suppose we'd best go back. It's almost dark." She turned,
facing into the wind. "Funny, you can almost—" A pungent,
instantly recognizable smell of ganja filled her nostrils and a
great billow of smoke appeared in the mid-distance. Almost
instantly a wave of orange and red flame appeared on the rim
of the slope, its billiance making the twilight sky seem midnight blackness by contrast. The wind whipped the fire forward with incredible speed, sending sparks and great plumes
of color and heat. She was too shocked to move, muttering,
"Oh, my God, oh, my dear God," again and again until her

feet seemed to move involuntarily, backing her up. There was a roar as the border of cane, not half a mile from them, caught. The flames began to advance with ferocious speed. "Archie. Archie, for Chrissake, come on. The cane . . ." But he stood transfixed, his mouth slack in childish wonder at the terrible beauty of the conflagration against the tropic sky. "Archie!" She pulled his arm, yanking him into the border. He lurched and stumbled, recovered himself, and lurched on. The stalks cut into their faces and arms. Another blast of wind enveloped them in smoke. Above the roar of the blaze she could hear him coughing, gasping for breath. She moved as quickly as she could without letting go of him, but she had no sense of advancing. Pushing branches and vines aside, feeling him bump into her, she had a nightmarish sense of being rooted to the spot, of not being able to move.

Reaching the gully at last, she stopped, panting, feeling her chest constricted with pain. She swallowed, tasting grit and soot, located the plank and reached back for him. He stumbled, lurching headfirst down the bank. She screamed, scrambling down, her knee crashing into a rock. He had rolled over and lay face up, his eyes staring at the sky. For a split second she thought he must have been knocked unconscious, but then she heard a muttering, wheezing sound coming from his chest as though the very air was suffocating him. She put her hands under his armpits and strained to lift him, but his weight made her tip backward. "Archie, help me. You must help me. Get up . . ." She strained to right him, panicked by the rattling noise coming from his chest. "Can't . . . can't . . ." He was convulsed with choking coughs, so powerful that they seemed to propel him forward before he fell back again. With a strength she had not known she had, she put his arm around her shoulder and hoisted him up, almost slipping again. Somehow they managed, half crawling, half climbing, to get up the bank and to the car. He collapsed onto the hood and began to slide to the earth. She reached for the door handle, found her hands sticky with blood or mud, and wrenched it open. "Don't fall, Archie. Just hold on. I'm coming. I'm coming to . . . get . . ." She almost collapsed under his weight but succeeded in getting him into the seat. "You're safe . . . you're . . ." Her heart pounded wildly. She felt in her pocket for the keys, panicked, felt again, and found them. "We're all right now." She coughed until she thought she might be sick, simultaneously turning on the motor and backing up into a clump of bushes. "We're . . ."

But as she righted the car and began to bounce over the road, gunning the motor, not daring to look back, she glanced across at him, doubled up, gasping, his head rocking forward, bumping into the dashboard. He made a frightening, gurgling sound and collapsed, his head rolling back onto the seat.

Seventeen

Ceci stood, ear to the door, listening. One hand stroked her throat, still feeling for her necklace with the silver heart. She felt superstitiously unprotected without it.

The voices from the front rooms were speaking in measured counterpoint occasionally jarred by Hilary's sharper tone. They must be discussing business again. The phone rang and she heard Vivian's high-pitched, almost hysterical greeting. A chair scraped. Footsteps went upstairs. There was a call to the servants, followed by descending footsteps. They must be going out.

She moved back to the bed, pulling the sheet up to her chin and closing her eyes. A kaleidoscope of events shifted before her—the horrible drive back to the house; the barking of the dogs when she'd pulled up to the big tree, circling her, sniffing the blood, almost knocking her down as she'd staggered out of the car; Archie being carried into the house by the cook and some unknown man who'd been summoned from Thelda's cabin; the way Archie had looked, a big puppet, a dead weight but immensely fragile at the same time; the chaos of the house. They had already been notified about the fire. Marsden had gone to inspect it. She must've passed his car on the main road without being aware of it. And Hilary, crashing about, screaming, asking questions. It had been

Vivian who'd taken charge. Like a good soldier under fire, she'd called the doctor, found extra pillows to prop Archie up and ease his strangled breathing, instructed Icilda to cover him with blankets because he was in shock. She'd held a glass of brandy to Ceci's lips, all the while answering Hilary's questions: no, there was no fire department; yes, the great house would be protected by natural and man-made fire-breaks; no, she didn't know if the crop was insured; and, finally losing patience, telling Hilary to shut up. Hilary had sobbed that she was being treated abominably and had gone off to put in a call to her father. It had occurred to Ceci—dimly, her head throbbing too much to sustain real thought—that Vivian's ability to cope was still there, like an atrophied muscle.

She had stared down at her muddy, bloodstained legs and muttered that she wanted to take a bath. Vivian had said she might have broken bones and should remain still until the doctor came. He'd arrived in what seemed like minutes, so she must've blacked out. It was hard to believe he was a doctor. He was younger than she, suntanned, wearing huaraches and a shirt printed with sailboats and palm trees. She thought he might be stoned. He'd glanced at her and said she might take a bath, then he had gone in to see to Archie. Icilda had helped her to the bathroom, worked her arms out of her dress, pulled down her panties and helped her into the tub. She was washed and patted dry and talcummed. Tenderly, as though she were a baby.

It was while she was being examined, sitting on her bed, naked except for the sheet she clutched to her chest, that she'd noticed the necklace was gone. "My heart!" she'd whispered. The doctor assured her that her heart was all right. She had some cuts and bruises. There would be a small scar from the gash on her knee. He'd just put three dissolving stitches into it, but she hadn't felt a thing. "My father?" she asked. He said he'd already told her that Archie was all right, but repeated it again. Archie was suffering from shock and smoke inhalation. Serious complaints for a man his age, but by no means fatal. Archie had been given a shot to calm him. "And these are for you . . ." the doctor had begun. "Tranquilizers. Take two now and . . ." She'd stared at the sailboat closest to his belly button. She didn't want any tranquilizers. She had to stay straight to . . . "And rest. Lots of rest," he'd advised. She'd nodded. Sleep was what she wanted, what she craved. At least it seemed to be the best way of avoiding confrontations and questions. She'd drifted off.

Then Marsden was standing over her. The light from the bathroom was shining into her eyes and she could only make out his outline. He asked, quietly at first, why she had taken Archie up to the fields, then, losing patience, screamed that she was a stubborn bitch. Surprisingly, it had been Hilary who'd come to her defense, pulling Marsden back, saying she couldn't imagine him talking to a woman that way before turning to her more pressing concerns about crop insurance. He must've said there was none because Hilary had begun to curse. And then she'd been left alone in the dark, listening to the dogs bark.

When she'd woken, sometime around noon she supposed, she'd gone into Archie's room. Marsden, Hilary, and Vivian were standing around his bed. They said they were glad to see she was feeling better and then turned their attention back to Archie. Archie, shrunken and disoriented, looked at the ceiling fan. Marsden's glance met hers in a brief look of concern, tinged, she thought, with guilt. Hilary broke the silence by laughing and saying that men were notoriously poor patients. Vivian jiggled Archie's foot. "He's always been a great baby, haven't you, Angus? Always been an actor. When he was a boy he could turn a runny nose into a death scene. Even then . . ."

"Even then . . ." Archie repeated slowly, as though trying to remember a series of numbers.

"Do you want anything?" Marsden asked.

Archie continued to look at the fan. "Please all leave," he finally whispered.

"He's still in shock," Hilary said. "Best let him rest. He'll be all right."

Ceci didn't think so. She was last out of the room, and as she pulled the door to, she saw Archie's shoulders begin to quiver. She thought he was about to go into another coughing fit, but then realized that he was silently crying. She went back to her own room, pleading dizziness. Between fitful bouts of sleep she listened to the lawn mower, the ringing telephone, the snatches of muffled conversation.

There was a tap on the door. "I think she's still asleep," Vivian said in a voice designed to wake her. Ceci did not stir. "When she wakes up, Icilda, give her something nourishing to eat and tell her we'll be back by nightfall."

Ceci waited until she heard the car being driven away, then got up and changed into the jade silk pajamas Max had given her last Christmas. She padded out to the veranda. The bay was calm. The large leaves of the sea grape hung limp in the humid afternoon air. Thelda, idle whenever she wasn't aware of being watched, sat with her feet dangling in the pond while a man in gum boots waded about skimming off the algae. Ceci moved to the shady side of the veranda, took a cigarette from the onyx container on the table, took a drag on it, and crushed it out in disgust. Her throat was still raw. She wished there was some way to contact Paul.

Not that he could do anything about the situation, just that it would be a comfort to talk to him. She had lived so many years without him, yet their encounter had made her know that he was the only one in whom she wanted to confide. He couldn't be more than a few hundred miles away, yet he might as well be on another continent. It was no good. She shouldn't see him again. She wouldn't. Again she picked up a cigarette, coughed as she inhaled, and studied it, counting the hours until their next meeting. Forty-six approximately, since she judged it to be around five o'clock Wednesday, and they were to meet at three on Friday. Was there such a thing as sensible love? Could you find the middle ground between elation and desolation? Punch an emotional time clock; "work" at a relationship, saying "this much I give and no more, my time's up"? It didn't seem so.

A pungent smell of roast pork and garlic was coming through the kitchen window. She realized that she hadn't eaten for a long time. Her mouth watered but she felt queasy. And she didn't want to encounter the cook. She must talk with Archie now, before the others returned.

She opened his door without knocking. Icilda was kneeling by his bed, her head almost touching the sheets. She seemed to be importuning Archie, not, Ceci hoped, about the damned plot of land. Perhaps she was just praying over him. She got nervously to her feet as Ceci came to the foot of the bed. "I'd like to be alone with Archie," Ceci said.

"He won't talk, miss," Icilda cautioned her. "He want nothin' but to get ready."

"Ready for what?"

"His journey," Icilda said, lowering her voice. "It all behind him now. He making his accounts. Getting ready."

"Don't be superstitious," Ceci hissed. "The doctor says . . ."

"The soul decide when it time to go, not the doctor. The soul . . ."

"Please leave us alone. You should know better than to talk that way in front of a sick person."

"Don't matter. He not hearing us now." Icilda lingered, waiting for her point to sink in. "Obedeah man say . . ."

"I don't care what he says. Please open the window. It's stifling in here."

"Obedeah man say . . ."

"Then go pray with the Obedeah man! Go pray to Jesus. Pray to both of them, but please leave us alone."

Icilda, drawing herself up with dignified self-righteousness, slipped out the door. Ceci opened the window, then pulled a chair up to Archie's side. "Archie, can you hear me?"

He was mortally tired. He heard his name but didn't want to answer to it. It had taken him a lifetime to build a wall of forgetfulness and indifference, and he wanted to put in the final brick. From behind closed eyes he felt light seeping in. He shivered, knowing that he was a wheezing old man back in the bed in which he'd slept as a boy. Full circle. Birth to decay. As Nanny Mary had said, "It not the same day the leaf drop in the water that it go rotten." He'd divorced three wives and buried one. He'd seen his firstborn son perhaps five times in his entire life. He had a daughter who knew his cowardliness better than most and as a consequence despised him. And another son. Marsden. A deceitful man. A cruel man.

Yet it wasn't so much what Marsden had done, but that he'd known he could pull the wool over Archie's eyes while doing it. And why shouldn't Marsden treat him as an object for manipulation and lies? Had he ever proven himself to be anything else? He may even have had another child—there'd been that fling with the little extra from Milwaukee. The one who'd turned up a couple of weeks after he'd had her and said she was pregnant and could he help her to find an abortionist and, though he'd believed he was the first or one of the first, he'd sent her off with a fifty-dollar bill and best wishes. Hadn't thought of her since.

"Archie? Please talk to me. Let me know if you can hear me."

His hand moved as though brushing away a fly. He remembered. He'd played some of his best scenes both on and off camera in the years of his bachelorhood. He'd been a master of the good-bye scene, stoking the flames of remorse by recalling the initial blaze of attraction, mentioning some incident that was sure to get the about-to-be-deserted woman teary-eyed—"remember the night we went grunion hunting in our evening clothes?"—then cutting her short with his debonair but poignant grin, implying that he was the one who suffered, struggled to keep a stiff upper lip because he was wise enough to know that all good things must, etc., when in reality he wished that he might have it done with so that he could have his morning coffee in peace. He liked it "Easy on; Easy off" —like a freeway advertisement for an eatery. He had thought of himself as a great lover, but had he ever really loved anyone but himself?

"Archie?" A pause. "I'm going to call the doctor," Ceci said, though she had no idea of the doctor's number.

"No," he said as he felt her get up. Dying wasn't a struggle. He had played the death scene in *Count of Deceit* all wrong. One didn't fight. One gave way. He saw that now. He had coasted along, frustrated, selfish, but in the last analysis quite content with his lot, able to sustain himself with trivial pleasures and creature comforts and the occasional pat on the back from a stranger. He had claimed to put his career above all else, but in that he had been most cowardly of all, sticking to films because theater work frightened him, falling back on roles he knew he could play, not because they were the only ones offered, but because he was afraid to fail. He had said, had actually believed, that he sought the respect of his peers, but secretly he had hankered after indiscriminate, ego-bathing public acclaim. He hadn't wanted to strive; he'd just wanted to be recognized. And, by God, he'd had some talent. Even Laughton had said that. He might have wiggled out of all other responsibilities and still been able to live with himself if he'd been true to his gift. That was the most unforgivable sin of all.

"Go away," he said in a weak, dirgelike voice. "I want to sleep." He would not throw away his last shred of pride by making confession to his daughter. Would not. But something between a sob and a moan came out. "When Phoebe had her first success—her first real success—in the West End, she asked me to come and see her performance. And I pleaded work. That was a lie. I didn't go because I was jealous of her."

"I'm sure . . ."

"Jealous of Phoebe! Who'd worked harder than I ever did. Who didn't have the slightest recognition till she was in her fifties. And the times . . ." he almost gagged, ". . . the times I didn't bother to send money for Eric. The times I pleaded poverty when—"

"Phoebe forgave you. I know she did." Ceci sat back down, reaching for his hand. "I know you loved Phoebe best of all."

"Not true either. I loved Marsden's mother more than any of them." He moved his head from side to side. "Or I wanted her because she didn't want me. And your mother. I treated Mabs abominably."

"She didn't think so."

"She was such a sweet-natured woman. All she wanted was to bring some order to my life because she considered me more attractive and gifted than she. She was wrong about that, but I never . . ." There was a gurgling in his throat. As his chest heaved with exertion, she noticed how bony it was. One of his legs had escaped the sheets, the pajama leg rucked up to expose a withered and almost hairless shin. She covered it, felt how cold it was, remembered his vanity at looking so

well in tights. "Do stop talking like this," she said, her eyes
watering. Then she said, with a light brittleness, as though
she were reading Oscar Wilde, "Self-pity is such a useless and
boring vice."

". . . I never let her know," he went on as though he hadn't
heard her. "Even from the first, when she'd come to arrange
my scrapbooks and put my accounts in order, I always made
sure that photos of the great beauties were in evidence, just
to keep her in her place. All she wanted was to be married to
me and to have a child. She wanted you very much. I was even
jealous of that." His voice was so low she had to bend closer
to hear him. "And when she turned up pregnant, I acted as
though she'd trapped me. Made her think it was a great sacrifice to do the right thing. I wanted someone to sleep with
who'd also run my house. Someone who wouldn't ask for
much. I got her on the cheap. Made her come to me for an
allowance. And after you were born I . . . what do you call
it now?" He looked at her for the first time. "I opted out. My
job was done after you were conceived. After that I just
turned up for the picture sessions. You were such a pretty
little girl. So cheeky." He began to wheeze again, an open-
mouthed expression of anguish on his face. "And with you
. . . I did that on the cheap too. In every way. I . . ."

"Archie, please. There's no need. Not now." She had
waited all her life to hear such admissions, but there was no
triumph in hearing them now. That Mabs had been pregnant
before they'd married confirmed what she'd always intuited,
but suddenly seemed inconsequential. It struck her as too
punishing to let him continue. "I'm sorry for taking you up
to the fields," she said at last. "Can you forgive me?"

"Doesn't matter," he wheezed.

"Has Marsden said anything to you?"

He turned his head to the wall. "Marsden won't say anything to me. He talked me into selling Vivie down the river.
He squeezed me out like an old lemon. He doesn't need me
now."

She got up. "You have to rest. As soon as you're better—
and that should only be a week or so—you can go home."

"Where . . ." he asked after a time, as though he'd lost the thread of the conversation, ". . . would that be?"

"Don't talk. Your voice is so scratchy. And you have to take care of your voice. After all," she reminded him, "you are an actor."

"Actor? No. Narcissist. Peacock. Show-off."

She bent forward to stroke his cheek. "You're all stubbly," she said softly. "When you wake up I'll come in and give you a shave."

He closed his eyes as if to dismiss her. She waited, but when he opened them again he seemed to have forgotten her presence.

"I'd like to call Phoebe in London," was the first thing Ceci said as Marsden stepped onto the veranda.

Hilary, who was a little distance behind him but had paused to inspect the pond, called out, "Will someone turn on the veranda lights? I think it's still scummy at this end."

"I hope you didn't disturb Archie," Marsden said. "The doctor said he needs complete rest."

"I said," Ceci repeated in a calm voice, "that I'd like to call Phoebe. I think it's important for Archie to see her now."

"Who's this Phoebe?" Hilary inquired, advancing to the steps.

Vivian had stopped by the flowerbeds and was picking dead leaves from the bushes. "Don't you remember?" she asked without looking up, "Divorced, beheaded . . ." She pinched off a blossom and brought it close to her face. ". . . died. Divorced . . . I told you the other night. It's Phoebe, Kay, Alicia Winterspan, and Mabs. Phoebe is—"

"I don't care who she is," Hilary snapped. "We can't have anybody here now. If my own mother came and asked for a sandwich I'd turn her away."

"Yes. Perhaps you would," Vivian mused, then, straightening up, "You look marvelous in green, Ceci. Or is it turquoise? Do turn on the light. Are you quite recovered now?"

"Yes, thanks, I'm much better." She got up, flicked on the lights, and turned to Marsden again. "About Phoebe . . ."

Marsden flung himself into a chair. His face was sallow and

sweaty. "Nightfall, and it's still so damned hot! Will someone call one of the servants and get me a drink?"

"Thelda! Icilda! Maurice! Where in the world . . ." Hilary pushed past Ceci and moved into the front room.

"If Archie's been asking for Phoebe, it's probably just the effects of the drugs," Marsden said. "The doctor said they'd make him disoriented."

"He isn't disoriented," Ceci said in a low voice. "He's profoundly depressed."

"Or else milking it. He's a pretty good actor, after all."

"He's a marvelous actor," Vivian asserted, climbing the steps with the flower in her hand.

"And I've seen him play all the parts," Ceci said. "So either this is his Oscar performance or he's in very bad shape. Personally, I don't want to gamble with . . ."

Hilary came out, ice bucket held to her chest. "We cannot, I repeat, cannot . . ." She slammed the bucket onto a table. "Ceci, do you always have to parade around as though you're ready for bed? I will not let you seduce Marsden into . . ." She turned her head from side to side. "Where is that girl? Where is the damned ice?"

"I'm not ready for bed, Hilary." Ceci smiled. "If I were ready for bed I'd be in the buff."

"Now, now," Vivian came to her, laughing, running her hand from the crown of Ceci's head and putting the flower behind her ear. "That's our little secret."

Marsden got up. "God save me from a houseful of women," he muttered, moving to the drinks' cart and pouring gin into a tumbler.

"Don't drink that without ice!" Hilary commanded, wheeling on him, and, as he swallowed a mouthful, "Why did I come to this godforsaken place? Why did I ask Daddy for that loan last night?"

Ceci leaned against a pillar, crossing her arms over her chest. "Marsden, I think we'd best have a talk. I think we'd best take a walk on the beach and have a—"

"How many times do I have to . . ." Hilary interrupted, now at the whimpering stage. "I want ice!"

"Listen, princess," Ceci said with strained patience, "a

word of advice: You can't treat the staff as though they were children and act like a spoiled child yourself. So either get over this pathological fixation with ice or move to goddamn Alaska."

"You . . . you . . ." The muscles in Hilary's throat stretched so taut that it seemed she might strangle. "Don't think we aren't on to you. Don't think we don't know about your dirty little escapades with Communists. *Married* Communists! You . . . slut!"

Ceci stepped off the veranda. "Are you coming, Marsden? I don't just want to talk to you about Archie. I want to talk to you about Al Lupon. And various other and sundry things." She began to walk toward the beach.

"What's this about Communists?" Vivian demanded.

"She's been . . ." Hilary began, but Thelda had straggled out, cigarette in hand. "Did you call, miss?" she asked. "I didn't hear straight away 'cause I'm on the back steps."

"You know there's no smoking permitted in this house."

"That why I'm on the back steps, miss," Thelda explained.

"Put it out immediately," Hilary said as though she were sleepwalking. "And get me some—"

"Ice? You want ice, miss?"

"Marsden and Cecily always used to walk on the beach together when they were young," Vivian said, sinking into a chair. "I used to watch them. Marsden always talked and Ceci always listened."

Marsden put down his tumbler and stepped off the veranda.

"If you let her talk you into letting anyone come to this house . . ." Hilary called after him.

"Yes," Vivian went on dreamily, "Marsden always talked and Ceci always listened. But everything changes. You'd best learn that, Hilary. Before it's too late." She picked up the tumbler and held it out. "I believe I will have a drink tonight. Either with or without ice. Will you join me, Hilary? Yes, I'll have a drink and then I'll go in and see our own John Barrymore."

Ceci walked with relaxed determination. Past the pool with the statue of the gasping Nereid, past the bauhana tree and the servants' cabins, down to the water's edge. A cool breeze blew in off the breakers, rustling the tops of the trees. She bent to roll up the legs of her pajamas, and as she straightened, throwing her head back to look into the spangle of stars, she felt Marsden behind her. "It's such a beautiful night," he said casually but with feeling, as though they were newly introduced passengers aboard a cruise ship.

"Yes."

"I don't suppose you see the sky much in New York."

"Hardly at all. We go out onto the terrace sometimes. We're high up, so we have the illusion of seeing it clearly, but compared to this . . ."

"Yes."

". . . it's a sort of orange haze. In any big city . . ."

"Of course. That's one of the reasons I've always loved it here."

She could feel the heat of his hand poised above her shoulder but he moved away without touching her, one arm stiffly held at his side, the other near his belt, poised and ready, as though he were on point, leading the way through a combat zone. She followed at a distance of several feet, listening to the waves. When he finally spoke, she had to move closer to hear him.

"How did you know about the crop?"

"It doesn't matter."

"It matters to me."

"Put it down to my acute powers of observation."

"Percy told you."

"No."

"You're lying."

"I don't lie."

A snort. "That's right. You don't lie. And you stayed two nights at Mrs. Cleardon's. To avoid the storm."

"That's my business."

"I see. My business is your business but your business is your own, is that it? Rather like what's mine is mine and what's yours is mine."

"I'm not after money, if that's what you think."

"Then why . . . ?"

"Let's just say I don't like the way you treat people."

"For example?"

"Aunt Vivian, for example."

"Whence this sudden concern, sister dear? *I'm* the one who came down here to take care of her; *I'm* the one who's managed to put the place in order and begun to restore the great house and . . ."

"You threw Jesmina out because she wouldn't kowtow to Hilary."

"Ah, I see," he said with gentle sarcasm. "You shop at Saks and Harrod's but you can't bear to see the suffering of the downtrodden. Or do you just have an abiding interest in those who'd like to be their new masters? Are you just hot for overeducated mulatto opportunists?"

"And Archie . . ." she began.

"I'm not the one who took Archie up to the fields and almost got him killed."

"I didn't come out here to trade accusations, Marsden." She curled her toes into the sand and lifted back the hair that had blown into her face. It was all getting off to the wrong start, but she couldn't help herself from asking, "Was it Strangman or me you were having followed?"

"Why should I have either of you followed? It's a tight little island. Word gets around. If you're stupid enough to have your assignations on a main road . . . . Though I suppose that's in keeping with your general sense of theatrics. You're a chip off the old block, aren't you? With your affairs and your snooping and your scenes at parties."

"In point of fact, I abhor theatrics. As for throwing that drink at you . . . I've never done anything like that in my life." She wrapped her arms around her breasts, enjoying the memory of it while realizing that it had been a reckless gesture.

"You were drinking, is that it? Another habitual family excuse."

"I'm a big girl. I take responsibility for my actions, even when I'm under the influence. I just didn't like the way you were treating—what's her name—Gloria?"

"What's she got to do with you?"

"Girls like that—girls who are passed around, who can't stand up for themselves . . ."

"Your compassion extends itself to them, too, does it? Is that because you've been passed around yourself?"

"I have never—" She broke off, looking out into the bay, thinking how ominous a beach looked at night because you couldn't judge the depth of the waves. This conversation was like that: she was already out of her depth, letting Marsden maneuver her into a defensive position by bringing up her peccadilloes, particularly her sexual ones, which seemed to interest him inordinately. "About Phoebe," she said. "I think it would be a good idea if I asked her to come. If anyone can help Archie, it's Phoebe. And I don't care what the doctor says. Archie is in bad shape. He doesn't want to live anymore."

"Spare me your mystic diagnosis."

"I wouldn't want him on my conscience, and I don't suppose you would either. If you don't care about his well-being, I should think the idea of having Phoebe come would still appeal to you. The faster he recovers, the faster he'll go back to Los Angeles. And then you could get on with planning your next crop."

"Those bastards," he muttered.

She didn't ask what bastards.

He picked up a stone and hurled it into the surf. "And then you'll be leaving the island, too?"

"I suppose so."

"Not that you're interested in my advice, but things are heating up here. It's not a safe time for you to be on the island."

"Are you threatening me?"

"Let's say your presence might not have a positive effect on your mulatto's rank and file. They may dream about pretty, rich white women, but it doesn't fit their party line."

"Oh, I don't know," she said lightly, brazening it out. "I don't think that sort of gossip could hurt him much. They like that sort of thing around here."

"Not when it comes to elections. Or do you picture yourself as the Great White Goddess *cum* First Lady? He won't go that far with you, you know. He already has a wife. And she's very popular with the masses—isn't that what you'd call them? If Vera Strangman found out about you, it might be unpleasant."

"I expect it would be equally unpleasant if Hilary found out about Gloria. Or your crop. Or the real nature of Al Lupon's business." For all she knew, Hilary did know about the crop and Lupon, but she didn't think so.

"About Lupon . . . how?"

"You introduced me to him, remember?"

"And," he said snidely, "your general powers of observation . . ."

"Precisely. You're in the intelligence business, aren't you?"

"I see the mulatto's infected you with his paranoia. He has to have some excuse for failure."

"All right, the information business. Anyone who travels a lot is in the information business if they don't spend their time exclusively in the Hilton lounge. You get chummy with bank clerks and airline stewardesses and professors on sabbatical. You get the lay of the land. I was passing through Managua just before the revolution. I talked to people—on the street, in the marketplace, in bars."

"I'm surprised you didn't go into the hills with one of the *comandantes*—eat beans and rice and learn to make Molotov cocktails. Or was there a party you just *had* to get to in New York or Paris?"

"I just meant that I figured out it was the end for Somosa before the boys from the State Department did."

"That wouldn't surprise me. Those assholes."

"So it wasn't hard to spot Lupon. Someone ought to tell him to go easy on the heavy gold jewelry. And then I checked him out with a couple of contacts in Miami and Las Vegas." Bluffing it out. Just like poker. She didn't suppose he could see her clearly in the moonlight, but her shoulders were quivering. She camouflaged it with an elaborate shrug.

Hands behind him, head down, as though considering, he moved away, did a half-turn and came back to her. "Lupon approached me. Two years ago he heard about my plans for the great house and thought it would be an ideal place for a casino. I didn't want to be in the life, Ceci. I just wanted to turn this place around, make it what it used to be, what it *should* be. I knew it would be a money-making proposition once I got it on its feet. But I didn't have the capital. That's all the crop was. A means to an end. I never intended to keep on with it." He wiped his hand over his eyes as though struggling to maintain dignity while making a confession. "In a way," he went on after a time, "I'm just as glad some wild-eyed subversive set fire to it. It's a financial disaster; but it guarantees that I'll get out. Hilary's father will kick in now. And I will get the great house finished. I've had setbacks before, but this is the only thing I've ever wanted: to see things the way they used to be. The only thing I've ever really *wanted*," he repeated.

"And you think Lupon will just let you walk away from it all?"

"It was a temporary business arrangement. It's been conducted to mutual advantage. Al understood that from the beginning. Now it's over. Al respects what I'm trying to do with the great house. He's a pretty decent guy, you know."

"I'm sure. But I don't think that has much to do with it." How could Marsden be so naive? Had wishful thinking let him convince himself that he could deal with the Mafia, then pick up his loot and say so long, it's been good to know you? She was about to question him about this when a wave hit her, soaking her pajama legs. As she hoisted up the waistband and then bent to roll up the cuffs of wet silk, she decided not to entangle herself with this particular problem. "I understand," she said as she straightened up, "that we all do things we don't want the world to know about; not necessarily because we're ashamed of them, but . . ."

"I'm ashamed of nothing. I've turned this place around. I've . . ."

". . . but because others might not understand. Hilary, for example. She seems to have led a rather protected life. If she found out about the crop—"

"The fields are already plowed over. There's no evidence. Besides, she'd never believe you."

"No, she probably wouldn't. Then again, I wouldn't want

to go to her. That would just muddy the waters. Once a suspicion is planted—well, even if she didn't call off the wedding, she'd always have something over you. That's not an auspicious beginning for a marriage. She might even hold up that loan from her daddy."

"What do you want?" he asked in a flat, calm voice.

"What do I want? Oh, love, peace, justice. Isn't that what all of us want?" She smiled, turning to him. He was staring into the dark waves, somber and stolid looking. His ramrod posture and close-cropped hair reminded her of his younger self: the cadet who'd talked about honor and foreign service appointments and tried to express his individuality by listening to Wagner and smoking strong French cigarettes. She wanted to ask him how he'd come to this particular crossroad in his life, but she knew he wouldn't be able to tell her even if he'd wanted to. He'd made too many rationalizations to remember the choices, the actions, the final fork in the road. His need and expectation of love must've been stifled in childhood, even before she'd met him. "Respect," or, failing that, obedience, had become its substitute. If he craved peace he must have considered it in a highly personal and very limited way: the time to sit on the veranda and enjoy the bay (which he would only allow himself five or six years hence, when he was recovering from his first heart attack). And justice? In his own distorted way he probably believed that he was struggling to achieve justice—the birthright of property and power Archie's neglect had deprived him of. Yes, she understood him well enough. Didn't women always "understand"? But the old adage was phony: to understand was not always to forgive.

"My wants are simple," she said. "I want you to stop trying to convince everyone that Vivian's crazy, and . . ."

"Aunt Vivian is not competent to—"

"I want you to rein Hilary in," she overrode him, "I want you to give Icilda that plot of land they've been farming since God knows when. I've already talked to Vivian about it and she's agreeable. I want you to let Phoebe come down, because I don't think we can handle Archie alone. And as far as the ganja crop goes—how you manage that is your concern. I'm not the one who wants to revive the bygone days of the Nettletons' glory. But I remember something you said to Thomlinson the other night, something about risk in proportion to gain. It seems to me that the risk outweighs the gain when you're dealing with the Mafia."

"I've already told you . . ."

"Yes. I expect you do want out." Another wave came in, splashing her up to her thighs, but she didn't move. "And another thing: I'm riding shotgun on this now. Don't try to screw around with Vivian's will. And be sure that Archie gets his proper share of the dividend checks. I too have powerful friends. And this won't be my last trip to the island."

"You've got it, sister," he said almost too quickly for her liking. "And in return: you won't—"

"Hasn't secrecy always been the hallmark of our illustrious family? I'm mute. And you know Archie won't say anything. He'll probably never even mention it to you."

"I wouldn't want Aunt Vivian . . ."

"No. Neither would I. We've both caused her enough grief one way or another. Besides, she loves you."

They both fell silent, listening to the surf.

"I'm aware of that. As soon as the great house is finished Hilary and I will move up there. I'll see that Vivian is taken care of here. You have my word." He offered his hand but she pretended not to see it.

"Shall we go back?" she asked.

"Yes. You must be chilly. Those pajamas . . ." He put his hand on her arm, chafing the fabric. She stiffened. Could she really have won out so easily? It seemed so, but she was wary. She turned without looking at him and walked back toward the house.

As they went up the embankment, slipping, trying to get a foothold on the powdery sand, the lights outside the servants' cabins illuminated his face, but his expression told her nothing. "I'm glad we've had this talk," he said, as though she were the wayward teenager who'd just come clean with Daddy. "When the great house is completed—six months, nine, depending on the money and whether the construction crews go on strike—I'll let you know. You might want to come down for the opening."

A burst of laughter from the veranda made them break contact. "Mrs. Cleardon, if I'm not mistaken," Ceci said.

"So it would appear."

Hilary was moving about in a whirlwind of agitated hospitality. "Oh, here you are," she called gaily as they approached. "We've been waiting for you. Aunt Vivian's down with another of her headaches, so Mrs. Cleardon and I are entertaining each other. Thelda, do go and see if Maurice has heated those hors d'ouevres yet." She turned back to Mrs. Cleardon, who was settled in Marsden's fan-backed chair, her eyes bulging, her tongue held between her teeth, the voluminous folds of her green and gold caftan billowing around her so that she resembled a large, inquisitive frog.

"Maurice is such a purist," Hilary went on, "I have to bribe him to freeze anything. He's absolutely opposed to freezing. But I've told him we have to have something on hand for guests."

"Uninvited guests don't deserve hot hors d'ouevres, Miss Berwith." Mrs. Cleardon smiled. "And I do apologize for dropping in unannounced."

"But that's what I love about the tropics," Hilary gushed. "The ease, the spontaneity."

"Ceci, my dear." Mrs. Cleardon held out her arms. "I only came by because I was concerned. The coconut telegraph has been rattling with all sorts of wild rumors, so I had to come and see for myself. What a dreadful accident. That awful fire! I won't even talk about the financial loss. The main thing is that you and your father are all right. Word had it that you were severely injured."

"No." Ceci let herself be hugged. "I'm all right. Archie is still very shaken."

"So we hear. I wouldn't dream of disturbing him. And you, Marsden," Mrs. Cleardon turned to him, clicking her tongue, "you must be very shaken as well."

"A year's harvest gone." Marsden shrugged, then took a chair.

"Yes. All that *sugar!*"

"After the shock I don't suppose there's much more than to be philosophical about it."

"That's the aristocratic response, Marsden," Mrs. Cleardon complimented him. "I remember shortly after I came to the island, my husband and I were visiting some friends—the Whiteheads, you wouldn't remember them, before your time —well, the Whiteheads had a fire in their fields and we all sat on their veranda and drank champagne and just watched it roar. One of the most impressive sights I've ever seen. Better than London during the blitz. Though I believe they were insured. Hilary tells me you weren't?" Her voice was soft with sympathy but her eyes glinted with curiosity.

"I still can't believe it," Hilary shook her head. "Ah, Thelda, there you are! With the hors d'ouevres. Please refill Mrs. Cleardon's glass, then be a good girl and run out to the cabins to see if . . ."

"Gladys," Mrs. Cleardon supplied.

"Yes. To see if Gladys would like to join us."

"Gladys is very taken with . . ."

With Percy, Ceci thought. But he's not here anymore.

". . . with native herbal remedies. She thinks your Icilda is a sort of witch, I believe. So Icilda's showing her how to brew some tea. For hives, I think it is. And Ceci, darling, I hope this nasty little incident with the fire isn't going to turn you against us. I suppose you had gone up there to get a really good view of the bay?"

"Yes."

"So lovely from the hills, isn't it?" Mrs. Cleardon smoothed her hair, braclets rattling. "So you'll be staying on, will you?"

Ceci's reply was interrupted by the sound of the dogs and a honking horn.

"Someone at the gates." Marsden got up, barely able to conceal his annoyance. "Thelda, will you go and see?"

Mrs. Cleardon shuddered. "You don't have a man on the property now, do you? I don't mean you, Marsden," she apologized with a little laugh. "I mean . . ."

"We've hired a new driver, but he hasn't moved in yet," Hilary explained.

"Well, Betty Sempill has gotten herself a security guard

and I hear that Lady Pembroke . . ." She broke off. "But there I go, being infected with their silliness. I'm sure it isn't necessary to have a guard. Especially if you have the dogs."

She got to her feet as the car pulled up to the big tree. "Oh, it's the police," she sighed, putting her hand on her bosom. "I'm old friends with Sergeant Owens. I suppose he's come about the fire."

The sergeant was a tall, reserved man with liverish circles under his eyes. He wore civilian clothes. His assistant was black, on the chubby side, squeezed into a short-sleeved uniform that might have been worn by a Disneyland guard. After polite introductions—Hilary in a welter of indecision as to whether law enforcement personnel should be offered drinks, Mrs. Cleardon pumping Owens for gossip—Marsden suggested that he speak to the men in the dining room. Ceci got up to join them, but was told that they would talk to her later. She sipped fruit juice while Hilary engaged Mrs. Cleardon in conversation about shopping—local stores versus the U.S. (which she called "the mainland")—and begged her help in making up the guest list for the wedding. "If you'll excuse me for a moment," Ceci said when she could stand it no longer, "Nature calls."

She paused near the dining room doors, feeling foolish because she wanted to eavesdrop, but reasoning that dealing with Marsden always required atypical behavior. "I don't think I can help you there," Marsden was saying. "Not that I wouldn't want to see the culprits brought to justice if, as you suspect, the fire was deliberately set; but I just can't believe . . . Sorry." He cleared his throat as though overcoming emotion, then spoke with a tough-it-out stoicism. "Main thing is that I've lost a crop. That's what concerns me now. Not revenge. Not even justice." His voice dropped. "Though, yes, there is someone who might be implicated. Though I can hardly believe—that is, I wouldn't want to believe . . ."

"Yes?" Owens prodded.

"Our former driver. Percy. Had to fire him just a couple of days ago. He seemed a friendly sort, but lazy. Though that's not the reason for his dismissal. But I really wouldn't want to think . . ."

"Why did you dismiss him?"

"I'm sorry to say we caught him dealing drugs. I know that's a common enough problem here, but . . ."

"But still against the law," Sergeant Owens reminded him.

"I'd hate to believe it was Percy."

"What's this Percy's full name?"

"I can't think . . . oh, Balstrum, Balstrait . . . Yes, that's it, Percy Balstrait."

"And his description?"

"Very tall. I'd say six foot three or so, extremely dark-skinned. No," he broke off, shaking his head, "it must have been that gang of disgruntled subversives. I told you about the graffiti on the gate, didn't I? 'Down with the rich.' Anyone of that tribe . . . but Percy? . . ."

Owens cleared his throat. "About his description . . ."

"I know who Percy Balstrait is," his assistant said.

Ceci stepped into the room. "Are you ready to talk to me yet? I'm really very tired and though I don't have much to contribute, I'd like to get it over with and go to bed."

The men got to their feet. "No, please," she continued, sitting down. "I couldn't help but overhear what you were discussing and I have to tell you that I picked Percy up on the road the morning of the fire. I don't believe he's implicated in any way. He wasn't angry about being fired, just sad." She tried to catch Marsden's eye, but he was concentrating on the flower arrangement in the middle of the table.

"Where did you take him when you picked him up, Miss Baron?"

"I dropped him on the side of the road, in toward Mo Bay. He doesn't have a car, so I don't see that he would have been able to turn around, get back to the fields, and set the fire. Besides, there were guards in the fields, weren't there?"

"He could easily have hitched a ride," the assistant offered. Owens shot him a look that let him know that his conjectures were out of place, then leaned forward, exchanging a sidelong glance with Marsden before beginning to ask Ceci, "Approximately what time did you and your father drive into the fields?" She answered his questions as concisely as she could, but noticed that he'd stopped taking notes. When she tried to reintroduce the subject of Percy, Marsden rose from his chair. "As you can see, my sister is exhausted. And my father is in no condition . . . Perhaps, since you've taken what information you need, you'll have that glass of sherry now?"

"Not while on duty, thank you all the same." Owens demurred, getting up. "We'll continue to investigate all leads, Mr. Baron. Sorry that your trip to the island has been marred by this, Miss Baron. I suggest you stay close to the house until your return to the U.S. You will do that, won't you? No need to show us out."

But Marsden insisted on walking them out while Ceci sat, examining the sunburned flesh of her arm and again straining to hear. Their brief, muttered exchange was overwhelmed by the more boisterous conversation on the veranda. Were the police on Marsden's payroll, too, or was she so enmeshed in suspicion that . . .

"Why did you try to finger Percy," she whispered as Marsden returned to the table. "You know . . ."

"I know no more than you do. It's quite likely that he did set the fire. You believe what you want to believe, Cecily. You've probably convinced yourself that no one with black skin can do any wrong."

"Don't be ridiculous. I believe no such thing. For chrissake, this isn't a racial issue, it's a question of character. Percy just isn't the type to—"

"Lower your voice. We have guests. Need I remind you—"

"I'm not interested in your lousy etiquette, I'm interested in the morality of—"

"Marsden, do come out!" Hilary trumpeted from the veranda. "Mrs. Cleardon and Gladys are getting ready to leave. Ceci?"

Ceci pushed past him, moving quickly to the veranda.

"Ceci, you're so flushed," Mrs. Cleardon exclaimed. "Are you sure you're feeling all right?"

"Quite all right. You must come back and visit us again in a few days, Mrs. Cleardon. And you too, Gladys." She looked down at Gladys, who was sitting on the steps, a jar of herbs held between her knees.

"Great to see you," Gladys drawled, tucking her hair behind her ears and squinting up at her. "Love your pajamas. You look like some Chinese empress who's been wading in the rice paddies."

"Time to go, Gladys," Mrs. Cleardon announced. "So sorry to fall in on you unannounced, Miss Berwith."

"Call me Hilary."

"Only on the condition that you call me Austin," Mrs. Cleardon insisted, offering a cheek to be kissed. "Say good-bye to Marsden for me."

"Shall I drive?" Gladys asked, feeling in her jean's pocket. "Hey, I've lost the keys again."

"No. I have the keys," Mrs. Cleardon assured her, digging into the folds of her caftan. "Just bring along your herbs, and . . ." She turned to Ceci, raising her arms.

"I said you must drop by because my father's first wife is coming to visit," Ceci said. "Phoebe Suffringham. You must know her. Or at least you'd recognize her if you saw her. She's a very fine English actress."

"Oh, I'm a fan of hers. I'd be delighted to meet her."

"Yes," Hilary enthused, as Mrs. Cleardon removed her hands from the sides of Ceci's face and started down the steps. "If there's enough time, I'd like to plan a little luncheon for Miss Suffringham. She's quite a celebrity, as Ceci says. And Mrs. Cleardon . . . I mean Austin." She laughed, almost executing a bow. "If you could just jot down some names for me. For the wedding reception," she reminded, seeing the blank look on Mrs. Cleardon's face.

"To be sure," Mrs. Cleardon called. "To be sure. Please give my regards to Mr. Baron and Vivian." She gave Gladys, who had stopped on the path, looking backward to Ceci with a who-knows-what's-going-on-and-who-cares smile, a gentle push.

"Is Phoebe really a celebrity?" Hilary asked cautiously as Mrs. Cleardon started up her car.

"Very much so," Ceci answered. "These days she's much better known than Archie." She put the back of her hand to her cheek; her face was flushed. "Phoebe did some series on the BBC a few years ago. Something about the Roman Em-

pire. And then she did a big movie in India. I haven't seen it
yet."

"I know who she is," Hilary cried. "Tall, white hair, a
funny nose?"

"That's probably her, yes."

Hilary looked about the veranda, nervously centering the
container of cigarettes and staring at the plate of hors
d'ouevres. "I know Mr. Cleardon said she's on a perpetual
diet, but she only ate one of the hors d'ouevres." She twitched
as the insect-killing machine zapped another bug. "Now
where is Marsden? It's so hard to find a man, isn't it? They're
always darting about like flies, except when you need them."
She laughed, met Ceci's eyes, and looked away, wanting to
mend the rift between them but not quite sure how to go
about it.

"You needn't worry about Phoebe coming," Ceci said. "She
won't require any special treatment. She's not like that."

"Of course not. The truly important people never are, are
they? I'm sorry I snapped about her but . . ."

"We're all tense these days. I think I'll go in and call her
now if that's all right."

"Sure. Go ahead. It's only a nine-hour flight from London
to Kingston, then a hop to Mo Bay," Hilary smiled brightly,
moving into the house, "so if she booked a flight tonight
. . . now, let's see . . . I should tell Maurice . . ." She came back
to the veranda. "If I got Maurice a kitchen helper he could
make fresh food whenever anyone arrived. What do you
think?"

"That's a good idea." She could hear that particular bird,
the one who took up his post at twilight and called "ah-ha-ha."

"Then I will get him a helper," Hilary said with resolve.
"And we'll have a luncheon—just for the ladies, I should
think—yes, a luncheon in Phoebe's honor. Oh, I wish I was
going to be here when she arrives, but then I've promised I'd
go and explain to Daddy about the fire and the loan. Personal
appeals are always best with Daddy. But I think I'll cut my
visit short. I'll be back in three or four days."

"I'm sure I can manage till then."

"I'll go and arrange the menu with Maurice now, in case

there's anything he needs me to get in New York. Dear me," she looked about with dizzy anxiety, "everything is such a mess! But, as Austin said, the aristocratic thing is just to carry on. I wish I've been up in the fields with you. We could have drunk champagne and watched it all go up in smoke."

"That's right," Ceci murmured. Only forty-two hours now. Then she would see Paul.

Eighteen

The clearing by the waterfall seemed deserted as Ceci pulled up, but moments later Winston emerged from the bushes wearing U.S. Army camouflage gear over a bright yellow T-shirt. "See you right on time, an' lookin' pretty as moonlight on water," he said, eyeing her appreciatively. As a matter of fact, she was twenty minutes late. He offered his hand to help her out of the Toyota. "You think anybody follow you?"

She shook her head. Hilary had gone to the airport by midmorning. Marsden had left the house shortly afterward for what must've been an important meeting, since he'd taken the Rolls. Still, the possibility that she might be followed had occurred, so she'd detoured before going to the Edisons' place to look for Percy. She had wanted to warn him that the police might be looking for him, but the news had apparently reached him already because she found no trace of him or his belongings. She'd backtracked to the village to look for Jesmina, thinking that she could remember which place was hers; but the jumble of shacks had confused her and she'd felt too conspicuous to continue her search. She'd spoken to an old woman who was weaving hats, and, in hopes that a purchase would ensure delivery of a message to Jesmina, bought one. She'd then driven down to the beach, waiting until there was no sign of traffic to return to the main road. When she'd turned off at the shallows, there'd been no adults about, just a group of boys playing cricket. Some had waved at her, but as she'd down-shifted and started up the dirt road to the waterfall, she'd felt a rock being pelted at the trunk of her car.

"Good you get in the habit of bein' careful," Winston advised. "Soon it come natural, you see."

She ignored his assumption that her meetings with Paul would be an ongoing thing and looked at him questioningly.

"Boss say for me to wait here with you. Not a good time for you to be goin' about alone. He's meetin' with some fellas come all the way from South Africa to talk to him, so he goin' to be a little late."

Part of her had expected this—it had happened often enough when they'd lived together—but her anticipation did little to soften her feeling of neglect. Another part, hidden from her understanding, half hoped he wouldn't come at all.

"Don't be mad," Winston coaxed, touching her arm. "I know he rather be here with you. It always somethin', isn't it, man? Man like the boss, everyone always waiting round for him, even . . ." He'd started to say 'even his wife' but changed it to ". . . even me. Spend half m' life waitin' for him. Lucky I'm such a good-natured fellow, huh?"

She acknowledged his grin with a half-smile. "It's just that I have to pick someone up at the airport at seven o'clock."

"Don't worry y' head. He be here soon's he can. Come, let's go to the waterfall. Cooler there."

She followed him through the bushes, found a large rock close to the bank, took off her shoes and rolled up the cuffs of her pants. "Here," Winston said gallantly, taking off his shirt and spreading it out for her. "You shouldn't get dirty." He moved a few feet away, leaning against a tree and tossing his pocketknife into the air. "You know this," he called over the rush of water, cutting off a length of thin vine and handing her a piece. "Chewstick. Bite on it till you make it like a little brush then scrub all round. It good for your teeth and gums."

She grimaced at the bitter taste. "Mmm. I seem to remember it."

"Yeah, that right. Paul tell me you live on the island when

you small, but he don't know you then." He chomped philo-
sophically. "Just think of it: You two little souls rompin' 'bout
not two hundred miles from each other, maybe dreamin'
'bout each other even then."

Though she and Paul had indulged in just such a fantasy
in a sentimental moment, she said, "You're full of bull, Winston."

He threw the chewstick aside, running his tongue over his
teeth and giving his most beguiling smile. "Had to learn me
romance, man. When I'm young I got no money to buy presents for the pretty women. All I got to endear m'self is me
mouth."

"I'm sure that must've been enough," she said coolly, too
impatient to enjoy the compulsive flirtatiousness so common
to island men.

"Yeah, once in awhile I get lucky and some kindhearted
woman take pity on me. Hey, we hear 'bout the fire up in y'
fields. Big fire, huh? Was anybody hurt?"

She was in no mood to discuss Archie. When she'd gone in
to see him that morning, there had been no apparent change
in his condition; indeed he'd seemed more wasted and depressed, unwilling to speak to anyone. "I don't think anyone
was hurt," she said, trailing her hand in the water. "At least
I didn't hear about it. I don't know about the fellows who
were supposed to be guarding the fields, but . . ."

Winston rubbed his chest and laughed. "Don't worry 'bout
that. Word say y' brother get some of his boys to start that fire.
Got to be true. Day after that big storm, those plants still
damp. They need a splash of gasoline here an' there to get
them goin'. Ah, so sad. So sad. All that good ganja going' up
to the sky." He winked. "Just ahead of the drug teams gonna
burn it up anyway."

"What do you mean?"

"Raids startin' up all over this coast, man. Narcotics boys
got them buzz saw with shoulder sling to cut down the
plants . . ." He mimed the swinging saw. ". . . little bombs
to blow up the private air fields, pa-boom!" His hands ges-
ticulated, arching into the air. ". . . doggies to sniff it
out . . ." He screwed up his nose and jerked his head for-

ward, sniffing. "Oh, yes, man," he laughed, delighted with his performance. "Oh, yes. But the guys with they private air fields have them truckloads of sand right by, fill up those holes, be back in operation the next day. Since your brother don't have him air field done yet, I don't guess what he's gonna do. Yeah, it's a very expensive game. The security police be runnin' round, burnin' up an' blowin' up, but they back off when it get rough. Say they don't want to interfere with civil rights. Not if it a rich man's property, they don't. They just be playing at cops and robbers, hide and seek. They be like boys in the schoolyard, only now they big boys so they gets the government to give them bigger toys to play. Yeah, yeah," he nodded again, "that be the word goin' down: Your brother get a warning 'bout the narcotics boys an' he beat them to the punch. But now the police be huntin' in the village an' the hills for what they call the per-pe-trator. An' all the people already nervous, ready to jump outta they skin. Trouble, trouble. It's worse in Kingston. Things hottin' up in Kingston. Air thick, just like before that storm. Very, very quiet. Peoples meetin' on the streets, then meltin' into the shacks. Only the radio goin'."

He made a fist and raised it to his mouth like a microphone, taking on the mock troubled tone of a reporter. " 'Things very, very tense in this biggest Caribbean island. Rumors goin' all around. Gas price goin' up; dollar goin' down.' "

He spat into the bushes and wiped his mouth. "It happenin' just like Paul say it goin' to," he said with bitterness. "Last election they blamin' everything on him, saying we in bad shape 'cause he spending on the schools and hospitals and such, sayin' the U.S. cut off our water because of him. No International Monetary Fund, no World Bank money, just because of bad Paul Strangman. Now what? They been drop-pin' sacks of dollars down from the sky, say we goin' to be a new economic miracle. Everythin' goin' to be better. But better never come. Everythin' the same. Worse. It was a bogus election. A mule can get elected if he has the right backing and enough money. Now maybe these fools see the truth. Me, I think that fine British education ruin Mr. Paul Strangman. He think he educate the people. He believe in this parliamen-

tary democracy. He want to be elected again. Me . . ." His eyes
narrowed as he looked up beyond the falls into the hills,
". . . I think we start up here. Gather the people round us.
Take it over. That's the only way."

"There you go, being romantic again."

"In the Sierra Mastra . . ."

"You're spoiling for a fight you can't win, Winston. There
can't be a revolutionary takeover here."

"Who say we can't win?" he demanded. "Who say?"

"I would for one. I expect Paul would, too."

Winston's features became clouded with frustration. "M'
grandfather have the right idea. He tell about the before-time
people who built their villages in the mountains."

"You mean the Maroons?"

"Yes. When I was a little chap, he tell me 'bout all the
battles."

"But that took place generations before he . . ."

"Once," Winston continued, caught up in his narrative,
"the governor come through our town and m' grandfather
dress up in his ambush dress. Tying bush, vines, and leaves
on his Sunday suit, puttin' a little tree on his back. I never
forget the sight. I tell him he look like the man I see on the
can of vegetables come from the U.S.A."

"You mean the Jolly Green Giant?"

"Sure." He chuckled softly. "But he not so jolly. When I say
that to him, he slap me hard. Ah, yes. Me grandfather in
ambush gear! He willin' to fight. You think all them boys in
Kingston slums not ready to fight, too?"

She felt they might be. But not in a protracted battle. "I
can't say," she begged off, wondering how long they'd been
waiting, feeling her impatience meld with anxiety about
Paul's whereabouts.

"Hey, cheer up. Boss be here soon." He moved to the edge
of the bank and squatted down on his haunches. "Here I am,
talkin' your pretty ear off while you just wanting to be with
your own thoughts." She said nothing. "I see a big change in
him these last days," he continued gently. "Before he see you
again, he's very down. Very down. It hard for him to talk to
the people. He don't say the same speech twice, and even the

ones who hate him never call him hypocrite. So you know it be hard for him, keepin' up the faith in everyone else. Hardest thing in the world to be keepin' up other peoples' spirits when you're down yourself. But since he get you back he got energy again. I see him revvin' up, ready to go. He's in a fightin' mood, and workin' so hard—taking little naps in the day, fifteen, twenty minutes—then ready to go again. Nothin' do it like the right woman. Maybe you stay up all night with her," he shot her a sly smile, "but it better than sleep."

She was gratified to know that he thought she had such a tonic affect on Paul. Through no conscious effort she'd won Winston over, and that pleased her too, because she liked him. She brushed back her hair and smiled. "Are you married, Winston?"

"Got me a wife somewhere."

"You misplaced her?"

"She misplaced me. I think she live in Toronto now. She's doing real well, I hear."

"You don't sound very upset about it."

He shrugged. "Lots of nice women around. I got me a couple of steady ones. Only ever loved one woman really, and she just a girl when I loved her." She nodded, encouraging him to go on. "We from the same village. Even when she small, she crazy to get married. Dress up her dolls in veils, even dress up the chicken and the cat. When we comin' on to sixteen, she make me so shy m' tongue cleave to the roof of m' mouth every time I look at her. I want to marry her more than almost anything. But also, I want to get away from the village. I work in m' father's carpentry shop, building caskets mostly. I hate the work an' hate m' father even more. He was a real *petit bourgeoisie.*" Ceci was amused by the precision of his pronunciation, knowing he must've learned it from Paul. "So," he continued, "I can't stay and let m' father rule me just to have a job to get married, so I promise her I go away, make m' fortune and come back. She promise she wait for me. But she lie. She didn't wait."

"How long were you gone?"

He looked sheepish. "Twenty years. She got six children by then, and her arms—used to have skinny, little arms—they

big 'round as a tree trunk. That don't stop me. She still put
me in a sweat. But she won't havin' nothin' to do with me.
Won't say 'boo' to me. She make me feel lower than a snake's
belly. But when I see her oldest, I think he must be mine
'cause he's a very handsome young man, and that fella she
marry look just like that chicken she used to dress up as the
groom."

He told the story with such mournful indignation that she
had to turn her head away and pretend to study a stone to stop
him from seeing her face. "And where did you go during
those twenty years?" she asked.

"You name it, I go there. Puerto Rico, New York, Miami,
Toronto. Sometimes I spend more time looking for work than
working, but I do it all—dishwasher, carpenter, short order
cook, stevedore. I sell hot stuff on the street. . . . I'm a bouncer
in a social club. I do what all a man with no education can do,
you know?"

She nodded. It was impossible to live in New York and not
be aware of that great tide of mostly young, mostly dark-
skinned, immigrant men. They came from Africa, Korea,
Central America, Hong Kong, the Mideast; but mostly she
was aware of those from the Caribbean. They hefted meat and
produce, drove trucks and taxis, played in steel bands, painted
apartments, went to City College to study business and computer science, dropped out, hung around the Off Track Bet-
ting stores, pushed racks of clothes along Seventh Avenue,
bopped down the streets gripping their "Third World Briefcases," transistors that blasted the air with mindless Motown
disco their American cousins were so fond of. (What was it
Paul had said? That it had taken three hundred years but
blacks had finally started to produce and buy lousy music.)
There was even a section in Brooklyn called the "Little Caribbean." There you could buy meat pies, coconut bread, ginger
beer, goat meat, reggae records, and, of course, ganja. She had
gone there once, alone, to see the Caribbean Day parade and
had found herself pushed to a side street where she'd stood,
surrounded by the oldtime residents of the neighborhood—
Hasidic Jews—the men sweltering in suits and hats, nattering
amongst themselves in sorrowful, philosophic voices; their

women, in wigs and shape-disguising dresses, rocking baby carriages, silent, incredulous as they watched their new neighbors rock and dance down the avenue: black women in elaborate tinsel headdresses, satin gowns, fishnet stockings, and bathing suits, near-naked men sporting painted faces, devil costumes with hose-length phalluses. In Manhattan she was less aware of them—they were the accented voices hawking handbags, belts, and cheap jewelry, seducing unsuspecting out-of-towners into games of three-card monte, asking "Where to?" when you got into a taxi. In Max's neighborhood she saw them hardly at all, and when she did they were reduced to hands cleaning up restaurant tables, opening apartment or hotel doors, passing the groceries in through the back door, giving back the change when you bought a newspaper or a pack of cigarettes. She wondered what would happen to them all—eager, adventurous, secretly fearful, ready to hustle but ill equipped—for, as the TV commercial for the *Wall Street Journal* put it: "There are millions of men and women chasing the American Dream; there's only so much of it to go around."

Winston was now telling and, she suspected, embroidering, a story of how he'd convinced a Miami cop to give him five dollars instead of arresting him for vagrancy. He was such a good story teller that she'd almost forgotten her anxiety about Paul, but something caused her to look up. Shielding her eyes against the glaring sunlight, she saw him, his thumbs looped into his belt, moving down the path. A shiver of joy and relief went through her. Their eyes met and he stopped, holding the glance with breath-stopping concentration until Winston realized that he'd lost his audience and spun around. "Hey, boss. You finally here. Meeting go okay?"

"Well as could be expected." Paul came to the bank. "Ceci, I'm sorry."

"It doesn't matter." Suddenly it didn't. The fact that he was here and safe was what mattered.

"Geoff's waiting in the jeep," he told Winston without taking his eyes from her.

Winston got up, wiping his hands on the back of his jeans. "A-okay. Let's get goin'." He jogged away, singing as he went.

"Who's Geoff?" Ceci asked as she put on her sandals.

"Just a friend."

"You mean a bodyguard, don't you?"

He shrugged, offering his hand to help her up. They were no more than inches from each other, but they didn't touch.

"You're tired," she said, noticing the veined whites of his intensely green eyes.

"It's been a rough few days." He had been under siege, deluged with phone calls, emergency meetings, policy decisions. Everything was coming to a head: the commercial bank lending rate had risen to 33 percent; the government was trying to refinance the foreign debt after admitting that 40 percent of the island's budget was going to pay it off; the Gasoline Retailers Association was threatening a shutdown; a coalition of unions was planning a general strike. Power cuts and water shortages would cause companies to close. If the hotel workers joined in, there'd be hell to pay. Stranded tourists would make international headlines. There would be demonstrations and possibly riots. Some advised him to remain above the fray, then step in afterward and call for a vote of confidence that could bring down the government. Others urged him to do what he could to calm the situation lest it get out of hand and result in bloodshed. And during all of it—listening to intelligence reports, going from one meeting to another, trying to decide his course of action—his thoughts had gone back to Ceci, recalling bits of their conversation, seeing her stretched out on his bed, remembering her smell, the feel of her thighs, the look of love in her eyes.

She looked vastly different from the image he'd been carrying in his mind. Her tailored blouse and slacks gave her body a lean, almost angular look; her nose had started to peel, but there was a touch of pale blue shadow on her eyelids and her lips were shining with some clear gloss; her hair, upswept and held with a silver and tortoiseshell barette, made her look cool even in the afternoon heat. She was quintessentially American: long-legged, seemingly independent, but pampered. A rich man's wife.

"I have so much to talk to you about," she said.

Vera had used those exact words last night when he'd

finally gone to bed. "Not now. Let's go," he said, leading the way through the trees.

He was sure Vera hadn't noticed anything strange about his behavior. She'd been through so many crises with him that she accepted his preoccupations with equanimity. Yet last night she had been troubled. She'd urged him not to make any public appearances during the demonstrations. She'd made her arguments calmly and intelligently—Vera was not one to pull out the emotional stops to get her way, which was one of the reasons he trusted her counsel, though he didn't always take her advice. Women were less inclined to take risks, to seize the main chance; though when the chips were down you couldn't maintain a movement, let alone start a revolution, without them. He'd told Vera he'd think about what she'd said. "So much for pillow talk," she'd sighed, turning off the light and leaving the room, saying her stomach was upset and she was going to get a piece of ginger root.

She must have showered, too, because when she'd come back to bed, turning her back to him and catching his foot between her calves in their usual sleeping position, she'd smelled of ginger and that lavender soap she got from England. Her breathing had been steady but he had known she wasn't asleep. He'd put his hand on her hipbone. "Don't worry about me," he'd said. "I wasn't worrying about you. I was worrying about me," she'd answered. He could feel her eyes staring into the dark. She said she'd gotten a letter from a friend, the widow of an internationally famous civil rights leader. "I was teasing her in my last letter, saying how she should get herself a lover. Of course, I know she can't do that. She couldn't risk the scandal if anyone found out. And the chances of her marrying are even worse. Who'd presume to fill the great man's shoes? She's still young and attractive, but I guess she'll have to spend the rest of her life making speeches and opening libraries. She's been turned into a national monument. It's as though everyone needs to see her grieving to keep his memory alive. I swear, she might as well have lived in India and been forced to practice suttee." He'd stroked her back. "Ah, thanks . . . there . . . no, lower . . . yes, right there near my tailbone." She'd laughed softly. "You must be trying to get round me for something, Paul. You never rub my back no matter how much I beg you. I wrote and told her that she and I should go off on vacation together. Change our names and act like a couple of wild divorcees out on a spree. That'll make her laugh. Of course," she'd added, "we'll never do it." He had dropped off the edge of consciousness then, barely caring when she'd pulled up her legs and rolled away from him.

But this morning she'd been amorous, clutching at him as Elliot knocked on their door complaining that he hadn't seen Paul "in a hundred years." He had started to get up but Vera had shooed Elliot away and guided his hand back under the sheets. Couldn't he let the representatives of the Teachers' Union wait just fifteen minutes? What he'd lacked in spontaneity he'd made up for in the will to please, and she too had been unusually intent on satisfying him, though afterward, when he'd wanted to linger, she'd said he mustn't make people wait too long. Yet even as he'd watched her get up and bend forward, easing her breasts into her bra, he'd thought of Ceci. It was only Ceci, ironically so disruptive to his life, who could give him that calm in the center of things. It was she who gave him energy and hope. He wanted and needed her, not just sexually; he needed her presence. He could get through anything knowing that she was there for him. He must convince her to stay on the island.

As he'd showered, he'd dismissed the idea as an impossibility. Later, cutting into his breakfast steak, it had seemed less an irrational desire, more an achievable goal. By midmorning, listening to organizers from Spanish Town, it had become a full-blown purpose, swallowing up all objections. He was so full of it that it kept him firm, balanced him, gave him an assurance that was perceived as cool detachment. He'd cut off the discussion, announcing that he'd made up his mind. To those around him he'd said that he would make public appearances, would try to quell whatever violence might erupt. He wanted to be there in the thick of it. He owed it to the people to do what he could to stop them from being beaten, arrested, or shot. The people would remember that when he called for the vote of confidence. He asked one of his aides to reissue a statement challenging the validity of the last voter registration. He knew the bastards had screwed around with that, not registering the young people because they knew that was where his strength lay. To himself he said that he would talk Ceci into staying.

Teddy was on the veranda, his revolver on the table, a stub of a pencil in his hand. "I'm working' on my' sums, boss," he called as the jeep pulled up. Paul, Ceci, and Winston got out. Geoff, the bodyguard, got into the driver's seat and started to drive the jeep around to the cook house.

"Come on out back, Teddy," Winston said, leaning on the railing as Ceci and Paul mounted the steps.

"But I'm figuring out the household accounts, like the boss tell me to."

"Dumb as you are you'll need me to help you," Winston said.

"I don't need . . ." A smile parted Teddy's lips. "Oh, yeah. Sure. You can help me." He picked up his revolver and moved off.

Paul went into his rooms, but Ceci lingered on the veranda, tapping the bird cage. The obviousness of the situation and the proximity of the other men made her feel awkward, but, hearing Paul lower the blinds and move into the bathroom, anticipation overcame embarrassment.

She shut the door behind her. The room, blinds seeping mellow afternoon light, seemed protected, intensely private. Paul had stripped off his shirt and was standing at the basin, splashing his face and chest. Seeing her watching him, he began to wash more slowly, throwing back his head. She went to him, leaning against the door jamb, prolonging the sweet agony of not touching.

"I think Winston's a little bit in love with you," he said.

"He barely knows me."

"He goes on intuition. Often too much so."

"I guessed that. He was telling me he thought you should go into the hills and become a guerrilla general or something."

Paul shook his head, throwing the towel aside and moving to his desk. He was glad Winston had hit it off with Ceci.

Relations between Winston and Vera were often strained. She was put off by his tall tales and sexual jokes and thought he played too roughly with Elliot. Winston in turn thought Vera was too much of a constraining influence. But Winston would feel that about any man's wife.

He took off one boot and then the other, holding the second one high and smiling at her before he let it drop. "Come here." He reached for her. "It seems like forever."

"For me too." She clung to him. He pulled back, cupping her chin, kissing her eyelids. "You look so elegant I hate to mess you up."

"Mess me up."

He undid her blouse, fingering the embroidery on her bra. "This was probably made by some poor Filipino who went blind making these tiny stitches."

"The best lingerie is made in America," she whispered as he bent closer, having trouble with the front clasp.

"Another capitalist conspiracy." He slid her pants down over her hips and stripped off his own, kneeling, one hand between her legs, the other sliding up from ankle to calf. She winced as he brushed the gash on her knee. "How . . . ?" He eased back onto his haunches, examining it.

"I'll tell you later," she breathed, reaching for his hands, guiding them to her waist and stepping backward until she'd lowered herself onto the bed, her feet still firm on the floor, her legs wide. He touched the wound tenderly, then buried his face between her legs.

"Plum jam," he whispered, moving up to kiss her face. "Made in the U.K. by Nettleton Limited."

"You are merry, m' lord." In a startling change, all anxiety had disappeared, leaving them playful, lighthearted.

"I am happy, madam. I am with you. That is, almost with you." He eased into her, slowly, in a stupor of possessive joy.

Working under him, she remembered waiting for him and her mood suddenly darkened. She slid her legs down from his shoulders, thrusting and twisting her pelvis. He took her cue and moved to bring her on top and she squatted over him, holding him tight, pulling on him, moving in easy teasing circles, wanting to get him first. He gazed up at her, providing himself for her pleasure, relishing her slippery hunger, daring her, urging her on. "Come on, lady," he whispered at last, "clear the fence." It triggered her. Hair swinging, eyes rolling back, she rocked onto him, coming down hard again and again, biting her lip to stop herself from crying out.

He pulled her down to him, kneading her back, soothing her until she subsided before lifting her into a kneeling position, clasping her hips from behind. She could feel only his finger moving in her cleft, and then his penis, stiff and steady —ah, ah, ah—an animal thrust demanding release.

They lay without touching, reentering the space of the bed, the room, the house, not speaking for a long time. She was glad they were silent. Even though she could feel that his mind had already turned to something else, she felt close to him. At one time she had been so insecure, so greedy for his love that his silences had seemed to deprive her; now she felt they granted access to deeper thoughts, longings, and confusions. Though they would always in some way be adversaries, she knew that he accepted her totally, as she accepted him. Max did not accept her; not completely. Neither her opinions, nor her wildness, nor her deepest sexual feelings. Max bought the popular myth of the simultaneous orgasm—how could that have become the ideal since it deprived you of the most intense awareness of yourself as well as your lover? Sometimes, to please him, she'd even faked it. With Max there was always a part of her that she held back, intuiting that real abandon would—though Max would rather cut his tongue out than admit such a fear—overwhelm him. Paul was never at risk of being overwhelmed.

Her hand reached for the tight curls at the nape of his neck, tugging on them, then pressing, feeling his skull. The awful fear came on her—the skeleton beneath the flesh.

"Why are you frightened?" His voice was husky. He didn't open his eyes.

"How did you know I was?"

"Because I can feel you."

"I was wondering what time it is."

"I don't know. It doesn't matter."

"I have to pick Phoebe up at the airport at seven. I lied to them at the house, told them I was picking her up earlier and taking her out to dinner."

"Who's Phoebe?"

"I've told you all about her, don't you remember? You even met her a few times."

"She was your father's first wife, wasn't she?"

"I've told you all about her," she repeated, hurt.

"Don't be so impatient. I remember now. She took care of you. She . . ."

Ceci sat up, wrapping her arms around her legs. "And I have to . . ."

"All right." He had an appointment in Kingston at nine and was relieved that he wouldn't have to risk hurting her feelings by cutting their meeting short. He opened his eyes. "You haven't told me how you got that cut on your knee."

She told him about the fire, about her confrontation with Marsden, which he listened to intently, interrupting only long enough to say she shouldn't trust anything Marsden had said and that he wanted her to leave that house as soon as possible. Finally she began to talk about Archie. "I never realized how much I cared about him. I don't think I've ever really considered his dying. The thought of it frightens me terribly. This morning when I went in to see him, he ordered everyone out of the room. Said he didn't want anyone in there, except Icilda. I found myself thinking, If Archie dies, I'll be an orphan. A thirty-three-year-old orphan." She laughed. "That I could feel that way . . . it proves to me that I've never really grown up. Or that I've missed some vital move in the cycle. Perhaps people who have children of their own don't feel—"

"It's the top of the hill. At a certain age we're up there. With the view. We might look backward but now we also see forward, down the slope—to the death of a parent, then to our own."

"And I find I can't talk to Archie, can't comfort him at all. I suppose that takes years of practice. I can't even tell him that I love him though I realize for the first time that I do. He's an old fake, but I love him. And the way he opened up to me —no, it wasn't really to me, it was to himself, but he knew I was there. I've always wanted to strip away all of his phony rationalizations and defenses, but now I see how much he needed . . ." She shuddered, gripping her legs tighter. "Now that he's without them, I wish he had them back. He seems so helpless."

"But if the doctor said . . ." he reasoned, caressing her foot.

"Paul, please understand. I feel as though I need help, too. That's why I've asked Phoebe to come. And there's this man I've been living with," she rushed on, not knowing she was going to mention Max until the words had already left her mouth. "His name is . . ."

"Do you love him?"

She paused, the vertical crease between her eyes deepening. "In a way. I . . ."

The *in a way* was enough. "I don't want to know his name. It's not important."

"I've been living with him for almost a year. We're very compatible. He's asked me to marry him."

"But you said you didn't love him."

"I said I loved him in a way."

"That'll never be enough for you."

She studied her knee. Why was he so sure that a marriage that admitted limitations worked for him but wouldn't work for her? Her frustration grew as she realized that she agreed with him.

"Even if he's rich, which I suppose he is," Paul went on, "you'd be running off to other places, or certainly other beds, inside of six months."

"How can you be so goddamned arrogant?"

"I'm just telling you what you already know." He pulled himself up to sit beside her. "You'll never be a hausfrau and you're not really a party girl, though you do a fine imitation. Why don't you get back to your writing, Ceci? Why don't you dig in on that one thing? You have the experience now and . . ."

"And I don't want you as a career counselor."

"And I don't want to argue. There isn't enough time." He leaned to kiss the gash on her knee as though she were a child who'd come to have a hurt made better. The tenderness of his

gesture made tears come to her eyes, made her feel grateful
and vulnerable and somehow patronized. Did he have any
idea how miserable she'd been these last days, not being able
to contact him? It was easy enough for him to dismiss Max,
but could he guess how she sometimes craved the comfort of
Max's "I'm available anytime" declaration? His hand slithered down her leg. She noticed he was getting another erec-
tion. "You," she said, "you think you can galumph around
like some Alpha male, beating his chest in front of the lesser
gorillas, hauling the female . . ."

"The most *desirable* female . . ."

". . . into your cave and . . ."

He moved like lightning, seizing her by the shoulders and
giving her one teeth-rattling shake. "Ceci. There isn't time for
this."

"What is there time for? Screwing and politics, right?" She
pulled free of him. "Or, in your case politics and screwing."

"I've never wanted to separate my priorities," he grinned,
still trying to lighten her mood, then, seeing the almost haggard expression on her face, "Why do you denigrate it, Ceci?
Why? When it's one of the things that makes you feel most
alive. Shouldn't we all try to do the things that make us feel
most alive?"

"Don't give me your 'sex as life force' lecture, Paul. Save
it for one of your novices."

"I love you."

It was the first time since they'd been back together that
he'd said the words, and she steeled herself against their im-
pact, demanding, "Is that supposed to make it all right? Kiss
it better?"

"I love you," he repeated. "I won't even say I wish I didn't.
And you love me. Don't complicate it," he added, almost as
if it was an order. "It's already complicated enough. So
don't."

They stared at each other, the look draining all irritation
until at last she lowered her head, looping her arms around
his neck, their foreheads pressed together. She could hear
Teddy's radio and the buzzing of a fly against the blinds. She
slapped at a mosquito and he moistened his finger with saliva

and rubbed the spot. They moved as a single body, easing back down, holding on. "What time . . . ?" she asked. "We have time." He held her tighter. "I know it's not true, but just now it feels like it." He sighed. "I was remembering the fireplace in our London flat."

She took his hand, rubbing the calluses, wondering where he'd gotten them. "How could you think of that in all this heat?"

"Sometimes, in front of that fireplace with you . . . I don't think I've ever felt so . . ."

"*Luxe, calme, et volupte,*" she supplied.

"Not just that. Hopeful." His fingertips brushed the translucent down on her arms.

"And when we were in front of the fire we used to talk about being in Jamaica. How you longed to get back. How we were going to swim naked in the moonlight and all that. My first night back, when I was walking on the beach alone, I thought about all that. All the things we were going to do."

"We can still do them."

"Oh, Paul. I'm afraid we're neither of us content by nature. In the London drizzle we longed for Jamaica. Here we are panting with the heat and you're dreaming of the fireplace." Safe in his arms now, she was determined not to look either backward or forward.

"You used to forget to open the flue." He laughed softly. "Twice we had to open the windows in the dead of winter because you'd just about suffocated us."

She pinched the flesh around his waist, and he grabbed her hand and brought it to his lips. "This man I met with today," he whispered, kissing her fingertips, "he's from the African National Congress. He's been running a bush radio station beaming into South Africa. It's time for them to make their move now, so he's going back to his home village. Poor buggers. They'll have to make concessions, but if they make too many concessions they'll be coopted by the powers that be and lose their own hard-liners. But they know they can't run the country alone." He sighed, considering, stroking her back absently. "Well, he can't expect a peaceful death. I wonder if I'll ever see him again."

"Then again, he might be the Minister of Culture next year," She snuggled her head into his neck, wrapping her leg around his and feeling the throb of renewed desire.

"No," he said slowly, holding her tighter, "it won't be that easy. They've got years of it ahead. God knows how much slaughter or how it will turn out in the end. Poor bastard. We ended up talking about England. Seems we used to go to the same pub in Notting Hill."

He was holding her so close that she was having trouble breathing. She moved her head, so that he saw the underside of her chin. Such a defiant chin. He used to tease her about it, calling her a boxer with a glass jaw. "Ceci. Cecily Baron."

"Paul Strangman." She took a deep breath, reaching behind her to come up with the tortoiseshell comb. "So this is what's been digging into my bum," she said, holding it up to the light.

He seized her hand, pulling her close again, looking into her eyes. "Stay on the island, Ceci. Stay with me."

Nineteen

"Thank god you're here," Ceci said, letting herself be drawn into Phoebe's arms and feeling the softness of her cheek and the comfort of her bosom. "It was too much to hope that you could get here so quickly."

"How is he?"

"Not much changed. Perhaps I've been an alarmist. The doctor was at the house again this morning and he said . . . but when I left, Archie still wouldn't speak and . . ." She was having trouble getting her thoughts in order ". . . I called the house from Paul's just before I came to pick you up and . . ."

"From Paul's? Ceci, you didn't tell me that . . ."

". . . Icilda said Archie was resting and . . . yes, from Paul's, I . . ." She felt someone brush past them, heard a curt "excuse me," and realized they were blocking the path of the other passengers. "I suppose we'd best move along. I'll tell you everything once we're in the car. Your bags?"

"Haven't got anything but this carry-on. Thought I'd buy some lighter clothes while I was . . ."

"Good." Ceci took it from her. "I spoke to one of the fellows in immigration, so we should be able to get through in no time. Here, up these stairs. Perhaps I shouldn't have asked you to come," she said as they passed the line of swaying girls singing their welcoming song, "but I was so . . ."

"Nonsense. I want to be here. I suppose Archie needs me, and if he doesn't, it certainly appears that you do." She followed her up a flight of stairs and into the large room with the immigration desks. When they'd joined one of the lines, she slipped her arm through Ceci's and gave her hand a squeeze. "My dear girl, you have been through it, haven't you? I know what you told me on the phone was only the tip of the iceberg."

"The very tip." She could tell from the stiffness of his neck and the slight inclination of his head that the man standing in front of them was listening to them. As the immigration clerk waved him forward, he turned and gave Phoebe a smile of recognition. "I think you've been recognized," she whispered. "And you do look wonderful, Phoebe. You really do." As Phoebe had gotten off the plane, Ceci had noticed her rose-colored suit, the way she'd descended the steps without looking down at her feet, and the graceful curiosity in the turn of her head, and she'd thought Phoebe looked like a much younger woman. Now she took in Phoebe's new hair style; close-cropped waves, redolent of the twenties, giving her face (which had been discreetly made-up), a natural lift.

"Thought I'd best doll myself up a bit. Not for Archie," Phoebe protested, "I started the redo a few days ago. It seems," she lowered her voice, "that I'm going to be made a Dame. Did I tell you? No, I don't suppose I did. I found out just after you'd left. Eric was all against it at first, said titles run entirely counter to every principle I'd ever espoused. But then I pointed out that it would improve my 'bankability,' as they say in Hollywood, so he came round. It was that Indian film that did it. Seems it's going to be nominated for an Oscar. Imagine," she laughed, "me with a title. If we feel earth tremors, we'll know it's Lady Mother turning in her grave."

"That's wonderful, Phoebe! Congratulations. Marsden's fiancée doesn't know what to think of anyone until she's read their press clippings, so your new celebrity will make things that much easier. And believe me, it's not going to be easy."

"I didn't think it would be. You don't suppose Archie will be upset by the news, do you?"

"At one time perhaps, but not now. Now I think he'll be pleased. Without betraying his trust, I think I can tell you about the things he said the other afternoon when . . ."

The immigration clerk shoved a ballpoint pen into the fuzz of his Afro and motioned them forward.

"I'll tell you later."

Ceci had driven slowly, talking all the while, but when they'd come within miles of the house there was still much to be explained, so she'd pulled off onto a promontory. Below them, past a wooded slope, was the ocean, and high above them, its columns becoming luminous in the growing darkness, was the great house. They continued to talk, their voices becoming more subdued as the light failed, until finally Ceci threw back her head, closed her eyes, and said, "And that's about it."

"And quite enough, I'm sure." Phoebe purposefully ground out her cigarette in the ashtray. " 'When troubles come, they come not as single spies but in battalions.' It seems impossible that so much could have happened in such a brief space of time, but then I've always found life like that. Long stretches of nothing, then everything coming to a head at once, so that you can't possibly assimilate it all." She inclined her head toward the half-opened window. "It does smell lovely here. That sea smell, and all the flowers. I have to pinch myself to realize that I'm here. I've imagined it most of my life, you see. Ever since I've known Archie." She ducked her head and tilted it, staring past Ceci up into the hills. "That great house. It's so very much as I'd imagined it that I feel I've seen it before. It's positively Gothic. Enough to make you believe in ghosts."

"We call them duppies here. Nervous as I've been these last few days, I think I've come to believe in them." She turned on the ignition and the headlights. "We really shouldn't be parked like this after dark. As I said, things are very uneasy on the island now. Paul says—"

"That's what I want to talk to you about some more. About Paul."

Ceci shut off the headlights and turned off the key. The foliage, briefly illuminated, now had a menacing look. The moon had disappeared behind a bank of clouds, and down the slope she thought she could see the glimmer of a campfire. She reached for Phoebe's cigarettes. "I don't know what to say. Except that I can't imagine being without him again."

"I'm sure he feels the same way about you. I don't doubt that." Phoebe flicked the lighter, studying the grim little lines around Ceci's mouth. "But how will you manage?"

"Paul says Winston knows of a house for rent just outside Montego," she said, thoughtfully blowing out the smoke and resting her head on the steering wheel.

"I wasn't talking about logistics. You've said the island depresses you. And you don't have any friends here. And if you stayed, you'd want to see Vivian, and from what you've told me about Marsden . . . You don't suppose you could be here secretly, do you? And what would you do with yourself?"

"What have I ever done with myself? Flitted about, never connecting with anyone or anything, bullshitting myself that I'm a citizen of the world. Never staying in one place long enough to even have any real friends. I used to con myself into believing that I was having a good time, that I was free. But I stopped having a good time years ago. I've never been committed to anyone. And I am committed to Paul. I'm even committed to his beliefs, though we always argue about them. I don't mean I buy them just because they're his, but because I share them. I would like to think I could make a difference."

"But what would you *do?*" Phoebe interrupted gently.

"I'll write. If I'm living alone, I won't have any excuse not to. And I want to support myself. I don't know if I can, but I really want to. Paul will help me at first."

"But you must try to imagine what it will really be like. No matter how much Paul wants to be with you, it's bound to be infrequent at best. It strikes me as a bit selfish on his part." Ceci's head lifted reflexively, ready to defend. "Not that Paul means to be selfish," Phoebe added. "But that's the way it's bound to come out. It would be bad enough to live with a man who's a public figure, but if he's a married man? In any affair with a married man, a woman must have very limited expectations, and a strong drive toward her own accomplishments, otherwise it's a lifetime of waiting around."

"I said I was going to write," Ceci insisted. "Don't you believe me?"

"And friends. She must have a few friends. Even then, when you love the man, you find yourself slipping away from all your self-imposed limitations. What if he's sick, or you are? You can't go to each other. What if you or he have a success? You can never publicly share it. At first that intensifies things, makes the moments together more precious, but after a time it's just miserable. You eat alone. Most nights you sleep alone. Waking up alone can be a relief if it's just a sexual fling, but if you love the man, it's hell to have him get out of your bed and go home. And you start to think about his wife. You envy her but you feel sorry for her. What felt reasonable and necessary in the beginning begins to feel like a sacrifice, you resent—"

"The only sacrifice I can see would be leaving him." Ceci stubbed out the cigarette. She suspected that Phoebe must be talking from personal experience, that she must have had a long and unhappy affair with a married man, but she was too caught up in her own dilemma to want to question her about it. "I know Paul cares about his wife, but he did—"

"Talk about getting a divorce? They always talk about—"

"Not *they*," Ceci insisted, *"Paul."*

"And you say he has a child?"

"Yes. Elliot."

"Ceci, can't you see? The sacrifice would be so unequal. You'll come to resent it despite yourself."

"What else can I do? I love him. I love him more now than I did before, though I didn't think that possible. And I'd rather have part of an exceptional man than all of an unexceptional one, because when I'm with him I do have all of him. I know I do." She had started out speaking in a protesting tone, but now she sounded almost serene. "I can't give him up."

Phoebe sighed. "It seems I've just broken one of my own cardinal rules: Never give advice about lovers or relatives.

And it sounds as though you've already told him you'll stay. Have you?"

"No. Not yet. We're to meet again in another four days."

"I won't say that this is a very inopportune time for you to make a major decision."

"I think you just did."

"What about your Max?"

"Telling him won't be easy, though I don't plan to tell him everything. Why hurt his ego? But, in a way, I expect he already knows I'm not coming back. We really should get going, Phoebe."

"Yes. Yes, of course. I'm anxious to see Archie. I just . . ." She touched Ceci's cheek and Ceci inclined her head, resting it on her shoulder. "I don't know why you're grousing at me, Phoebe. Haven't you always been the one who's encouraged me to follow my passions and to live independently and devil take the hindmost?"

"Guilty as charged," Phoebe said. "Though that all seems terribly theoretical now. Now I just feel like a mother hen. S'pose there is a natural conservatism that creeps in, no matter how much I fight it."

"I've always thought of you as my mother in a way, though I don't suppose I could ever talk to my own mother this openly."

"No, lovey, you have enough problems. If you'd been born with my nose . . ." She brought her face close to Ceci's until the tips of their noses touched. "Shall we go?"

Ceci murmured "Thank you for coming" before she pulled away and turned on the motor.

"It'll be hard to look Marsden in the face, knowing what I know," Phoebe said as they bumped onto the road.

"Don't worry. Marsden never looks anyone in the face. And Hilary won't be back for a few days, so things should be relatively quiet."

There was no response but barking from the kennels when Ceci honked her horn at the gate. She got out, opened the gates, and drove up to the big tree. The lower floor of the house was ablaze with lights and Vivian was waiting on the veranda. As Ceci and Phoebe got out, she came toward them, pausing midway on the gravel path, then hurrying to them with a burst of precipitous steps. She was wearing a good but sadly unfashionable print dress and an armada of little ships sailed across her corseted hips and trussed bosom. "Aunt Vivian," Ceci said, "this is Phoebe Suffringham. I believe you've met before."

"Decades ago," Phoebe extended her hand. "It was very kind of you to invite me, Miss Nettleton." She looked into Vivian's face, immediately focusing on her good eye.

"It's Mrs. Pinto," Vivian corrected with pride. "I suppose Angus forgot to tell you that I'd been married. And, in point of fact, I wasn't consulted about your visit." Ceci bit her lip, realizing that anxious though she was to protect Vivian's rights, she'd neglected to ask her permission. "Which doesn't mean to say that I'm not pleased to receive you," Vivian continued, "because I am."

"How is Archie?" Phoebe asked.

"I'm sure I don't know. He's closeted himself in there with Icilda and pretends to be asleep whenever anyone else comes into the room. His supper tray came out empty and there was enough on it to feed a horse, so he must have his appetite back."

"Aunt Vivie," Ceci said gently, grieved to see that Vivian was acting like a child who was jealous because her sibling was getting too much attention. "You know Archie's had a terrible shock."

"Ceci seems to think that Angus is at death's door, though I'm inclined to believe that he's just having one of his snit fits. Since you were married to him, you'll know what I mean. Nevertheless, I'm sure it will be beneficial for him to see you again."

Phoebe turned at the top of the stairs, exchanged a quick glance with Ceci, and said, "What a lovely place you have here, Mrs. Pinto. The scent from the garden mixing with the scent of the ocean, and this diamond-clear night sky . . . it's magical."

"Perhaps you'd like to walk around the garden with me."

Vivian smiled. "I've neglected it pitifully of late and our last storm flattened . . ."

"Indeed I would love to see the garden. I putter about in the garden myself, but perhaps later. Just now, I'd like to see Archie, if I might."

"Of course. In this house the people come and go, but my garden is always here." Vivian settled into a chair. "Ceci will show you in. If you don't mind, I'll wait out here. Our new driver took our girl Thelda into Sav la Mar to do some shopping hours ago and they haven't returned. And my nephew was supposed to be home for supper and he hasn't returned, so I shall station myself here and play Penelope."

Ceci put Phoebe's bag on a chair in the front room and led the way up the passage. She tapped lightly at the door and heard what sounded like the shifting of furniture on the other side. "So this is where he was a boy," Phoebe whispered, looking about her with the rapt curiosity of a bride. "Perhaps he's in the bathroom," Ceci ventured, then, more impatiently, "Icilda, will you please let us in." Icilda opened the door, staring nervously at them. "This is Miss Suffringham, Icilda. Phoebe, this is Icilda. You've often heard me speak of her." "To be sure," Phoebe said softly. "It's a pleasure to meet you, Icilda." Still Icilda made no move to let them in. "Pleased to make your acquaintance, miss. He sleepin'." Ceci motioned her aside.

"Archie? Archie, can you hear me?" Ceci asked, reaching the foot of the bed. "Archie, please wake up. There's someone special to see you."

Phoebe stood, one hand on her breast, the other reaching to touch Archie's forehead, her eyes filling with tears. Archie opened his eyes slowly, inspecting the face bent to his with a long and penetrating stare, as though trying to understand what place and time he'd woken up in. "Is it you?" he asked.

"Yes. It's me."

"But you've let your hair go white." He struggled up on the pillows, pulling the front of his pajamas together. "Why didn't anyone tell me you were coming?"

"It's a surprise. I'm between plays and Cecily called and said you weren't well, so . . ."

He shot Ceci a stabbingly accusatory glance. "Now you've gone and worried her."

"I would have been more worried if I hadn't come. Are you feeling any better?"

"My chest feels like a perforated bellows," he wheezed, fondling her hand. "My throat feels as though it's been stripped raw. I . . ."

"There, there." She sat on the bed, smoothing his few wisps of hair back from his forehead. He reached up, patting them back into place, managing the ghost of a smile as she shook her head at his vanity. "Aren't you glad to see me, Archie?"

"Always a pleasure, old girl. Always a pleasure." He eased backward, pulling her with him, his hands clutching her back.

Ceci turned to Icilda. "I think we'd best leave Father and Miss Suffringham alone for a bit," she suggested, rolling her eyes toward the door. Icilda reluctantly followed her out. "You rings the bell for me," she called over her shoulder. "Anythin' go wrong, you . . ."

"Icilda!" Ceci said. "Come."

Walking through the dining room, Icilda asked if Ceci would like anything to eat. She asked for a sandwich and went out onto the veranda. Vivian was still stationed in her chair, looking out into the darkness. "Archie seems much better," Ceci said, putting her hand on Vivian's shoulder. "Perhaps I was too much of an alarmist."

"You don't know Angus as well as I do."

"Let's say we know him differently."

"And you were feeling guilty about having taken him up to the fields."

"Perhaps. I'll carry Phoebe's bag up for her. Where have you put her?"

"In the guest room opposite Hilary's."

"Are you upset because Phoebe's here? I apologize for not asking you directly."

"It's not that. Her presence makes me thoughtful. She was always held up to me as what a woman shouldn't be. But she seems to have fared quite well, doesn't she? I shall never forget—Mother almost fainted away when she met her.

Angus was half-sozzled. He actually snapped Phoebe's garter in front of us and she just made goo-goo eyes at him. She was quite the hoyden then. She still has a bit of flash, doesn't she? No, I'm not annoyed with you. Or Phoebe. It's just that Marsden said he'd be home for supper. And Thelda and that new boy have gone off. And I think I'm getting another case of the spots." Vivian closed her eyes, putting her middle fingers on the lids.

"I shouldn't worry about Marsden. Perhaps he decided to have dinner with whomever he was meeting."

Vivian shook her head, rejecting all comforting possibilities. "No. Marsden is very punctilious. He doesn't like to see me worry. He would have called."

"I'll have Icilda make you some tea," Ceci said, turning away.

Icilda had already started up the stairs with Phoebe's bag and a set of fresh towels. Ceci went to her room and sat on the bed. After a time she got up, stripped off her clothes, and stepped into the bathroom. Phoebe's words about Paul seemed to fill her head as she bent, wrapping it in a towel. But as she stepped into the spray, leaning against the tile and letting the warm needles play on her, she thought of nothing but Paul's words. And his touch. And the times they would have together now. Not just time for bed. They would walk and talk and discuss things as they'd done in the past. Paul had even said that they might be able to travel together. And when she wasn't with him, she would work. He had always taken an interest in her writing, always read, encouraged, criticized. Sometimes his criticism had been too painfully on the mark, but she'd been younger then, more defensive, more eager for approval. It would be different now. Because he did care about what she accomplished, more than any of the others, he did care. And, not to put too cynical a cast on it, he would have to care because—Phoebe had been right about this—he'd need her to be independent and able to function without him. It might not be the best of all possible worlds, but it was the best world she could hope for because he would be a part of it.

Putting on her robe, she went to the desk and took a sheet

of Vivian's heavy Nettleton House stationery from the drawer. "Dear Max." She bit the end of the pen. The blank page stared up at her. Dear Max. She felt as though she were trying to write a letter of condolence to a bereaved friend—only clichés came to mind. She scratched at her shoulder and saw the tiny welt where Paul's teeth had broken her flesh. She looked at her own teethmarks on the pen. She tried again. She pushed the paper aside.

He was *dear* Max and he'd been more than just another port in her continuing storm. Indulgent not by nature, but because he was in love with her. Did she want a trip? Call the travel agent. A new dress? That summery thing they'd seen in Bergdorf's window would look great on her. A bracelet? A house in the country? A baby? Nothing would please him more than to start a second family now that his kids were in college and rarely bothered to call. He'd been available to her twenty-four hours a day, every day. Couldn't she wake him up when she'd had a nightmare, or interrupt his conferences when she needed to talk? Hadn't he offered to come to the dentist when she'd had root canal? Hadn't he, once, even humbled himself to go to the drugstore and buy Tampax when she'd started her period early? Dear Max. But how could any relationship survive such an inequality of feeling? Her stomach rumbled and she was reminded that she was hungry. She crumpled up the paper. Tomorrow she would find the right words.

A sandwich and a glass of milk was waiting on the dining room table. Hearing low voices in the front room, she looked in and saw to her utmost surprise that Archie and Phoebe were sitting on the sofa. "Ceci, please join us," Phoebe said, looking up. "We'd been wondering where you'd gotten to. Archie insisted on getting out of bed. I 'spose he needed a change of scene. Looking at the same four walls can be depressing." As though she were still in a chilly climate, Phoebe tucked a blanket around Archie's shins. They all chatted for a bit, but when Ceci went to the bar to fix Phoebe a drink, Archie and Phoebe dropped their voices, like adolescents trying to snatch a moment of privacy in the presence of their chaperone. Ceci excused herself, picked up her sandwich, and went into the kitchen.

Icilda stood near the stove, her wizened face shining in the steam jet from the kettle, eyeing Maurice's Cuisinart, electric knife sharpener, and blender as though they were instruments of torture. Vivian sat at the table smoothing the pages of a book she hadn't the concentration to read. "Mind if I turn on the radio?" Ceci asked. "I'd like to find a newsbroadcast." A duet of remonstrance (Icilda reminding her that the radio belonged to Maurice; Vivian saying her nerves couldn't stand the noise) made her shut it off after a few bars of music. She ate her sandwich—Vivian telling her not to leave the crusts and Icilda urging her to have another glass of milk—and announced that she was going to bed. "I shall wait up for Marsden," Vivian said. Ceci asked if she should stay up with her but was told there was no need; Icilda would keep her company.

Ceci put her head into the front room, saw that it was empty and went to her room, feeling somehow superfluous. Archie was with Phoebe; Icilda with Vivian. Paul, she imagined as she got into bed and turned off the light, Paul was probably with Vera. But Winston had said that Paul was now only sleeping four or less hours a night. She pulled the pillow to her chest. It was better to think of him still up and working.

Some time later she woke, hearing a noise from the front of the house. Feeling her way along the darkened passage, she saw the light in the dining room and heard hushed, confidential female voices. The centerpiece had been moved to the sideboard and a confusion of boxes, albums, and snapshots littered the table. Vivian, her hair braided, a worn dressing gown over her button-up nightie, sat close to Phoebe, who had changed into a peignoir of honeymoon splendor. Icilda, still dressed in her uniform but barefoot, stood behind them. Ceci smiled. Phoebe had ingratiated herself, and was now enjoying the ritual she'd missed half a century ago: the showing of family photos to the new in-law.

"I hope we didn't wake you," Phoebe said.

"No. I was restless. How's Archie?"

"He's resting comfortably. Vivian's been showing me these

wonderful old photos. Look at this, will you? That's you and Marsden."

Ceci took the photo. They were standing by the pond. Marsden was dressed in his summer whites, his cadet's cap at a jaunty angle, his arm around her. She, stringy and gangly but almost reaching to his shoulder, looked up at him admiringly, her shoulders hunched to conceal the knobs of childish breasts.

"And this one. Look at this. That's your grandfather and Archie when he was a boy." The photo was sepia-toned, showing palm trees, the cane fields, the bent backs of workers and, in the foreground, a gaunt man in shirtsleeves and jodphurs, astride a horse, a silver flask in his hand, the shadow made by his pith helmet obscuring his face. Next to him was his miniature, a boy in jodphurs and pith helmet, sitting on a donkey. "Doesn't Archie look grand?" Phoebe asked, though, to Ceci's eyes, boy Archie looked decidedly spoiled and disinterested. "And here's another . . ." But Ceci's ears had already picked up the howl of the dogs and a car motor. "That'll be Marsden," she said, moving quickly through the front room.

But from the veranda she saw the police car bumping down the slope and Sergeant Owens getting out of it almost before it had drawn to a stop. "Miss Baron," he said with military correctness as she hurried to meet him. "I'm so glad to have a word with you first." His eyes were even more puffy than they'd been at their first meeting and his jacket looked as though it had been slept in. "The fact is . . ." His Adam's apple bobbled as he swallowed. "The fact is that your brother has been killed."

Twenty

They sat in the front room, silent and watchful as strangers on a train that had unaccountably stopped between stations. Only Icilda moved—a slow swaying from side to side in rhythm to a low, keening sound.

"And you say it was near Mandeville?" Archie asked.

Ceci stared at the floor. They had already heard that it was near Mandeville. They had heard it twice. But she understood the need to have the details repeated. Details might help to make it real.

"Yes. Near Mandeville. About six o'clock as well as we can make out. We didn't report to you earlier because there was some difficulty with identification, and, as you've probably heard from the news broadcasts, we've had quite a bit on our hands."

"No, we hadn't heard," Ceci said. "What's going on?"

"Gas stations are closing down. Strikes have started in Kingston. It could turn into a general strike." Owens looked above their heads, as though he were reporting directly to the image of Sir Isaac. "We've had quite a lot on our hands, and frankly we expect it to get worse."

"When will you bring us his body?" Vivian asked.

"I'm afraid there's some difficulty there, too, Mrs. Pinto. You see . . ."

"There really isn't any body," Owens' less sensitive associate began before he was stopped by a quick turning of his superior's head.

"As I explained," Owens went on, "it was a powerful explosion. The bomb was detonated as he turned on the motor just after he'd stopped for gas. When an explosion like that happens, there's an instantaneous fireball, nothing . . ." He paused, wanting to spare them the more gruesome details. "At first we thought the employees at the station might be implicated, but that seems unlikely since they were both injured in the blast. The younger man may lose his hand. It seems more likely that the device was set hours before. One of our demolition experts is checking that out. You said you didn't know Mr. Baron's destination?"

"It was Kingston, wasn't it, Auntie?" Ceci asked.

Vivian remained mute, her good eye marooned in her pale face, the poor one veering off, seeking something on which to focus.

Owens buttoned the jacket he'd unbuttoned moments before. "We'd like to shed some light on this." As though taking his injunction literally, Ceci leaned and turned on the table lamp.

"He only said he was going to Kingston," Vivian said after a time. "Our bank is there. And the company that's putting in the swimming pool, I believe. But how can there be no body? There must be. . . . We have a family cemetery, you see, and we can't . . ." Phoebe left Archie's side and moved to Vivian, kneeling and wrapping her arms about her legs. Icilda's keening increased in volume.

"If you could provide any appointment book, any notes of Mr. Baron's," Owens said. "Not now, of course. But later, when you're calmer. And I'd like to talk to that new driver you said you'd hired."

"He's not here," Ceci said. "He and the housegirl left this afternoon and haven't been seen since."

"His name?"

"I don't know his name. I wasn't here when he was hired. I believe he was hired by my brother's fiancée . . . I really don't know," Ceci concluded, wanting them to leave.

"But . . . who . . . would . . . ?" Vivian's eyes were dry but her question came out in sobs.

"The suspects are numerous," Owens said.

"Could include anyone who ever worked for him. Could just have been some guy who saw the Rolls and wanted to get him, or he could have been the target of some terrorist," his associate put in. "But our prime suspect is that fellow Mr. Baron mentioned the other night. Percy Balstrait. We'll have a few questions to put to him when we catch up with him. Mr. Baron said he was the one who serviced the Rolls, so . . ."

"I've already told you—" Ceci began, then, hearing another choked sound from Vivian, "Gentlemen, I think it best that we conclude this now. My aunt . . ."

Icilda's eyes were bright with panic. She inched over to stand in front of Archie, muttering in patois. "There, there," Archie soothed, getting to his feet and placing his hands on her shoulders. He stood perfectly still, commanding attention until all eyes focused on him. "I think it best to tell you something, Sergeant Owens." He paused for what seemed an inordinately long time, so that Owens shifted impatiently, leaning forward. "There is no point in your searching for Percy," Archie said, drawing himself up, "because Percy is here and has been here for several days." Icilda began to wail. "It's all right, Icilda," Archie assured her, "It's all right. They're not going to harm him." He looked at Ceci for the briefest moment, then turned to stare at Owens. "Percy was very frightened, so naturally he came back here. Icilda confided in me, so I took Percy in. He's been hiding in my room."

Owen's mouth was tight with exasperation. "We've had men searching the parish, men whose services are needed for countless important jobs, and you've been harboring the man you've asked us to search for? That's an obstruction of justice, Mr. Baron. That's a bloody stupid thing for you to have done. You people . . ."

"I can assure you that no one but myself was party to any of it," Archie said. "If I have violated any law by giving asylum to a man who's been in our employ since his boyhood . . ."

"Whatever the legality," Phoebe asserted, "Archie did the moral thing. The only right thing."

"Icilda," Vivian said in an injured tone, "I've never known you to keep a secret from me before. How could you have . . ."

Owens wiped his hand over his mouth. These goddamn planter-class dinosaurs! They were positively schizophrenic. They wanted you to protect them from their servants, then they turned around and messed everything up with their noblesse oblige. And how could you expect to get the truth out of them when they didn't even tell it to their own family? "Let's get a look at this Percy. And let's make it quick."

"No, no," Icilda quaked. "They take him, they put him in jail. I never get him back."

Archie pried Icilda's hand from his arm. "No such thing, Icilda. I give you my word no harm will come to him. Go in and get him now. Nobody's going to take him anywhere. I'll see to that."

Owens motioned Icilda out of the room with a brusque wave of his hand. He was tempted to tell this bungling old fool that his grandiose promises of protection would mean little if Percy didn't have a tight alibi; but in fact, he had few suspicions of the driver's guilt. Owens had had enough for one day. Besides, it was only the nouveau Americans who minded if you drank on the job. He unbuttoned his jacket again. "I'll take that whisky you offered earlier, Miss Baron."

"Of course," Ceci said, her voice polite, mitigating the shock she felt at Archie's revelation. Relieved as she was to know that Percy was safe, she couldn't help but notice, as she crossed the room, the upward thrust of Archie's chin and the triumphal defiance in his eyes, as though he were some patriot going to the gallows. He was the wastrel who'd finally redeemed himself, cutting loose from the familiar shores of habit and launching himself on the uncharted seas of action. She didn't doubt that he was aware of the adoring look in Phoebe's eyes. But as Vivian whispered an almost inaudible

"Oh, God, my dear, little, Marsden!" Archie's face crumbled and he sank down on the couch, holding his head in his hands.

Ceci shook the water from her ears and looked seaward. She had never swum this far into the bay before. Her breath was labored and there was a cramp in her leg, but she wanted to push on to the point of exhaustion, to distance herself as much as possible from the house. She knew that Vivian was up in Marsden's room, packing up his things. She had offered to help, but had been vastly relieved when Vivian had said no, that Ceci had taken her share of responsibility by calling Hilary.

The conversation with Hilary, made the morning after they'd heard about Marsden, had exhausted Ceci as much as a full day's work. After several attempts, she'd gotten through, carefully editing herself to provide the facts but omitting the grisly details. Hilary's father, Mr. Berwith, had come on the line almost immediately, ordering Hilary to hang up and demanding a complete retelling. By God, he'd yelled, he was coming straight down. Ceci had explained that flights were being canceled, that there would be no funeral, but he'd said he would be down anyway. He would be down with his lawyer and a private detective. He hung up on her when she questioned the possibility as well as the wisdom of that plan. Later he called back and, after an initial apology, settled into his natural métier: a bullying discussion of property. He would hold the Nettletons personally responsible if anything happened to Hilary's BMW or any of the rest of her possessions, a complete list of which he had already drawn up. His lawyer would be in touch. And no, Ceci could not speak to Hilary. Hilary was under sedation, and when she recovered, he was sure that she'd want nothing more to do with Jamaica or the Nettletons. Ceci had almost been relieved when the phones had gone dead shortly after his call.

She turned onto her back to float, letting the water support her and staring up into the sky. It was a bright, clear sky, as it had been yesterday and the day before that. Another joyously bright day that Marsden would not see. She half wished that Owens had had the imagination to lie and present them with an empty casket. That would have helped. They would have been able to plan a funeral. As it was, she couldn't quite believe that Marsden was dead. He had been, like some astronaut, blasted into space by some terrible explosion, his sins and ambitions disappearing along with his guts, bone, flesh, and fingernails. Whenever she tried to comprehend it, her mind skidded away in disbelief and settled on their last conversation. She knew she had not said or done anything to harm him, but still she felt a lingering sadness, remembering the touch of his hand (which she had shrugged off) and the way he had looked into the waves, saying that the restoration of the great house was all he'd ever wanted. She squinted at the sun and felt her hair swaying against her cheek, wondering how they had all gotten through the last few days.

Vivian, who must be feeling the shock and loss more than any of them, had behaved with a stoic self-discipline. If she cried, she must've done so in her rooms. She had put on a good black dress, so ill-fitting that the buttons pulled against her bosom, and, as far as Ceci knew, she had not taken it off even to sleep, because in the mornings it looked rumpled and was covered with lint. Vivian made lists of things to do, which she showed to no one. She worked in the garden until she was red in the face. She asked Ceci to call Sergeant Owens and find out the name of the gas station attendants who'd been injured in the blast so that she might send a basket of fruit and a check to their families. Even after Ceci explained that the telephone lines were down, she still persisted in her request. Apart from this, there was no discussion of Marsden or his death; no discussion of anything, really. They all went in and out of their separate rooms, and when they did bump into each other, the talk was about food, the puppy, the weather, and whether Percy should risk going to Sav la Mar for gasoline and supplies.

At first they had kept the radio on almost all the time, galvanized by what Phoebe, reverting to her Irish roots, called "the troubles." Between interludes of incendiary reggae and a smattering of international news, they heard of strikes, demonstrations, and the cancellation of flights. The fire in their fields was reported as having been set by terrorists

and was said to mark the beginning of trouble in their parish.
Marsden's death was also announced. (Reporters had come to
the gates and been shooed away by Percy.) The announcer
said in respectful tones that the life of Marsden Baron Nettleton, "heir to one of our island's most respected families," had
been snuffed out in a mysterious bomb blast in his Rolls-
Royce. The third time they had heard it, Archie had snapped
off the radio and commanded that it not be turned on again.
Looking at Archie's haggard face, Ceci had known that there
was nothing for it but to comply with his wishes; so, during
the daytime, she and Phoebe listened secretly, while Archie
was bathing or taking his nap. But news of Marsden's death
had soon dropped from the headlines, to be replaced by
broadcasts of power failures, looting, the imposition of cur-
few, and three violent deaths in the capital.

Before the phones had gone dead, Maurice had called to say
that it was too dangerous for him to come to work, and
though no one seemed to have any appetite, there was a great
to-do about food. Phoebe believed that concern for the stomach showed a healthy survival instinct and hoped that cooking
smells would relieve the emotional gloom of the house. She
and Icilda shared kitchen duty, Phoebe turning out one of
Archie's favorites, shepherd's pie, and, until the bread ran
out, making stacks of sandwiches that sat about until they
dried up and their crusts curled. Icilda, her lips always moving in silent prayer, made a potful of curried goat. Ceci
obliged by forcing down a helping, but afterward the odor of
the curry lingered in the air and made her stomach turn. The
puppy, too, was a diversion. Everyone made suggestions
about his name until Archie, over Icilda's objection, chris-
tened him Duppy. Archie insisted that Duppy be allowed to
sleep in his room (an honor that, Ceci suspected, Phoebe
shared, since she'd heard her creeping down the stairs after
lights out). They all played with Duppy and tried to train
him, though it was left to Icilda and her husband (who'd
wandered over from the cabins the night they'd heard about
Marsden's death and had become a permanent fixture in the
kitchen) to mop up the puddles.

Fear could be kept at bay during the day—indeed the glorious sunlight and gentle breezes seemed to mock it—but after dark it became palpable. The others crept off to bed, but Ceci stayed up as long as she could, washing dishes, trying to read (Vivian had, surprisingly, left a copy of the writings of Krishnamurti as well as a Bible on Ceci's night table), listening to scratchy 78s of "Someone to Watch Over Me" and "Till the Clouds Roll By" with the volume turned down, or just sitting on the veranda until midnight, when Percy took over guard duty at the gates from Icilda's husband. Then she would wander off to her room and, after checking the candles, matches, cigarettes, and bottle of whisky next to her bed, she would lie down in the darkness, holding Maurice's transistor close.

One ear tuned to any sound from outside, she would listen, switching the dial from station to station, desperate for news. Paul Strangman had broken up a near-riot at the bauxite mines. . . . Paul Strangman was quoted as saying . . . Paul Strangman was expected to address a mass rally in Kingston. There didn't seem to be any chance that Paul would meet her as planned. She wasn't even sure that she'd risk leaving the house to meet him, though Percy had made the run into Sav la Mar and, for an exorbitant price, had managed to fill the tank of her Toyota and buy two five-gallon tins of extra gasoline. (Percy had also heard rumors that Marsden's black Toyota had been found parked near the jetty, apparently abandoned by Thelda and the new driver. Understandably, Percy hadn't wanted to go to the police station to check out the rumor.) After a few swigs of whiskey, Ceci would drop off, but the slightest sound would wake her like a splash of cold water on her face and she would start up: Am I safe? Are the others safe? Paul, where are you? Are you safe?

Like the others, she napped fitfully in the afternoon, and, upon waking, came, groggy and bleary-eyed, to the kitchen where Phoebe, wearing a muu-muu that Icilda had fashioned for her out of a sheet, puttered about making tea. Sometimes they would exchange furtive words about what Ceci had heard on the radio, particularly about Paul. It was some relief just to mention his name. Wise Phoebe would pat Ceci's hand or smoothe her hair and say nothing. Perhaps, Ceci thought, real compassion was always silent; yet she felt that if she had to endure another day of fearful waiting and desultory conversation she might explode.

She turned in the water now, arms cutting, legs still heavy but maintaining a rhythmic kick. She had no desire to go back to the house, but she couldn't swim all morning, and she was feeling weak, probably because she'd yet to have breakfast. Stopping again, treading water, she glanced toward the shore and saw Phoebe and a tall black man standing near the cupola. She thought . . . she blinked, her eyes smarting with salt water . . . yes, it was: it was Teddy. The distance back assumed incredible proportions. She plunged in, pushing herself with her last burst of energy. As she waded out, chest heaving, pulling up the sagging bottom of her suit, she saw that Teddy had moved to the big tree.

"This young man," Phoebe said nervously, handing her a towel, "He says he has to talk to you privately. Is he all right?"

"He's from Paul," she said, moving past her. Phoebe reluctantly stayed where she was, glancing back toward the house.

"Yes? Yes?" Ceci swallowed, still trying to regain her breath.

"I come to take you to the boss, but I don't have no car. Can we use your car?"

"Yes, but . . ."

"You got gas?"

"I've got gas, but where . . . ?"

"Don't you know, man?" Teddy asked almost contemptuously. "They got him. The boss in Kingston hospital."

"What?"

"He talkin' at a big demo. Someone in the crowd got him. Shot him. Shot Winston, too."

"Is he all right? Is he alive?"

"Last I hear. You want to get dressed? You want to come?"

"Wait right here." She ran at full tilt, calling to Phoebe as she passed her, "Paul's been shot. I'm going to Kingston."

"What shall I tell . . . ?"

"Tell them anything. I don't care. I'm going."

Twenty-one

Ceci watched through the spattered windshield as Teddy walked to the delivery entrance of the hospital, said a few words to the guard, turned, and motioned for her to come. She opened the car door, putting her handbag over her head as protection against the drizzle, wondering why it was so heavy, remembering that she'd persuaded Teddy to let her carry his revolver. Her legs felt wobbly. Apart from a few roadblocks where they had been stopped—Teddy frisked, she interrogated—the countryside had looked normal; but as they'd approached the city, the stench of gasoline and burning rubber from the stacks of tires the demonstrators had set up against the police was still heavy in the air. The streets were littered with debris, windows shattered. A couple of cars were smashed, overturned, looking like metal corpses. Threatened with a car search that could have held them up for hours, she'd taken the risk of slipping a twenty-dollar bill to the officer in charge, begging him to let them pass because they were on their way to see a dying relative. An anxious look—compassion for her story or fear of taking the bribe?— had crossed the man's face, then he'd waved them on. Within another mile, everything seemed normal again, except for the eerie quiet and the fact that more stray dogs than people were on the streets.

She stepped into the deserted hallway. Fluorescent light bounced off the waxed floor; cardboard boxes were stacked against the walls. She supposed they must be near the kitchen because she could hear a muffled clatter and there was a cooking smell not altogether camouflaged by the liberal use of disinfectant. She tugged at her skirt. She had put on the first thing her hand had touched—a green halter dress, which, she'd realized later, had shrunk in the wash and had a safety pin in the hem. She followed Teddy up a flight of stairs, through swinging doors. They pressed their bodies against the wall as they heard shouts from an intersecting corridor and saw interns rolling a gurney. They waited, then went through another set of swinging doors into the intensive care unit. One in a series of doors was open—through it she glimpsed a family ranged around a bedside—absolute silence except for the hiss of a respirator. Up another corridor, Teddy's sneakers squeaking on the linoleum, she with her head down, barely noticing the ABSOLUTELY NO VISITORS sign. A guard sat at a desk, his face propped on his chin, his eyes closed. He opened them just long enough to recognize Teddy and wave him on. She didn't know if she was alarmed or blessed by the slack security. They turned into another hallway. Teddy stopped short, stretching back his hand, looking from left to right. "Maybe you wait in here. I get you when the coast is clear. You all right?"

She nodded and slipped past him into the "staff only" room. He shut the door behind her. There were two plastic bucket chairs pushed up against a barred window, locked cabinets, a sink, shelves of bandages, towels and bottles, the glint of some steely apparatus shining through its plastic cover.

Impossible to tell how long she waited, holding her breath whenever she heard the slightest noise outside, as though she could render herself invisible by not breathing. The light was beginning to fade, but she was reluctant to turn on the overhead lamp. She could detect a trace of cigarette smoke in the air. The nurses probably sneaked in here for a smoke. She reached into her purse, dismayed when her fingers touched the revolver, found an unopened pack and lit up, feeling guilty as a schoolgirl hiding in the coat room. Her hands were steady, but her chest felt painfully constricted. Stupid for her to have such anxiety. Teddy had said Paul was all right. The radio had said he was. Both might have been lying.

There was a burst of laughter outside the door, then footsteps hurrying away.

She stepped on the butt of the cigarette, waited, picked it up, wrapping it in a piece of cellophane and looking about for the trash can. She lifted the lid and dropped it in, averting her eyes. If she saw so much as a bloody bandage now, she might crack. She sat back down, turning her head to look out the window.

The door opened soundlessly. She spun around to see a tall mulatto woman momentarily illuminated by the shaft of light from the hallway. The woman stepped in and shut the door behind her. For a split second Ceci thought she must be a nurse; then she caught a whiff of perfume—L'Air du Temps? —saw the glint of silver bracelets; realized that what she'd taken for a uniform and cap was a pale yellow shirtwaist dress and matching silk scarf. She stood up, staring into intelligent, slightly protruberant dark eyes and a small but full-lipped mouth that opened, closed, opened again, and finally managed to speak. "Miss Nettleton?"

"No. It's Baron. Nettleton is just the family name."

"Yes." Vera's voice was controlled and mellow. "Yes, I think I knew that."

They continued to stare at each other until Ceci could no longer contain herself. "Is he . . . ?"

"He's out of danger, but he's lost a lot of blood. The second bullet lodged near the shoulder blade and they had difficulty getting it out. Part of the bone is shattered." Vera swayed almost imperceptably, reaching for the door handle.

Ceci picked up her purse from the chair. "Would you care to sit down?" she asked. The polite restraint of their conversation made her feel as though she was losing her mind. This woman might be attacking her, calling her a whore; instead she came forward, sat, crossed her legs, and asked, "Would you happen to have a cigarette? I shouldn't be smoking but . . ."

Ceci offered the pack and rummaged for her lighter.

"No, thank you. I have one. I really shouldn't . . ." Vera lit the cigarette, looked at it, blinked. "I haven't heard the radio for hours. How many . . . ?"

"The last I heard, the riots had stopped. Seven dead."

"Seven? They killed seven? Lousy sons of bitches!"

"That's what it said on the car radio."

Vera leaned forward, studying her hands. When she finally spoke, she seemed to have forgotten Ceci entirely, muttering to herself. "Well, our security reports told us . . . I asked him not to go, but then, as his mother says, even as a boy she couldn't stop him from . . . Elliot's the same. Last year he swam out way beyond the limit. I punished him, but it does no good . . . he's got it, too, that awful physical courage." She looked around her. "They don't know yet if he'll have the full use of that arm . . . if the bone . . . It's useless to say anything to him. Once he's made up his mind . . . but you probably know that about him." Her gaze settled on Ceci's knees and when she spoke again, there was a firmness in her voice, as though she had been challenged. "But nothing is possible if fear of the consequences is stronger than the desire to do the right thing. He was right to . . ." She took a long, reflective drag on the cigarette, automatically waving the smoke away from Ceci's direction. "What was I saying? Yes, Paul's mother. She's gone down to the car. The reporters are probably all over her now. I must . . ." She looked at the cigarette, disgusted. "I shouldn't be . . ."

"You'll have to put it out on the floor."

Vera did so and, as she raised up, studied Ceci's face. "You're very beautiful."

There was another pause that seemed to stretch time, Ceci wanting to turn her face away but holding the gaze. "You've known?" she asked quietly.

"About you? Yes. Paul told me about you before we were married and . . . You mean about your being back on the island? Well, I've lived with him for a long time. At first I didn't know it was you, I just knew. I suppose because he seemed so . . ." She struggled for the right word. ". . . so optimistic about everything. And then, quite by accident, I ran into a colleague of mine, a sociology professor, and he was gossiping about a party he'd been to in Mo Bay and he mentioned meeting you so, yes, I knew."

"I didn't come back to see Paul. We hadn't even seen each other at the time of that party. We met quite by accident."

"Of course," Vera said softly, though Ceci could tell that Vera didn't believe her. "May I ask if you plan to stay on the island?"

"I'm not sure of my plans. I haven't . . ." How was it possible for Vera to maintain such poise? Not that it was really poise; it was a vast fatigue and disorientation, perhaps an emotional equanimity that rivaled Paul's physical courage —but here she was, calmly asking questions about travel plans while her eyes conveyed a rising panic, asking the real questions: Are you going to make my life miserable? Are you going to destroy my family? Are you going to keep sleeping with my husband?

"I know that Paul is in love with you," Vera said after another pause.

"He loves you, too," Ceci blurted. "When he speaks of you . . ."

"There you have the advantage. Obviously he does not speak of you. You look as though you are about to cry. Please don't do that. Crying doesn't help anything. And, while I'm aware of the fact that Paul loves me, I know that he is in love with you. That is the reality; and I pride myself on being in touch with reality." Vera's face was impassive except for a movement of her nostrils. They dialated and compressed, sensing danger, betraying her passionate response. Ceci thought it was one of the most beautiful noses she had ever seen.

"Did you expect me to hurl myself on the floor?" Vera continued, "To cause a scene or insult you? People are dying on this island, Miss Nettleton. I can't indulge in some petty argument about who's sleeping with whom. In the scheme of things . . ." Vera straightened her spine. "There are far more serious considerations. In the scheme of things . . ." But it was too much. She covered her face with her hand and turned away. Ceci reached out, almost touching her before realizing the inappropriateness of the gesture. What she meant to be comforting might be seen as condescending, and Vera was not a woman to whom one condescended or offered trivial comforts. She could already see that.

"I'm sorry," Vera said tightly, reaching into her purse and taking out a small package of soda crackers. She peeled off the cellophane and wiped her eyes with the back of her hand. "I shouldn't have smoked that cigarette," she muttered. "And the smell of hospitals always makes me . . ." She bit into the cracker. "The nausea didn't last this long with Elliot. I suppose . . ."

Ceci felt the bottom of her stomach drop into her guts. "You're . . ."

"About seven weeks. Elliot's very excited about it. I wasn't going to tell him so soon, but he was very upset about Paul last night, so I told him. I think it will be good for Elliot. Paul dotes on him so much that he's in danger of becoming a little egomaniac."

Ceci wanted to ask if Paul knew about the pregnancy but couldn't bring herself to. He couldn't know; no, he couldn't know.

Vera wiped a crumb from her mouth. "I didn't mean to play on your sympathies, Miss Nettleton. Should Paul decide to leave me, I'm not without . . ."

"Please don't . . ." She had wanted to say "please don't call me Miss Nettleton," but that was a ridiculous thing to say.

"I wanted to see you. I realize that was foolish and self-punishing of me, but I wanted to see you. Perhaps you can understand."

"Yes, I understand. Am I . . . ?" Ceci began, ready to ask if she could see Paul now, knowing that she would see him no matter what Vera said.

"Not really," Vera cut her off, misinterpreting. "I thought you'd be blond, and more fragile looking." She smiled at her own cliché, rising to her feet. "I must go. Paul's mother is waiting in the car with Elliot, and Elliot's very upset because the doctors won't let him up to see Paul." She went to the door and turned back. "You said seven people had been killed?"

"That's what the radio said."

Vera's eyes moved away from her and her hand came up to her throat. Ceci realized that Vera had mentally left her and was probably already phrasing what she would say to the press or how she would explain things to her son. She wondered how Vera could bear the weight of it all.

"Seven, and they don't know about Winston yet," Vera said to herself, "so . . ."

"What did you say?"

"Winston Lewis, Paul's bodyguard. He died about an hour ago."

"Oh, no."

"That's right, you must've known him. I was with him, but he was unconscious most of the time. When he came to, he kept asking about Paul. They were very close. I suppose you knew that, too. He didn't like me very much. He looked so disappointed to see me there." She shook her head and pressed her lips together, her brow furrowing as she made an inventory of what she had to do. "Winston didn't have any family that I know of. Just Paul," she muttered, straightening up. "Paul doesn't know about Winston yet. I don't presume to tell you what to do, but I don't think it's advisable to tell him about Winston just now."

Ceci nodded as she got up, holding onto the back of the chair. She wanted to say a hundred things: that she was sorry, that she did love Paul, that she didn't need instructions about what to say to him, that Winston had been a fine man, that . . .

"Oh," Vera said, finding the pack of cigarettes still in her hand, walking back and depositing them on the chair, "I almost took these by mistake."

She had already closed the door behind her before Ceci could speak.

Ceci remained standing, spinning but numb. She sat back down. Waiting. Only waiting. Though, when a thought finally formed itself, she saw there was no need to hide anymore. She could go out into the corridor. It was getting dark in the room. Still she sat. Just as she was about to get up and turn on a light, Teddy opened the door. "I'm sorry," he whispered. "I don't know how it happen, but . . ."

"Can I see him now?"

"Sure." He held the door open to the phorescent glare of the corridor. "I don't know how she . . ."

"That's all right. It's not your fault," she said as she moved past him. He smiled so easily at her forgiveness that she supposed he hadn't yet heard about Winston.

"Come on, this way," he said. She followed him down the corridor, almost bumping into him as he made a sharp right turn. Geoff, the bodyguard who'd driven the jeep the last time she'd seen Paul, was sitting in a plastic bucket chair, ostensibly reading a comic book. He did not look up as Teddy reached for the door handle and said, sotto voce, "I wait here. Don't be too long. He still punchy an' they come to check him all the time."

The single light on the bedside table showed the paraphenalia of steel, plastic, bottles, and dangling tubes. His leg was drawn up, making a tent of the sheet so that she couldn't see the upper part of his body. At the sound of the latch clicking, he lowered it. He was naked to the waist. She supposed they couldn't get a pajama top over the cast that swathed his arm and shoulder. There were more bandages crisscrossing his chest. Without moving his head, he opened his eyes. His speech was low and slurred. "You got here."

"Yes."

"You shouldn't have risked . . ." Trying to pull himself up, a guttural hissing sound such as she'd heard in their lovemaking came from between his clench teeth. "My brave girl." He sank back.

"Don't move." To stop him from talking, she told about the ride, the news reports, how she'd bribed the officer at the roadblock, all the time rooted to the foot of his bed, one of her shoulders drawn down with the weight of her bag. Staring at the yellowish pallor of his skin, seeing the beads of sweat like tiny seed pearls on his forehead, her voice broke. "I love you. I was so frightened."

His eyes focused on her, then rolled back, trying to figure out his own sequence. "Winston must've told Geoff to get you. I don't think I . . ." He forced his eyes open. "I think they gave me too much anesthetic when they . . ."

"Probably had to to knock you out."

"Mmmm. I hate to . . ."

". . . go under," she finished it for him.

"Ceci, come. Come round to me."

She moved to the dark side of the bed, looking into his eyes and then slowly lowering her head to his chest, seeing a smear of antiseptic paint that had escaped the bandage, bringing her cheek close enough to feel his chest hairs. She could smell his sweat now, even through the barrier of antiseptic. She thought she could feel his heartbeat. His hand, light as a child's, came to rest on her head and a silence settled over them.

" 'Blue were her eyes as the fairyflax/Her cheeks like the dawn of day/And her bosom white as the hawthorn buds/ That ope' in the month of May,' " he murmured after a time.

She raised her head a fraction. She had never heard him quote poetry before.

"Before your time," he said. "Before my time. The detritus of a colonial education. I learned it when I was about ten. I had no idea what a hawthorn bud was."

"They should have taught you to duck instead." There was an ache in her back and a crick in her neck from trying to stay in the crouching position.

"As they wheeled me into the operating room, I turned superstitious. I thought, if I can remember that poem I'll live." As she straightened up, looking behind her for a chair, his hand dropped from her but his voice insisted, "Don't move away from me."

"I'm just getting . . ." but she was arrested by his face again, irresistibly drawn to him, wanting to hold him to her in a crushing embrace. Her hand trembled as she wiped the hair back from his brow and kissed his eyelids. "Did you lock the door?" he whispered.

She moved out of the protective circle of light and to the door, listening for outside sounds before feeling for a lock. "There isn't a lock," she whispered, turning back to him.

He smiled for the first time—an incredulous, triumphant smile, brought on by her presence and the continuing surprise of finding himself alive. "Winston won't have to make up any tall stories about this one," he said. "It happened so fast. I was up on the platform, speaking, when the microphones went dead. I turned to check out the sound man . . ." he paused, seeing it again, struggling for breath, "and I saw Winston. He was right next to me. The crowd was hooting and yelling because the sound had cut off, so I didn't hear the shots. There was this look on Winston's face—as though he'd suddenly *seen* something. He threw himself across me. I realized he'd been hit. But it wasn't until we both went down that I knew I'd been hit too."

"You don't have to tell me now," she said, though she wanted to hear.

"And the lug is lying across me and I can smell his breath and he's . . . saying . . . 'This is it, boss,' and smiling at me . . . smiling, Ceci! . . . smelling of onions and rum—and I put my hands on his back and I feel this wetness and it's sticky and . . ." He lay perfectly still, trying to master his pain with immobility, and she stared at him, her hand over her mouth. ". . . and I thought yes, this is it, and then I didn't come to until I was going into the operating room . . . ah . . ."

"Don't . . ." She tilted her head back against the door, swallowing hard. Tears overflowed, rolling into her ears and hair.

"Don't you. Don't cry now. Come here. Come lie next to me."

"Paul, we can't."

"Come."

She got the chair and pushed it underneath the door handle and then came to the bed, bending to slip off her sandals. His hand reached to touch her, then fell back onto the bed. "Don't move," she begged him. "Promise you won't move." Gingerly, she put one knee on the bed, then lowered herself. She squeezed next to him, lying stiffly on her side, one arm pressed beneath her, the other carefully draped across his hip, as though they were on a raft and she was trying to protect him from the waves. Her foot kept slipping off the bed. "Put your leg across mine. My legs are all right," he whispered. She did so, and it moored her, letting her ease into him bit by bit—her foot on his ankle, her thigh across his, belly to hip bone, breast against ribs—a clinging but relaxed huddling, giving a sense of blind security. No sound but the buzzing of a fly, trapped between window and screen, troubled the prolonged silence. They were together. Everything was all right.

Finally, her pinioned arm cramping, prickling with pins and needles, she shifted, painstakingly inching it out from under her, gently moving her leg. Even this slight movement away from him caused her to sob "I'll always love you," as she moved into him again. He heard the resignation in her voice. "Don't say always. Always is far away." His breath was moist on her forehead. "When I was going under, it was so clear. Ceci . . . you and I . . . you'll see . . ."

She touched her finger to his lips. She couldn't bear to hear what he would say. It would be some fantasy of their future —an expectation of lovemaking, a shared meal, a trip—which she would seize upon and embroider in painful detail for years to come; or, worse yet, a passionate but impossible pledge of an entirely different life. Having come so close to death, he might offer that to himself and to her, momentarily obliterating thought of his son, now being driven through the deserted, riot-torn streets, relinquishing his eight-year-old independence to once again seek the comfort of his mother's breast; or Vera, her hand folded across her belly, protecting the life within; or the thousands of Winstons, Jesminas, and Percys. Paul would not desert them. She could not love him if he did.

There was a tap on the door. She got up in slow motion, disengaging herself, surprised at the strength of his hand as he held onto hers. "Don't drive back tonight," he said. "Stay at a hotel in the city. Tomorrow . . ." His head moved impatiently and he clenched his teeth. She went to the door, heard Teddy say something unintelligible but urgent-sounding from the other side, and tapped to let him know she'd heard.

Swiftly and noiselessly, she went back to Paul's side. They clutched at each other, unmindful of his pain. His cheekbone was hard against hers and he whispered furiously into her hair, "We'll . . . we'll . . . tomorrow . . ." She pulled back slowly, shaking her head. They looked into each other's eyes. It seemed that their entire lives—seconds, weeks, years—

were concentrated into this exchange of looks, that they understood not only what had been, but what was, and was not, to be.

Another tap, more insistent this time, and she wheeled around, picking up her purse and shoes, not daring to look back.

Twenty-two

The doors of the Pegasus hotel opened before them. Ceci felt a blast of cool, scentless air and the carpet beneath her feet. A man in livery reached for her overnight bag but she pulled it close to her chest, feeling another man come behind her, stopping Teddy with a nervously interrogative "Sir?" She stumbled forward, the sole of her sandal turning back against her foot, before regaining balance and saying, "Come on, Teddy," as she moved across the lobby.

The quiet, clean spaciousness, the soft lighting, the banks of flowers and businessmen lounging on low couches, sipping drinks, gave her a sense of eerie deliverance. Not fifteen minutes before, when they had yet to see this oasis of high-rise buildings, they had seen flares, stopped, and been approached by uniformed men with automatic weapons. As they'd questioned her, she'd stared out of the car window to a group of barefoot men and women huddled around a fire next to a wall lurid with graffiti, one of the women gyrating drunkenly to transistor reggae, a child wailing, his belly and genitals exposed.

At the registration desk a young mulatto who'd straightened her hair into an approximation of the style Farrah Fawcett had made popular years before glanced up, ironing her look of surprise into one of bland welcome, and, without looking behind her, tapped her ring on the plate glass of the manager's office.

"I'd like a room."

"Did you have a reservation, miss?"

"No, but . . ." Ceci touched the plastic frames of her sunglasses, aware that, under the circumstances, dark glasses might appear not just an affectation, but perhaps threatening. It would be better to establish eye contact. But too many tears seemed to have dried her eyeballs and her lids were puffy. She pushed the frames tigher onto the bridge of her nose, looking past the clerk to the cubbyholes that housed the room keys. "It seems you have rooms available."

The manager joined the clerk. Ceci could feel him watching her as she bent, her hair falling about her face, then dug in her bag, found her wallet, took out a handful of credit cards, and threw them onto the marble countertop. A brown finger sorted the plastic, selected one. "American Express. Don't leave home without it," the manager chuckled. "Have you any photo I.D.?" She rummaged again and came up with a New York driver's license. The manager glanced up, reconciling the disheveled woman before him with her calmer likeness, and pushed the license back. "Will that be a single or a double room, miss?"

"A single. No . . ." She glanced back. Teddy stood directly behind her as though guarding her, rubbing one tennis shoe against the other, biting the lining of his cheek. "Two rooms. You will stay, won't you, Teddy? You must be exhausted."

"One room for you and one for your driver?" the clerk asked, clicking a ballpoint and reaching for registration forms. There was the twitch of a smirk as she asked, "Adjoining rooms?"

"*Please.* Any two rooms."

The manager palmed the plastic. "If you'll be kind enough to wait for just a few minutes. I'll have to check your card."

"Look, the card is all right. If you could give me the keys I'd . . ." She squeezed her eyes shut, regaining composure. "If we could just go to our rooms and have a scotch and . . ."

"Terribly sorry, miss. We can't provide room service. And

the rooms will have to be made up. We're having some staffing difficulties today."

That meant that some employees were still out on strike, or fired, or trapped in their houses. Or perhaps the riots were still going on.

"If you'd care to go into our cocktail lounge and have your drink, this will only take a moment. I'll have someone come and get you as soon as your rooms are ready."

"Are the phones in service?"

"Yes, miss, but there's a wait in getting through."

"And the airlines?"

"Some flights resumed tonight. Back to normal schedule tomorrow for sure. If you'd care to step into the cocktail lounge."

"Since you're checking my card, I'd also like to get the equivalent of a thousand dollars U.S. in cash. You do provide that service, don't you?" She made her voice sarcastic, querulous, the American tourist strained to breaking point by native inefficiency. The manager responded to the intimidation. "I'll do what I can, miss, though I don't know if . . ."

"Yes. Do what you can," she said wearily.

"We provide all services, miss, but just now, as you must know, we're having some little difficulties."

"If you'd care to check local references, you may call Nettleton House in Westmoreland Parish."

The manager almost bowed. "Your cocktails while waiting will be courtesy of the hotel. Thank you for . . ."

"Good. We'll be in the lounge. Teddy?"

As they crossed the lobby she saw a potted tree and remembered Winston's story about his grandfather's ambush gear. How lonely Paul was going to be without Winston and his stories.

The lounge was smoky but almost deserted. Tiny round tables were dotted with candles. The Muzak oozed a soupy string version of "All You Need Is Love." In the dim light Teddy seemed to disappear except for his clothes. His hand flashed in the candlelight, picking up one peanut, then another, gathering a handful. "Hungry," he explained

apologetically. The waiter took their drinks order. Ceci stared
at the candle flame. She took off her glasses, drank her water
chaser first, asked for another glass of water, and drank that
down before picking up her scotch and rolling the glass across
her forehead. Paul was in that hospital room. She was here.
She knew that she was here, in the cocktail lounge of the
Pegasus hotel, because she could hear the ice cubes rattle.

She looked up at the bar, the mirror behind it, the shimmer-
ing bottles, the recessed lights, the men's backsides on the
stools. There was a lone woman, tight skirt pulled high to
accommodate her crossed legs, her back and arms creamy in
the dim light, her hair a halo of bronze fluff. She was half
turned, her cheeks dented, pulling on her straw, though her
glass was already empty. Feeling eyes on her, she swung into
profile, self-consciously sweeping back her hair, still making
slurping sounds like a child playing with a milkshake. She
raised her eyes coquettishly, surprised to meet the gaze of
another woman. Ceci lowered her head, but not in time.

"Don't I know you?" the woman called over to her. "Don't
I know you?" She slunk off the stool and wobbled to their
table, pulling at the vertical creases in her skirt. "Sure. Sure
I do." She smiled as gratefully as if they'd been old school
friends bumping into each other after years of separation.
"We met at Austin Cleardon's. I remember. I don't suppose
you remember me. I'm Gloria. And you're . . . ?"

Ceci picked up her glasses. Teddy half rose, then reached
to the next table for another bowl of peanuts.

"Mind if I sit?" Gloria asked, doing so. "How great to see
you! Are you stranded here too? I was supposed to leave,
when was it? Three, four days ago. Yeah." She pulled on the
straw again. "But then all the flights were canceled. It was like
being in prison or somethin'. They told us not to go out on
the street. I don't even have a pair of panty hose left without
a run in them." Ceci gazed at her intently. Improbable as it
was, Gloria did not seem to have heard about Marsden's
death. But Gloria was the sort of woman who would hide
under the covers during a storm or turn off the TV during
a crisis. Then again, judging from the puffiness of her face,
Gloria had spent the last few days in semi-conscious drunken-

ness and might have only the foggiest notion of who Ceci was. "And nothing to eat but sandwiches and fruit!" Gloria went on. "They gave everyone a big basket of fruit. All wrapped up with a bow. Must've had 'em ready beforehand. It's really been scary." She giggled. "Scarier than livin' in New York. But I met this real nice guy. He just came in on a flight a coupla hours ago. He's in the little boys' room now, but he'll be right back. You're Cecilia, aren't you? I met you . . . ?" Gloria went blank.

"Yes." Ceci put down her drink. The Muzak seemed to be stuffing her ears, blocking thought. She grasped Teddy's arm and shut her eyes. "I'm sorry, Gloria. We were just about to leave."

"Hey, don't leave," Gloria insisted. "Where the hell would you go anyway? There's nothing to do but party here. We can go up to the bar on the roof. You can see everything from there. Last night there were fires all over. No, night before. You could see them. Hey . . . here's my friend."

Ceci opened her eyes to the waistband of a pair of putty-colored slacks and a lime T-shirt with an alligator logo, its open neck bristling with dark hair and a gold medallion.

"This is Al," Gloria said, leaning into him. "Al's a real sweetheart. A real gentleman. He's been so nice to me, haven't you, Al?" She nuzzled her face into his midsection and held up her glass. "Do you s'pose I could have another one of these?"

Ceci's legs took responsibility for her body and got her up. "I'm sorry. I'm very tired. Good night." She nodded at them. "Gloria. Mr. Lupon."

"You know him already?" Gloria was delighted. "How do you know each other? Mrs. Cleardon?"

Teddy touched Ceci's arm. "I'll go see about the rooms." He moved a chair out of her way and walked off. She collected her bag, nodded again, and moved after him.

"Hey, don't go," Gloria implored. "It's fun up on the roof. You don't happen to have an extra pair of panty hose, do you?"

Ceci reached the entrance to the lounge before Lupon caught up with her. "I'm sorry," he said, glancing back to the bar, so that for a split second she thought he was apologizing for having picked up Gloria. "Sorry . . ." He touched her shoulder, his hand gaining weight and insistence as it slid down her arm and seized hers ". . . about your brother. If there's anything I can do . . ."

"How did you know?" formed in her mind, but never reached her lips. Gloria had said he'd flown into Jamaica hours before, so he couldn't have heard on the radio, or . . . She turned slowly, looking into his face. His eyes were bloodshot, melancholy and defensive. "Your *half*-brother," he corrected himself as though relieved by the difference. He removed his hand, wiped it on his trouser leg, then put it back on her forearm. She stared at it: beefy, rings shining, smelling faintly of cologne. "I don't know why he burnt those fields," he added, almost to himself. "That was a dumb thing to do."

There was a skidding shudder in her stomach, saliva gathered in her mouth, and, as she thought, so it was you, she felt she was going to vomit. She made no attempt to move, but, as though sensing her revulsion, he let go of her and stepped back, his head sinking almost to his chest. He brought it up, ran his tongue over his front teeth, turned and looked back at the tables. "Can't keep a lady waiting."

If she could make it to the desk, she would be all right.

The clerk was in a strained, slow-speaking transaction with a pair of Japanese businessmen. Teddy leaned on the counter, his rear end jutting, one hand stuffed into the back pocket of his jeans, breaking through a rip. He straightened. "If you think you be okay, I leave you now."

"But where will you . . . ?"

"Got a sister in town. Prob'ly she scared. She got kids. If you be okay . . ."

She couldn't tell if he was telling the truth. "Will you be safe out there? It's probably still . . ."

"Sure. I be okay." Teddy slid his hand into his jacket and carefully, so as not to expose his revolver, drew out the car keys.

"Please wait long enough for me to get the money. I want you to take it to someone in the village."

The manager moved to them, setting out the credit card,

bank form, keys, and cash. "We could only give you seven hundred and fifty, miss," he said apologetically. Ceci nodded and began to count the cash. She asked for an envelope. The clerk, much put upon, grunted and moved off. Ceci stared at her arms. Her skin was dry and peeling and as she scratched it, flakes of skin came off on her fingertips. The clerk placed an envelope on the counter and began an assiduous examination of her nail polish. Ceci put most of the cash into the envelope, sealed it, addressed it with Jesmina's name, said "You can find her in the village" and pushed it and the remainder of the cash along the counter. "That's for you, Teddy." He reached, but stopped himself, shaking his head. "Takin' money you don't earn is begging. It's counter-revolutionary."

"Teddy, that's such a dumb line."

"No line, man," he said, adamant and sullen. "It got to start somewhere." He touched his heart.

"But will you take this?" She picked up the envelope.

"Sure." He looked around the lobby. When his eyes came back to rest on her face, they still had a look of suspicious contempt. Then he smiled. "Pleased to make your acquaintance, miss. Hope to see you soon."

"Are you sure you'll be all right?"

"If the boss okay, we all okay. Right?"

She moved to kiss his cheek but he turned away, suddenly shy.

"Thank you, Teddy."

He turned, loping across the lobby with a bouncy swagger, head high. At the entrance he turned, clenching his fist and raising his thumb before brushing past the attendant and pushing open the doors for himself.

Ceci turned back to the desk. "I would appreciate it if you'd ask your switchboard operator to start trying the following numbers." Much as she wanted to, she could not leave the island until she had gone back to the house to see that everything was taken care of. To see Archie and Vivie, Icilda and Phoebe. To see the cupola again. "In Westmoreland Parish . . ." She gave the number at the house. "And in New York, area code 213 . . . no, that's California. In New

York, area code 212, then 782 . . . no, 873 . . ." A whirl of numbers, past ones of her own and those of old lovers, mixed in her head. She picked up the pen and let her memory make the connection with her hand. "Yes. That's it. Thank you so much. I'll be in my room."

The girl picked up the slip of paper, studying it. "We hope you will enjoy your stay at the Pegasus," she said in the cheerless, quonky voice of a computer. "Is this your first trip to the island?"

"No. My last."

The elevator delivered her up. It was swift and clean and silent and her sobs bounced off the walls, rolling back, engulfing her.

Twenty-three

Phoebe stepped onto the veranda and looked at Archie, asleep in the fan-backed chair, Duppy stretched at his side. She turned her eyes away, taking in the blistered statue of the Nereid, the overgrown bushes, and the slimy pond. Neither the house nor the grounds had been kept up to the standard she'd witnessed when she'd first come to the house over a year ago. Even Vivian had slackened her gardening efforts, letting the natural growth encroach on her flowerbeds, though, to Phoebe's mind, the place now had a lusher, more homey look.

"Dozing?" she asked, putting her hand on Archie's shoulder.

"Dozing?" he said indignantly, opening his eyes. "Not a bit of it. I was learning my lines." He felt on his knee for the script, looked about and found it on the table.

"Have you been tippling with that weedy Mr. Pembroke again?"

"You know better than to ask me that. I never drink while I'm working. Pembroke did come by. The chap's so lonely I felt it was only decent to spend a few minutes with him. Couldn't just turn him away. Besides, when you're out traipsing, he's the only one about who's intelligent enough to stop my brain from going rusty."

She held her purse to her bosom and looked out at the bay. "Isn't it lovely this time of day."

"You'd best ask that new girl to put up some more of that punch. Whose idea was it that she freeze it in the ice trays?"

"Mine."

"Well, Pembroke likes it fresh. Like a bloody supermarket around here these days. Frozen punch!"

Phoebe put down her purse, drew out her glasses and cigarettes, and reached for the script. "So, how's it coming? Shall I run lines with you?" She ran her finger down the open page and, without waiting for his reply, began. "Ah yes, here it is. . . . You begin with . . ."

"I know it. I know it."

She waited, watching him look out toward the cupola. The sunset glow made his eyes shiny and opaque, his lids flickering as he forced his memory. " 'Will the king come, that I may breathe my last in wholesome counsel to his unstaid youth?' "

"Yes. Then York says, 'Vex not yourself, nor strive not with your breath; For all in vain comes counsel to his ear.' "

Archie shifted in his chair. " 'O, but they say the tongues of dying enforce attention like deep harmony; Where words are scarce they are seldom spent in vain; For they breathe truth that breathe their words in pain. He that no more must breathe . . ."

" 'Must *say*.' "

" 'He that no more must *say* is listen'd more than . . .' " He reached down and began to fondle Duppy's ear. "Oh, bugger this, Phoebe. We can do this after dinner. Tell me what's been going on up at the great house."

She reached for a cigarette, looking at him over the rim of her glasses, discipline fighting with indulgence. "You must get the words down, Archie. For your own comfort. It's been years since you've trod the boards. You can't just stop in the middle and say 'cut' when you're on stage, you know."

"Is it the perpetual function of a wife—even an ex-wife— to inform a man of what he already knows?" he asked peevishly, and then, with a sidelong, teasing glance, "The character I'm playing is dying, isn't he? If I dry up on the lines, I'll just die a bit sooner."

"Your obligation to the other actors, to say nothing of your obligation to the audience, or William Shakespeare . . ." She broke off. "All right. I'm not your custodian. I'm not even in the scene, so if it's a balls-up . . ." Why was she letting her anxiety run away with her. Archie would be fine. He would be more than fine. He had another week to get his lines down before they flew back to London for rehearsals. It was just that she'd pulled a few strings to get him the part. More than a few strings; she'd more or less maneuvered it. The young director, hoping for an offer to film the stage production of Richard II, had fallen all over himself to get her to take the lackluster role of the Duchess of Gloucester. She'd said her acceptance was contingent on the "proper casting" of the role of John of Gaunt, and who better to play that role than Archie Baron? It was the sort of nepotism she'd always despised, but being a Dame must be worth something. Though she'd always shied away from any exploitation of her private life, she'd even gone so far as to suggest that the publicity people might make some capital of the fact that she and Archie had once been married and would be appearing together for the first time in over forty years. The important thing was to get Archie back to work.

During the first six months they'd been reunited, when they'd stayed at her country house, Archie had been an angel of consideration. Marsden's death, and news from California that his old dog Horton had to be put to sleep, had thrown him into a period of soul searching. He was more contemplative than morose, taking long walks in the countryside, staying up until the wee hours to talk to her. He began to read a great deal—Chekhov and Proust, books on politics and history, poetry. He had even gotten through the first thirty pages of *The Second Sex*. When Eric and his family had come to visit, Archie had been a model of *pater familias*. He'd built the fire, carved the roast, served the drinks, and dandled his great-grandchild on his knee. Later, in bed, he'd embraced Phoebe with great fervor, whispering about the simple joys of family life. But then Phoebe had a television job offer that was too lucrative to turn down, so they'd returned to London. And

Archie's self-sufficiency, as well as his self-examination, came to an end.

He moped about, complaining of the weather and his sinuses, grousing whenever she went to work. When she arrived home she was likely to find the flat in a mess, and Archie still in his robe and slippers. His helplessness maddened her. He could not iron a shirt or make a bed. When pressed, he would start to help her with the washing up, but would invariably wander off by the time she got to the pots and pans. Even when they went out, things were not much better. He said he felt like odd-man-out socializing with her friends. After evenings at the theater, they would barely get into the taxi before he started denigrating the performances (betraying, Phoebe knew, not so much his critical sense as an envy of which he was but dimly aware). At first she had reproved herself, thinking that she'd lived alone too long and had become too set in her ways. But finally she'd had to admit that loving Archie would be a lot easier if she didn't have to see him every day. If she could help him out of retirement and he could score a single hit, that might open up future work, not only in London but in Hollywood as well.

"Then York says . . . ." Her finger went down the page, " 'Tis breath thou lack'st, and that breath wilt thou lose,' and you say, 'Methinks I am . . .' "

"I know it, woman. I know it," he said impatiently. "And speaking of breath, that's the fifth cigarette I've seen you with today. You said you were going to cut down. Do you think it's pleasant to wake up next to someone wheezing away like a broken penny whistle! It's a disgusting habit."

"Granted." She took a long, satisfied drag.

"So, tell me, how were things up at the great house?"

"Everything in top form. Mrs. Cleardon says they have reservations months in advance. That article in *Town and Country* did the place a world of good. She's such a dynamo, isn't she? I can't imagine why she didn't go into business before. The happy coincidence is that she doesn't have to put it on, she really loves waltzing around making sure everyone's enjoying himself. If she'd been born in another era I daresay

Austin Cleardon would have made a first-class madam. It was a stroke of luck that we found her."

"Or she found us."

"In point of fact, she was Ceci's idea, remember? We'd never have been able to get it off the ground if Ceci hadn't convinced you and Vivie to sell off some of the property and convinced Austin to invest. And Austin's honest and a ball of energy."

"Too bloody much energy if you ask me. She's always dashing about, mutton done up like lamb, those dreadful false eyelashes that look like caterpillars crawling across her face. And once she buttonholes you, you can give up on the next half-hour."

"I notice you're not so critical when you see her. In fact, you fairly ooze charm and compliments."

He purred like a great fat cat. "Bit jealous are you, woman?"

"Dear me, no. You may flirt with Austin Cleardon as much as you wish."

"I don't flirt with her. I just flatter her a bit. To retain decent business relations."

Phoebe wet her lips and turned them in a half-smile. It was his old game: the rogue with the scolding wife. But if it was necessary for him to have the remembered vibration of his power over women, so be it. She didn't mind playing. It was the sort of weakness one learned to accommodate, probably not as irritating as being with a man who sucked his teeth or sat about watching telly all day. "Why don't you come up to the great house and see what's going on for yourself, Archie? It's so much better than getting your gossip secondhand."

"Because I'm working!" He grabbed the script from her. "It ought to be perfectly clear to you that I'm working." He studied the page. He had a terrible aversion to going up to the great house. Seeing it disoriented him; made him (he who prided himself on being the least superstitious of men) feel as nervous as some native who believed in the duppies. A month ago, when they'd come back for the grand opening, he had gone along. He had put on his tuxedo and zipped Phoebe into an artfully draped, plum-colored evening gown that made her look slim and aristocratic. He had stood in Vivian's doorway fortifying himself with punch while Phoebe clucked and cooed, wiping the excess rouge from Vivian's cheeks and persuading her to borrow a pair of sheer black stockings. And Percy, so proud of his new suit that he seemed incapable of natural movement, had driven them up the hill in the rented limousine.

They had made an impressive entrance, gliding under the great moonlit columns into a room resplendent with chandeliers, burnished picture frames, banks of flowers, silver, crystal, and more well-cared-for womanflesh than he'd seen at the best of the Hollywood parties back in the good old days. The opulence had fairly dazzled him. And as he'd looked up at portraits of Sir Isaac and Lady Maude, which Mrs. Cleardon had persuaded them to part with because they gave just the right tone to the lobby, he'd felt sure that he experienced more pride and satisfaction than flinty-eyed Sir Isaac would ever have allowed himself. And yet . . . as the music had changed (Vivian had wanted a string quartet; Mrs. Cleardon had insisted on reggae and they'd compromised: Scarlatti giving way to the drums, flutes, and guitars of bleary-eyed native musicians) he'd found the room stifling, suddenly claustrophobic. He'd excused himself from a tourist who'd already taken off his tie and was trying, with that awful, prying American friendliness, to talk to him about his "feelings." He'd shouldered his way through the crush of gyrating buttocks, dodged another stranger who wanted to talk about fishing, and waved off an anorexic brunette who said she'd just seen a rerun of *Reign of Terror* and thought he was absolutely marvelous.

He'd drifted out to the portico, then walked down the sloping lawn. Leaning against a tree, he'd watched the clouds move across the face of the watery moon and had heard, above the thrump of the music and laughter and tinkling of glasses, a single birdcall. It seemed to mingle with whispers and produced a feeling of ineffable sadness. If only Marsden could have been here, he'd thought. Marsden might have been miserable, misguided, a petty tyrant, but the restoration of the great house had been his dream. And Marsden had been his son. It was a dreadful thing when the death of a child preceded that of the parent. Or if Ceci had come. He hadn't believed her excuse that she was tied up with a writing assignment. That wouldn't have stopped Ceci from doing what she wanted to do. If only . . .

No. He didn't want to go up to the great house again. Even in the sunlight, with those well-heeled tourists thwacking golf balls around the course or lazing near the pool, happy and harmless as hippos in a mud hole, the place had too many shadows for him.

"Well," Phoebe's voice interupted his thoughts, "I hesitate to tell you about it because I know how much you were against it, but Austin's idea of turning the overseer's house into a shop is working out marvelously."

"It's enough we have to run a hostelry; do we have to peddle things too?"

"You have no head for business, Archie. Never did. Never will."

"She only thought up that shop because she had to find something for that Gladys creature to do."

"Yes, Gladys is in her element, but it's Icilda who really gets the attention."

"Why a woman of Icilda's age would let herself be gotten up in that silly colonial costume and put a bandanna on her head and sit there dipping weeds out of jars is more than I can understand!'

"She loves it."

"Practicing medicine without a license, that's what I call it."

"Don't be silly. It's no more than showing them how to make herb teas. The guests love chatting with Icilda and then Gladys writes up the 'prescription' in calligraphy with that violet ink and . . ."

"At ten dollars a jar? Gladys is probably telling them it's an aphrodisiac and taking another ten under the counter. She's probably still working on an aphrodisiac for Percy."

"I don't think that'll do her any good. Icilda tells me that he's still mooning over that woman who went off to Miami."

"In the meantime, I'm sure Gladys is comforting herself by nipping off into the underbrush with the bellhops."

Phoebe laughed. "No doubt. The important thing is that it's all running smoothly. It'll be making a thumping profit this time next year and you won't have to concern yourself with anything but going over the books." She took the script back from him. "Now you can devote yourself to your career."

"If Ceci could see it," he grumbled. "Ceci wouldn't like that plush upholstery in the lobby any more than I do. If Ceci would come down . . ."

"Archie, you know how Ceci feels. I don't think she'll ever come to the island again."

"She said she'd would. She said . . ."

"She said she'd come if there was anything wrong with Vivian. But there isn't anything wrong with Vivian, is there? And now," she hurried on, "let's get back to these lines. Why don't you take the long speech, the 'This other Eden, demi paradise.' Do go on. Ah, very well." She slapped the script against his chest. "Find your place and look at it again. I'll just go and see to dinner. If Vivian's awake shall I invite her out for drinks?"

"She's awake. She sat out here for most of Pembroke's visit, potting marigolds. She was going on about the elections." He wiped an imaginary speck of dirt from the script.

Phoebe brought her head up sharply. "Yes?" When Ceci had run off to the Kingston hospital during the riots, Phoebe had told Archie about Ceci and Paul's affair. Since then, he had never made direct reference to it. She didn't suppose that this had anything to do with lingering racist attitudes, but rather reflected the typical Nettleton trait of avoiding anything that smacked of unpleasantness or deep emotion.

"Yes, Vivie was going on about the elections, banging the trowel about as though it were a weapon. First she started talking about Strangman. She kept calling him 'that man.' I haven't heard that expression since FDR was alive. And Pembroke sat there fiddling with his knees and she kept pressing him to tell her who he was going to vote for. When he said Strangman, she did a complete aboutface, said Strangman was the only hope for the island and that defending the status quo was what caused people to ossify. That's Viv for you. She's never had the courage of a conviction. She's in her room now." He shook his head. "I looked in on her about an hour ago. She's writing to Ceci. Writing a bloody volume. Sitting there scratching away like a demented chicken."

Phoebe looked out at the water. The sun was almost touching the horizon, sending firelike streaks across the bay. "I only hope there won't be any more violence," she said after a pause. "If he'd been able to call the election just after the last disturbances he might have had a chance."

"He could hardly call an election when he was at death's door. Seems as though everything was on his side except the timing."

"But now there're all these rumors that they haven't registered the young people. If there's fraud there . . . I don't see how he can win without the young peoples' vote."

"He's a cheeky blighter, that Strangman. I think he might just win. Course if he does, the property taxes will go up. I don't like that. Still, I'll bet you a fiver."

"You already owe me more than a fiver. I bought the groceries yesterday." She'd said a few silent prayers for Paul Strangman, but she couldn't bring herself to make a wager on his future. Since she'd been back on the island, she'd sent Ceci every clipping she could find that concerned Paul Strangman. Except the one that showed him with his wife and the new child. She wondered if Ceci would keep them and put them in a scrapbook as she herself had done with Archie's reviews. Somehow she didn't think so.

"Yes," Archie went on, cradling the script to his chest and lowering his head so that his mustache grazed it, "Vivian's writing to Ceci. And by the time she finishes the letter, Ceci will undoubtedly have flitted off somewhere else and she won't know where to send it."

"Don't exaggerate. We know where Ceci is, Archie. She's in Manila doing interviews for that article about Filipino women."

"And who's interested in that?"

"A couple of million people I should think. Me being one of them."

"Damned stupid if you ask me. Ceci's thirty-four now, isn't she? She's floated around for over a decade and now, at an age when most women decide to settle down, she decides that she needs a career."

"A purpose," Phoebe said softly.

"Even a blind man could see that Max is mad about her and he looks to have enough money to sail us all into the indefinite future in grand style. And Ceci loves nice things. I know that much about her. Though I don't suppose that if she married him he'd put up with her trotting about the globe, taking all sorts of risks and leaving him alone."

"Oh, I imagine Max would put with up almost anything Ceci did. He's intelligent enough to know that giving her free rein and providing a nest for her to come back to is his only chance of holding on to her. But that isn't enough for her."

"It's that old perverse streak of hers. That banging her head against the bars of her crib," he said with increasing agitation.

"What?" Phoebe asked.

"When she was just an infant . . ." Archie began, but broke off in exasperation.

"Speaking of perversity, I wonder why parents, even those who've been less than successful in their own marriages, are always so anxious to see their children rush to the altar."

"Surely by this time," Archie continued, seemingly oblivious to her barb, "she should have enough sense not to give up a veritable mansion and a man who dotes on her to go and live by herself in a grubby little studio."

"It wasn't little and it certainly wasn't grubby. It's quite spacious by New York standards and Ceci's made it very attractive, within her means."

"You know what I mean," Archie insisted. "She's thirty-four now. Didn't you tell me she's thirty-four?"

Phoebe sighed. She wasn't the only one who repeated herself. "It takes some people longer than others to sort out their lives," she said with a pointedness that she knew was likely to be ignored. "And why can't you give her the benefit of the doubt? She desperately needs to prove herself to herself. She wants to feel that she's steering her own course; that she makes a difference in the world."

"Well, her timing is off. Socially and personally. People younger than Ceci aren't rushing about full of wild-eyed idealism anymore. She said herself that she could have gotten a staff position on that fashion magazine. But no, she wants to be a political reporter. That's still primarily a man's world. That's what I was trying to explain to you about her perverse streak." Looking out of the corner of his eye, he saw Phoebe's expression harden and decided not to pursue the point. "Of course," he said, "if she has no real passion for the man . . ."

"Dear me!" Phoebe laughed. "If real passion was the requirement for marriage, the whole world would stop."

"Then again . . ." He settled back into his chair, feeling that he had maneuvered her into conceding his point. ". . . Max may yet wear down her resistance."

"I shouldn't think so." She might have sounded smug had it not been for a note of sadness in her voice. When, on their way back to Jamaica, she and Archie had stopped overnight in New York, Max's limo had picked them up at the airport and they'd been driven first to Ceci's apartment—a walk-up building on Twenty-third Street and Ninth Avenue. Ceci, dressed in corduroy pants, bulky sweater, and flat-heeled shoes, her hair tied back with a ribbon, had looked both younger and healthier than she had the year before. Her face no longer had a chic thinness, but this, she'd explained, was because she'd grown "fat" from sitting at her typewriter and eating too many take-out pizzas. She'd shown them around her studio, pointing with pride to the plastering job she'd done on the crumbling walls, the arrangement of dining room table, file cabinets, and bookshelves that constituted her "office," the lovely crimson and blue Oriental carpet she'd bought at cost from a designer friend. She'd offered them the use of the double bed that was pushed into a corner and, laughing at the "bull eating prickles" expression on Archie's face, had said that her friend Max was looking forward to meeting them and would provide accommodation more suitable to visiting British celebrities.

As Phoebe had settled into one of the butter-soft leather
chairs in Max's living room and made appropriate noises
about the beauty of his furnishings, Max had draped his arm
over Ceci's shoulder and praised her taste. But if there was
any electricity between them, it had been a one-way current.
The meal of scampi, pilaf, and salad, which Ceci had prepared, had gone well. There had only been a couple of flare-
ups: the first when Max had said that Ceci was pig-headed not
to accept a word processor he'd wanted to give her. Ceci,
obviously enjoying the self-deprecating irony of her remark,
replied that taking handouts was counter-revolutionary and,
since Shakespeare had written with pen and quill, her portable Olympia was more than equal to her tasks. Max had then
told of how, quite by accident, his car had been stalled in
traffic near the United Nations just as a demonstration had
been breaking up and he had seen "his rebel girl" in the
crowd. He'd offered her a ride, but Ceci had said she'd rather
walk because she couldn't see the world through the smoked
glass of a limousine. "But," Max had said, patting Ceci's hand,
"I wouldn't love her so much if she was a pea-brain who spent
her afternoons at Elizabeth Arden." Ceci had laughed too,
though less heartily.

Phoebe and Ceci had left the men and gone to the terrace,
ostensibly to smoke, but really to have a private conversation.
Ceci had assured her that she was doing fine. She'd approached her writing in a businesslike way, using every possible social contact to secure jobs, though she was still far from
being able to support herself in the style to which she'd become accustomed. And if Ceci had sounded a trifle too bright
when she spoke of making ends meet or hustling free-lance
assignments, her voice was calmer and more convincing
when she'd said that she had an increasing sense of directing
her life; that there were days when her confidence actually
out-distanced her insecurity. "No more neti-neti," Ceci had
said, almost to herself, though Phoebe had no idea what that
might mean.

A chill wind had come off the East River and Max had called
them in for some brandy. Ceci, getting up, wrapping her arms
around her breast and leaning on the railing, had said how

lucky Phoebe and Archie were to be heading for the sun. Her eyes had taken on a wintery expression. "I can imagine it," she'd said softly, "The cupola and the bay and . . ." Max had called again. But Ceci hadn't needed to go on. Phoebe knew who Ceci was really imagining.

They'd finished their nightcap. Phoebe would have been willing to sit up and talk into the small hours, but Archie had begun to nod off, jerking to attention every few minutes but finally giving way to snuffling noises that sounded suspiciously like a snore. Max had shown them to their room. Archie had insisted on keeping the light on in order to read an article Max had given him about how to combat jet lag, but had promptly dropped off, leaving Phoebe wakeful, full of an anxious maternal concern about Ceci's future. Later, her bladder tortured by the third bottle of Max's vintage wine, she had sought the bathroom across the hall and, starting out of their room, had seen Ceci and Max standing at the end of the passageway. Ceci seemed to be saying thank you, and Max, with almost paternal affection, ran his finger down Ceci's cheek, kissed her lightly, and walked off. Ceci then let herself into another of the guest rooms.

Pulling up her nightdress and sitting on the commode, Phoebe had thought of a performance she'd given years ago —a reading of the letters of Heloise and Abelard—and how, after the performance, she'd come into the alley near the stage entrance to find a handsome, well-dressed woman with intelligent eyes and a rather world-weary face. The woman had pressed Phoebe's hand and said, "Thank you for your performance. You know, there really are great loves. Impossible loves. Our modern world tries to make us forget that." Flushing the toilet, averting her eyes from the image of the old woman's face that had nothing to do with her real self, Phoebe had thought, Ceci will never settle for a marriage where there is an imbalance of feeling, a marriage that would leave parts of her nature unsatisfied while putting a strain on others. She will never settle for a good relationship, no matter how comforting, when she has known real love. Paul Strangman was and would continue to be, a central fact of Ceci's life.

"What's that you just mumbled?" Archie asked, calling her back from her reverie.

"I didn't know I'd mumbled anything," Phoebe sighed. "Though I was thinking about that aphorism about time healing all wounds. Trouble is, it says nothing about the scars."

"You're getting as bad as Vivian. I have no idea what you're talking about."

"Doesn't matter." She started to get up. "I could be wrong. No one can predict the future."

"Listen, Phoebe, I didn't mean to be hard on the girl," Archie grumbled. "It's just that—"

"I understand." Phoebe settled into her chair again, reaching for his hand. "It's because you love her so much."

Archie cleared his throat. "It must be the cocktail hour," he said impatiently. "Look, the sun's almost down."

"Not just yet," Phoebe said softly; then, remembering how the waning of the day affected him, asked, "Would you like to go in now? Shall I turn on the lights?"

He turned to her, studying the rosy light on her face, seeing how it smoothed out the wrinkles and made her eyes shine. "You look very pretty in this light, old girl. I didn't like it that you let your hair go white, but now I've gotten used to it, I think it's rather becoming." By way of saying thank-you, she let her hand slip to his knee. "Ah, none of that yet," he chided her, getting up. "Why don't I run that long speech? See how much of it I have under my belt." He handed her the script and clutched the back of his chair. " 'Methinks I am a prophet new inspir'd, And thus expiring . . .' " he began slowly.

She brought the page close to her face in the fading light. He paced back and forth, arms behind his back, feeling his way until the power of the words took him up, carrying him like a wave. When he reached, " 'This fortress built by Nature for herself, This happy breed of men, this little world; This precious stone set in the silver sea . . .' " his voice became rich with a tender authority. She put the script on her lap, watching him, wondering if he'd been teasing, pretending that he hadn't studied, or if he was having an attack of inspiration. How could she have doubted? He was going to be good, very good.

He went on, cueing himself, backtracking to find the right inflection but retaining his emotional involvement, so that by the time he had come to the end of it, steadying himself against the table, his voice breaking on the line, " 'Live in thy shame, but die not shame with thee!' " his eyes were moist and she felt a terrible ache in her throat. " 'Convey me to my bed, then to my grave,' " he concluded with hoarse dignity, " 'Love they to live that love and honor have.' "

"That was lovely, Archie. Quite, quite lovely," she said at last.

He straightened up, pinching his nose and winking at her. He was no weakling man, swept away by emotions. He was an actor taking possession of his craft. "Had you going, did I?" His heart was beating against his ribs. "Not a bad part, is it? Got that onion at the end; should make 'em weep. Well, the softies like you, anyhow."

"Quite, quite lovely," she repeated. "Would you like to go in now?"

"Not just yet." He sat down, leaning forward, his hands on his knees. "Beautiful this time of day. Shame to miss the end of it. Let's wait here together till it's well and truly dark." He took her hand. "See, see over there, Phoebe, that curve in the bay where the trees come almost to the shore and the last rays . . . Good show, wouldn't you say? A thoroughly good show."

FOR THE BEST IN PAPERBACKS, LOOK FOR THE

In every corner of the world, on every subject under the sun, Penguin represents quality and variety—the very best in publishing today.

For complete information about books available from Penguin—including Puffins, Penguin Classics, and Compass—and how to order them, write to us at the appropriate address below. Please note that for copyright reasons the selection of books varies from country to country.

In the United Kingdom: Please write to *Dept. EP, Penguin Books Ltd, Bath Road, Harmondsworth, West Drayton, Middlesex UB7 0DA.*

In the United States: Please write to *Penguin Putnam Inc., P.O. Box 12289 Dept. B, Newark, New Jersey 07101-5289* or call 1-800-788-6262.

In Canada: Please write to *Penguin Books Canada Ltd, 10 Alcorn Avenue, Suite 300, Toronto, Ontario M4V 3B2.*

In Australia: Please write to *Penguin Books Australia Ltd, P.O. Box 257, Ringwood, Victoria 3134.*

In New Zealand: Please write to *Penguin Books (NZ) Ltd, Private Bag 102902, North Shore Mail Centre, Auckland 10.*

In India: Please write to *Penguin Books India Pvt Ltd, 11 Panchsheel Shopping Centre, Panchsheel Park, New Delhi 110 017.*

In the Netherlands: Please write to *Penguin Books Netherlands bv, Postbus 3507, NL-1001 AH Amsterdam.*

In Germany: Please write to *Penguin Books Deutschland GmbH, Metzlerstrasse 26, 60594 Frankfurt am Main.*

In Spain: Please write to *Penguin Books S. A., Bravo Murillo 19, 1° B, 28015 Madrid.*

In Italy: Please write to *Penguin Italia s.r.l., Via Benedetto Croce 2, 20094 Corsico, Milano.*

In France: Please write to *Penguin France, Le Carré Wilson, 62 rue Benjamin Baillaud, 31500 Toulouse.*

In Japan: Please write to *Penguin Books Japan Ltd, Kaneko Building, 2-3-25 Koraku, Bunkyo-Ku, Tokyo 112.*

In South Africa: Please write to *Penguin Books South Africa (Pty) Ltd, Private Bag X14, Parkview, 2122 Johannesburg.*